THE SOUND OF A SCREAM

Books by John Manning

ALL THE PRETTY DEAD GIRLS

THE KILLING ROOM

THE SOUND OF A SCREAM

Published by Kensington Publishing Corporation

THE SOUND OF A SCREAM

JOHN MANNING

PINNACLE BOOKS
Kensington Publishing Corp.
www.kensingtonbooks.com

PINNACLE BOOKS are published by

Kensington Publishing Corp.
119 West 40th Street
New York, NY 10018

ISBN-13: 978-1-61793-978-5

Printed in the United States of America

ONE

As Daphne stepped off the train, the howl of a distant animal briefly obscured the sound of the wind. But still the wind was there, tossing her long auburn hair in front of her face and whistling through the wooden slats of the platform. Daphne shivered as she looked from one end of the station to the other. There was no one to greet her. There was only the heavy orange October moon hanging in the purple-black sky.

She wasn't sure what to do. A shade was pulled down at the ticket booth across the way with a sign that read CLOSED. Only one other person had gotten off the train with her at this windswept, god-forsaken station, a man whose footsteps now echoed ahead of her as he quickly crossed the platform toward the parking lot.

Daphne shivered again and looked up at the sky. It had been raining when they left Boston, but here it was only damp and cold. Still, she knew the rain was coming, racing along the coast as if trying to catch her, a mad, determined stalker. As the train had pulled into the village, Daphne had looked down from the craggy cliffs at the roiling Atlantic crashing far below her and shivered in her seat. Mother Angela had warned her it would be this way: "Why else do you think they call it Point Woebegone?"

Taking a deep breath, Daphne stepped across the platform and down the wooden steps to the parking lot, carrying her small suitcase at her side. Despite the fact that they had promised a car would meet her here, no one was waiting in the lot for her either. Perhaps the car was just late; perhaps the train had been a few moments early and all she needed to do was wait and someone would come. After all, the people who had summoned her here from Boston, who had been so eager for her arrival, couldn't have forgotten about her. Still, as the shadows flickered in the windy moonlight, Daphne couldn't shake a sense of foreboding. There was something about this place that she didn't like, didn't trust. She should never have come. She should have listened to her instincts and said no when Mother Angela had brought her the letter.

"Excuse me," came a voice, startling her out of her thoughts.

Daphne looked around. It was the man who had gotten off the train ahead of her. He was standing next to a car in the deep shadows of the parking lot.

"Are you in need of a ride?" he asked.

"I was supposed to be met here," Daphne told him.

The man smiled. He looked to be in his early thirties, tall and handsome and red-haired. "Well,

I can't imagine a more inhospitable place to be stood up. There's a reason they call this Point Woebegone, you know."

"So I've heard."

"I'd be happy to give you a ride into town," the man said.

Daphne hesitated. "I—well, I should probably just wait. . . ."

"It's going to rain soon."

Daphne wasn't used to strange men offering her rides in their cars. In fact, not once in her twenty-two years had she ever been in a car with a man—except for old Father O'Donnell, and then there were always two or three of the other girls as well, plus Mother Angela, who, despite being relatively young (Daphne thought she was probably mid-forties) proved a stern chaperone. Daphne wasn't so naïve that she didn't realize she'd grown up extremely sheltered. She knew there was a big, wide world out there she had yet to experience. Part of her reason for accepting this job was so that she could finally leave the safe confines of Our Lady's School for Girls and enter the real world. Not that the "real world" was something Daphne particularly wanted; she had been quite happy at Our Lady, and would gladly have remained there even though she had graduated. She had no calling to become a nun herself, but she would have been glad to help the sisters and teach the younger girls. But one day Mother Angela had brought her a letter from a man who lived on the rocky northern Maine coast, in a place called Point Woebegone, and who was offering her a job as live-in governess to his young son.

It was crazy, Daphne thought. She'd never heard of this man, this Peter Witherspoon. But one of the school's benefactors had recommended her for the position, Mother Angela explained, and she urged Daphne to take it. "It's time for you leave us, my dear," the nun had said. "There is more for you to see and know in this world."

And so Daphne had come. It hadn't taken the real world long to rush up and meet her. Just minutes after she stepped off the train, here was a strange, handsome man beckoning her to his car, and despite her hesitation, there was a stirring somewhere down deep inside Daphne that she didn't want to admit.

"I should wait," she said finally.

"All right, whatever you say," the man said, smiling, giving her a little bow, then turning around to unlock his car door.

Just then, as if in a movie, the black skies opened up and pelted the ground with a cold, hard rain. The raindrops felt like ice pellets as they slapped against Daphne's face.

The man, about to enter his car, looked back at her over his shoulder.

Daphne ran toward him.

"I guess—I guess I should take you up on your offer!" she called, and he smiled—kindly, she thought. She hoped.

He hurried around to open the passenger side door. She thanked him and slid into the warm, dry, leather-fragranced interior. She'd managed to see the word BOXSTER on the back of the car as she passed. She thought that meant the car was a Porsche—she'd seen pictures on the Internet—

and she was pretty sure Porsches were expensive cars.

"Thank you," she said as the man settled into the driver's seat and closed his door.

"Not a problem." He smiled over at her, his teeth very white in the dark. The rain pounded hard against the roof of the car. "And you needn't fear accepting rides from strange men here in Point Woebegone. We might be a little cold and raw in these parts, but our hearts are pretty warm."

Daphne gave him a small, tight smile. The man's words were reassuring, but she still wasn't comfortable accepting a ride from a man whose name she didn't even know.

Almost as if reading her mind, her savior from the rain remedied that problem. "Allow me to introduce myself. I'm Gregory Winston." He smiled, flashing that white smile again. "The third, if you're keeping count."

"Daphne May," she told him.

"Now that's a pretty name. Your full name? Or is that just one of those sweet-sounding first-and-middle-name confections?"

She laughed. "No, it's my full name. May is my . . . last name."

As Gregory started the ignition, Daphne didn't add that it wasn't a real last name. At least not for her. It was simply the name given to her by the nuns, since they'd found her on their doorstep on a bright sunny morning in the month of May. The note pinned to her bassinet read: *Her name is Daphne. Please care for her well.* The nuns had done so, despite urgings from the local bishop to put her up for adoption. They'd raised her, taught her, loved her. Especially Mother Angela, who'd pulled Daphne to her small bosom before she'd gotten on that train and held her so tight that Daphne thought they might fuse that way, and nothing or no one would ever be able to part them.

As the Porsche glided smoothly out of the parking lot and onto the dark road, Daphne missed Mother Angela with a sudden and terrible fierceness. Here she was, in a strange man's car, heading to a strange house, all by herself, in a place she'd never been before. She'd never done anything on her own in her life. Mother Angela—born Angela Mastroianni, the only child of devout Italian immigrants—had always been with her. Mother had been like a real mother, there when Daphne took her first baby steps to the proud moment when she received her diploma, a graduate of Our Lady's Teacher's College. Mother had loved all the girls, but always seemed to make Daphne feel as if she mattered most. She guessed that's how all the girls felt.

Daphne looked out through the watery car windows and blinked back tears.

The other sisters had been disappointed that she didn't want to become a nun herself. But Mother Angela had supported her. "It is not your destiny, my dear," she said. "As much as we would love to have you here with us always, God has other plans for you. You will see."

"Are you staying at the inn?" Gregory asked her, interrupting her memories. "It's in the center of town."

"No," Daphne replied, removing a piece of paper

from the pocket of her coat. "The address is . . . well, all it says is Witherswood, Cliff Road."

The man looked over at her, without a smile this time.

"You're going to Witherswood?"

"Yes. That's the address I have here."

"Whatever for?" He immediately lifted his hand in apology. "That's none of my business, I'm sorry. It's just that—"

"Just that what?"

The car hit a hole in the road and rainwater splashed against Daphne's window. She pulled back slightly in surprise.

"Well, I just didn't expect a pretty young girl just off the train to be heading to Witherswood. But now I understand why there was no car as they promised you. Poor old Pete seems to be forgetting more and more these days."

"Pete? You mean Mr. Witherspoon?"

Gregory nodded. "Good old Pete owns half this town." The smile had returned as he looked over at Daphne and winked. "I own the other half."

"Oh," Daphne said in a small voice. She had expected from the car that Gregory was a wealthy man. "Well, all I know is Mr. Witherspoon has hired me as a governess for his eight-year-old son, Christopher."

Gregory made a short, whistling sound. "Governess to young Christopher! Well, you *do* have your work cut out for you."

"What do you mean?"

"Have you ever met any of the residents of Witherswood?"

"No."

"Then it's not my place to say." He looked over at her with sympathetic eyes, then returned his gaze to the road. "And as much as I'd like to be gallant and drive you right up to the front door of Witherswood, I'm afraid it would harm your new employer's opinion of you if they saw you get out of Gregory Winston's car."

"Why is that?"

"Nothing to trouble your pretty mind over. Up ahead is the Woebegone Inn. I was planning on stopping there for a little dinner myself. You can get a cab there—which I hope you'll allow me to pay for, since I'm being such a cad and not driving you the whole way."

"Oh, no, I have money," Daphne said. Mr. Witherspoon had sent not only the train ticket but also two hundred dollars for traveling expenses. He seemed to be a very generous man.

But also a rather . . . well, peculiar one, if Gregory Winston could be trusted.

The question was, how much *could* Gregory be trusted? As they pulled up in front of the inn, Daphne was eager to get out of the car. No doubt there were reasons why the Witherspoons wouldn't approve of her being seen with this man—reasons Daphne didn't much care to speculate about. She should have braved the rain and waited at the station. Surely the car would have shown up eventually.

After switching off the ignition, Gregory quickly jumped out and ran around to open Daphne's door, opening an umbrella over her head. They hurried into the inn, splashing through puddles and mud.

The place was dark, paneled in deep brown, hung with fishing nets and buoys and life pre-servers. The floorboards were uneven, warped from decades of sea air. A grizzled old man with skin like leather greeted them and, recognizing Gregory, waved them inside.

"I have my own table," Gregory told her with a grin, his cheeks dimpling. "Will you join me for a quick drink?"

"No, thank you. Where do I get the cab?"

Gregory pointed to a sign on the wall reading TONY'S TAXI. "There's the number," he said.

"I'm sorry" Daphne said, "but I don't own a cell phone."

He looked at her with some surprise. Daphne understood why. It wasn't often these days that a twenty-two-year-old didn't have a cell phone. But such things were not regulation at Our Lady.

The grizzled old man had overheard her. "I can call the cab for ya, sweetheart. But it's prob'ly gonna be about forty minutes or so. With the rain, Tony's bound to be kind of busy tonight."

Gregory gave her a look of understanding. "You see, there's only one cab driver in Point Woebe-gone. You must remember this is a seasonal town. During the summer Tony has a couple of helpers. But after Labor Day, it's just him and his rebuilt 1980 Mercedes Diesel."

"Oh," Daphne said, in another small voice. "Then I should call Mr. Witherspoon. I'm sure he will send a car."

"Witherspoon?" The old man lifted bushy white eyebrows. "You're not going out to Witherswood, are ya?"

"I am indeed."

He laughed, and Gregory joined. "There's no phone at Witherswood. Never has been. I suspect the new misses has a cell, but there's never been a phone line out to that house, not as far back as I can remember, and that's a long time."

"I'm afraid you'll just have to join me after all," Gregory said, gesturing to his table, "and wait for Tony to arrive."

Daphne sighed and followed him past a blazing fireplace, which lit the room with an orange glow. At a small, round, oaken table off to the side, Gregory held out a chair for Daphne to sit down. She took her seat, setting her suitcase alongside her.

"I'll be right back," Gregory said. "I'll save Maggie the chore of coming by to take our order. What would you like, Daphne?"

"Nothing, thank you," she said.

"Nothing at all?"

She suppressed a shiver. Even with the fire, Daphne hadn't been able to shake off the chill of the damp, cold night.

"A cup of tea would be nice," she said.

Gregory smiled and headed toward the kitchen.

She would pay for the tea herself. She did not want to be in this man's debt. More than ever, she wished she had waited at the station. This was not a good way to start her new life here in Point Woebegone, to be sitting in a dark inn with a man her new employers didn't like, didn't trust. The "new misses"—Daphne assumed that was Mr. Witherspoon's wife—was probably sitting at the station right now, wondering where she was, and when Daphne failed to show up, she'd report back to her husband that their new governess must have missed the train. Oh, this wasn't good. This wasn't good at all.

She glanced around the room. There were only a few other diners. A man and a woman, probably in their sixties, eating what looked like fried fish and mashed potatoes, not speaking, not even looking at each other. A large man in rolled-up shirtsleeves, his arms adorned with tattoos of anchors and swordfish, hulking over a very frosty mug of beer. And, way in back, in the shadows, another man that Daphne strained to see—

She made a small gasp.

It wasn't a man.

It was . . . a *clown.*

How very odd. Who would come to a place like this, dressed like a clown, with big orange hair and a bulbous red nose and a polka-dotted shirt, and sit all by himself in the very last booth? He didn't seem to be eating or drinking anything either, just sitting there, the glow of the fire picking out his hair and nose and clammy white face from the shadows. His mouth was painted in a crazy blue grin.

And he was looking at her.

Daphne shuddered, dropping her eyes to the table. She'd always been scared of clowns, ever since Mother Angela had thrown a birthday party for her when she turned five, marking the day not of her birth, of course, but the day her bassinet had been left at the sisters' door. In had trundled a man with hair as bright as this clown's, and feet as big and floppy as she was sure rested under that table. The little five-year-old Daphne had screamed when the clown's unearthly white face had come toward her. The poor man hadn't meant to frighten her, but he had, nonetheless—and she'd spent the rest of her party on Mother Angela's lap, her face buried in the brown cloth of the nun's habit.

"Here you go," came Gregory's voice as he set a teacup steaming with hot water down on the table in front of her. With his other hand he set down a basket of tea bags. "You can have your choice."

She smiled and chose chamomile, tearing open the paper wrapping and pressing the tea bag down into the water with her spoon.

Gregory took his seat. "I don't know where Maggie is. The cook said she took a quick break for a cigarette and hasn't come back."

The tea tasted good, warming her as she drank it.

"Will he let me know when the cab is here?" Daphne asked.

"Oh, sure. But in the meantime, if I can give you just a bit of advice, just relax a bit." Gregory smiled. "You might as well, because you won't have much chance to relax once you get to Witherswood. I can tell you that much."

Daphne kept her eyes on Gregory. She didn't want to have to look at the clown sitting in the booth again.

"You keep talking as if I'm headed to Castle Dracula or something."

He laughed, showing those dimples again. "The comparison isn't so far off."

It was Daphne's turn to laugh. "Ever since I've arrived, it's seemed like there was some big mystery to this town. I must admit, it's quite the place."

"Point Woebegone? If you mean the weather, you haven't seen anything yet, Daphne. Wait until the winter rolls in."

She held Gregory's gaze and lowered her voice. "Well, is it common for clowns to walk around and come in here and sit in the booths?"

He looked at her strangely. "Clowns?"

"Look behind you."

As she said it, she moved her eyes back to the booth. But the booth was empty. The clown was gone.

"I don't see any clowns," Gregory remarked.

"He was there just a moment ago. He must have left—"

Gregory was looking at her with a strange look on his face. "You mean a clown with makeup and—"

"Yes! He had orange hair and a red nose—"

Gregory shook his head. "Can't see how somebody looking like that could come in and out of here without being noticed."

Daphne stood and took a few steps so she could see the booth more clearly. It was definitely empty.

"I swear I saw a clown sitting there," she said, retaking her seat.

"Maybe you did. Or maybe . . ." Gregory's voice trailed off. "This place—this town—sometimes does things to a person's imagination."

"What do you mean?"

"I mean, it's so isolated and all. Popular in the tourist season. But off-season . . . it can be pretty lonely."

"Why do you live here then?"

His eyes turned to fix on her. "My father was born here, and his before him. I went away for a while, but I came back. My father was a grounds-keeper. Now I own half the town."

"You've mentioned that," Daphne said, wondering why it was a fact that seemed so important to him.

He was still looking at her. "Are you sure you know nothing about Witherswood or the people who live there?"

"Nothing."

"So what brings you here? If I'm being too nosy, tell me to butt out."

"It's all right." Daphne took another sip of tea. "One of the benefactors of my school recommended me for the governess position, and Mr. Witherspoon wrote offering me the job."

Gregory's brow wrinkled. "He offered you the job without even meeting you?"

"That's right."

"And you accepted it without meeting him?"

Daphne set down her teacup. She was warm all of a sudden. She felt uneasy, frightened. She wished she were back at Our Lady. She wished she and Katie and Ann Marie were sitting around, watching television, or playing Ping-Pong, or pre-paring Sunday's liturgy with Mother Angela.

"Excuse me," she said suddenly. "The ladies' room?"

Gregory gave her that sympathetic smile again. "Right over there, through those doors."

Daphne stood and hurried across the wide, warped floorboards. She passed the couple eating their fish and potatoes. Neither looked up at her.

Her heart was beating in her ears. Gregory's questions had disturbed her. They pointed out just how crazy she was for coming here. Accepting a job from a man she'd never met? Moving hundreds of miles away from everyone she knew and loved? If Mother Angela hadn't advised her to do it, she would never have done so. She wanted to believe that Mother was right, wiser than she—but right now, as she heard the rain start beating on the roof of the inn again, she couldn't shake her doubts.

She headed down a short hallway that led to two doors. The sign on the first read BUOYS. The second read GULLS. She pushed open the latter.

She could see someone's feet in the lavatory's only stall. The feet were wearing white shoes. Waitress shoes, maybe? What was her name . . . Maggie? Taking her cigarette break in the lav? She appeared to be sitting on the toilet.

Daphne steadied herself at the sink, splashing some cold water on her face. Why was she so suddenly so frightened? It was more than just Gregory's questions. Was it that clown? Daphne just felt so odd, so peculiar. She felt out of time and place. Her reflection in the mirror told her that she looked the same as she had that morning. Her hair was still long, auburn, and parted in the middle. Her eyes were still green. But she was different somehow. She felt as if the moment she had stepped off that train, she had become a different person.

A sound from the stall made her turn.

A thud.

The woman sitting on the toilet had leaned—fallen?—against the side of the stall.

Daphne's eyes dropped to the floor.

A small stream of dark blood was running across the tiles from under the stall, and had nearly reached Daphne's feet.

"Dear God," she gasped.

She rushed around to the front of the stall. The door was not locked. She quickly pushed it open.

There, on the toilet, fully dressed in a white waitress uniform, slumped a woman who must have been Maggie.

This was why she hadn't been around to take their order.

Someone had slit her throat.

Maggie's eyes stared at Daphne with the glassy sheen of death.

Daphne screamed.

TWO

The police were asking Daphne all sorts of questions. What was her name? What was she doing here? How long had she been in the bathroom? Had she seen anyone leave? Had she ever seen Maggie before in her life?

Daphne's mind was reeling. She answered the questions as best she could, then suddenly felt faint. She struggled to hold on to consciousness but lost the battle. If not for Gregory catching her, she would have fallen flat onto the wooden floor.

When she came to, she was in a booth. The same one, she was certain, where she'd seen the clown.

"The clown," she said suddenly.

"Take it easy, Daphne," Gregory was telling her. "It's okay. Damn, what a terrible way for you to start your life here in Point Woebegone."

"No, please," she said. "Please, you must tell the police officers I need to talk to them again. The clown I saw . . ."

"The clown you thought you saw . . ."

"I *did* see him!" Daphne stood, thankful that her knees didn't buckle again. "I saw a clown! He was here, in this booth, and then he was gone. Slipped out without anyone noticing! Right before I found the body!"

A police officer had overheard her, and strolled over to the booth. "Evenin', Greg," he said, and Gregory nodded to him. The officer looked about seventy, with a craggy face and a thick white walrus moustache. "Miss May, do you want to add something to your statement?"

"Yes," she said. "I do."

She told him about the clown. As she spoke, she noticed the cold, hard stare he gave her. The policeman didn't say anything. He wrote nothing down. But his mustache twitched several times.

"What has Mr. Winston been telling you about Point Woebegone, Miss May?" the policeman finally asked her.

"I told her nothing about any of that," Gregory said, impatient at the implication.

"About any of what?" Daphne asked.

"She's tired," Gregory said. "She had a very long train ride here from Boston, and then Pete stands her up at the station."

"*I saw that clown!*" Daphne insisted.

"I didn't say I disbelieved you, Miss May." The policeman handed her his card. "I'm Sheriff Joseph Patterson. I've been sheriff here in this town for a very long time. I've seen an awful lot, so I'm not apt to disbelieve anything. Do me a favor, however. When you get up to Witherswood tonight, you tell Pete what you saw here. *Everything* you saw here. And you call me later and tell me what he says."

"Joe," Gregory said. "What are you trying to do? Get the kid fired on her first day on the job?"

"I just find it interesting that a girl hired to work at Witherswood starts talking about clowns after finding Maggie with her throat cut open."

"I don't understand," Daphne said.

"You just go on and get up to Witherswood, little girl," the sheriff said. "In fact, I think Tony's waiting for you out in his cab right now."

She picked up her suitcase. Gregory placed a hand on her forearm.

"Are you all right?"

"The sisters taught me never to lie," she replied, managing a small smile. "So I'll tell you the truth. No, I'm not all right. But give me some time, and I'll be fine."

"I wish I could drive you. . . ."

Daphne shook her head. "I think my arrival is going to be stressful enough. I don't know what Mr. Witherspoon has against you, Mr. Winston, but I shouldn't stir things up any more than they already are." She smiled at him. "Thank you. You've been very kind." She took a few steps toward the door. "Oh, I didn't pay you for the tea—"

"Please," he said. "Don't worry about that."

She sighed. "Thank you." She turned the sheriff. "I hope you find whoever did that to that poor girl. It's horrible. My heart aches for her family."

"She had none," Sheriff Patterson said. "Nobody really—since she came up here with that—" He broke off his sentence, seeming not to want to say any more.

Daphne held his gaze. She wanted to ask him what he had been about to say, but then decided against it. She hurried out to the taxi.

One more mystery about the place she would now call home.

And she hadn't even gotten there yet.

Tony was a pudgy little dark-haired man, leaning against his old yellow Mercedes. "Terrible thing about Maggie," he said. "She was a good girl. Good heart. Been through a lot, poor Maggie has. I heard you found the body."

Daphne shuddered. "Please. I'm sure you understand. I don't want to talk about it."

"Sure, sure," he said, smiling sympathetically at her. He opened the back door and she slid in. Then he clambered into the front seat. "You should just go home and take a nice long hot bath. Just relax and put it outta your mind."

She managed a small smile but made no reply.

Tony started up the cab. Daphne inhaled the acrid odor of diesel fumes. "Now where am I taking you, miss?"

"Oh, the innkeeper didn't tell you?" Daphne asked.

"No, miss, he did not."

"It's Cliff Road. Do you know it?"

"I sure do, miss. I know every road and alleyway in Woebegone. What number Cliff Road, miss?"

"It's a place called . . . Witherswood."

Daphne saw Tony's eyes widen in the rearview mirror as he stared at her.

"Witherswood? You're going to . . . Witherswood?"

"Yes," she said.

Tony arched a bushy eyebrow at her in the mirror, but said nothing more. He drove off into the night, and she felt strangely as if all of the sympathy he'd shown her had suddenly evaporated in the last few seconds.

The rain had eased up. The wipers needed to flick only every few minutes. The moon slipped out from beneath the dark clouds, making Daphne think of a shy child peeking around a corner past his bedtime. She wondered if little Christopher Witherspoon was shy. When she'd asked Mother Angela why the boy wasn't in regular school, the nun had replied that she did not know. All Mr. Witherspoon had said was that he wanted his son homeschooled.

Daphne rested her head against the window. The moon's light was hesitant, but it was enough to illuminate the jagged wet rocks on the side of the road and the crashing sea beyond. The white caps of the waves seemed unbearably cold to Daphne. She listened as they crashed on the beach far below.

She had never seen anything like what she had seen in that bathroom. The only dead person she had ever seen in her life had been old Sister Agnes, and she had died at age ninety-two peacefully in her bed, clutching her Rosary beads. Daphne closed her eyes, afraid she might faint again, as the image of Maggie's bloody body came back into her mind. So sheltered she had been at Our Lady. She had always feared what was out there in the big wide world. Now, just hours after leaving her safe little cocoon, her fears had been realized.

She tried to focus on the road on which they were traveling. Cliff Road was exactly what its name promised: a long, winding route that ran from the village along the cliffs, becoming narrower and narrower as it made its way higher and higher. Finally, up ahead, Daphne could see a house at the very precipice of the cliff, silhouetted against the moon. It seemed less of a house than a painted backdrop for one of the stage productions she and her friends had put on at Our Lady.

"Look, miss," Tony said, breaking the silence, "I don't usually pry into my customers' business. In fact, I never do. But tonight, I'm going to give you a tip."

"What's that?" Daphne asked.

"You take care of whatever business you have up at that house and then you hightail it outta there," the cab driver said. "Don't ask no questions of anybody. Don't look any of them too long in the eyes. Just do what you came to do and then get the heck out."

Daphne kept her eyes on the dark house. As they drew nearer, she could see that it was huge. There had to be at least fifty rooms. Only a few windows were lit, however. Most of the place seemed to squat in darkness. From the west end of the house rose a tower that seemed to pierce the heavy gray clouds that still drifted across the sky.

"I'm going to live there," she told Tony in a small, frightened voice.

The driver shook his head. "Well, I feel sorry for you, miss. I really do. I worked for Pete Witherspoon once, on one of his boats. He owns most of the town's fishing fleets, and he thought he owned me. Don't let him do that to you."

Daphne made no reply. They pulled up in front of the house, and she stepped out of the car. She handed Tony five dollars. The ride had only cost three.

"I shouldn't even take a tip from you," Tony said, but made no effort to give Daphne any change.

The cab made a screeching U-turn on the wet road and then headed back down into the village. Daphne was left alone in the dark, a light mist on her face. Below, the monotonous crash of the waves nearly drowned out the sound of a far-off foghorn.

Daphne knocked on the door.

It was a great oak door, carved with an intricate design of flowers and leaves. In the center of the door was engraved the image of a swallow, its long tail reaching toward the knob. Elaborately inter-twined with the swallowtail in great effusive curli-cues was the letter *W*.

No one appeared to have heard her knock.

Daphne grabbed hold of the large brass knocker that hung above the W and pounded as loudly as she could.

A horrible thought occurred to her.

What if no one was home?

What if the reason no one had picked her up at the station was because they had gone away? What if she was up here at the top of this cliff all by her-self?

All by herself—with a killer running on the loose who liked to slice the throats of young women?

Again the image of Maggie's dead, bloody body, her glassy, staring eyes, overpowered her, and Daphne felt as if she might get sick

She knocked again, more frantically this time, and called out, "Hello? Please! Is anyone home?"

At last she heard movement from inside the house. She breathed a sigh of relief.

The door began to open. It creaked, as doors always did in scary movies. And it opened slowly, just like in the movies, too, and Daphne half expected to see Lurch, the ghoulish butler from *The Addams Family,* one of the occasional movies Mother Angela would permit the girls to watch on Netflix.

But instead Daphne saw a young woman, probably only a few years older than she was, pretty and blond with large breasts.

"Are you Daphne?" the young woman asked.

"Yes, I'm Daphne May."

"Oh, welcome to Witherswood!"

The young woman practically leapt at Daphne, throwing her thin arms around her and pulling her into the house. "I've been waiting all day to meet you! Welcome, welcome, welcome!"

Daphne managed to say, "Thank you," before the young woman was hugging her again. Her impressive breasts crushed between them. Daphne realized her new friend wore no bra under her thin pink T-shirt. Having spent her life in a convent, Daphne couldn't help but be a bit embarrassed.

"I'm Ashlee," the young woman declared. "What a miserable night for you to arrive. All this rain and wind! But then again, they don't call it Point Woebegone for nothing!"

"No," Daphne said, trying to smile. "I guess they don't."

Ashlee was looking out the door. "Where's the car? Did Axel just drop you off then pull around back?"

"I came by cab," Daphne explained.

The young woman's eyes widened. "Cab? You took a cab from the train station? Whatever for?"

"There was no one at the station waiting to meet me."

"No one waiting? But that's crazy. Axel went out to get you. It was in his daily assignment book. I know, because I wrote it in there."

"I'm sorry," Daphne told her. "But no one was there."

"Well, that's inexcusable!" Ashlee's pretty face was twisting into a deep frown, the blood rising to her cheeks. "You come all the way up here from Boston, taking a job here without even knowing anything about this place, and no one meets you when you arrive. That's simply inexcusable."

"It's all right," Daphne sad.

Ashlee was shaking her head. "It is *not* all right! Things need to start changing around here. I don't like the way this house is run. Not at all!"

Daphne didn't know quite what to say. She agreed that it was pretty lousy to leave her stranded at the train station on her very first night in town. But she couldn't start criticizing her employer right off the bat. Besides, maybe this Axel, whoever he was, had car trouble. Maybe there was a perfectly logical explanation.

"I'm sure there's a reason," Daphne said. "I'm sure it wasn't deliberate. Just an oversight."

"Even if so," Ashlee said, "it's still unacceptable. I tell you, if I were the one making decisions in this house, an awful lot of heads would roll around here."

Daphne allowed her eyes to look around the room. They stood in a large foyer, with an enormous staircase off to her right, ascending to a railed landing where several doors led to what she presumed were different wings of the house. Ahead of her lay a grand parlor, with bright orange flames crackling in the largest fireplace Daphne had ever seen. Off to her left was a corridor lined with large stained-glass windows. The images cut into the colored glass were, of course, swallows.

"You probably want to wash up and rest a bit before you meet the family," Ashlee was saying. "And I'm sure you have to pee!"

Daphne smiled. The girl certainly was blunt.

"It would be good to maybe change my clothes," she said.

"Of course." Ashlee took her bag, which Daphne had set at her feet. "Let me carry it for you. You must be exhausted."

Daphne smiled. "That's very sweet of you, but you don't have—"

"I want to!" Ashlee bounded toward the staircase. "Come on, I'll show you to your room."

They headed up the stairs, Ashlee scampering in front, Daphne following.

She was surprised how anxious she was to meet the family. So far there had been no sign, no sound, of anyone else in the house, but Daphne assumed they were here somewhere. Mr. and Mrs.

Witherspoon and the little boy, Christopher. Why was she so anxious? She supposed it was natural to worry about meeting people who had hired you, sight unseen. And besides, she had plenty of reasons to be a little more anxious than usual this night. Finding a corpse could do that to a person.

Outside, the rain had started up again, harder than ever. Daphne could hear it rapping against the windows on the landing.

"Your room is through here," Ashlee was telling her. "Just three down from Christopher's."

"Is he home?"

Ashlee laughed, but didn't pause in her hurry down the corridor or turn around to look at Daphne. "That boy is always home!" Her laughter echoed in the quiet space. "Poor little monster never gets out of this mausoleum. It's the way his father wants it, but I think it's crazy."

Daphne was about to ask Ashlee what her job was here at Witherswood. It seemed odd that she would be so outspokenly critical of her employers when they could come walking around the corner at any moment. But they had arrived at Daphne's room, and Ashlee walked inside, switched on the light, and exclaimed, "Ta-da!"

By anyone else's standards, the room was probably moderately sized. But to Daphne, accustomed to sharing a room with two roommates most of her life, it was a suite for a princess. A large canopy bed, draped in pink and covered with a white velvet duvet, stood beside a white chest of drawers. The windows overlooked the estate. Even in the darkness Daphne could tell she'd be able to look out those windows and see the cliffs and the At-

lantic Ocean beyond. The crash of the surf rose
clearly to her ears.

Ashlee had opened a door and flicked another
light switch, revealing a gleaming bathroom of blue
marble.

"Is that . . . just for me?" Daphne asked.

"Of course it is!" Ashlee laughed. "Sweetie, we
all have our own bathrooms here!"

She was quickly moving out of the bathroom
and opening another door. A large walk-in closet.
Hundreds of padded hangers awaited Daphne's
clothes.

Daphne smiled. "I don't think I'll be needing all
that room," she said, setting her single small suitcase on top of the bed.

"We'll go shopping and get you lots of new
clothes!" Ashlee exclaimed. "Oh, Daphne, it is *so*
good to have someone my age here at last! I'm so
happy you've come to live with us!"

She leapt at her again, embracing her, squeez-
ing her in a tight hug. Daphne couldn't have
found the breath to speak even if she had known
what to say.

"Now, I've got to get downstairs," Ashlee was saying as she let her go. "Come down whenever
you're ready. I'll round up the family and let them
know you're here!" She was hurrying toward the
door. "And don't worry, I'll speak to Axel and find
out what happened and give him a piece of my
mind for not getting you at the station."

"Please don't cause any trouble on my account,"
Daphne said.

But Ashlee was already out the door.

Left alone, Daphne took a deep breath and sat

down on the bed. Idly she caressed her suitcase, all that she had left from her old life. There were a couple pairs of jeans, several blouses and skirts, a couple of sweaters, underwear, stockings, and a paltry set of cosmetics and toiletries. There was an address book and a pair of sneakers. And there were photographs, of Mother Angela, and Kate, and Ann Marie. That was all. Other than the clothes she was wearing and the tiny gold chain and locket around her neck, that was all Daphne owned in the entire world.

She fingered the locket, then looked down and snapped it open.

Inside was a small piece of fabric.

It was purple brocade, the last remnant of the blanket she had been wrapped in when she was left outside the door of Our Lady's School for Girls. Over the years the blanket—really more a large swatch of fabric that an actual blanket—had frayed and worn, and finally Mother Angela had suggested she dispose of it. But she had let Daphne keep a small cutting from it, because Daphne, feeling sentimental, had declared it was the only tangible connection she had to her real parents. Her mother, she believed, had handled that fabric, had wrapped Daphne in it, before placing her in the basket and leaving her at Our Lady.

She snapped the locket shut again.

For more than a decade now she had worn that locket close to her heart. She supposed it was silly. She was a practical young woman. She didn't believe in luck. She believed in fate. She believed in prayer, but only if you were willing to do what you needed to. You couldn't depend on God to do it for you. God only helped those, Daphne believed, who helped themselves.

For growing up in a convent, Daphne wasn't really all that religious. The sisters who had instructed her had been unusually independent of the local bishop, and while they'd taught the required religion classes and taken the girls to Mass every Sunday, they hadn't spent a lot of time on dogma. Mother Angela wasn't a dogmatic person. She believed in sin, she said, but not in sinners. No one was all bad. No one was all good, either—except Christ and Our Lady, of course. But Mother Angela was an imperfect human being, she told Daphne, and so she didn't sit in judgment of anyone. She had brought Daphne up to be the same.

Daphne closed her eyes and listened to the crash of the waves far below. As soon as she did so, the horrible image of Maggie's bloody body came right back to her, and she realized she hadn't told Ashlee what had happened. Partly because the young woman had given her barely any time to speak for herself. But also partly because, Daphne realized, it would have meant explaining she'd been at the inn, and that it had been Gregory Winston ("the third, if you're keeping count") who had actually given her a ride from the station. And she knew her new employers, for whatever reason, did not care for Gregory.

She'd have to tell them, though. Her name was going to be in the papers tomorrow. There had been a reporter at the inn, and while Gregory had kept her away from Daphne, Sheriff Patterson had said the police report would include Daphne's name, and the police report was public record.

She stood. Better get unpacked and washed up, then head downstairs. She snapped open her suitcase and carefully placed her jeans and underwear in the bureau and hung her blouses and skirts in the closet. She barely took up one drawer and used just three hangers. Washing her face, she looked again at her eyes. They seemed far more bloodshot and tired than they had when she'd glanced in the mirror at the inn. Of course, that was right before she'd found the dead body. Once more, she shuddered.

She took a comb to her long straight hair. The soft lighting in the bathroom picked up golden highlights in her auburn tresses. She decided she wouldn't change out of the green plaid knee-length skirt she was wearing—it was her nicest skirt—but she'd change her blouse. She selected a white one, with brown stitching around the collar and sleeves.

One more glance in the mirror. Bloodshot eyes or not, it was time to go downstairs and meet the people who had brought her here.

Heading out her door, she found the corridor as quiet as it had been earlier. If she didn't know better, she'd think she was the only person in the house. She wondered how many people lived here. All Mother Angela had known about were Mr. Witherspoon and his son. She'd mentioned the boy's mother had passed away. But Gregory had said there was a new Mrs. Witherspoon. So young Christopher had a stepmother. Was there any other family? Daphne didn't know. Then there would be servants. Whether they lived at Witherswood or came just for the day, Daphne had no clue. But in a place as big as this house, she expected there'd be at least some live-in staff. There would be a cook and a housekeeper and a grounds-keeper and a chauffeur. Was Axel, the man Ashlee mentioned, the Witherspoon chauffeur? And just what was Ashlee's position here anyway?

Daphne presumed she'd find out soon enough. Taking another deep breath, she began her walk down the long, dark, unnervingly quiet corridor.

She wasn't sure she could ever get used to living in a place as large or as grand as this. The dormitory at Our Lady had been spartan. She felt as if she might get lost here.

Somehow the idea of getting lost inside Witherswood terrified her.

Daphne smiled to herself. She was feeling edgy. Why wouldn't she be? She had just seen a murdered woman. Never in her life had she ever seen such a thing. And she hoped she never would again—though she was certain she'd never forget it.

She prayed once again that the police would find the person who had killed poor Maggie. And she prayed that a house as large as Witherswood would have an impressive and efficient security system.

She was nearing the staircase when she heard her name.

Daphne paused. Had she heard someone call her? Or was it the rain?

She listened again. Nothing. So she resumed her walk.

"Daphne," came a voice once more.

This time it was clear. Someone had spoken her name. Whether a man or a woman, she couldn't tell. It was little more than a whisper, but it was distinct. And nearby.

"Hello?" Daphne called. "Is someone calling me?"

"Daphne," the voice came again.

It seemed to come from the room to her right. The third door, in fact, from hers. Ashlee had said it was the boy's, Christopher's.

"Hello?" Daphne called again, taking a couple of steps toward the room.

"Daphneeeeeee . . ."

This time the voice drew her name out into many syllables. It was obvious someone knew she was there. It must be the boy.

"Christopher?" she asked, approaching his door. It was ajar. Although the room was dark, she detected motion inside. "Yes, it's me, Daphne. I'd love to meet you."

She knocked on the door. But there was no response.

She waited. "Christopher?"

Laughter. The boy was inside the room, and he was laughing at her. Low, soft, hushed. But he was laughing all right.

Mother Angela had urged her to be firm with the child. She had to set parameters right from the start. She should be warm and friendly, but also clearly set the ground rules. Daphne was to be in charge. She was the authority. It was the only way homeschooling could work. The boy would likely try to test her, Mother Angela had warned. Daphne had to establish that she was the boss, not the other way around.

Daphne held on to that advice as she paused at the boy's door. She'd have preferred to turn and leave. She didn't like intruding into the boy's room. But Christopher had to know he couldn't manipulate her. He couldn't play games.

"Well," Daphne said, pleased that her voice sounded steady, "if there's a joke, why don't you share it?"

She pushed open the door. The room seemed empty. Daphne stepped inside.

"Christopher?"

She looked around. Through the dimness she could make out the boy's bed, and a desk, and a standing globe. There was little else discernible. But she was certain she'd seen motion in here a few moments before.

Then she heard the laughter again.

It was coming from the closet. If it was like hers, it was a huge, cavernous place, and the boy could be hiding among clothes or boxes. There was no way Daphne was being drawn in there. She decided she'd deal with Christopher later. There would be other opportunities to set the ground rules.

She turned to leave, but then the voice came again: "Daphneeeeeee . . ."

She stopped. She couldn't walk away while the boy was saying her name. That just wouldn't do. Steeling her nerve, she turned on her heels and strode quickly and decisively over to the closet.

"Okay, Christopher, it's time we made our acquaintance," she said, her hand on the closet door. "I'm going to be your teacher and you're going to be my student, so we might as well—"

She pulled open the door and stared into the darkness.

"Christopher?"

From the back of the closet she heard movement. The boy was hiding on her. Lifting her hand to the wall, Daphne hoped the light switch was in the same place it was in her own closet. It was.

She flicked it on.

And standing no more than two feet in front her, staring directly into her face, was a clown— with its bright white face and big orange hair and bulbous red nose and grinning blue mouth.

THREE

She must have screamed, and then she must have fainted, because the next thing Daphne knew she was on the floor, and a woman was kneeling beside her, a woman she didn't recognize, and the woman was shaking her.

"Come now, what's wrong?" the woman was asking. "What's wrong with you?"

Daphne tried to sit up. As soon as she did, the memory of that hideous clown came back to her, and she started to tremble again.

"No," she muttered. "Get it away from me! It killed that girl. . . ."

"What girl are you talking about? Who killed a girl?"

Daphne looked up into the woman's face. She was an older woman, maybe sixty, her gray hair tied behind her head in a tight bun. Her hair was pulled so tight, in fact, that her skin seemed to be stretched, her thin eyebrows drawn up in an expression of perpetual surprise.

"That clown," Daphne managed to say, and cast her eyes back toward the closet.

The woman stood. "What are you talking about? I heard you scream, and rushed over here."

"I opened the closet and saw a clown standing inside," Daphne said. But the light was now off— she had turned it on, she was sure of that—and she could no longer make anything out in the gloomy darkness of the small space.

"Of course you saw a clown," the woman said. "You saw this."

She reached into the closet and switched on the light again. Daphne gasped and recoiled, certain she'd spot that monstrous creature again standing there.

But there was no clown.

At least, not a living, breathing one.

At the far end of the closet there was a small plastic figure of Ronald McDonald, the fast-food chain mascot, propped against a collection of other toys: Rollerblades, board games, a baseball mitt, half a dozen teddy bears.

"No," Daphne said, standing up now and looking inside the closet, her eyes trained on the Ronald McDonald doll. "That's not what I saw. I saw a real clown. . . . It was as tall as I was . . . no, taller!"

The older woman narrowed her eyes at Daphne. "It's not heartening for me to think that my young nephew is going to be supervised by such an unstable teacher such as yourself." She sniffed. "I assume that is who you are. Christopher's new governess?"

"Yes," Daphne said, suddenly feeling terribly embarrassed.

Had she, in her anxiety over meeting the family, not to mention the lingering terror of finding Maggie's body at the inn, imagined she had seen a clown? Had she looked in the closet, spotted that silly doll, and then hallucinated?

But someone had called my name, she thought. *Someone lured me in here.*

"I am Abigail Witherspoon," the older woman said. "My brother informed me you would be arriving today. I expected a seasoned, unflappable professional. Not a silly little girl."

"I'm sorry, but I truly thought I saw—"

"You will need to be on your guard much more than that," Abigail told her. "It is only a fair warning. Christopher is known for his pranks. It's why he was tossed out of that school in Portland, for all the mischief he caused. But I assume my brother has told you all of that."

In fact, he hadn't. Daphne knew practically nothing about the boy. Or his father. Or this very strange house called Witherswood.

"I will do you a favor, Miss May," Abigail said. "I won't report this little episode to my brother. It would upset him to think he might have made a mistake. But I give you some important advice. Do not let your emotions get the better of you in this house. It would surely mean your downfall."

Daphne didn't reply. What was there to say? She felt silly and foolish to have been fooled by a toy. If she *had* been fooled. She hadn't hallucinated someone calling her name. Of that much she was sure.

"Come along," Abigail said briskly. "I was heading downstairs, where I understand the entire clan has gathered in the parlor to meet you."

"Thank you," Daphne said, taking a deep breath. "Thank you for not saying anything for now."

"You will either prove first impressions wrong," Abigail said, "or you will be gone from here in two weeks' time."

She whisked out of the door. The older woman was wearing a gold paisley caftan, tied at the waist with a black sash. She walked ahead of Daphne, choosing not to speak further. Daphne followed, trying to force the image of the clown from her mind. *I imagined it. I was freaked out about what happened at the inn.*

But then who lured me into that room?

They made their way down the stairs, back into the foyer where Daphne had arrived. They crossed the marble floor toward the parlor, where the fire still blazed and cast a flickering golden glow over the room. Only a few dim amber lamps had been lit, so the light in the room was muted, dominated by shadows. But even before they had entered, Daphne could see the room was filled with people.

"Daphne!"

The voice was familiar and, given what Daphne had just gone through, welcome. Ashlee bounded up to her, grasped both her hands in her own, and gave her a huge smile. She still wore the same blue jeans but had changed out of her flimsy T-shirt into a bulky green turtleneck sweater.

Abigail Witherspoon retreated to a far corner of the room, pouring herself a glass of brandy and then taking a seat. Meanwhile Ashlee was leading

Daphne through the center of the room, past the
curious eyes of half a dozen others, all of whom
were partially concealed by shadows. They headed
for a man who was seated in a large wingback chair
beside the fireplace. He was smoking a pipe. Fluffy
rings of gray smoke floated up past his head in
steady succession.

"Pete," Ashlee said, "may I introduce to you
Daphne May?"

The master of Witherswood turned to look up
at her. His hair was snow white, a big thick mane
combed back from his forehead and reaching all
the way down to his collar. He was clean-shaven,
and his face looked both incredibly young and un-
speakably ancient at the same time. His skin might
not have been wrinkled in the slightest, but it was
as thin as tracing paper. Even in this light Daphne
could detect the intricate network of blue veins
and red capillaries crisscrossing just below the surface of the skin. But Mr. Witherspoon's eyes were
those of a child's, big and round and bright, filled
with curiosity at seeing Daphne, like a little boy
might be when presented a new toy.

"Welcome to Witherswood," Peter Witherspoon
said in a raspy voice, tattered by years of tobacco
smoke. He stood briefly, to accept Daphne's hand
in his right hand, while holding his pipe out in his
left.

"Thank you, sir," Daphne replied.

The old man sat back down. "Have you met the
terror yet?" he asked before replacing his pipe in
his mouth.

Daphne's heart jumped a little. She had met a
couple of terrors so far.

Ashlee laughed. "No, Pete, she hasn't met Christopher yet." To Daphne she said, "He'll be down momentarily. At least I hope he will. He's a bit of willful child, as you'll see."

Daphne just smiled. She thought it odd that servants like Ashlee called Mr. Witherspoon "Pete." She wondered what she would call him.

"May I extend you my apologies about for my driver's inaction this afternoon." Pete said. "I have been informed he failed to meet you at the station."

"It's all right, Mr. Witherspoon. It was no problem to take a cab."

"No, it's not all right. He had explicit instructions to pick you up. Ashlee said she wrote them in his book. He claims to have missed the entry, but I have checked, and it was right there. In red ink, in fact. There was no way he could have missed it. It's not like him to be so neglectful, and he has been disciplined."

"Oh, I don't want to cause anyone any trouble," Daphne said.

The old man lifted a hand, fingers twisted with arthritis. "He is the one who caused the trouble."

Ashlee seemed to sense Daphne's discomfort, so she took her by the arm. "Let me introduce you to the rest of the clan," she said, leading Daphne toward the others. "Everyone, this is Daphne May, and I'd like you all to welcome her to Witherswood."

Now that her eyes had adjusted somewhat to the dimness of the firelight, Daphne could make out the others, all of whom stared at her as intently as their patriarch did. "This is Louella Kent," Ashlee said, gesturing to a plump woman of about fifty, who looked up at Daphne with kind eyes and a dimpled smile. "Pete's younger sister."

Daphne shook Louella's hand. "Very nice to meet you, Mrs. Kent."

"And you, too, my dear, welcome," she said.

"And next to her is her son, Donovan," Ashlee said.

Daphne's eyes moved over to the young man in the next chair. Donovan Kent was incredibly handsome, probably twenty-six or twenty-seven, with thick black hair and blue eyes that seemed to burn holes through the near darkness. He stood and clasped Daphne's outstretched hand between both of his.

"Welcome to Witherswood, dear Daphne," he said warmly.

"And this is Donovan's fiancée, Suzanne," Ashlee said, continuing on with the introductions.

A pretty Asian woman, probably Korean or Japanese, greeted Daphne with a rather pinched smile. Daphne smiled back.

Daphne noticed how Pete Witherspoon's bright childlike eyes stayed fixed on her the whole time she was moving about meeting the family, studying her as he puffed on his pipe. It made her somewhat uneasy to be looked at like that.

"Over here we have Ben Witherspoon, Pete's nephew," Ashlee was saying as she and Daphne took a few steps around a coffee table. A tall blond man stood and Daphne grasped his outstretched hand.

"I hope my little cousin doesn't run you too

ragged," Ben said, giving her a friendly smile. "If you ever my help in corralling him, please don't hesitate to call."

"Oh, thank you," she said shyly.

"And in the corner over there . . ." With a rather dismissive wave of her hand, Ashlee indicated a young man who Daphne now noticed was seated in a wheelchair with his face averted from the rest of them. ". . . is Gabriel Witherspoon, Ben's brother."

The man in the wheelchair didn't look up at her, just lifted a few fingers as if to wave to her. Daphne started to walk over to him so she could take his hand as she had all the others, but Ashlee stopped her, shaking her head. Instead, she took Daphne's arm once more and led her back toward Pete by the fire.

"And I see that you've already made the acquaintance of Abigail, since you came in together," Ashlee said, nodding over at Abigail Witherspoon, who sat drinking her brandy.

"Yes," Daphne said, "We met upstairs."

She looked over at the older woman, but Abigail did not return her gaze.

"So that does it for the Witherspoons," Ashlee said as they returned to stand at Pete's side. "Except for Christopher, of course."

"And Mrs. Witherspoon," Daphne said.

They were all quiet, looking at her. Pete Witherspoon's bright eyes seemed to grow even wider as he looked up at Daphne.

"Your wife," Daphne said, looking down at the old man in the chair. "Where is your wife?"

Suddenly she was startled by a bolt of laughter

from behind her. It was Ashlee. She was looking at Daphne with the most amused expression on her face.

"Sweetie, you silly goose! *I'm* Pete's wife!"

Daphne felt her cheeks burn with embarrassment. Behind her she could hear the others chuckle. But no one laughed harder than Pete Witherspoon.

"I'm sorry," Daphne said. "I assumed . . . oh, dear, please forgive me, I'm sorry."

"No apologies necessary, sweetie," Ashlee said. "I guess I don't look like your typical 'mistress of the great house.' " She let out a whoop of laughter again. "That's why I was so pleased that someone my age was coming to live here!"

Daphne tried to smile. She couldn't help but notice the way the others were looking at Ashlee. The men seemed somewhat embarrassed. Louella Kent looked troubled or possibly worried about something, but both Abigail and Suzanne looked outright disdainful. Daphne intuited there was not a lot of love in the family for Pete Witherspoon's young bride.

"Of course, Suzanne isn't *that* much older than I am, are you Suzanne?" Ashlee said, smiling a sweet little grin over at the woman seated beside Donovan. "But see, Suzanne went to Vassar and I can't even do long division, so I'm sure my incessant blatherings must bore her—and everyone else in this house—to tears."

"Don't worry, Ashlee dear," Suzanne said, standing up and walking across the room to tend to the fire, which was starting to sputter. "You are *never* boring."

"You are so sweet to say that, Suzanne," Ashlee said.

They hate each other, Daphne realized.

Donovan had come over to the fireplace to help his fiancée, and probably show his support of her, Daphne thought. "Ashlee, baby, you brought a whole new life to this house when you arrived," he said, placing his arm around Suzanne's shoulder. "We can't thank you enough."

Daphne suspected he was being sarcastic.

"It's true," Ben said, standing now himself, and helping himself to a glass of brandy. "This house was rather boring until Ashlee arrived. Just all of us doddering around, running the family business. But then Ashlee came, and since then we've had Lady Gaga playing at all hours and rap music filtering in from the garden. . . ."

Daphne couldn't tell if Ben was perturbed by all that, or if he truly enjoyed the way Ashlee had livened up the house.

"Well, you see, Daphne," Ashlee said, "my dear and most beloved husband is rather old-fashioned. He has never allowed a television set in Witherswood, let alone a telephone. I've respected that, but I told him he couldn't keep me from listening to my music, could you, Petie-poo?"

Daphne noticed the way Pete was watching and listening to all of this, his eyes big, soaking up everything. Ashlee leaned down and gave Pete a kiss on his forehead. The old man chuckled, as if relishing some secret only he understood.

"Now, listen here, everyone," the family patriarch said, looking around the room. "Daphne is in charge of Christopher. She had in her charge at Our Lady's School no less than twenty girls at any given time. She knows how to keep children in line."

"And that cousin of ours has a habit of stepping *out* of line," Donovan said.

"Tomorrow, my dear," Pete continued, "we will go over the specifics of what Christopher needs, both in the house and in his studies. But you are to be his authority. It is you who will have charge over his daily routine."

"I hope to live up to your expectations of me, sir," Daphne said.

His eyes sparkled. "Mother Angela spoke with such praise for you."

The old man's words were filled with genuine warmth, Daphne thought. She smiled. "She taught all of us well," she said.

Pete was nodding. Daphne noticed Ashlee reach over and stroke his hand.

"Daphne dear," came the meek voice of Louella Kent behind her. Daphne turned around to look at her. "I wonder if you heard all the sirens when you came through town. I heard sirens about an hour ago, so many I thought the whole town must be on fire." The woman shivered. "Did you see any commotion?"

Here it was, the moment Daphne had been dreading. She'd have to tell them now about what had happened at the inn.

And who she was there with.

"As a matter of fact," she said, pleased that her voice was steady, "I did see considerable commotion. It was really quite unnerving, and it's why I haven't really been very grounded since I've gotten here."

She noticed the expression in Pete's saucer eyes had changed from amusement to one of deliberate caution.

"You see, when I didn't see anyone waiting for me at the station, I had to accept a ride to the inn, where I was told I could get a cab."

No one seemed to question from whom she had accepted a ride, much to her relief. For now she could sidestep that little detail. Perhaps, in fact, they never had to know she had accepted a ride from Gregory Winston. She might not ever see him again.

"Well, while waiting at the inn for a cab, I went into the ladies' room and I—"

She couldn't say the words. She began to tremble.

"It's okay, Daphne," Ashlee said, putting her arm around her.

Ben Witherspoon and Donovan Kent also approached her, as if to offer support.

"I went into the ladies' room and found a girl had been murdered inside," Daphne blurted, glad to have gotten the words out, but realizing the bitter taste they left on her tongue.

"Murdered!" bellowed Pete Witherspoon, who stood from his chair.

"Dear Lord!" Louella Kent uttered, a fluttery hand to her chest.

The rest seemed shocked into silence.

"Who . . . who was it? Do you know?" Ashlee asked.

Daphne looked at her. "A waitress. Her name was Maggie."

"Oh, no," Ashlee said in a small voice. She let go of Daphne and knelt by her husband's chair. Pete sat back down and began stroking Ashlee's hair.

"Maggie was a friend of Ashlee's," Ben explained softly to Daphne. "She came up here from Florida after Ashlee married Uncle Pete."

"Oh, I'm so sorry," Daphne said.

"This must be terrible for you, too," Donovan said to Daphne. "You poor girl. On your first night here to have to see such a thing. If we had known, we wouldn't have subjected you to this big introduction meeting. Here, please, take my chair."

"I'm fine, thank you," Daphne said. "It did shake me up, quite a bit." Her gaze caught that of Abigail, who was now staring at her. "But I promise I won't let it interfere with my job, Mr. Witherspoon."

She looked back over at Pete. His bright eyes now seemed terribly dim. It was as if someone had pulled a plug and all the life force had just drained out of him.

Ashlee stood. "Do they have any idea who killed her?" she asked Daphne. She, too, seemed a pale copy of the vibrant person she had been just moments before. "Did they catch anyone?"

"I don't know," Daphne replied. "At the time, they had no leads. At least none that the sheriff mentioned when he interviewed me."

At this Abigail Witherspoon stood and approached her brother. "If they interviewed her," she told Pete, "then her name will be in the papers. They'll say she has come to work here."

Pete groaned.

"And they'll also note that Maggie was a friend of Ashlee's from Florida," said Suzanne, from across the room, standing apart from the family she was planning to marry into.

Pete let out a long sigh.

"Maggie and I haven't been in touch for a while," Ashlee said. "We had . . . a bit of a falling out. But, yes, I suppose the newspapers will make the connection between she and I." She looked over at her husband. "I'm sorry, Pete."

"It can't be helped," he said at last, standing again. He knocked the last of the tobacco from his pipe into an ashtray. "Whenever there is a killing within fifty miles of here, they will bring our family into it. It's just the way it is." He turned and looked at Daphne. "I'm sorry you had to experience that, Daphne. I hope you will not let yourself be broken by it."

"No, sir," she said. "I won't let it get in the way of my job."

He nodded, reaching out to his wife. Ashlee took his arm to steady him as he walked. They moved across the parlor toward the foyer.

"I need to be alone for a bit," the old man told his family over his shoulder. "The plans we had had for this evening will unfortunately be canceled. I am not up for any festivities tonight. Expect to have the sheriff here tomorrow, asking questions."

Daphne saw Abigail shudder.

"Daphne," Pete said, directing his final point to her. "I trust you will find everything you need in your room. Sleep well, my dear. I guess you'll meet my son in the morning. You've had enough terrors for one day."

"Yes, sir, thank you. I'm sorry that I was the bearer of such unpleasant news."

"We all should get some rest," Pete said. "Good night everyone."

The others bid him good night as well, and Pete and Ashlee left the room.

"Well, that sure put a damper on our little party, eh?" Donovan said wryly. "We had cook prepare a whole feast in your honor tonight, my dear." He lifted a glass of brandy in Daphne's direction. "All that pork loin going to waste."

"Well, we still need to eat, don't we, darling?" his fiancée cooed, walking over to stand next to him.

Daphne noticed, however, that Donovan Kent's eyes stayed locked on her own. He winked. Daphne blushed. *Is he flirting with me?*

Suzanne noticed, and shot Daphne a look. Daphne quickly turned away.

"Well, I suspect Daphne could probably use something to eat," Ben said, offering her a kind smile. "I imagine you've had nothing all day."

Her stomach was indeed empty, and she'd heard it growl now and then. But with all that had happened she hadn't much thought about food. Her appetite wasn't exactly ravenous after seeing the body of a girl murdered in cold blood.

"Why don't we go into the dining room and have something to eat?" Ben suggested. "It might not be the big celebration Uncle Pete had in mind, but . . ."

"I don't know how you can think about eating at

a time like this," Abigail snapped at her nephew.
"You know what this latest scandal in the village
will do to us. Pete is right! Every time there's a
tragedy they blame us."

"Now, Aunt Abigail, we still have to eat," Ben
said.

"He's right, Abby," her sister, Louella, said, somewhat timidly, as if she didn't want to offend her
older sister. "Cook has prepared all that food. . . ."

"You can all sit down and break bread and make
merry," Abigail said, "but I am far too shaken up. I
am going to my room."

Daphne noticed she snatched the bottle of
brandy and took it with her as she left.

"May I?" Ben was asking.

Daphne looked over at him. He was offering his
arm to her to escort her to the dining room.
Daphne accepted.

Of all of them, only Ben seemed genuinely per-
sonable. Louella was a frightened mouse, Donovan seemed a bit of a player, or at least an
incorrigible flirt, and the rest bubbled over with
anger and discontent. Daphne thanked God that
at least two of the people in this big gloomy old
house, Ben and Ashlee, seemed as if they might
become her friends.

"Aunt Louella," Ben was asking. "would you
wheel Gabe into the dining room so I might show
Daphne the way?"

"Of course," Louella said, approaching her other
nephew in the wheelchair.

Daphne had almost forgotten about him. He
had sat there, off in the corner, not saying a word,
not even looking up at them.

But when his aunt approached his chair, his eyes suddenly lifted to her. "I can wheel myself," Gabriel said suddenly. "There's nothing wrong with my arms."

"Oh, of course," Louella said, jittery and flustered.

Daphne watched as Gabriel wheeled himself forcefully out of the parlor and into the corridor beyond. Donovan and Suzanne had already departed, and Louella trundled her way out as well. Daphne noticed she was very large in the posterior.

"It must all seem like a terrible nightmare for you," Ben said as he led Daphne out toward the dining room.

She sighed. "It hasn't been easy."

She wondered if she should tell him about what she thought she had seen in Christopher's room earlier. But she remained so confused about what was real and what was not, she decided to hold her tongue. At least for now. She was pretty sure she could trust Ben, but she wanted to wait and make sure. And also make sure she wasn't going a little crazy. She hoped after a good night's sleep she'd feel more like herself.

But she decided she couldn't wait about one thing. There was something that puzzled her terribly, and she wasn't sure she could sleep at all if she didn't know the answer.

"Ben," she asked, as they neared the dining room, "why would the sheriff come here tomorrow to ask questions? Why did your uncle and aunt say that whenever anything bad happens, your family gets blamed?"

Ben stopped walking. He stood beside Daphne, deathly still.

"Why would there be any connection to this family in regard to Maggie's death? I realize Ashlee was a friend of hers, but there seems to be much more than just that. What was it that made everyone in the parlor so upset?"

Ben smiled down at her. "You poor girl," he said. "No one told you, did they?"

Daphne looked up at him. "Told me what?"

"Twenty-five years ago, there were other murders in Point Woebegone. A number of grisly, terrible murders."

He looked at Daphne, seeming unable to say what else needed to be said.

At last he forced himself to speak. "And those murders were committed by . . . Peter Witherspoon."

FOUR

"No!" Daphne exclaimed. "Mr. Witherspoon committed murder?"

Ben was shaking his head. "Not Uncle Pete. His father. My grandfather." This was clearly very difficult for Ben to talk about. "Peter Witherspoon Senior was a terribly sick man. It's not easy knowing you're descended from a serial killer."

Daphne felt faint again. "A serial killer? He actually was a . . . serial killer?"

Ben nodded. "Among his victims were some in his own family. My father, John Witherspoon, his eldest son, for example."

"That's horrible!"

"He only killed Dad after he'd found out the truth." Ben looked as if he might cry. "So you see . . . this is what has upset everyone. The village hasn't forgotten that terrible period. Many still blame our family. It's why Uncle Pete has never allowed a telephone here, so we can't be reached by reporters. They even had ways of discovering unpublished numbers. And it's why, when we were growing up, no newspapers or telephones were permitted for my brother or me, or for Donovan. Uncle Pete didn't want us to know the full details of our family's horrible legacy until we were adults. When the murders occurred, we were children. We didn't fully understand everything that was happening. It's why Uncle Pete brought Christopher back from school, too, so he could be home-tutored. He had hoped, that far away, the memory of the murders of Point Woebegone wouldn't be brought up. But Christopher found something on the Internet and called asking questions. That's when Uncle Pete decided to bring him back here, where there's no connection with the outside world."

It explained so much, Daphne thought. And it might also explain why Mr. Witherspoon had hired her—a girl who had very little experience of the world herself, who wouldn't be bringing in too many questions with her, or possibly be a spy for some newspaper or magazine.

"I'm sorry I made you talk about all of that," Daphne said.

"It's okay," Ben said, but he seemed to be glad to be done with it. They resumed walking. "Someone had to tell you eventually. I wonder when Uncle Pete planned on telling you. He might be angry with me for jumping the gun, but I'll explain to him, after everything you've been through today, it was only fair you knew."

He paused, looking down at her.

"I hope it doesn't make you leave us," Ben said.

She smiled weakly up at him. "To be honest, I don't have anywhere else to go."

It was true. She couldn't go back to Our Lady.

Mother Angela would expect her to stick this out. To make the best of it. It was, she'd tell Daphne, her calling.

They entered the dining room. The others had already taken their seats around the table while a couple of servants, hunched old men with silver hair, served the food. The smell of the roast pork suddenly made Daphne hungry, despite everything that had happened today. She took a seat beside Ben at one end of the table, where she had a good view of the others. No one spoke much during dinner; obviously the fear of their old family scandal being dredged up again weighed heavily upon them.

As she ate, Daphne looked around the table. Louella was one of those women who, on first glance, didn't seem particularly fat, but on second and third look, seemed to be barely contained in her clothes. As she reached across the table for another helping of mashed potatoes, a bowling ball of fatty flesh swung from her arm. Her wide bottom seemed squeezed into the chair. Yet she seemed pleasant enough, smiling up at Daphne now and then with lips smeared, not exactly evenly, with bright red lipstick. She certainly seemed far more amiable than her stern sister, Abigail, who, Daphne presumed, was upstairs polishing off that bottle of brandy.

Several times in the course of dinner Daphne noticed Donovan look up at her and smile. Once he even winked. She didn't have a lot of worldly experience, and certainly she had none with men. She'd never had a boyfriend, even though the girls at Our Lady had all insisted she was the prettiest of

them all. There just had been very little opportunity to meet boys. Occasionally, some of the boys
from neighboring parishes came in for programs,
and once, Daphne had become friends with a
young man named Kevin O'Connell, a redhead
with a smattering of freckles, and she'd thought
maybe she'd felt the first stirrings of a crush. But
that had been when she was eighteen. Three years
had passed, and there had been no one else.

Yet no matter her inexperience, she knew one
thing: Donovan Kent was definitely flirting with
her.

She knew for sure from the surly looks his fiancée, Suzanne, kept giving her. Suzanne would
notice Donovan smiling at Daphne and then turn
her own steely-eyed stare onto the girl. Daphne
thought Suzanne didn't have to worry. Daphne
might be pretty, but Suzanne was a knockout.
Long, shiny black hair, the most intense black al-
mond eyes, the perfect figure. Daphne figured
Donovan was just one of those guys she'd seen on
TV: an instinctive flirt. She was certain it was harm-
less.

Still, she had to admit that Donovan was perhaps the handsomest man she'd ever seen in her
life. Tall, with thick wavy dark hair, he had deep-set
blue eyes that danced when he looked at her. A
strong jaw, a cleft chin, broad shoulders. The black
T-shirt he wore under a blue blazer couldn't dis-
guise a well-worked physique. Donovan was so
handsome, he could be a model.

As she finished the last of her dinner, she realized he might actually be a model. She had no
idea what any of these people did for a living.

Maybe they were rich enough that they didn't have to do anything. Odd that they all still lived in the same house; brothers and sisters she could maybe understand, but cousins? It seemed the four children of the horrible Peter Witherspoon Senior—Pete Junior, Abigail, Louella, and Ben's late father, John—had never left Witherswood. Instead, they had married and raised children there—at least all of them but Abigail, who was apparently unmarried.

The hunched-over waiters took her empty plate and replaced it with a slice of apple pie, a piece of cheese melting over the top of the crust and a large dollop of whipped cream smack in the middle. She didn't think she could possibly eat it, but Ben told her to have a bite at least. Cook made an awesome apple pie.

She complied. And indeed it was wonderful.

Daphne looked over at Ben. He wasn't as handsome as his cousin Donovan, but he certainly wasn't unattractive. He had extraordinary blue eyes and a classic Roman nose and, like Donovan, was very fit. The short sleeves of the shirt he was wearing were completely filled by large, baseball-sized biceps. Ben's blond hair was buzzed close to his scalp—a solution, Daphne surmised, to a slightly receding hairline.

Finally her eyes moved over to the last person at the table. The silent, withdrawn Gabriel. He ate slowly, deliberately, and never once lifted his eyes to the others at the table. It was hard to get a good look at him, since he kept his head down so much, but Daphne finally was able to see that, like the other men, Gabriel was a very attractive man. Like his brother Ben, he had blond hair, but kept it long—in fact, now that Daphne looked closer at him, she could see Gabriel's hair was drawn back into a small ponytail behind his head. He shared with his brother another trait as well: those big arms. Clearly he'd kept working out his upper body despite being in a wheelchair.

Daphne wondered how Gabriel had become disabled. His defensiveness about being wheeled into the dining room earlier suggested to Daphne that it had not been a condition he'd been born with. He seemed, in fact, resentful of being in that chair, and perhaps it was that resentment that kept him so withdrawn into himself.

"Well, that was a fine meal," Donovan announced. "Cook has outdone herself."

"Yes, it was delicious," Daphne said.

"If you need anything now, my dear," Donovan said, "please don't hesitate to call."

Suzanne stood up and left the table without saying a word. Donovan winked at Daphne, then stood up and followed his fiancée out of the room.

"You'll find my cousin is a bit of a flirt," Ben said, walking with Daphne out into the foyer. Louella had stayed at the table for a second wedge of pie.

"Is he?" Daphne played clueless. "I hadn't noticed."

"Watch out for him."

This wasn't Ben speaking. It was a new voice. Both Daphne and Ben turned around. It was Gabriel, wheeling himself out of the dining room.

"Tell her, Ben," he said. "Tell her all about Donovan."

Ben sighed. "She's had enough family history for one night, I think."

"Two words for you, dear brother," Gabe said as he rolled past them, not making eye contact with either of them. "Kathy Swenson."

Ben was silent as they watched Gabe continue on down the hall, until he turned at a far corner and disappeared from view.

"Who's Kathy Swenson?" Daphne asked.

Ben smiled sadly. "The only girl Gabe ever loved. And Donovan stole her away."

"Oh, that's terrible."

"We were all kids. Teenagers. More than ten years ago now." He sighed. "But Gabe never forgets."

Daphne did a little math in her head. If they were teenagers more than ten years ago, that meant Ben, Gabriel, and Donovan were all probably in their late twenties. That wasn't really so much older than she was, but she still felt like a child.

"Listen, Daphne, may I give you a bit of advice?" Ben asked.

"Of course," she said.

He looked down at her kindly. "Tomorrow, and the day after that, and next week, we will keep on moving further and further away from this terrible night. Once again the tongues in the village will stop wagging, the sheriff won't be coming up here to ask questions, and life will resume a degree of normalcy at Witherswood."

"I look forward to that," Daphne said. "But what's the advice?"

"We shouldn't allow you to forget that you have a rather daunting task ahead of you. My little cousin Christopher can be a handful. He hasn't ever gotten over his mother's death a few years ago. It was quite tragic."

"The poor boy."

"And ever since, he's been acting out. Uncle Pete was too old, in my humble opinion, to have a child, because now that he's hit seventy he just doesn't have the energy or the patience to give Christopher the attention he needs. So you'll have quite the job reaching him, let alone teaching him."

Daphne smiled weakly. "So what do you suggest?"

"It's what Uncle Pete said earlier. You are his authority. Let him know from day one that you're in charge. That he can't boss you around or manipulate you—or try to scare you."

"Scare me?"

Ben laughed. "Have Ashlee and Suzanne tell you how he scared them when they first came here. Just pranks. But elaborate ones. It's pretty amazing what that kid can concoct. It's his way of trying to have the upper hand."

Daphne was nodding. So maybe there was more to her so-called hallucination earlier than she realized. Maybe she'd been too quick to write it off as her imagination. She thought about describing what had happened to Ben, but decided against it. Already Abigail thought she was a flighty scaredy-cat. No use making Ben think so, too. She'd just take his advice. She'd be firm with Christopher, and find out what she could.

"Thanks, Ben," she said. "I'll set the ground rules right away. It's good advice."

He smiled. "Well, sleep well tonight, Daphne. Or at least try to."

"Thank you. I will."

"Oh," he said, remembering something. He reached inside his jacket pocket and produced a small silver flashlight, just about four inches long. "Here's a little welcome gift for you. You'll find we lose the power often up here, so it's a useful tool to keep on you."

Daphne accepted the flashlight. "Well, thank you."

Ben winked. "Don't want you to find yourself alone in the dark."

She smiled as he headed off.

Donovan might be the more traditionally handsome, but it was Ben she watched as he walked away, her heart filling up with something . . . something she couldn't quite describe. She had never been in such close contact with so many handsome men before. Daphne felt warm, tingly.

Until she suddenly shook her head to free herself of such foolish romantic notions.

She noticed that Ben and Gabriel had gone in one direction, Donovan and Suzanne another. She guessed that the different families had different wings in the great old house, and shared the parlor, dining room, and kitchen.

Suddenly she was utterly and completely tired. Exhaustion threatened to knock her over like a charging quarterback. With the exhale of one long, weary breath, she headed up the grand marble staircase back to her room.

But first, before she crawled into bed, she thought she might pay a call on the one remaining member of the family she had yet to meet.

Daphne paused outside Christopher's door. It

was now completely closed. She could hear music coming from within. A small, tinny sound, barely audible, that only the utter silence of the corridor could permit her to hear. Daphne raised her hand and knocked.

The music went on. It was some kind of rap or hip-hop, she thought. She knocked again.

Still the music continued without any movement from within. It occurred to her then that the softness and tinniness of the music suggested it emanated from a set of headphones, plugged into the boy's ears. With that cacophony blasting into his ears, Christopher wouldn't be able to hear her knock.

She was about to forget seeing him this night and head back to her own room, when suddenly Ben's advice came back into head. She shouldn't barge into the boy's room, but she felt she ought to confront the situation right then and there. She was his governess after all; Mr. Witherspoon's letter to Mother Angela had said she would have charge over both the boy's studies and his domestic chores. And tonight he'd stated clearly that she was to be the authority in his life. She figured she'd start now.

She placed her hand on the doorknob and turned.

Suddenly a cold shiver went down her back.

That awful clown might be standing behind that door.

No, she told herself, that was one of Christopher's elaborate pranks. And she would ask him about it, right now.

She opened the door.

As she had suspected, the eight-year-old was lying on his bed, earbuds tucked snugly in his ear, as he tapped, tapped, tapped on an iPad. He looked up at her in sudden surprise—a look of stunned horror—big round brown eyes staring out from white sockets in the shadows of his room.

"Christopher, I wanted to come in and introduce myself," Daphne said, loudly.

The boy, eyes still wide, removed his earbuds.

"I'm Daphne. I'm your new governess."

"And that's the last time you'll ever just walk into my room without knocking," he said, furious.

"Oh, but I have knocked. You just couldn't hear me."

He moved forward on the bed and Daphne got a better look at him. He was a fat little kid, with a mass of brown curls and freckled, pudgy cheeks.

"Doesn't matter," he spit. "If I don't answer the door, then I want to be left alone."

"Nope," Daphne replied. "That's not how it's going to work. If you want to be left alone, I'll respect that. But you've got to tell me so when I knock."

"But if I'm listening to my music I won't be able to hear you."

"Then listen to it at a slightly lower volume."

Daphne stood at the end of his bed, facing him. She was pleased with herself that she didn't tremble or hesitate. The boy saw that she was serious. He groaned.

She figured she'd won the first battle of wills. But she suspected there many more to come.

"We can get more acquainted in the morning,

but I wanted to come in tonight and at least say hello." She smiled as her eyes narrowed at him. "Since, after all, when you called to me earlier this evening we never actually got a chance to meet."

He made a face at her. "I never called to you."

"Come on, Christopher. I heard you. Your door was ajar, you heard me walk by in the corridor, you called to me, I came in here. . . ."

"I was out at the stables."

"Then who was calling my name from your room?"

A crooked smile suddenly made its way across the boy's chubby face like an eel swimming through water. "Maybe it was the ghost," he suggested.

Daphne smirked. "You'll have to think up a better excuse than that."

Christopher lay back on his bed, seeming to enjoy the conversation now. "No, it's not an excuse. You mean no one's told you about the ghost that haunts Witherswood?"

"No, but I expect you're about to."

He laughed. "I wouldn't want to scare you on your first night here!"

"Of course you wouldn't."

"But there really is a ghost. I've seen it many times. And I know who it is, too."

Daphne sighed. "Who is it, Christopher?"

"My grandfather."

Daphne didn't reply right away. After what she'd just learned about the boy's grandfather, Pete Witherspoon Senior, she felt a little unnerved taking the conversation in that direction.

"I think you're a very imaginative, clever boy.

Too clever for your own good." She turned to leave. "So long as we understand each other, I'll say good night for now and you can go back to—"

"I think I've scared you after all."

Daphne turned back to look at him. Had he seen her faint earlier? Had he been hiding in the room when she opened that closet door and saw what she thought she saw? Had he had a good laugh at her expense, his prank having succeeded beyond all his expectations?

But how could that have been a prank?

That clown was real.

And far too tall to be a little boy dressed up.

"No," Daphne said, but her words no longer had the authority of a few minutes earlier. "You haven't scared me, Christopher."

"Did anyone tell you that my grandfather was a serial killer? He killed seventeen people, mostly little kids. One of the adults he killed was his own son."

"This is not something I wish to speak about," Daphne told him.

The boy laughed. "My father thinks I know nothing about it. But there are ways of getting onto the Internet even when he thinks he's proofed the house from any wireless intrusion. I've read all about Grandpa. Fascinating guy."

"Christopher, that's enough."

"Do you know how he'd kill the kids? He'd cut them up into little pieces and feed them to his dogs. The police dug up more bones on our estate than you can find in most cemeteries. I'm sure there are still more out there if we just went out and looked."

"Okay, from here on in, ground rule," Daphne said loudly, trying to regain the upper hand. "We will not talk about this—ever! Your father does not wish it brought up."

"But there's one more detail you're going to love, Daphne. Really!"

"Good night," she said firmly and walked briskly toward the door.

"Do you know how good old Grandpa would get the kids to come to him?" Christopher was asking.

Daphne's hand was on the doorknob. She didn't want to know the answer. She wanted out of that room more than anything before that hateful little boy could speak another word.

"They all came to him," Christopher said. "All sorts of kids just flocked to see Grandpa. Boys and girls, black and white, rich and poor. From all around they came just to see him. So he had quite the selection from which to choose the best dog food."

Daphne was moving through the door, but Christopher went on speaking, shouting now so she'd be sure to hear him.

"And do you know why the kids came to him, Daphne? Do you know why?"

She was almost out into the corridor.

But she wasn't quite fast enough.

"Because, Daphne," Christopher said, exultant, "he was dressed like a clown!"

FIVE

Daphne could hear the boy's laughter echoing in the dead-silent house as she ran down the corridor back to her room.

What a mess she'd just made of that first encounter. It had started out well, but she had let Christopher get to her. She had handed over all control to him.

But he had frightened her. She couldn't deny that.

Was what he had told her true?

Had Pete Witherspoon Senior really dressed as a clown to lure his victims to their deaths?

And did his ghost really haunt this house?

Slamming and locking her door behind her, Daphne had another terrifying thought.

Did his ghost haunt the entire village?

Is that what she had seen at the inn? That clown sitting in the last booth? Had it really been the ghost of the serial killer who had once lived in this house?

"And if so," Daphne whispered to herself, trembling as she leaned up against the door, "is his ghost killing again?" She thought of Maggie, her throat sliced in the stall of the ladies' room.

This was all absurd. Completely and utterly absurd. She pulled herself away from the door and switched on the lamp in her room, taking comfort in the golden light that suddenly surrounded her. She didn't believe in ghosts. That wasn't the way Mother Angela had raised her. She had raised her to believe in God, and to believe in herself. She had taught her to be strong and confident. "There is nothing you can't handle," the good mother had taught her. "Nothing you can't accomplish. You just have to believe in yourself." Others might try to distract her, tempt her, confuse her, scare her, Mother had said. But Daphne only needed to trust her own heart and mind. Then she could never go wrong.

This was just Christopher's way of trying to scare her, Daphne reassured herself. There was no doubt a perfectly logical explanation for the strange things she'd seen, heard, and encountered tonight. Maybe the clown she had seen at the inn was merely stopping by on his way to some child's birthday party. And in her anxiety over Maggie's murder, she'd imagined that little clown doll in Christopher's room was the same figure she'd seen at the inn. Christopher had no doubt been hiding, and had seen her faint—so now he was just making up stories to scare her further.

She decided to take a shower. A hot shower would feel good, and calm her down. It had been a long day, after all. Stepping into the stream of water, Daphne let out a long sigh. She was truly and utterly exhausted. Every muscle in her body seemed to ache. She closed her eyes and lifted her face directly into the shower, letting the water cascade over her eyes, her nose, her cheeks. In that moment, she was back at Our Lady, in the shower she shared with her roommates, and Katie and Ann Marie were out waiting for her in the game room, *Harry Potter and the Goblet of Fire* next up in their Netflix queue.

But in the next second Daphne remembered she was alone in this dark room, and with the steady stream of the shower, she couldn't see or hear if anyone was creeping up on her. *That's crazy*, she told herself. *I locked the door.*

Still, she felt tingly enough to quickly switch off the shower, hop out onto the marble floor, and towel herself dry. Wrapping the towel around her head, she walked around the room to peer into all the deep blue shadows. Convinced she was alone, and scolding herself for acting like a child, Daphne finished towel-drying her hair, slipped into her flannel nightgown, and finally crawled into bed.

She was asleep moments after her head touched the pillow.

So quickly did she fall asleep that she was unable to separate what was real and what was a dream. She sat up in bed, looking toward the window. There was someone looking in at her. But that was impossible. She was two floors up.

But someone was there—a woman—and she appeared to be screaming, although Daphne couldn't hear her.

Daphne got up, out of bed, and began walking across the floor. Her room seemed different. Larger, wider, deeper. It was also hot, oppressively hot. She moved over to the window and tried to open it—but it was no use. The windows were locked.

She was in danger, she suddenly felt. Something was in the room with her.

Daphne took a deep breath. She fumbled in the dark for a lamp but couldn't find one. *If I can just get a light on, I'll be okay.*

But as far as she could tell, all the lamps were gone. No furniture was left at all, in fact.

Her room was as barren as—a cell.

Stop it! I'm dreaming!

She tried to force herself awake.

If only she could find a light . . .

Then, ahead of her, seemingly a long way off, Daphne saw a flicker, like the small flame of a candle.

Someone was in the room with her.

"Hello?" she said, in a tiny, terrible voice.

She moved toward the light, taking several steps, then stopping, then taking several more, stopping, then several more steps after that. Surely she should be reaching the far wall by now. How large could this room possibly be? It seemed to Daphne that she walked and walked and walked . . . and there was no end to the room. It defied logic. And still the flicker of light seemed the same distance away.

She heard something. A scuff.

Someone *was* in the room with her.

In the darkness.

"Hello?" Daphne whimpered.

The flicker of light seemed to be moving toward her.

It *was* a candle. As it came closer, Daphne could make out a hand carrying it, and then . . . a face. . . .

A face she knew.

In that last glimmer of candlelight, Daphne saw something that went far, far beyond the scope of her young, innocent imagination. All the nameless terrors she'd ever felt, all the creeping anxieties she'd ever experienced, all of the doubts and fears and nightmares of her life came rushing wickedly into the candlelight before her. The face in front of her began to scream, its mouth growing wider and wider until the sound itself began to take shape and crowd everything else out of the room. Daphne clapped her hands over her ears and began to scream herself.

She opened her eyes and looked down at the pink light that was striping her white sheets.

It was morning.

And she had had a dream. A terrible dream.

One that was fading from her memory even as she tried to hold on to it. All she knew was that it had frightened her, and badly.

And why not? After what she had experienced the night before, no wonder Daphne had nightmares.

Outside, the dark rainy night had been succeeded by a brilliant sunny morning. Birds chirped in the trees. The fragrance of sea air filled the room, and the crash of the surf was louder than ever, without any rain or wind to obscure its sound. It was just before seven o'clock.

Daphne was dressing when she heard a soft knock at her door.

"Are you awake?" came a whispered voice.

Daphne unlocked the door and opened it. It was Ashlee, beaming up at her with a smile that seemed to reflect the cheeriness of the morning outside.

"Good morning," Daphne greeted her.

Ashlee came into the room. She was wearing a ruffled white blouse over blue jeans. She was barefoot.

"Did you sleep okay?" the lady of the house asked her. "The storm finally let up."

"Yes, thank you," Daphne said, not entirely truthfully, but not wanting to admit to having had a nightmare on her first night in the house.

"Good." Ashlee grabbed her hands in hers and smiled up at her. "I'm so sorry that Pete and I cut your welcome party short last night. It's just that the shock—"

"I understand," Daphne said. "It must have terrible learning about your friend's death."

Ashlee suddenly looked near tears, the way she had last night. "What's worse is that Maggie and I had fallen out of touch. You know, running this house for Pete and all, I didn't really have time to go out with her and do all the things we used to do."

"Well, that makes sense. I'm sure she understood."

Ashlee shook her head. "I'm afraid she didn't. Maggie was resentful, I think. Here I was living at Witherswood, with servants and cars and drivers at my disposal. And she was still working as a waitress."

Daphne made a sympathetic face.

"We started out together, you know. Went to

high school together in Florida. We were like two peas in a pod back then." Ashlee looked out toward the cliffs. "Times change."

"I just pray they find the person who did it," Daphne said.

Ashlee whipped her eyes back to Daphne's. "Indeed! I hope they find him and give him the electric chair!" Her lips tightened into what seemed like some kind of cruel smile. "Although the state's preferred method is lethal injection. I hear that's not as painful."

Daphne shivered. Ashlee's usually sweet demeanor had darkened. She supposed it was only natural, given the fate her old friend had suffered.

"Well, enough of that," Ashlee said, shaking off the darkness that had momentarily clouded her face. "I came here to make up for ditching you last night. I've had cook prepare us a little breakfast that we can eat out on the cliffside terrace. Before you get down to your duties, I thought we could get to know each other a little better."

Daphne was very grateful. Ashlee was a bright spot in this gloomy old mansion. Sitting with her out on the terrace, watching the white waves hit the rocks below, sipping hot coffee, and enjoying the best homemade raspberry croissants she'd ever tasted, Daphne finally found herself laughing—for the first time since her arrival in Point Woebegone. Ashlee was a good storyteller. The tale of how she'd met Pete Witherspoon—she'd been his waitress at a restaurant when he was in Florida on business—was a doozy, and Daphne couldn't help but laugh out loud as she told it.

"Well, my boss had told me Pete was a 'vic,' "

Ashlee was saying. "A very important customer. I was rushing around, trying to make sure he and his party had everything they needed. I was told to make sure Mr. Witherspoon was treated like a king. Well, I found out he was certainly very regal— and by that I mean demanding—when he gave me his order." Here her voice deepened into a delicious impersonation of her gravel-voiced husband. " 'Now, make sure the meat is done only slightly medium rare, not medium rare, mind you, young lady, or heaven forbid just plain rare. There is a very fine middle ground, where there is no more than one-quarter of an inch pinkness. Do you understand? Just slightly medium rare.' "

Ashlee stood up, demonstrating with a tray of croissants the way she had brought Pete his plate of slightly medium-rare beef. "So I come along, after our chef had spent such care making sure the order was prepared just right, and Pete is sitting there with those damn long legs of his sprawled out into the aisle. And I come by just like this—" She pretended to bump into Daphne's feet. "And boom! I trip over those long legs and go sprawling right down, flat on my face!"

Daphne laughed. "And his steak?"

"It went skidding across the floor!"

"Oh no!"

"But here's the best part." Ashlee seemed unable to contain a rush of laughter for a moment. "I actually went chasing after the steak, picked up in my fingers, brought it back to the table, and showed it to Pete. 'But look, sir,' I told him, 'it really was exactly one-quarter-inch pink!' "

"You didn't!" Daphne laughed.

"I did." Ashlee sat back down at the table. "Of course, my manager came out and fired me right on the spot. Pete very gallantly insisted I be reinstated, and then asked me my name. The next day he called for me at the restaurant and asked if he could take me out to dinner to make up for his ungainly feet. Of course I agreed." She smiled dreamily over at Daphne. "And the rest, as they say, is history."

"It's a wonderfully romantic story in its own way," Daphne said.

"I'm glad you think so," Ashlee replied, taking a sip of her coffee. "Not everyone in the family agrees."

Daphne had seen the disapproval of Ashlee last night in the eyes of some of them. But she feigned ignorance. "I'm sorry to hear that," she said.

"You might as well know the family dynamics, since you're going to live here." She buttered a croissant and took a bite. "Pete controls the family fortune, so his sisters and his nephews are all constantly watching out for themselves around him, not wanting to get cut out of the will. Of course, the bulk goes to Christopher." Her eyes danced a moment as they looked over at Daphne. "And any offspring that Pete and I might have, of course. Which is why they don't like me much. They thought Pete was through making babies. And then he gets married again."

"Are you . . . ?" Daphne asked.

"Not yet." Ashlee giggled. "But just because he's seventy years old doesn't mean you can count Pete out quite yet in that department."

"In what department?"

Ashlee hooted, taking Daphne's question as a joke. "But I'll give you one bit of advice. Watch out for Abigail. She's the worst. A miserable old spinster. Probably never had any in her entire life."

"Had any what?" Daphne asked.

Ashlee looked at her as if she thought Daphne might be joking again. Then she realized the new governess really didn't understand her innuendo.

"Sex," Ashlee told her. "She's never had sex." Suddenly a smile stretched across the young woman's face. "Oh, I forgot. You grew up in a convent."

Daphne felt her cheeks flush. "I'm not always so naïve," she promised. "But . . . I guess there are some things I have to learn."

"Don't worry about it, sweetie." Ashlee smiled kindly. "So . . . if I can be so bold—should I assume you've never had any either?"

Daphne's cheeks burned hotter. She just shook her head.

Ashlee smiled. "That'll change. I saw the way Donovan was eyeing you last night."

"But he's engaged!"

"That's never stopped him before," Ashlee quipped.

Daphne drew her shoulders up. "Well, it would certainly stop me."

"Good for you, sweetie. But I didn't necessarily mean Donovan. I just meant I saw how he looked at you. You're an extremely pretty girl. I'm sure lots of guys will look at you the same way now that you're out of the convent."

Daphne just laughed awkwardly and looked away.

"In fact, I'll bet even on your way over here, you attracted some attention from the male citizens of Point Woebegone."

Daphne looked at her. Could she possibly know that Gregory Winston had given her a ride? Could the sheriff have mentioned it? Given that the sheriff was coming by later today, Daphne figured it might be wise to admit it. And surely if there was a sympathetic ear in this house, it was Ashlee's.

"Actually," she said, "not that there was anything to it"—was there?—"I did get a ride from the train station to the inn from a gentleman who said he knew Mr. Witherspoon."

Ashlee's eyes twinkled. "You were holding back on us last night, Daphne. You didn't tell us this part."

"It's just that—well, I didn't want to add any further distress after breaking the news about Maggie."

"How could you cause distress by telling us a man had given you ride?"

"Well, the man indicated . . ." Daphne's voice wavered. What exactly had Gregory said? "He implied that Mr. Witherspoon wouldn't approve of seeing me arrive at Witherswood in his car."

Ashlee leaned in close. "What was this man's name?"

"Gregory Winston."

Ashlee laughed out loud, harder and harsher than her usual laugh, a sound like breaking glass.

"Gregory Winston! Indeed, Pete would have been fit to be tied if he saw you drive up to Witherswood in Gregory's car." She lowered her voice. "Though I sure wouldn't have. I think Gregory is dreamy. So gorgeous. Don't you think?"

Daphne blushed again. "Why doesn't Mr. Wither-spoon like him? I assume it has something to do with business. Gregory said that Mr. Witherspoon owned half the town, and he owned the other half."

"That's part of it," Ashlee acknowledged. "Gregory keeps trying to buy properties from under Pete, keeps trying to woo away our employees at the cannery and the fishing fleet and the various restaurants we own on the coast." She sat back as a plump woman came by and cleared away their plates and freshened their coffees. "But that's not all of it. Their history goes back a lot further than that."

They were silent until the server had finished brushing the crumbs from the table and then trundled away toward the kitchen, leaving them alone on the terrace.

"Of course, this all predates me by many, many years," Ashlee continued. "But as I understand it, Gregory's father once lived and worked at Withers-wood. He was the groundskeeper. In fact, I believe that Gregory was born on the estate and spent much of his youth here." She paused, her eyes moving off to look beyond the cliffs. "Then . . . well, the tragedies happened."

Daphne thought she knew what Ashlee meant by the "tragedies," but she held her tongue.

Ashlee looked over at her. "I told Pete he was wrong not to tell you the history of this house before you made the decision to come here or not." She smiled kindly. "Ben informed me that he told you about Pete's father and the terrible things he did."

"Yes, he told me," Daphne said, and shuddered again as the memory of those horrors intruded onto what had been, until this point, such a pleasant morning.

"He was right to. He felt that Pete and I should know that he'd broken the news to you. Pete will be angry at first, because he felt you should only learn about it in time, and that he should have been the one to tell you. But I think he'll also feel relieved that Ben took that terrible responsibility from him."

"It must be so horrible for you all to live with that knowledge," Daphne said.

Ashlee looked at her with cold eyes. "The legacy of that monster lives on in everything we do in this house. The family can't seem to escape him."

"Christopher knows all about it," Daphne told her. "Last night, I visited him, and he seemed to take some enjoyment in revealing the details."

"Of course he knows," Ashlee said. "Pete is a fool if he thinks he can keep the knowledge from him. Pete doesn't understand we live in a world now where secrets aren't as easily kept. Please, Daphne, don't let whatever Christopher said trouble you. He's a very disturbed boy. If I had my way, he'd be in a mental hospital somewhere. The boy needs treatment." She sipped her coffee. "I'm sure that's why he hates me, because he knows I think he should be sent away to be helped."

"Hate is a strong word."

Ashlee laughed. "You've met him. Is it not accurate in his case?"

Daphne sighed. "He does seem to have a tremendous amount of anger bottled up inside him. But I guess ever since his mother died . . ."

Ashlee set her coffee cup down hard on the table. "Sweet, sainted Peggy. Everyone loved Peggy. And of course I can never be as good as Peggy." She laughed, that harsh sound again. "Except Pete. Pete thinks I'm every bit as good!"

This new side of her friend disturbed Daphne. Not that Ashlee's resentment wasn't in some ways justified. She was being judged by people who distrusted her, after all, people who actively disliked her and who compared her to the memory of a woman who had died. It must be very difficult to live in a house filled with such attitudes. But Ashlee's harshness in the face of such grievances was a marked contrast to her usual sunny, cheery disposition. It left Daphne uneasy.

Just at that moment, they were joined on the terrace by Ben and Gabriel. Ben was dressed in riding clothes and Gabe was, as usual, hunched over in his wheelchair, keeping his eyes averted from anyone else.

"Good morning, ladies!" Ben announced. "A beautiful autumn day! Would either of you like to join me for a ride around the estate?"

"That's very tempting," Ashlee said, "but I have a million items on my to-do list today."

"I have to begin lessons with Christopher," Daphne said. "Besides, I don't know how to ride."

"I'd love to teach you," Ben said, giving her a wide grin and a wink. "Some morning when my cousin has a day off from his studies."

Daphne smiled, and felt that tingly little feeling in her chest again.

Ben grabbed a cup of coffee and headed off into the yard toward the stables.

Ashlee was smirking at Daphne, watching her eyes follow Ben across the grass.

"Sweetie, you'd be wiser to stick with Donovan," Ashlee told her.

Daphne looked over at her startled. "What?"

Ashlee's smirk widened. "Donovan might have a fiancée, but at least he plays on your team."

"I don't understand."

Ashlee let out that whooping laugh—the lighter, happier one. "Of course you don't! Ben's gay, sweetie! I assume even a convent girl knows what gay means!"

"Oh," Daphne said, her cheeks flushing yet again.

"I know," Ashlee said, shaking her head. "Handsome, charming, all-around good guy, but..." Her voice trailed off. "He'll make some guy a great husband, but for you, sweetie, he's going to be just a really good friend."

"That's ... that's all I had in mind." Daphne looked away in embarrassment. She noticed that Gabriel had wheeled himself off to the far side of the terrace, where he sat watching his brother mount his horse.

"Poor Gabe," Ashlee whispered, leaning toward Daphne. "They say he was a terrific horseman in his day."

Daphne eyed the young man in the wheelchair. Gabriel's gaze was fixed on Ben far off across the grounds. Ben and his chestnut-colored horse suddenly bolted across the lawn, galloping along the cliffs. Daphne's heart broke for Gabriel. It was obvious he so wished he could still ride. She thought about asking Ashlee what kind of accident had left Gabriel wheelchair-bound. But Ashlee was standing now. Their breakfast was over. Daphne realized it was time she got to work. She had a meeting with Mr. Witherspoon at ten to go over Christopher's studies. And then, at noon, the first official sit-down with the boy—a moment Daphne was not looking forward to. At all.

But one question still lingered. As she and Ashlee headed into the house, passing through the dining room and into the great foyer, Daphne decided to inquire about one point that had gone unexplained at breakfast.

"Ashlee," she said quietly, after making certain no one was around. "There's just one other thing. . . ."

"What's that, sweetie?"

Daphne hesitated, then proceeded. "You said that Gregory Winston lived here until the time of the . . . the tragedies. What happened then? What caused him and his father to leave Witherswood?"

"I thought you knew," Ashlee said. "I see that Ben didn't tell you everything."

She motioned Daphne over to a small niche beside a grandfather's clock. There they had a modicum of privacy.

"You see," Ashlee said, her voice dropping to a whisper, "Gregory Winston's father—and his mother too—were the last two victims of Pete Witherspoon Senior. Their throats were cut on the very spot we're standing now!"

SIX

Daphne had barely recovered from the news when the sound of the heavy knocker on the front door reverberated throughout the foyer.

"That would be the sheriff," Ashlee said, as a tall, skeletal man walked in from the study to answer the door. "And that would be Boris," Ashlee added as an aside to Daphne. "Our butler. I don't think you met him last night."

Daphne thought Boris wasn't that far off from the image of Lurch she'd expected to answer the door last night. She was glad it had been Ashlee. Boris was gaunt and gray, with cadaverous cheeks and deep-set eyes. She wasn't sure if it was the sight of him or the news that Gregory Winston's parents had been murdered right where she was standing that made her suddenly start trembling from head to toe.

"Show the sheriff into the parlor, Boris," Ashlee was saying. "Hello, Sheriff, how are you?"

"Well, under the circumstances, Mrs. Witherspoon, I've been better," he said. Daphne remembered his twitchy white moustache.

"I understand," she said. "We're all devastated here. I'll get my husband. You don't need anyone else in the house, do you?"

"Not at the moment. Just some perfunctory questions. You know I hate to disturb Mr. Witherspoon with this, but it has to be done."

"We understand."

The sheriff noticed Daphne. "Though it might be good to speak with you again, Miss May," he said. "Since you were there."

"If you insist," Daphne said, trying to get her trembling under control.

"Listen, Sheriff, one favor before I go get Pete," Ashlee said. "Just a simple request, really. Daphne and I aren't mentioning that Gregory Winston gave her a ride last night. It was all completely innocent. You know how that would upset Pete, and Daphne's just started here. You don't want to make her job any more difficult than it already is, do you? Is that okay?"

Daphne wanted to throw her arms around Ashlee and kiss her. The sheriff nodded. "I don't see why we have to mention that detail," he said.

"You're a sweetheart," Ashlee said, and bounded up the stairs to get her husband.

The butler had come up behind them without making a sound. "You can wait in here, sir," Boris said, in a voice that sounded far too high and squeaky to be coming out of such a ghoulish face. He gestured with one extremely long arm and a deathly white hand toward the parlor.

The sheriff headed inside. Daphne figured she might as well join him, and get this interview over with. She didn't know why she had to go through this again. She'd already told him everything she knew. But she headed into the parlor and sat down on the sofa. The sheriff walked over to the French doors that looked out onto the cliffs, flipped out his cell phone, and began speaking to some deputy, telling him he was "on point" and would be "back soon." As he did so, there was movement off to the side of the room, and Daphne looked up. Old Boris was conferring with a much shorter, much stouter man. Together they looked like— what was that old comedy team?—Laurel and Hardy. One tall and lean, the other short and fat. And to Daphne's dismay, both men kept looking over at her.

Then came the sound of footsteps on the great staircase, and through the lobby came Mr. Witherspoon, in a gold satin smoking jacket and a gold ascot tie. He was striding as quickly as possible, which for a man with obvious arthritic pain, was rather impressive. Ashlee followed behind. The sheriff flipped his phone shut.

"Sheriff Patterson," Mr. Witherspoon said in greeting.

"Pete, I'm sorry to have to come up here, but you know how it is."

"Of course." The old man eyed Daphne. "Why is my son's governess here?"

"Well, since she was at the crime scene, I thought I might get her story again."

Pete arched a white eyebrow. "I thought she gave you a statement last evening."

"I did, Mr. Witherspoon," Daphne said. "I'm not sure what more I can—"

The sheriff raised a hand. "Please, Miss May, I just want to point out something that you said last night and see what Pete makes of it."

Mr. Witherspoon looked over at Daphne. His hard eyes had softened, and he looked sad. "I owe you an apology, my dear," he said. "I understand you have only just learned the parts of our family history that cause us all such pain. I should have informed you myself. I would have, in time, but this horrible thing has forced it to the surface before I was prepared to explain it all to you."

"That's all right, sir," Daphne said.

The sheriff's mustache twitched. "So she didn't know anything about your father's crimes before she came here?"

"That is correct," Pete told him.

"So," the sheriff continued, "to be clear, she had no idea about any details of the murders last night when she was at the inn, and found the body?"

"No," Daphne said, answering for herself this time. "I hadn't even met anyone here yet. I had just arrived. I knew nothing!"

It seemed so long ago. In such a short time so much had happened. So much had she learned. So much horror . . .

"Well, then, what you said to me last night, Miss May," Sheriff Patterson said, pulling a small notebook from his front shirt pocket and glancing down into it, "becomes even more curious."

"What is it that I said?"

"Yes," Mr. Witherspoon said, his voice dropping to a low growl. "What was it that she said to you?"

The sheriff looked from Daphne over to the old man. "She told me that just before she found the body, she had seen a clown sitting in one of the booths."

"Dear God!" Mr. Witherspoon croaked, and grabbed the side of a chair. Ashlee helped him sit down.

"It's true then?" Daphne asked in a small voice. "The killer . . . dressed as a clown when he killed his victims?"

"He did indeed," Sheriff Patterson said. "Seems to me, Pete, that what we may have here—and I stress 'may have,' because it's too soon to know—is a copycat killer. Someone who's playing off the terrible memory of what happened here in Point Woebegone twenty-five years ago."

"No," Pete said, covering his face in his hands.

"It'll be okay, sweetheart," Ashlee said, kissing her husband on one of his sunken, wrinkled cheeks.

"I have my people on high alert, stationed all across town, on the lookout for anything or anyone suspicious," Sheriff Patterson said. "And I'll post a couple of deputies down the hill from Witherswood, just to be on the safe side."

"You don't think anyone would come up here, do you?" Ashlee asked.

The sheriff shrugged. "I don't have any reason to think so, Mrs. Witherspoon. But if what this young lady says is true, if there really was some freak dressed as a clown in the inn last night, then we have to consider the possibility that someone is trying to somehow evoke the murders that took place here a generation ago."

"Why would anyone want to do that?" Pete

croaked, his voice ragged with pain and grief and memory.

"There are a lot of sickos out there, Pete," the sheriff told him.

"Of course," Ashlee said, trying to look on the bright side, "there is always the possibility that what Daphne saw was just a strange and terrible coincidence."

"Meaning?" the sheriff asked.

"Meaning that maybe the clown she saw was some guy on his way to or from a kid's birthday party, and it was all an innocent coincidence that he stopped in at the inn on the same night someone killed poor Maggie."

"Yes," Daphne said hopefully, grateful to Ashlee for voicing the possibility. Even though she knew it was absurd, she couldn't help but feel responsible somehow for bringing the family such pain and distress, since she was the only one who had seen the clown and she was the one who had brought the news to their attention. "Maybe," Daphne said, "the clown I saw has nothing whatsoever to do with any of this."

"Maybe," the sheriff said, but he didn't seem convinced. The way Pete sat in his chair, rubbing his forehead with his gnarled hand, suggested he wasn't convinced either.

"Well, I feel better knowing there are deputies keeping an eye on the house," Ashlee said. "Is there anything else you need from us this morning, Sheriff?"

"Not unless anyone here has any information that might shed some light on things," he said. "Maybe some of the others . . . ?"

"We discussed it last night, all of us," Pete said, looking over at the sheriff with tired old eyes. "No one had any clue as to who or what might be doing this, or why."

"Maybe I should speak with them. . . ."

"No," Pete said curtly. "There is nothing to be learned from them."

"All right," Sheriff Patterson agreed. "But if you learn of anything, let me know as soon as possible. The killer, if he is really trying to copycat your father, might get in touch with you somehow. Or someone else in the family. I'd suggest you all be on the alert for anything unusual."

"Of course we will be," Ashlee said.

"And you, too, Miss May," the sheriff added. "If he was aware that you saw him last night and knows that you were on your way here, he may try to contact you in some way."

"Me?" Daphne asked, suddenly terrified. "You think he might try to contact me? Why?"

"Who knows? We just all have to be on alert. I'd suggest that when you leave the grounds of Witherswood, you never travel alone. Always go into town with someone. At least until we better understand what we are dealing with."

Daphne felt new fear rush through her. Was this what her life in this house was going to be like from now on? Constant terror?

"Sheriff," Ashlee said, "we will do anything we can to help you. I know I speak for the entire family. But I'm also speaking for myself, because you know Maggie was an old friend of mine. I want to see her killer brought to justice."

"And you told my deputy on the phone that you

knew of no one who had any grudge against her, no one from her past who would want to harm her?"

"No one," Ashlee said. "Maggie was a doll. Everyone loved her." She paused, and Daphne saw the sadness cross her face. "Of course, she and I had been out of touch for the last year or so, which means I can't speak to whatever might have been going on in her life more recently than that."

The sheriff was nodding. "All right. I guess I've taken up enough of your time. Keep me informed of anything you hear or see, even if you think it's irrelevant or insignificant. I'll be the judge of what's important. All right?"

Pete nodded. He didn't stand or speak as the sheriff headed out of the parlor. Ashlee walked him to the door.

"Miss May," Pete said when they were alone, his voice cracking.

"Yes, sir?"

"We might as well speak now about Christopher's studies."

"Yes, of course."

He looked at her. Daphne's fears dissipated as she looked upon Pete's face, which was filled with so much sadness. As distressing as all this was to her, it was far more difficult on Pete. Taking a long breath and then exhaling slowly, he spoke of his son's struggles in school. Christopher was a very bright boy, he told Daphne, but ever since his mother's death he had withdrawn, become antisocial. He acted out at school, got into fights, caused trouble. Pete had felt it was best to have him homeschooled. Christopher had also, his father admitted, begun finding out bits and pieces of the family scandal, and Pete suspected this, too, had caused the boy to act out.

"If I may, sir," Daphne said, not wanting to interrupt but feeling she had no choice, "I think he's discovered more than bits and pieces."

She told him about her encounter with the boy the previous night. Pete shook his head in a mix of anger and weariness.

"He is incorrigible," the old man said. "I'm sorry for his behavior. I'm not surprised, however, that he has learned all that I wanted to keep from him. When the boy sets his mind to something, there is no stopping him."

Standing with some difficulty, Pete produced his son's academic records. Daphne perused them. It was clear from these reports that Christopher was indeed very bright, though his emotional problems kept him from fully applying himself. She went over the curriculum that Pete, along with Christopher's former teachers, had put together. She had been given an outline when Pete made the job offer through Mother Angela, and Daphne felt she could handle the curriculum. The academic subjects, that was. She would have no trouble teaching and tutoring the boy in mathematics, history, English composition, and science. But she knew Christopher needed more guidance than that.

His father agreed. "But what more can I do? I try to talk with him, but he rebuffs me. He is hostile to Ashlee, thinking she is trying to replace his mother, so he is hostile to me." He sighed. "My nephew Ben suggested that I have the boy speak to a counselor, perhaps even a psychologist. I am reluctant to do so, however, for the idea of a stranger coming into my home and inquiring about my family is abhorrent to me."

"And yet," Daphne said, "you brought me here, and I am a stranger."

He looked over at her. There was something in his eyes, but whatever thoughts were in Pete's mind he kept to himself.

"You must wonder why I chose you," he said, looking away from her.

"Yes," Daphne admitted. "I do."

"When I brought Christopher back to Witherswood, I began to look around for a governess. One of your school's benefactors, someone I trust completely and who I have known a long time, recommended you as the ideal teacher for my son."

Daphne smiled. "That was kind of him. Or her, I suppose. I'd like to know the identity of this benefactor so I might say thank you. He or she must know me well to have recommended me for the position. But Mother Angela said she did not have a name to give me."

Pete was staring at her. "Was she good to you, Mother Angela? Did she raise you well? Were you happy in her care?"

Daphne's smile broadened. "Oh, yes, very much so. It was difficult growing up, not knowing who my parents were, or where I came from. But Mother Angela made it seem all very natural that I should live at Our Lady. She was as much a real mother to me as any real mother, I should think.

Took care of me when I was sick. Helped me with homework. Took me, along with the other girls, on trips. Yes, I was very happy there with her."

Suddenly a terrible wave of homesickness washed over Daphne. She wished she were back at Our Lady, doing chores, taking walks, sitting in the little nook next to the chapel, having long conversations with Mother Angela about everything and anything, from what it might be like to travel in the space shuttle to how best to cook beets.

"I am glad to hear it," Pete said. "I can't imagine what it must be like not to know anything about one's family." He paused. "In some ways, it might be a blessing."

Daphne understood why he would say such a thing. There was still so much she felt she needed to know about the murders that took place here by his father's hand. She didn't want any more surprises flung at her by Christopher. She needed the facts if she was to deal with the boy effectively. But she couldn't bring herself to ask Pete about it, especially not now, with the possibility of a copycat killer on the loose.

They went over specific lesson plans, and Daphne agreed to draw up a syllabus for each subject. Science would be the most difficult, Daphne thought, given that they had no lab or equipment, but Pete told her anything she thought they'd need, he'd buy. She told him that often the most instructive lessons didn't require expensive equipment. A simple walk through the woods on the estate could explain things like photosynthesis and chlorophyll. Pete said he liked the way Daphne thought.

They agreed the first official lessons with the boy would commence the next day. That would give Daphne time to plan out some lessons. Pete encouraged her to return to the boy's room and try to engage him again. Tonight, he said, the family would have the dinner they'd planned for last night, and Pete himself would lay down the rules of how the boy should behave with his new governess. He hoped that would make their relationship easier.

Daphne wasn't sure.

Gathering the academic records and lesson plans up in her arms, she thanked Pete and told him she'd get to work right away on the syllabi. He smiled weakly, and bid her good morning. Daphne lugged the materials out of the parlor and into the foyer.

She was about to head down to the study, where Pete had told her she could use the computer, when she was startled by a hand on her shoulder. A white, cold hand that made her jump.

"Miss May," came a high-pitched voice, and Daphne looked up to see the cadaverous face of Boris the butler looming over her.

"Yes?" she said meekly.

"I wanted to welcome you to Witherswood. I had the night off last night, so I wasn't able to greet you then."

"Thank you," she said, looking up at his sunken eyes.

"And I would like to welcome you as well," came another voice, this one from somewhere below and behind her. Daphne spun around. Standing on the other side of her was the small, squat man

Boris had been talking with earlier. He had a round, fat face and piercing black eyes that were small and round like buttons. He was completely bald—in fact, he seemed to have no hair anywhere on his body. His pudgy arms were hairless and he had no eyebrows or eyelashes. His skin was a bright pink.

"My name is Axel," the little man said. "I'm the family's chauffeur. And I must apologize to you as well as offering a welcome, for apparently I left you waiting at the train station last night. I'm very sorry that you had to take a taxi."

"It's okay," Daphne said.

These two creeped her out. They stood on either side of her, far too close. She felt as if they were pinning her between them, She clutched Christopher's academic files tightly to her breasts, almost in protection.

"I cannot understand how I could have made such an error. Boris and I usually have the same night off, when we visit my sister Hulga over in Bangor. I swear that I looked at my logbook yesterday morning and saw nothing scheduled for last night. But subsequently Mr. Witherspoon showed me that indeed there was something written there. It was instructions to pick you up at the station. It was in Mrs. Witherspoon's handwriting, and she told me she wrote it there two days ago. So somehow I must have looked at the page wrong, or perhaps I looked at another page. My deepest apologies."

"It's really okay," Daphne said again.

"I just hope it doesn't keep us from being friends," the little man said, smiling up at her. His fat cheeks dimpled, and he revealed a set of yellow, pointy teeth. Daphne recoiled.

"No, please, don't worry about it," she said, "Now, if you'll excuse me, I need to start preparing Christopher's lessons."

The two strange men backed away and Daphne hurried down the corridor to the study. Inside the room, she spread the files onto the large table and began sorting them. She tried to keep her mind on the job at hand, but a thought had begun to trouble her. She supposed it had come into her mind when Mr. Witherspoon asked her about Mother Angela. He'd wanted to know if Mother had been good to her. And Daphne said yes, oh yes, she had been very good to her.

But now she couldn't help but wonder.

Had Mother Angela known she was sending Daphne to a house that had been the site of grisly murders some twenty-five years earlier?

Not that it mattered, really. Mother had likely checked out Mr. Witherspoon to make sure he was who he said he was. The school benefactor, who-ever he or she was, no doubt assured her that Witherswood would be a fine place for Daphne to live. But did no one raise the issue of the murders? If Christopher had found information on the killings so easily on the Internet, had no one at Our Lady done so as well?

And even if that wouldn't have been enough to stop them from sending Daphne here, why wouldn't Mother have warned her—prepared her—for what she was about to discover?

Maybe Mother didn't know. Maybe the benefactor hadn't told her.

Daphne suddenly felt the need to talk with Mother Angela. But she had no cell phone. That was something Our Lady had not provided. Maybe Ashlee would let her use hers at some point.

Flipping open the first of the files—mathematics—Daphne began to make some notes. She spent more than an hour doing this, finally getting lost in her work, thankfully forgetting about dead waitresses and murderous clowns and strange men with pointy yellow teeth. For the better part of an hour she was back to being just a teacher, the profession she'd wanted to pursue ever since she was a young girl. She'd imagined herself teaching a class of children—third or fourth or fifth grade—not just one emotionally disturbed boy. But she would do the very best job she could.

She heard the deep chime of the grandfather clock from the foyer, twelve gongs signaling noon. She lifted her head and glanced out the windows looking toward the cliffs. In the distance she could see Ben returning from his ride, galloping across the golden field toward the stables, which were beyond her view. She smiled. She was glad for Ben and for Ashlee. She felt she could trust them, that she could talk to them. The rest of the house, she wasn't so sure about. Mr. Witherspoon was a good man, she thought, deep down. But his rigidity was a problem. How could he deny his son the professional mental help he so clearly needed?

As she continued gazing out the window, Daphne saw someone else moving across the field. Walking, however, not riding a horse. The figure was far away, sometimes obscured by the tall yellow grass. It seemed to be a man. It might be Donovan, or another servant she hadn't met. But as the figure kept approaching—walking, it seemed to Daphne, directly toward the windows of the study—she thought maybe it was Pete. The man wore a dark shirt and pants, and had a full head of white hair. Even from a distance, he seemed to resemble the master of the house.

Had Mr. Witherspoon gone for a walk? But it seemed impossible. She had left him sitting in the parlor. This man, whoever he was, had come from some distance across the field. There was no way Pete, who had trouble walking, could have left the house, gone that far across the field, and then headed back. Only an hour and half—maybe even just an hour and fifteen minutes—had elapsed since Daphne had left him. But the more she watched the man approaching, the more he looked like Pete.

He was close enough now that Daphne could see he carried something in his hands.

She strained to see.

Suddenly she made a little gasp.

The man was carrying an ax.

He kept walking closer. His shock of white hair, so much like Pete's, seemed to glow in the bright sunlight.

And now Daphne could see that he was smiling.

She could see something else, too.

His dark shirt wasn't dark at all.

It was a white shirt.

A white shirt—drenched in blood!

SEVEN

"Somebody, come quick!" Daphne shouted, leaping from her chair, sending several files scattering to the floor in the process, their papers fluttering in the air like giant butterflies. "Please, someone! You've got to help him!"

She ran into the corridor. Boris moved toward her at a snail's pace, his walk truly like that of the living dead. But Ashlee now appeared as well, and she sprinted past the butler to join Daphne in the doorway of the study.

"What's wrong? Daphne, what's wrong? You look white as a sheet!"

"Outside!" Daphne pointed toward the window. "Mr. Witherspoon! Outside! He's hurt—bleeding!"

"Pete?" Ashlee hurried into the room. "Where? But it can't be Pete! I just left him in the dining room!"

"But I saw him. . . ." Daphne stepped back into the room. "At least, it looked like him . . . An older man . . . bleeding . . ."

Her eyes searched beyond the windows in vain,

however, for a sign of the bleeding, smiling man. There was nothing. The tall yellow grass in the field blew in the breeze undisturbed. No one was standing there any longer.

"It looked like Mr. Witherspoon," Daphne said, her voice low. "I swear it looked like him . . . and his shirt was covered with blood."

"Oh, no, no," came a voice.

Daphne turned. Boris had reached the doorway now. He stood there, shaking his head. He had heard what Daphne had just said. And he looked terrified.

"He's returned," the butler rasped in that eerie high voice of his.

"Stop that, Boris," Ashlee said. She smiled over at Daphne. "You must have imagined it, sweetie."

"Who does he mean?" Daphne asked. "Who does he mean has returned?"

"Boris believes in all sorts of things. Don't pay any attention to him," Ashlee said, casting the butler a reprimanding look.

"With all due respect, madam," Boris said, "I've lived in this house much longer than you have, and I have seen things. Things that cannot be explained."

Daphne shuddered. "Do you mean . . . ghosts?"

"Call them what you will," the butler told her, "but I know what I have seen. Just as you know what you have seen."

"Stop it, Boris," Ashlee scolded. "Daphne's just arrived here. Are you trying to frighten her?"

The butler lifted his chin. "Just trying to be honest with her."

"Please leave us alone," Ashlee said. "We don't

need your superstitions here right now. They are not helpful."

Suddenly they were joined by another voice, rounding the corner into the study. It was Ben, still in his riding clothes.

"What's wrong? I heard Daphne scream, even from outside," he said.

Ashlee sighed. "She just had a fright, that's all. Nothing to it."

Boris just harrumphed and turned and left the study.

Daphne locked eyes with Ben. "I thought I saw a man . . . possibly Mr. Witherspoon . . . outside in the field. He looked to be bleeding."

"A man?" Ben asked. "I was just out there. . . ."

"Yes," Daphne said, suddenly hopeful. "He appeared from the same direction from which you came riding. He appeared shortly after I saw you. He walked from that direction straight toward the house. As he grew nearer, I saw that his shirt was covered in blood."

Ben's face paled. "And you say . . . he looked like Uncle Pete?"

"Yes," Daphne said. "He was still at some distance, but I could have sworn it was him."

"Dear Lord," Ben said, and pulled out a chair, sitting down hard.

Ashlee sighed. "But it couldn't have been Pete. He's in the dining room, having a cup of tea. I just left him. Go see for yourself."

"I did see him," Ben said. "I saw him sitting there as I came into the house. He asked me to find out what was wrong down here." He shook his head. "I hate to tell him."

"Then don't," Ashlee said. "Why disturb him more? The sheriff was here earlier, dredging up all that terrible history. . . . He's still pretty shaken up."

"Why would this disturb him so much?" Daphne asked.

Ashlee tried to smile over at her, but Daphne could see she was upset. "Wouldn't it disturb you, sweetie, if someone said they had just seen a vision of you walking through the field, your shirt covered in blood?"

"I won't say anything," Ben told her. He looked up at Daphne. "The only man in the field when I came through was old Tom, the stable hand. Maybe you saw him."

"Was he bleeding?" Daphne asked.

"No," Ben replied.

"Does he have white hair?"

"Well," Ben said, "I suppose it's white. Maybe more gray, I guess. Pretty thin on top."

Daphne shook her head deliberately. "The man I saw had thick white hair."

Ben just sighed, covering his face in his hands.

Ashlee approached and gave Daphne a quick hug. "You're still upset about last night, sweetie. Who wouldn't be? You discovered a woman's murdered body. That would be enough to keep me on edge for months! And the sheriff only made things worse with all his talk this morning."

"I . . . I just don't know," Daphne said.

Ashlee smiled at her. "You must have seen old Tom. If you ask me, his hair is white, not gray, and in the sunlight maybe it looked whiter than it is."

"Well, if it was Tom," Daphne said, "I suggest

you go out to the stable and see if he's hurt himself." She paused. "Though he didn't seem to be in any pain. He was smiling."

Ashlee and Ben exchanged looks.

"Look, sweetie, for now, I don't want to upset Pete any more than he already is. He's not a well man. I'm going to tell him you tripped and hurt your ankle. That's why you cried out. He didn't hear what your actual words were. I'll tell him you're fine now. You just called out in surprise."

Daphne turned away. "Do whatever you think best."

"Thanks, sweetie." She gave Daphne another quick hug, then hurried out of the study.

"Last night, I thought I saw a clown in Christopher's room," Daphne told Ben once they were alone. "I was convinced that it was my imagination. I'm not so sure today."

Ben stood, looking at her sympathetically. "Maybe the light on old Tom's shirt made it look as if he were bleeding. You said it was at a distance. . . ."

"I know what I saw!" Daphne said, her voice rising. "And I think you know that I saw it, that I'm not crazy."

Ben sighed. "No, you're not crazy."

"Boris said he's seen things in this house. Is that true?"

"He does say that, yes."

"Have you seen things?"

He hesitated. "No, well, nothing like what he describes. And nothing like you just saw." He walked over to a tall cabinet with two front doors. He placed his hands on the knobs of the doors.

"But in a gloomy old house like this one, especially a house where such terrible things occurred, it's hard not to . . . sometimes . . . see something . . . and wonder."

He opened the doors of the cabinet. He removed an old, tattered photograph album, the kind with black pages, where the photos were held in place with small triangular fasteners. He placed the album on the table and flipped it open. Daphne walked over to stand beside him. She looked down at the page he was showing her.

"Mr. Witherspoon," she said.

The picture was of Pete, possibly ten years ago. His hair was still as white as ever, but his face seemed somewhat fuller. He stared into the camera with an intense look in his eyes.

"Yes," Ben said, "that's Peter Witherspoon." He paused. "But not the Mr. Witherspoon you know. Not Uncle Pete."

Daphne gasped, as the meaning hit her. "You mean, it's—?"

Ben was nodding. "Yes. That's Pete Witherspoon Senior. Uncle Pete's father. My grandfather." He drew in a tight breath. "The murderer of seventeen people, three of them in this very house."

"That's the man I saw," Daphne said, in a voice barely above a whisper.

Ben closed the album. "Uncle Pete has always hated looking in a mirror, knowing how much he resembles his despised father."

"Then I saw a ghost," Daphne said. "And last night, the clown . . . that was him, too. Appearing in the form he used to murder his victims."

Ben returned the album to the cabinet. "Do you believe in ghosts, Daphne?"

"I never did until today," she said.

He smiled sadly. "Then maybe . . . maybe there's a more logical explanation."

"How could there be a logical explanation? I'd never seen a picture of Pete Witherspoon Senior before you just showed it to me. So how could I imagine seeing him?"

Ben sighed. "Well, you've seen Pete Witherspoon Junior. You thought it was him you saw, after all."

Daphne closed her eyes. "But Pete Junior is sitting in the dining room having a cup of tea. You said you saw him yourself."

"Yes, I did."

"I know what I saw."

Ben smiled again at her. "So, if you think you saw a ghost, what will you do now?"

"I don't know," Daphne said.

"If I truly believed I saw a ghost, I wouldn't stick around that place."

Daphne covered her face with her hands for a moment, then removed them, looking imploringly over at Ben. "There's nothing I can do. I can't leave. I can't go back to Our Lady. I've graduated from the school. I don't want to be a nun." She laughed at the absurdity of her situation. "So the only place in the world I can be right now is right here, in this dark old haunted house where seventeen people were killed."

"Just three were killed here," Ben reminded her. "The rest were killed in the village."

"I wish Mother Angela had prepared me for all this," Daphne said.

Ben put his arm around her shoulder. "I can't believe the people at that school would allow you to come here not knowing this family's history. That was irresponsible of them."

"I have to believe Mother Angela didn't know," Daphne said, suddenly close to tears. "I need to call her at some point."

"So why don't you?"

"I don't have a phone. And the house has no landline."

Ben gave her a quick squeeze. "Well, I have a phone. You can use mine anytime."

"Thank you."

"Look, Daphne," Ben said, letting go of her shoulder and sitting on the edge of the table to look her in the eyes. "It's really not such a bad place. Granted, the murder at the inn has dredged up all this terrible stuff once again. But when things get back to normal, you'll see, we're not all so bad."

She tried to smile.

"Ashlee's a sweet kid, no matter that my aunts don't care for her. And Christopher . . . well, he's a handful, but you may be just what he needs. Someone who can make him a priority. I think Uncle Pete, in his own grief over his first wife's death, dropped the ball with Christopher. The kid needs a friend. I've done what I can, but he trusts no one right now. Maybe in time, he'll trust you."

Daphne thought of the lonely, scared little boy

upstairs, still deep in grief over the loss of his mother.

"I'll teach you to ride," Ben promised. "And in the winter there's some great skiing and ice skating not far from here. In the summer, Uncle Pete opens the pool on the estate. I go down to Portland a couple times a month, just to get some city life, you know, and you are more than welcome to come with me. And I think you know . . ." Here he smiled widely. "I think you know you'll be safe with me."

She smiled back.

"Okay, then," Ben said, standing up. "You're not running out of here quite yet, then, right?"

"No," she said in a small voice.

"Good deal," he said, and winked at her. "Now I've got to go change out of these riding clothes. See you at dinner. I hear cook is making a special feast!"

Ben headed out of the room.

Daphne decided the only thing to do for the moment was to get back to work. She gathered up the papers from the floor and rearranged them on the table. She sat back down to continue working on Christopher's lesson plans. But she made sure this time to sit facing away from the windows.

Work had always been her way out of stressful situations. Whenever she was anxious about something—her grades, a minor squabble with Katie, the occasional melancholy that set in when she dwelled too long on her unknown past—Daphne had always taken refuge in her schoolwork. She hadn't been one of those kids who put off studying for tests until the last minute. She actually enjoyed studying, reading, taking notes, making outlines. It was her way of calming her mind. So it was now, too, preparing Christopher's lessons. Thinking about square roots and long division—and the history of Western civilization and how to teach composition—got her mind far, far away from any thoughts of ghosts. And she was glad about that.

She spent most of the rest of the afternoon that way, stopping only for a brief lunch, which she ate in the kitchen with cook—Daphne found out the large, red-cheeked woman's name was actually Frances. Then, after finally putting Christopher's lesson plans away, satisfied she had enough planned with which to start the next day, she took a long walk around the grounds. She saw nothing to frighten her. No renegade clowns. No men in bloody shirts. Just beautiful, rolling countryside. The leaves on the trees were fading to reds and oranges, and the grass was so yellow that it seemed almost on fire. The setting sun cast an amber glow across everything, from the dark stone of the house to the red wooden stables to the gray cliffs that dropped precipitously to the crashing ocean below.

Maybe it was my imagination, Daphne thought at last. Maybe Ashlee was right. Who knew what kind of effect seeing a woman with her throat cut open had had on her, or how long those effects might last?

After all, Mother Angela had always said Daphne had a florid imagination. Daphne would write the most elaborate stories in composition class, about elves and secret tunnels through mountains and

Shangri-las filled with exotic birds and rivers that ran with gold. Mother used to say that Daphne could conjure up the most extraordinary tales, that she rivaled the Brothers Grimm, that she had, by far, the liveliest imagination of any student she'd ever worked with.

Maybe she was just conjuring up stories again.

She held on to this belief—this hope—all through dinner. No one mentioned a word about anything distressing. No ghosts, no murders, no sheriffs, no clowns. And Daphne was grateful for that. Although Abigail just sat there glowering at her, and poor Gabe simply continued his pattern of not speaking a word, everyone else chatted amiably with Daphne. Louella told her how lovely she thought her blouse was, and even Suzanne talked about taking a walk with Daphne down to the pond at the far end of the estate: "It's so very pretty down there—you'll love it." Maybe that was because she didn't notice the sly little smiles her fiancé Donovan kept giving Daphne, and the wink he gave her as he passed the garlic mashed potatoes.

Christopher, however, was the biggest surprise. When he came into the dining room, all four feet of him, he approached Daphne like a peer of the queen's court. He bowed to her and took her hand and kissed it.

"My official welcome to my new governess," he said, his button eyes shining.

Daphne had smiled, but she didn't trust him. At one point during dinner, Mr. Witherspoon had addressed his son.

"Just so that we go on record here, Christopher, in front of the entire household," the old man

said, "you are to give Daphne your full coopera-
tion and obedience, and treat her with complete
and total respect, accepting her authority as you
would mine. Is that very clear?"

"But, of course, Father," the boy replied. "I am
most anxious to learn all that Miss May has to
teach me. I am sure the breadth of her knowledge
and experience is impressive. How fortunate I am
to be her pupil."

Daphne and Ben exchanged small smiles. The
kid was such a player.

After dinner, Daphne asked Ben if she could
take him up on his offer to use his phone. He
obliged immediately, handing over his BlackBerry,
but he explained that reception wasn't great out
here on the point, and the best place to get the
most bars was up in the tower room. He offered to
take her there, since Daphne had yet to climb
those particular stairs. The entrance to the tower
was at the far end of the front foyer. Unlike the
grand marble staircase that led to the second story
of the main house, these steps were narrow, and
iron, and spiral. As Daphne and Ben ascended,
their footsteps clanged against the metal and echoed
in the darkness.

Ben explained that when the house was first
built, in the late nineteenth century, the tower had
been used as a lookout for incoming ships. Mr.
Witherspoon's great-grandfather had been a sea
captain, Ben said, and his servants—as well as,
sometimes, his wife—would climb these stairs to
keep an eye on the ocean to spot his ship returning
to the harbor. Eventually, old Amos Witherspoon
was lost at sea. But for many years afterward, his

grieving widow, Millicent, a recluse who grew slightly mad, had continued her treks up these stairs, night after night, so she could stand in the tower room and scan the seas for a sign of her late husband. She was known to call out, "There he is! Amos returns!"—sending chills through the entire house.

The tower room was a round space about fifteen feet in diameter, sparsely furnished with plain sofas against the stone walls, and a round table with a lamp placed directly in the center. Narrow rectangular windows evenly spaced around the entire room looked out over the cliffs and the roiling sea beyond. Ben left Daphne alone to make her call, after first switching on the lamp, which cast an amber glow across the room.

For a moment after he left, Daphne hesitated. The sound of the waves from far below reached her ears.

Then she pressed the digits of the number for Our Lady's School for Girls.

It was the private number for the sisters' residence. She recognized Sister Therese's voice when she answered, and after chatting happily with her for a few moments, she asked to speak with Mother Angela.

"Daphne! My child!" the good mother said exultantly when she came to the phone. "I am so happy to hear from you. How are you, my darling?"

"I am fine, Mother," Daphne told her, and quickly related a bit of her trip, and some about the house and its people, and the challenges she faced with Christopher.

"You will rise to the challenge, my dear," Mother Angela said. "Do you remember how well you worked with that little girl whose father had been killed in Iraq? How she blossomed with you as her tutor?"

Daphne did remember little Heather Marie. But she faced more challenges here at Witherswood than she had even with a little girl grieving a father killed in war.

"Mother," she finally said, "I must ask you something."

"Of course, my dear, anything."

"Did you know the history of the Witherspoon family? Did you know about the murders?"

The nun fell silent on the other end of the line. "Oh, my darling child. Yes, I knew. And my heart broke not telling you ahead of time."

"How could you let me come here without preparing me?" Daphne was near tears. In a trembling voice she told her how she had discovered Maggie's body, and how the sheriff thought there might be a copycat killer loose. She told her how frightened she was.

Mother seemed to be close to crying herself. "My poor child. How I long to take you in my arms and console you. I had no idea ... none ... that the history of that family would revisit in such a terrible way. My poor, poor child."

"Were you told not to share the information with me?"

Mother admitted she had been. "Mr. Witherspoon is a good man. I spoke with him ... at length." Her voice trembled. "He asked me to let him tell you, in his own time and his own way. He . . ."

Suddenly Mother's voice faded. Daphne looked at the phone. The number of bars had dropped from three to two. She walked to the other side of the room.

"Mother? Are you there?"

"Yes, my darling" she replied, her voice coming in stronger once again. "I am always here. No matter the distance, I am always here."

"You felt you could trust Mr. Witherspoon? You felt sending me here was still a good idea even knowing what you knew about the family history?"

"I did, Daphne. And I do trust Mr. Witherspoon. He is a good man. You can trust him as well."

"How can you know for sure? You have never met him!"

Silence on the other end of the line. The reception was fading again. Daphne rushed to the center of the room.

"Daphne, my dear, I couldn't hear what you said."

"I asked how you can be so sure to trust him, when you've never met him. He seems like a good man, but this house is filled with so many mysterious people . . . so many secrets."

"Oh, my dear, I can make out only every other word you're saying," Mother Angela lamented. "All I can tell you is that I sent you to the Witherspoons because it is your destiny to be there. It is meant to be. God's will, Daphne."

"God's will? What do you mean that it's my destiny to be here?" An idea flickered in Daphne's mind. "Are you saying that this place has something to do with my past? Is this where my parents came from? Point Woebegone?"

"I can't hear you, my darling. Are you still there?"

"Yes, Mother I'm here! Oh, please tell me more!"

But the connection was gone. Daphne immediately hit redial, but the call wouldn't go through. There was barely one bar left on the phone. After three more tries, she gave up, and walked back down the stairs of the tower, listening to the echo of her footfalls against the stone walls.

She returned the BlackBerry to Ben and thanked him. He asked if it was good to speak with Mother Angela. Daphne said it was and it wasn't. She didn't feel like telling him any more.

Crawling into bed, Daphne stared wide-eyed at the ceiling. What had Mother meant, that it was her destiny to be here? What had she meant, that it was God's will?

The wind picked up then, howling through the eaves of the house. In the wind, she heard her name. It must be her imagination, she told herself, holding the locket that she wore around her neck in the palm of her hand, the locket that held the last physical link to her origins, to who she really was.

But then her name seemed to get louder behind the wind. "Daphneee, Daphneeeeee . . ."

She refused to be unnerved by it. She had a feeling that she'd better to get used to hearing her name when the wind blew. It might be her imagination. But it might also be the ghost of Pete Witherspoon Senior, the serial killer. Or it might be Christopher, taunting her. Or it might be the spirit of crazy Millicent Witherspoon, wanting Daphne to find her lost husband.

It might be anything, in fact.

All Daphne knew for sure was that it was her destiny to be there.

EIGHT

The days passed uneventfully after that. Daphne began her lessons with Christopher, which went better than she had feared. The boy could be exceedingly pleasant at times, complimenting her on her dress or her hair, and other times terribly sullen, barely speaking when she asked him a question. But, perhaps heeding his father's words, he did the lessons she gave him, completed his homework, and didn't argue when she told him it was time for bed.

One night she heard the faint buzz of Christopher's music after the lights went out. Daphne knocked on his door as she'd told him she would do. When he didn't reply, she went inside, as she'd also told him she would do. He was lying in bed with his earbuds plugged into his iPod, his eyes closed. Daphne tapped on his shoulder and he jumped. "I'll make a deal with you," she said. "You can listen to your music for a half an hour after the lights go out, but no longer." He started to protest, but she said he could take the deal or leave it.

He'd agreed, and so far, he'd kept his end of the bargain. The music always shut off half an hour after Daphne heard it go on.

Gradually, over the course of a few weeks, she settled into a routine. Breakfast with Ashlee and Mr. Witherspoon in the dining room. Sometimes Ben or Louella or Donovan or Suzanne would join them. Never Abigail or Gabe. There were no more family meals as there had been in the first couple of days. Cook made food each day and each member of the household ate when he or she pleased. Daphne took lunch at twelve-thirty, when she gave Christopher a half-hour break. Dinner she usually ate on the terrace, often with Ashlee and Mr. Witherspoon or Ben, sometimes all three. She had come to like Ashlee a great deal, even if their lives had been very different growing up. Ashlee's parents had divorced when she was eleven, and her mother had worked as a stripper to pay the rent. Ashlee said she never quite followed in her mother's footsteps, but cocktail waitress wasn't far up the ladder from stripper, and she'd understood that to get the best tips she had to flirt extravagantly and show as much skin as the law allowed. By the time she'd met Pete, she explained, she was trying to make something of herself, landing a job in a respectable restaurant and taking computer courses at night. Meanwhile, her mom had gotten cancer, and so Ashlee was supporting her as well. "Pete was a godsend," Ashlee told her. "He saved my life." She smiled sadly. "He understood what cancer does to a family. His first wife—you know, sweet, sainted Peggy—died of cancer."

Daphne realized Ashlee still had a hard time

reconciling the memory of her husband's first wife with their time together now. She supposed it must be like living with a ghost. She felt badly for Ashlee, since it was obvious she was deeply in love with her much-older husband. And Daphne was sure Pete loved her back just as much. She wondered what that was like, to love a man and have him love you in return.

Yet . . . was there a reason for Ashlee's fears? Daphne remembered that strange moment one night a couple of weeks earlier, when she'd walked in on Mr. Witherspoon in the study. He had been sitting in a chair, holding a photograph in his hands, just staring down at it. He'd been startled when Daphne had come in behind him, and she'd apologized. He said not to worry, but he quickly tucked the photograph into his jacket pocket. Daphne had caught a glimpse of the photo when she'd come upon the old man. It showed a young woman—but it wasn't Ashlee. It was an older photo, of a woman Daphne didn't recognize. Might it have been, she wondered, the same woman she'd seen in several photographs throughout Christopher's room? Might it have been Mr. Witherspoon's first wife, Peggy, Christopher's mother? Daphne recalled Ashlee's bitterness regarding "sweet, sainted Peggy," whom no one thought she could compare with. But her husband didn't share their view, Ashlee had insisted. He loved her just as much as he'd loved Peggy. If not more.

Maybe that's just what Ashlee wanted to believe.

After dinner, Daphne usually returned to her room to read, or sometimes made her way to the library, on the other side of the study. Here all sorts of ancient volumes were crammed in the floor-to-ceiling bookshelves. The room seemed musty and damp. First editions of Dickens and Twain and Hawthorne and Poe. Old Bibles and prayer books. And in the midst of them all, in a nook specially prepared by Ashlee, a shiny new twenty-seven-inch iMac.

"Ben and Donovan and Gabe all have computers in the rooms, but Pete won't let me bring 'one of those goddamn machines' into our room," Ashlee had told her with a laugh. "So I installed mine in the library. It's a beauty, isn't it? Expensive, yes, but Pete said I should only have the best. Feel free to use it, Daphne, anytime!"

Occasionally Daphne had signed on, but there was little reason to do. She no longer even had an e-mail address, having lost that privilege when she left Our Lady. So she'd check the news, or the weather, or Google a recipe to give to cook. Twice she'd gone on to get additional information to help in a history lesson with Christopher. But other than that, there wasn't much need for a computer. . . .

Except . . .

One night, having downloaded some background on Paul Revere's ride for the next day's lesson, Daphne had hesitated before signing off.

Her fingers had hovered over the keypad as the Google search engine waited on the screen.

Despite the sudden trembling of her hands, she slowly typed in a string of words. Witherspoon. Murder. Point Woebegone.

She was ready to press SEARCH when she suddenly pulled back.

Ashlee would see. Daphne didn't know how to hide searches. Ashlee would see that she had searched out information on the serial killings that had taken place in this town. In this house.

Not that Ashlee wouldn't understand. But Daphne deleted the words anyhow. Quite possibly, she wasn't ready to read any more details about what had happened here twenty-five years ago.

She'd received a letter from Mother Angela a few days after their telephone call. It was brief, but Mother had reassured Daphne that she was always there for her, that she loved her as she would her own daughter. She apologized again for not telling her about the Witherspoons' terrible family history, and stressed that she was certain that she could trust Mr. Witherspoon. "He is a good man," Mother wrote. Daphne could only hope she was correct.

Not that she thought he wasn't. Old Pete Witherspoon didn't say much, and kept to himself mostly, but he had been good and honorable in all his dealings with Daphne. Indeed, as the third week of her residence at Witherswood neared completion, Daphne could actually say that she was beginning to enjoy her life there. The food was terrific, her room was comfortable, the grounds were awesome. And except for the surliness of Abigail, who continued to glare at her whenever they passed in the hallway, everyone else was pleasant, or at least tolerable. Even Gabe didn't unnerve her as much as he had in the beginning. She felt sorry for him, and went out of her way to bid him good day whenever they came into contact. It seemed to be having an effect. The young man in the wheelchair had started to mutter a "good morning" or "good evening" in response to her greetings.

This past week, Donovan and Suzanne had gone off on a trip to Seattle, so for the duration Daphne hadn't even had to contend with any leering winks. That was a nice change. And while she continued to keep on her guard with Christopher, Daphne thought even the boy was warming up a little. He'd smile at little jokes she made during their lessons, and one day even paid her a bit of a compliment that seemed genuine, and not just for show. Daphne, Christopher said, was better at explaining long division than any teacher at his old school. They were all "dumb-asses" up there, he said. And Daphne was not a dumb-ass, he told her. She smiled, taking it as a real, honest-to-God compliment.

It was a Saturday, and the trees outside the house were on fire with brilliant reds, yellows, and oranges. The smell of autumn was in the air, and Ashlee suggested they go into Point Woebegone for lunch. Daphne had been into the village only for brief trips in the past few weeks: a couple of times with Ashlee to the grocery store, and once with Ben to a tack shop. Never had she gone in just for the fun of it.

"We might as well go now," Ashlee said, "before everything shuts down. In the winter Point Woebegone closes up. It's a real ghost town."

Daphne was excited by the idea of it. A trip off the estate sounded like a terrific break from her routine. They hopped into Ashlee's white BMW Z4, specially built with pink leather interior. The day was cool but sunny, so they figured they'd put the top down. As the wind whipped their hair, the two young women sped down the winding road, the crashing sea off to their left, into the village of Point Woebegone.

"We should do a little shopping, too," Ashlee said. "Get you some new clothes. Sweetie, those same old skirts and sweaters are starting to get a bit threadbare!"

Today, in a rare change, Daphne was wearing jeans. She smiled. "I can't afford new clothes yet," she said. "I'm still saving."

"Sweetie, my husband pays you every week and you get free room and board!" She laughed, looking over at her through a pair of oversized pink sunglasses. "Splurge a little!"

"Well, maybe one outfit," Daphne said.

"We can put it on my charge and you can pay me later."

"Oh, no," Daphne said. "I couldn't do that."

She was very strict about her money. Mother Angela had opened a savings account for her a long time ago, and Daphne had deposited whatever small money she'd made doing odd jobs back in Boston. Now Mr. Witherspoon deposited her check into that same account every week, and Daphne kept track of her funds the old-fashioned way: with a savings passbook. Her salary was quite generous for a first-time tutor, and it was true that she had virtually no expenses. She'd have quite the savings in a very short time. She guessed that was another reason Mother Angela had wanted her to take this job. What other girl with her lack of experience would land a job this lucrative? She supposed she could splurge a little. She'd use her debit card. She wouldn't let Ashlee put anything on her account.

Ashlee took her to a little boutique where the clothes seemed far more expensive than they were worth, and far more sexy than Daphne was used to. "Go ahead, try this on," Ashlee urged Daphne, pushing a short polka-dotted skirt at her. Daphne blushed, arguing that it wasn't her. But she tried it on anyway. Looking in the mirror, Daphne watched as Ashlee stood behind her, twisting her hair into a new, funky style. In her short polka-dotted skirt and new hairdo, Daphne didn't recognize herself.

"I can't believe you talked me into buying that!" Daphne said, laughing, carrying her new purchase as they headed to Rico's Raw Bar on the beach.

"What would all the good sisters back at Our Lady say?" Ashlee hooted.

"Exactly!" Daphne burned with embarrassment thinking of the look that would cross Mother Angela's face if she saw her in that skirt. Why had she bought it? "I'll never have a chance to wear it," Daphne told Ashlee.

"Oh, I don't know about that," she said, telling the maître d' they wanted a table for two. "I'm sure something will come along."

That's when Daphne saw him.

Sitting at a small table with a very lovely blond woman was Gregory Winston.

"Well," Ashlee said, her voice lowering, "look who's here."

Daphne said not a word as the maître d' led

them to their table, which, as fate would have it, was just opposite Gregory's. There was no way they could avoid him now. Gregory looked up, noticed Ashlee, and smiled politely. Then his eyes moved over to Daphne's. She saw recognition in his gaze, but he simply looked away and continued his conversation with the woman at his table.

"Oh, isn't he being gallant," Ashlee said, smirking, as they took their seats. "Pretending he's never seen you before. Afraid I'd rush back to Pete and spill the little secret you two share."

"We don't share any secret," Daphne said. "He gave me a ride. It was all very innocent."

"Mmhmm," Ashlee said, winking at her and giggling. "Come on, Daphne. He's a total hunk. If I wasn't a happily married woman, I'd be all over him."

Daphne said nothing. The waitress came to take their orders. Ashlee ordered them both margaritas, with salt. Daphne had no idea what a margarita even was. Then they'd have mussels and lobster rolls and coleslaw.

"You are totally checking him out," Ashlee told her.

"I am not," Daphne said. In fact, she was doing her best not to look over at Gregory's table. She had to admit, however, that she was very curious to know who the woman he was lunching with was. His girlfriend? Whoever she was, she was extremely pretty, with gorgeous tanned legs that she kept crossing and uncrossing as if she was displaying them in her white denim shorts.

The waitress brought their drinks and Daphne took a sip.

"Careful, sweetie," Ashlee told her. "There's alcohol in there, you know."

"Alcohol?" Daphne asked.

"Yeah, maybe you've heard of it?"

"I've never had an alcoholic drink in my life," Daphne admitted.

Ashlee smiled. "Just sip it slowly and you'll be fine."

Within a few minutes Daphne had a light-headed feeling she'd never experienced before. She felt giddy.

"He is pretty handsome, isn't he?" she asked Ashlee.

"Who are you talking about?" Ashlee asked. But she was kidding. She knew who Daphne meant.

"Why doesn't Mr. Witherspoon like him? I mean, he grew up at Witherswood. And his parents—"

She couldn't bring herself to say what had happened to Gregory's parents. Murdered, in cold blood, by Pete Witherspoon Senior.

"Well," Ashlee said, "it seems that Pete and his brother discovered their father's crimes, and didn't report him right away to the police. They were trying to get him to give himself up on his own." She took a sip of her margarita. "It was in that small delay that Pete Senior killed Gregory's parents. So Gregory has always believed that if my husband only acted more quickly, his mother and father would be alive today."

"I imagine Mr. Witherspoon feels terrible about it," Daphne said.

Ashlee sighed. "He did. Until Gregory started buying up half the town. He became a self-made millionaire buying and selling real estate. He made himself Pete's biggest competitor. Swore to drive Pete out of business. He bought a rival cannery in the next town over to compete with the Witherspoon interests. He bought all of the commercial fishing fleets that the Witherspoons didn't already own. He bought restaurants to compete with ours." She smiled. "In fact, we're eating in one of Gregory's restaurants now."

"He owns this place?"

Ashlee polished off the last of her margarita and signaled to the waiter that she wanted another. "He sure does. He bought Rico's about a year ago. Pete was eager to get his hands on it when Rico finally retired. It's a Woebegone institution. But Gregory beat him to it." She smiled. "So you can see, his sympathy for Gregory has dried up. That happens when someone's trying to ruin your businesses."

"You knew he owned this place," Daphne said, "so you came in here figuring there was a good chance we'd run into him."

Ashlee smirked. "They have the best mussels in town, sweetie. Oh, look." She nodded her head toward Gregory's table. "His lady love is leaving."

Daphne turned to see. Indeed, the leggy blonde had stood and Gregory had stood as well, kissing her on the cheek before she sauntered out of the place. His eyes flickered over to Daphne's table at that point.

"Gregory! Yoo-hoo!" Ashlee was waving.

"Why are you doing that?" Daphne whispered.

"Gregory! How are you, Gregory?"

He smiled, and Daphne remembered his dimples. He walked over to their table, all six feet of him, broad shoulders, cleft chin. His green eyes sparkled. The afternoon sun caught highlights in his red hair.

"Good day, Ashlee," he said, shaking her hand. "What a nice surprise to see Mrs. Pete Witherspoon in my restaurant."

"You know I adore the food here. Especially the mussels." She smiled. "Gregory, I'd like you to meet Daphne May. She's Christopher's new governess. Daphne, Gregory Winston."

He shook Daphne's hand. "Charmed to meet you," he said smoothly, as if he'd never seen her before. "Welcome to Rico's, and to Point Woebegone."

"Thank you," Daphne replied, and was aware her words were just a trifle slurred.

"Are you enjoying your new student?" Gregory asked.

"Oh!" Ashlee suddenly interjected. "My phone!" She started digging through her purse. Daphne didn't hear a ring. She assumed it must be vibrating. "So sorry, but I just must answer this." She withdrew an iPhone and tapped on it, pressing it to her ear. "Mama? Mama, is that you?"

Daphne realized Gregory was looking at her. She felt herself blush.

"Mama, hold on a second, I'm in a restaurant," Ashlee said into the phone. Then she looked over at Daphne and Gregory. "I'm so sorry, I've got take this call. My mother's been sick, you know. Gregory, be a doll and keep Daphne company for me while I go outside and talk, okay?"

"It would be my pleasure," he said.

Ashlee winked at Daphne and hustled out of the restaurant, the phone at her ear. Daphne started to say something, to get up and follow her, then just sat still, her eyes cast down at the table.

"Enjoying your margarita?" Gregory asked.

"I've never had one before," Daphne said.

He grinned. "That doesn't answer the question."

"I don't know. I feel a little . . . woozy."

His smile widened. "Drink a little water. It will keep the woozy from getting woozier."

She did as he suggested.

"How are things going at Witherswood?"

"Okay," she said.

"Christopher cooperating?"

"He's coming around, I think," she told him. "Everyone is very nice."

"Everyone?"

Daphne smiled. "Well, Abigail Witherspoon seems hostile to me. And Gabriel Witherspoon is a bit . . . reclusive."

"And Donovan Kent?"

"Why do ask about him?"

Gregory sat back in the chair. "He just has a certain reputation as a lady-killer."

The word made Daphne shudder.

"Well," Gregory said, "not literally."

"No," Daphne said, taking another sip of her margarita. She felt as if she needed it. "The literal killing was done by his grandfather."

"So I see you've discovered the backstory of the Witherspoons."

"It must be horrible," she said, her eyes making contact with Gregory's for the first time since he sat down with her.

"You mean about my parents?"

"Yes," she said, and she felt as if she might cry. The alcohol was making her very emotional all of a sudden. "To have to live with that all your life . . ."

"It was horrible. You're right about that."

"And now . . . I understand why you and the sheriff were so concerned when I said I saw a clown that night at the inn. He said there might be a copycat killer. . . ."

Gregory moved in closer to her. "Look, Daphne, there has thankfully not been a repeat of what happened that night. It could just have been a co-incidence. Please don't let that worry you too much."

She smiled weakly. "I can't help it. I think about it a lot."

"You poor kid," Gregory said. "Coming into this completely unaware. Going to live in that strange old house, cut off from the world." He sighed. "And having to put up with the freaks in that house . . . Abigail . . . Donovan . . . Pete himself."

"Mr. Witherspoon has been very kind to me."

"Has he?" He snorted. "Actually, I'm sure he has been kind. How else to get you on his side?"

"He doesn't know I know you," Daphne revealed.

"He will now. His little jailbait bride will tell him we met here today."

"No, I told Ashlee I had met you soon after I arrived. She's kept it a secret. She doesn't want anything to upset her husband. She loves him very much. And she's been a very good friend to me."

Gregory eyed her. "You trust her?"

"I do. She and Ben. The only ones in the house I trust completely."

Gregory was nodding. "I was never sure what to make of Ashlee. She shows up here in Point Woebegone a couple of years ago, the new child bride of old Pete Witherspoon. Everyone assumed she was just a gold digger."

"That's so unfair. You should see her with him. She's so kind and gentle to him."

"Well, she'll find out the same way that poor old Peggy did that no one can trust Pete Witherspoon."

"What do you mean?"

"I'm just saying. . . ." He sighed, as if considering whether he should say anything further. "Well, since Ashlee has been good to you, then maybe at some point you can be good to her. You don't have to say this came from me, but you can tell her that the whole town knew that Pete was never faithful to Peggy. He continued to see his old flame, the girl he was going to marry until her family took her away after the scandal with Pete Senior emerged. They wouldn't let their daughter see the son of a murderer, and forbade her to marry him. But Pete found her, and they continued seeing each other for years, until Peggy found about it."

"That's terrible," Daphne said,

"And so one more tragedy at Witherswood, one more instance where Pete Witherspoon was left with blood on his hands."

"I understand that he may have broken Peggy's heart, if he was cheating on her," Daphne said, "but surely you can't blame him for Peggy's cancer."

"Cancer?"

"Yes. Peggy died of cancer."

Gregory sat back in his chair. "They told you Peggy died of cancer?"

Daphne nodded. "Yes. Ashlee told me."

He looked off through the restaurant toward the front door. Ashlee was still outside on the sidewalk, the phone to her ear.

"I wonder if that's what they told her," Gregory mused. "If that's how she really believes Peggy died."

"How did Peggy die if it wasn't cancer?"

Gregory returned his eyes to her. How green they were. How beautiful. How easily Daphne could just fall into them. Her mind seemed to whirl.

"When Peggy learned of her husband's affair with his ex-flame—a girl named Maria, I believe, a beautiful girl—she was devastated." Gregory looked extremely sad as he told this tale. "She had hoped that giving him a son might break the spell Maria held over Pete, but no such luck. Peggy had thought the affair was over, but then she discovered Pete had gone to see Maria, wherever she lived then. He confessed he still loved Maria, and always would. It drove Peggy over the edge."

"What did she do?" Daphne asked.

Gregory paused. "Have you ever been to the tower room at Witherswood?"

"Yes," Daphne told him.

"Well, one terrible stormy night, Peggy climbed up the stairs to the tower room. Flinging open one of the windows, she wedged herself out onto the ledge, and then she jumped. It was a long fall to the ocean below. A few days later, her body washed up on the rocks."

NINE

"That's terrible!" Daphne gasped.

"It might officially have been a suicide," Gregory told her. "But in my mind, and in the minds of many others, it was one more death that could be laid directly at Pete Witherspoon's door. Not Pete Senior, mind you. Pete Junior. He may not have been the monster his father was, but his own weak nature and his appalling lack of conscience had resulted in the deaths of at least three people—my mother, my father and his wife Peggy—just the same."

Daphne was unsure how to respond. She supposed Gregory had a point. But was it fair to hold Mr. Witherspoon responsible?

"I feel quite certain that Mr. Witherspoon has lived with tremendous guilt about these things," she said. "He may have made decisions and choices that were not the right ones. But he never wanted these terrible things to happen."

"I wonder if you'd be so understanding and compassionate if it was your own parents you found bleeding to death on the marble floor of Witherswood."

Even in the floaty haze caused by her drink, Daphne regretted her words. "You may be right, Gregory," she said. "I guess I was just trying to see things from Mr. Witherspoon's perspective. I'm sorry if I seemed insensitive."

He smiled at her. "Not at all. In fact, you sounded very sensitive. Like someone who still sees the good in the world, and in other people, even after terrible things. And that's rather refreshing, to tell the truth."

"Well, I suppose I can't fully empathize with what you went through because I never knew my own parents."

He asked what she meant, so she explained her background and the mystery of her origins. She even added the comment that Mother Angela had made that Point Woebegone was Daphne's destiny. Did he, she wondered, have any knowledge about a girl born here twenty-two years earlier? Maybe a child given up by her mother and sent to Our Lady's School for Girls in Boston?

Gregory smiled. "I wish I did. It's a small village and I know just about everyone. But I was a boy of about ten twenty-two years ago, so things like that wouldn't have been part of my experience. Still, in a town this small, stories get repeated, and I haven't heard anything about a baby girl being given away."

"It was just a shot in the dark," Daphne admitted.

Gregory suddenly reached across the table and took her hands in his. In Daphne's slightly buzzy perspective, the action was enormous and significant, and she felt tingles from her scalp down to her toes.

"Would you have dinner with me this week?" he asked. "I'm not sure how you'd square it with your boss, but maybe Ashlee would help you out. She seems to be pretty cool."

Daphne couldn't speak for a moment. "Why would you want to have dinner with me?" she asked in a very small voice.

"Because I think you need to get out of that house more often. Because I think you could use some more friends. And, to be honest, because I'm intrigued by you. The whole mysterious background thing. And because it's rare to meet someone these days so essentially decent and genuine as you seem to be."

Daphne could feel her cheeks blush. "But what will . . . your girlfriend think?"

"My girlfriend?" Gregory sat back in his chair, letting go of Daphne's hands. He looked puzzled. "Oh, you mean Candace? The woman I was having lunch with?"

"The woman you kissed good-bye."

He grinned. "On the cheek." He laughed. "Candace is my night manager. She runs this place for me at night. She's not my girlfriend."

"Well, she's very pretty."

Gregory's smile grew kinder. "She is, indeed. But I'm a little weary of women who are all about being pretty. Or who try too hard at it. I'm more intrigued by those who don't have to try at all, who are just pretty by nature."

Daphne saw Ashlee coming through the door from outside. "Ashlee's coming back," she said.

"Then answer me quickly," Gregory said. "Will you have dinner with me this week? Or will it be too difficult for you?"

"I—I don't know . . ."

"She's almost to the table."

Every nerve seemed to be jangling in Daphne's body. "Yes!" she blurted.

"What night?"

"Wednesday," she said, for no real reason. It was just the first day that popped into her head.

"Okay. I'll meet you here at seven. Does that work? You'll be finished with the kid by then?"

She nodded. "But if something comes up, there's no way I can get a hold of you."

He shrugged. "Then I'll just have to understand."

"Look at you two!" Ashlee said, striding up to the table. "Gabbing together like you've known each other for years!"

Gregory stood. "I look forward to more such opportunities to get to know you, Daphne." He gave Ashlee a smile. "As always, a pleasure, Mrs. Witherspoon."

With a little salute, he headed off through the busy restaurant.

Ashlee sat back down. "He's dreamy."

Daphne just smiled.

"Don't you think?" Ashlee asked.

"He asked me to have dinner with him."

"Excellent!"

"I'm not sure I should go. Knowing how Mr. Witherspoon feels about him."

Ashlee scowled. "Pete doesn't have to know."

"But if he finds out, then I'm risking my job."

"I'll handle Pete." She leaned in across the table. "You cannot turn down a date with Gregory Winston III. He's a catch, Daphne."

Their meals arrived. Ashlee ordered them both another margarita, despite Daphne's protests. This second drink put her over the edge. She was laughing and talking loudly like she had never done in public before. She barely tasted her meal. The mussels slid down without her even being aware of them. She wolfed down the lobster roll. When a little burp involuntarily escaped her lips, both she and Ashlee burst into silly giggles.

Finally they staggered out of the restaurant. Or, more accurately, Daphne staggered. Ashlee steadied her with a hand on her elbow.

"Good thing I'm driving," Ashlee said. "Geez, girl, you can't hold your liquor very well."

"I tol' you," Daphne said. "I never had a drink"— except she pronounced it "shrink"—"before in my life."

"Well, I think a cup of joe is in order then," Ashlee said. "Tell you what, sweetie. Just wait for me over there on that bench, and I'll run into Woebegone Java and get us both some coffee."

"Okey dokey," Daphne said, feeling as light as a feather. She figured she could float over to the bench instead of walking.

Ashlee stood watching her as Daphne made her way to the bench. When she got there, she turned around and waved to her friend. Only then did

Ashlee head back down the street toward the coffee shop.

Daphne sat. She tried to steady her vision. She burped again, and chuckled to herself.

The town was rather quiet. Daphne guessed it was because the season was coming to an end. Most of the tourists had already left. A few shops already had signs in their windows: THANKS FOR A GREAT SEASON. SEE YOU IN APRIL. But there was enough still open to keep a few people wandering through downtown. A couple of ladies pushing babies in strollers passed Daphne by. Kids on their bikes shouted out to each other. A man with a couple of toddlers, a boy and a girl, turned the corner, the three of them stopping frequently to peer into shop windows. A few yards away from Daphne stood a young woman playing a violin, an upside-down top hat at her feet. Ashlee had mentioned that Point Woebegone drew a lot of street musicians and performers, at least in season. As the man with the two kids walked past the violinist, he dropped a dollar into the hat. The young woman smiled and thanked him.

It was only when the violinist had finished her piece, and put down her instrument momentarily, that Daphne heard another sound. A tinny bit of music, a tune she thought she recognized. What was it? She strained to listen. It seemed to be getting closer. Through the fog of the alcohol, she tried to place the tune. Then it hit her: it was "Pop Goes the Weasel." She used to have a jack-in-the-box back at Our Lady that played that tune when you turned the crank. "All around the mulberry bush, the monkey chased the weasel," the tune went. "The monkey thought it was all in fun. . . . Pop! goes the weasel!" And at "pop" the silly face of a monkey puppet had popped out of the toy.

Daphne noticed the two kids walking with the man had stopped at the corner, and were looking down the side street. It seemed that was where the music was coming from. The children seemed excited, jumping up and down and pointing. "Pop Goes the Weasel," in endless repetition, was indeed getting louder.

Daphne watched.

And suddenly her blood ran cold.

Coming around the corner, being greeted enthusiastically by the boy and girl, was a clown.

In one hand, he carried a small CD player, from which the music was emanating, and in the other hand he carried a fistful of colorful balloons.

Daphne shrunk back on the bench. The clown looked exactly like the one she had seen at the inn that night. The night Maggie was killed. He had a mass of orange hair and a big red nose and a terrible blue grin painted on his deathly white face. His outfit was yellow covered in green and red polka dots, and on his feet he wore enormous purple rubber shoes. It had to be the same clown she had seen at the inn. It had to be!

The children were squealing as the clown bent down and handed each one of them a balloon. Daphne watched in horror as the creature patted each child on the head with his enormous white-mittened hand. All the while "Pop Goes the Weasel" kept playing.

The man with the children exchanged a few words with the clown. Daphne was just far enough away not to be able to hear what was said, but the tone seemed friendly enough. She wanted to stand and shout, "Get away from him! He's a murderer!" But her fear—and the alcohol—kept her frozen to the bench.

She watched as the man and the children moved off. The clown turned slowly. Then his eyes fell on Daphne.

He knows, she thought. *He knows I saw him at the inn.*

The clown began to approach, that inane tune still playing, over and over.

With incredible effort, Daphne forced herself to stand. She thought she might fall over, but she found her balance, and started to walk away in the opposite direction of the clown. She couldn't bring herself to look back at the creature, but she could tell he continued to approach because the music was getting louder. Daphne walked faster.

She passed the violinist, who was setting her instrument on her shoulder to start a new piece. Daphne caught her gaze, but she couldn't speak. The violinist just stared at her. *She knows, too*, Daphne thought. *She's in on it! She wants the clown to get me!*

She was in no state to separate paranoia from real danger. She just began walking even faster. The music followed her. Finally, she began to run.

The wind whistled in her ears. She ran to the end of the block, then turned a sharp right, onto the street from which the man and the two kids had emerged. The ladies with the baby strollers had turned down there, too. Maybe they were still there. Maybe there were people Daphne could run to for help. But the street was a dead end in a gravel parking lot. There were a few cars, but no sign of any people.

Daphne could hear the music behind her.

All around the mulberry bush, the monkey chased the weasel. . . .

The clown had followed her around the corner!

The monkey thought it was all in fun. . . .

Daphne sprinted into the parking lot, praying that someone was in one of the cars.

Pop! goes the weasel!

The cars were empty. At the far end of the parking lot was a tall wooden fence. Beside it sat a Dumpster, stinking of trash and spoiled food.

Daphne stood there, at a loss, not sure where to run next.

That's when she realized the music had stopped.

She spun around. She was alone on the block. The clown was gone.

In relief, she leaned against the side of the Dumpster, breathing heavily. The thing stunk, but she needed the support, otherwise she feared she might fall to the ground.

Had she imagined it? Were her nerves working overtime again with her too-vivid imagination?

No, she had heard the music plain as day. The clown had followed her.

Or had he?

She was so confused. Was it the alcohol? Was that why she felt she couldn't tell what was real, and what was just in her mind?

Daphne looked around. The day was quiet. The sun had dropped lower in the sky, casting long shadows across the street. The only sound was a low rustling of leaves from the trees. Around her, an occasional red or yellow leaf floated to the ground. The block was utterly peaceful.

But in her head, she still heard the music. *All around the mulberry bush* . . . She tried to push the sound away, but it kept playing in that terrible loop in her head.

It's the alcohol, she told herself. It had to be. People hallucinate on alcohol. She'd seen enough television shows to know that. Instead of a pink elephant, she'd seen a clown.

That had to be the explanation.

She pressed her fingers to her temple. Her head was splitting now. She had to find the strength to walk back to the bench. Surely Ashlee had returned with the coffees by now, and was no doubt looking for her.

If only she could make the music stop in her head . . .

She took her fingers away from her temples.

The music, she realized, was not coming from her head.

It was coming from behind her.

From inside the Dumpster.

With a sudden gasp, Daphne pulled herself away, looking back at the foul-smelling receptacle in horror.

The music played on.

All around the mulberry bush, the monkey chased the weasel. The monkey thought it was all in fun. . . .

And then—on the note of "Pop!"—the clown burst up through the top of the Dumpster, its horrible blue mouth curled in an evil smile.

"Pop goes the weasel!" the thing croaked.

This time, being so close to it, Daphne could see that behind the clown's hideous blue lips lurked a set of very yellow, pointed teeth.

It gnashed them at her.

Daphne screamed once; then everything went black.

TEN

She woke up in her bed at Witherswood.

Her head throbbed. Ashlee stood over her, applying a cold, wet cloth to Daphne's forehead. Daphne could sense other people in her room, but her vision was too blurred to make them out.

"What . . . what happened?" she managed to ask.

"It's all my fault, sweetie," Ashlee was saying. "I should never have bought you that second drink."

"It is quite unacceptable that Christopher's governess was out in the village getting drunk." Even in her haze, Daphne recognized the voice of Abigail. Now the older woman loomed into her view, her stern, wrinkled face twisted in revulsion. "Isn't it bad enough that we have the gossips in town wagging their tongues about the murder of that barmaid? Now they're carrying on about the new governess. It is unacceptable!"

"Like I said, Abigail," Ashlee growled, turning to her, "it was my fault. Don't blame Daphne."

Abigail sniffed. "Well, I've always known you were two of a kind."

"What the hell is that supposed to mean?" Ashlee asked, aggressively taking a few steps toward Abigail. "I know you've never liked me. Why don't you just come right out and tell me how you feel?"

"Now, now, ladies," Ben suddenly interjected, and Daphne felt pleased that he was there, too. "This isn't the time or place. Back to your corners."

"Aw, come on, Ben, I was looking forward to a good cat fight." It was Donovan's voice, and now he, too, appeared in Daphne's view. He looked down at her and winked. "Poor little governess. I'll have to keep it in mind that you're a lightweight when it comes to alcohol."

"Back off, Donovan," Ashlee said, returning to Daphne's side and turning the cold cloth over on her forehead. "Not every female appreciates your lechery, you know. Just ask Suzanne."

Donovan laughed and moved away.

"I'm so sorry, sweetie," Ashlee whispered down to Daphne.

Ben came into view. "I guess this is what happens to convent girls who try to move into the real world a little too fast." He smiled sympathetically down at Daphne. "Don't worry, though. It will pass. I know it doesn't feel that way right now, but it will."

"My brother should be told of this," Abigail was saying, from somewhere across the room.

"I swear, Abigail," Ashlee said, spinning on her, "if you say anything of this to Pete . . ."

"You'll what?" the spinster spit back. "You have nothing to threaten me with."

Daphne saw the cloud that passed over Ashlee's

eyes, and heard her mutter, under her breath, "That's what you think."

Apparently, however, Abigail didn't hear, because she just went on about how she felt Mr. Witherspoon should be told about the behavior of their new governess—as well as that of his wife.

"Aunt Abigail," Ben said, sounding reasonable. "Uncle Pete is not feeling well. This whole thing with the possible copycat killer . . . it's got him very upset. There's no need to upset him further. The girls just went into town for a little fun. Daphne's not used to drinking. I suspect, given how she's feeling right now, she won't be imbibing again very soon."

Abigail said nothing in reply.

"I think this whole copycat-killer thing is bogus," Donovan said. "I mean, we're just basing it on Daphne saying she saw a clown at the inn. . . ."

A clown.

Suddenly it all came back to her.

Once again Daphne heard the terrible music. And saw the clown popping out of the Dumpster, gnashing its sharp teeth. . . .

"It's still out there!" she suddenly blurted, sitting up, the cloth falling from her face. "The clown! I saw it again!"

The others all looked at her, openmouthed.

"I did see it," Daphne said. "It followed me. It was going to attack me. Then—then—I blacked out!"

She saw the looks those in the room gave her. Abigail folded her bony arms across her chest and pressed her lips together so tightly that they turned white. Donovan, leaning against the windowsill, smirked. Ben let out a long sigh. And Ashlee sat down beside her on the bed and took her hands into her own.

"Sweetie," she said. "It was the alcohol. It made you see things."

"No . . ." Daphne's head throbbed harder. "I'm sure it was real. . . . It jumped out of the Dumpster at me. . . ."

"Out of the Dumpster?" Donovan hooted. "That's a good one!"

"Knock it off, Donovan," Ben said. "Can't you see she's upset?"

"If you ask me, that girl is not right in the head, and not fit to be teaching Christopher," Abigail snorted.

"Well, no one's asking you, Aunt Abigail," Ben said, sitting down alongside Ashlee on Daphne's bed. "You sure you saw a clown?" he asked her. "Or could it have been the effects of the alcohol?"

"I . . . I . . . I saw it," Daphne managed to say, falling back into her pillows and closing her eyes.

"She thought she saw a clown the very first day she got here, in Christopher's room," Abigail told them. "There was no clown. I was there."

Ben was looking at Daphne. "At that point, you had no idea about our grandfather's history of dressing as a clown, did you?"

"No," Daphne said in a small voice.

Ashlee smiled. "But she had seen the clown at the inn. That's what stayed in her mind."

Ben was studying Daphne's face. "Maybe it was just a hallucination," he said, "but I think we ought to let the sheriff know what Daphne thinks she saw."

"Oh, but Ben," Ashlee said, "that will just bring him back up here, and get Pete all upset again."

He sighed. "Maybe Daphne and I can go down to the sheriff instead, when she's feeling better."

Ashlee sighed, dropped Daphne's hand, and stood up.

"Come on," Ben said. "I can't chalk up to coincidence Daphne seeing a clown, not knowing a thing about Grandfather's history, and then Maggie gets murdered. Maybe what she saw today was just a lingering anxiety over all of that." He turned his eyes back to Daphne. "But maybe not."

"This is all just unacceptable," Abigail said again and huffed out the door.

Donovan laughed. "I do like to see Aunt Abigail in the midst of one of her tizzies. She's always so amusing."

"I think we ought to let Daphne rest," Ben said, standing. "When you feel up to it, maybe tomorrow morning, we can go down to the sheriff and make a report," he said to Daphne. Turning to Ashlee, he continued, "And for now, we don't have to get Uncle Pete upset."

Ashlee smiled weakly at him.

"Come on, Donovan, let's give Daphne some quiet time," Ben said, gesturing to his cousin to head out of the room. "You know what a hangover feels like."

"I do indeed," he said, following Ben. He looked back at Daphne and winked. "But if you need a little comforting, babe, just knock three times on the wall."

Daphne groaned.

After the men had left, Ashlee replaced the

cloth on Daphne's head. "I'm sorry again, sweetie. I should have known you weren't used to alcohol."

"It's okay," Daphne said. "You were just trying to make the day fun."

"We'll go slower next time."

"Wait," Daphne said, stopping Ashlee from leaving. "Tell me . . . how did I get here? How did you find me?"

"I was looking for you. You weren't on the bench. And then I heard you scream." Ashlee made a face of concern. "I ran around the block and saw you lying in that gravel parking lot. I got to you as quick as I could. You were passed out cold."

"And there was no one around me?"

"No one."

Daphne sighed and closed her eyes.

"Sweetie, there was no clown. In fact, I remember distinctly. The top of the Dumpster was closed."

"I don't understand," Daphne said, hot tears burning her eyes. "I can't tell what's real and what's not anymore."

"Just rest now, sweetie." Ashlee turned once again to leave.

"Wait," Daphne said. "One more thing."

"What's that, hon?"

"If I was passed out cold, how did you get me back to the car? We were parked quite a distance away. . . ."

Ashlee smiled. "Well, eventually I got you on your feet. You don't remember walking?"

"No. All I remember is that . . . that thing . . . and its teeth. . . ." She grimaced, fighting back the terror. "And then I woke up here."

"Just rest, sweetie," Ashlee told her. "Don't worry about anything. You're safe now."

The young mistress of Witherswood smiled kindly at her, then flicked the light switch and closed the door behind her as she left the room.

In the darkness, Daphne wondered, *Could I have imagined it all? Am I maybe starting to lose my mind?*

She sat up in bed.

No. It was real.

And if the sheriff could find that man and those two kids—and the violinist, yes, the violinist!—they could confirm that there really was a clown, that Daphne wasn't crazy.

The violinist would have seen me run away. She would have seen the clown following me!

The thought that she had witnesses reassured Daphne in a strange sort of way. She lay back against her pillows and closed her eyes. All she wanted was sleep.

She was safe here. Ashlee had said so.

Within moments, Daphne was asleep.

Her dream began with the sound of shovels, the stabbing of earth. A dark blue night. The moon as odd voyeur, glinting off the blades of the silver shovel in her hands. The eye of the sky was a hole into the heavens.

As before, Daphne couldn't tell where the dream ended and real life began. She peeled away sweaty sheets from her body, placing her feet against the cold wooden floor, and got out of bed. She pulled on a pair of pants and then plunged headfirst into the blue of the night. She made her way across the estate to a cemetery, a place she had never been, but she knew right where to go and begin digging.

Embraced by the sweet, damp, blue fog skin, Daphne dug up the graves, all of them, pulling the children from their coffins. Whose children they were and what connecton they had to her, she had no idea, but she dug up many of them, all perfectly preserved, beautiful children in their coffins. One little girl she took in her hands and shook. The little eyelids fluttered, like moths, and opened. The girl looked up at her.

Daphne awoke in a start, trying to remember the dream and figure out what it meant. But it was gone by the time her eyes were fully open.

It was a Sunday, so that meant no schoolwork for Christopher. Daphne still felt a little achy when she awoke, but a hot shower reinvigorated her, and she hurried downstairs to grab coffee. She skillfully avoided seeing anyone, waiting until Abigail and Louella had finished their breakfast. Ashlee and Pete were nowhere to be found. That was just as well. Gripping her mug of piping-hot coffee, Daphne made a beeline up to Ben's room, and told him she was ready to go talk to the sheriff. He nodded. "Then let's go," he said.

Although it was a Sunday, Sheriff Patterson agreed to meet them at his office. On the car ride into town, Ben looked over at Daphne and asked if maybe all this was too much for her, if she ever thought about going back to Boston.

"I'm not sure they'd take me back," Daphne said. "There's really no place for me there anymore. I've graduated from the affiliated teachers college, and I'm not continuing any studies through the auspices of Our Lady. I'm certainly not looking to become a nun."

Ben smiled. "See what happens when you knock back two margaritas? You become all dedicated to the worldly life."

Daphne managed a smile. "Being a nun was never my calling, even though I lived with the sisters all my life." She looked out through the window toward the jagged cliffs they'd just come from, and she caught a glimpse of the dark shape of Witherswood on the edge. "Besides, Mother Angela says my destiny is here."

"Lucky you," Ben said, and laughed.

At the sheriff's office, Daphne gave her story. Sheriff Patterson's bushy mustache twitched a few times as he listened, but, to Daphne's surprise, he wrote nothing down. When she was finished, he called one of his deputies over and asked him to go through the licenses of street performers.

"Anybody who sings, dances, plays an instrument, or otherwise entertains on the street has to have a performer's license," the sheriff explained. "I don't recall any clown."

"But he was there," Daphne insisted, and repeated that either the man and the children or the violinist could vouch for her.

"No way to find the man and the kids," the sheriff said. "At least not any sure way. They could have been tourists just passing through. But as for the violinist . . ."

Sheriff Patterson lifted a piece of paper from the folder his deputy had just placed on his desk.

"April Flynn," he said. "She's been out there play-ing Mozart since last May. I'll give her a call. See what she saw."

"Thank you," Daphne said. "She had to have seen him. He was coming after me, trying to ter-rorize me. And he had long pointed sharp teeth."

She saw the look the sheriff exchanged with Ben.

"You don't believe me!"

The sheriff ignored her comment. He just began turning papers over, one after another, in the folder.

"Ben, you believe me, don't you?" Daphne asked.

"I believe that you saw something," he replied.

"Nope," the sheriff said, closing the folder. "No license for any clown."

"If some madman was going to start murdering people dressed up like a clown, he wouldn't apply for a license from the town," Daphne snapped.

Sheriff Patterson shrugged. "Look. I appreciate the tip. I told you I wanted you to keep us in-formed of everything. So I'll follow up. I'll ask around. If there was a clown parading around Main Street yesterday, people would've seen him."

"Ask the violinist! April! Ask her!" Daphne said, almost shouting.

The sheriff gave her a crooked smile. "I intend to. Now, thanks for coming in, Miss May."

Back at Witherswood, Daphne decided the time had come to find out a little bit more about the vil-lainous Pete Witherspoon Senior, who had killed seventeen people dressed as a clown. Under the pretense of doing preparation for Christopher's next lesson, Daphne arranged to use the computer in the library. The house was very quiet. Everyone seemed to be in his or her own room. Except for Ben, who had gone to Portland for the evening to see friends. He'd invited her to come along, telling her she'd have fun, but she'd declined. Ben said it might do her good to get out of the house. But Daphne had other plans for the evening.

She had just brought up Google and her fingers were hovering over the keypad, ready to type in her search request, when suddenly very cold hands pressed themselves against the back of her neck and her shoulders. Daphne let out a small gasp.

"So sorry," came a man's voice from behind her. "I didn't mean to startle you."

Daphne turned around. It was Donovan. She glared at him, then turned back in her seat toward the computer screen.

"Somehow I think you *did* mean to startle me," she said.

He removed his hands. "Oh, now, Daphne, darling. You've been here more than a month now, and every time I smile at you, or just try to be friendly, you give me the cold shoulder."

He walked around to lean against the desk, facing her. He was pouting comically.

"I'm sorry, Donovan, but I'm trying to prepare Christopher's lesson."

"I was thinking of going for a walk along the cliffs," he said. "Pretty soon it will be too cold to go out there. Want to come along?"

She gave him an icy stare. "Why don't you ask Suzanne?"

"She's already gone to bed." He smiled, and showed off those dimples. Daphne had to look away. He might be revolting, but he was still ridiculously handsome.

"I need to do some work," she said.

Suddenly, before she even knew what was happening, Donovan reached over, placed his hand on her cheek, and pulled her in toward him, attempting to kiss her. Daphne recoiled, and when she had shaken his hand free of her face, she looked up at him with fire in her eyes, and slapped him across the face.

She could see the slap stung. Donovan's hand went to his cheek. His eyes burned.

"What's going on in here?"

This was a new voice. Daphne looked around.

Suzanne.

Donovan's fiancée was standing in the doorway, wearing a pink flannel nightdress, and she was shooting daggers from her eyes.

"Daphne was procrastinating on her lesson plans," Donovan said. "You really should get back to work now, Daphne." He moved away from the desk, going over to stand by Suzanne's side.

Daphne saw the accusation in Suzanne's expression. She wanted to speak the truth, to tell her what Donovan had just done, but she held her tongue. She spun around in her chair and faced the computer screen.

"Come on, Donovan. Let the little governess do her work," Suzanne said acidly.

From the corner of her eye, Daphne saw the two of them leave.

But seconds later, Donovan had stuck his head

back into the room. "You'll pay for that," he whispered, and then was gone again.

Daphne's heart was beating in her ears. She wanted to get out of this house! Ben had asked her if it all was too much. Yes, yes, it was. She felt as if she might cry.

Taking a deep breath, she resumed her Internet research.

What she discovered did not change her desire to leave Witherswood. In fact, it only made her want to bolt more.

There were plenty of news stories on the Internet about the murders in Point Woebegone twenty-five years earlier. Actually, they began twenty-five years ago but continued for two years after that. The last killings, those of Gregory's parents, had taken place twenty-three years previous, almost to the very day. It was on a night much like this one that a panicked, desperate Pete Witherspoon Senior, discovered by his sons to be a murderer, had lashed out. He killed his elder son, John, and then, stumbling upon the Winstons, had slaughtered them as well. He'd slit both of their throats, and they'd bled to death on the floor of the foyer. The police had questioned Boris, the butler, about whether he had heard anything, but he said he did not. Reading between the lines, Daphne seemed to gather that the police doubted Boris's story, remarking how loyal he had always been to the master of the house.

Pete Senior had fled into the woods, and it had been Pete Junior who apprehended him, and held him for the sheriff. How terrible that must have been for Mr. Witherspoon—to have to hold his own father, a serial killer, and await the arrival of the police. Again Daphne's heart went out to him. But, if Gregory was right and the younger Pete had known his father was the killer, even for just a brief time, his failure to turn him in immediately meant that not only were Gregory's parents killed, but Pete's older brother, John, as well.

It occurred to Daphne as she sat there reading the news articles online—frequently glancing over her shoulder to make sure no one saw what she was doing—that John, being the oldest, would have been the one to inherit the family businesses, or at least take the lead on them. That was how things usually worked. But with John's death, Pete became the sole proprietor of the family businesses, though she had seen Abigail's name on the Witherspoon business letterhead as well, as a partner.

But as terrible as these last three murders were, it was the fourteen previous ones that really devastated her. That was because the victims were all children. What a sick man to end the lives of children! And yes, as Daphne read in article after article, he had frequently dressed as a clown to get their attention. It was during high summer tourist season, when all sorts of street performers strolled down busy Main Street. A funny clown—with balloons—would waddle through the crowd, spot a child standing all alone, and cheerfully offer him or her a balloon. A number of witnesses on different occasions would report seeing a child walk off with a clown—a child whose body would be found, hours later, with his or her throat slit from ear to ear.

In one case, a little girl by the name of Audrey Kearns, just nine years old, was found—Daphne gasped—in a Dumpster on a side road off Main Street.

She strained to see the grainy image of the street on the screen. It was clear enough for her to realize it was the same side street, same parking lot, if not the very same Dumpster, where she had seen the clown.

More than ever, she believed there was a copycat killer on the loose. But so far he had not struck again. Was he waiting?

Daphne shuddered as a thought occurred to her. Was he waiting for her?

She had told the sheriff about seeing him at the inn, after all.

Suddenly Daphne felt terribly frightened. But she forced herself to read the last of the articles.

Once police realized it was a clown who was killing children, Pete Senior ditched the costume, and found other ways to get his victims. Shopping malls, grocery stores, bus stops. In all, fourteen bodies were found—but in the period of those two years, another seven children went missing from the surrounding towns. Police wondered if Pete had been involved. They never found out, however, nor were bodies ever found.

Pete Senior certainly planned to tell no secrets. He said nothing once he was apprehended, not even to his court-appointed lawyer. People were screaming in the street to hang him, but Maine has no death penalty. Pete saved them all the trouble. Apparently planning for such an eventuality, he had secreted several Seconal tablets somewhere on his body—investigators suspected in his rectum—and that night, in his cell, he swallowed them. He was dead when the guard came by in the morning.

The sheriff at the time was roundly condemned for allowing this to happen, and when he ran for reelection the next year, he was defeated—by a man named Joseph Patterson.

As for the Witherspoons, a final article in the set Daphne's search had located revealed that the family, deep in shame, had withdrawn to Witherswood and was rarely ever seen in the village. The little boys, Donovan, Gabriel and Benjamin, were homeschooled by tutors. Pete Junior saw to it that monetary gifts were made to all of the victims' families—including, it was noted, to the uncle and aunt who had taken in the Winstons' little son, Gregory.

But even that financial gift would not be enough for Gregory to forgive Pete for his delay in action. No amount of money could ever replace a mother and a father.

Daphne understood that part all too well.

It was almost one o'clock in the morning when she shut off the computer. As she did so, she heard the front door open and close. Padding slowly through the dark house, Daphne peered into the foyer, and saw Ben returning from his night out.

"Still up?" he asked.

"Working on Christopher's lesson plans," she said. She knew she could trust Ben, but she just didn't want to talk about all that death right at the moment.

They headed into the parlor and sat opposite

each other on two sofas that flanked a long glass coffee table. Ben told her he wished she'd gone with him to Portland. He and his friends had gone out to dinner and seen a movie. "Sometimes you just have to get out of Point Woebegone," he said.

"Why do you stay here?" she asked.

"I'll leave eventually," he said. "I suppose when I find the right guy."

"Wouldn't that be easier to do in Portland than up here?"

He admitted that it would, but he felt he couldn't leave Gabriel. "You know, ever since his accident . . ." His voice cracked a little, in emotion. "When our mother died a few years ago, she asked me to always look out for Gabe, so I feel an obligation."

"How did Gabriel become disabled?" Daphne asked.

"We were out riding." It was clear that Ben had a difficult time recounting the events of that day. "The three of us. Me, Gabe, Donovan. We were all in our late teens. We were racing to see who could get to the point first, and Donovan was in the lead, I was next, and Gabe was coming in third. It hadn't been a good day for Gabe. He'd seen Kathy Swenson that morning."

"His girlfriend," Daphne said. "The one Donovan stole away."

"That's right. He'd run into her in the village. She wouldn't speak to him. After stealing her away, Donovan had dumped her, and now she blamed our whole family, said we were cursed. She was crazy to ever get mixed up with any of us."

"Poor Gabe."

"Yeah, he really loved Kathy. Anyway, he and

Donovan get into a fight about it, Donovan being a jerk and telling him the best guy had won and the best guy had dumped the chick because she wasn't worth it after all." He frowned. "Donovan can be a real prick at times."

Daphne just smiled.

"So I break them up, suggest we all go for a ride to cool down their tempers. Off we go—and right away Donovan is bragging he's going to win, and I think it just pissed Gabe off. So all of a sudden there's Gabe slapping his horse to go faster. He's determined to beat us both. He passes me by, but then, before he can pass Donovan—he's down." Ben grimaced. "Part of me has always wondered . . ." His voice trailed off.

"Wondered what?"

"I shouldn't say it. I have no proof. But I've wondered if Donovan moved his horse deliberately into Gabe's, so he couldn't pass, and then, not meaning to, of course, caused Gabe's horse to stumble." His voice was thick with emotion. "I remember seeing my brother's body fly through the air like a rag doll."

"Oh my God," Daphne said, her hand covering her mouth.

"He broke his spine. For a while, however, the doctors were optimistic that he'd walk again. The spine healed very well. But he never could walk despite what the doctors had said. And so Gabe just spiraled down into a depression that he's never really gotten past. It's been almost a decade. But I think he lives that day over and over in his mind."

"No wonder he seems so withdrawn."

Ben sighed. "And you know, it goes back even before that, too. Gabe was never as good in his studies as I was in mine. Our tutor was always telling him he wasn't as smart as me. And the girls always seemed to prefer Donovan to him. So Gabe had a chip on his shoulder even before his accident. Probably more than any of us, he really resented being cooped up in this house, never being able to socialize in the village, because of Uncle Pete's lingering shame over his father's deeds. Our mother acquiesced to everything Uncle Pete wanted, because he was paying the bills."

"If you were all always cooped up here, how did he meet Kathy Swenson? How did Donovan get the chance to steal her away?"

"Well, by the time we were teenagers we were permitted to go to certain events, like the annual town fair, and some of the summer festivals. We were the mysterious boys from Witherswood." Ben laughed. "People both wanted to meet us and feared us."

Daphne was quiet a moment. "You know, Ben, you asked me if all of this was getting to be too much for me, living here. I want to say it's not. But . . . it's hard, sometimes."

He smiled sympathetically, reaching across the coffee table to take her hand in his. "I'm sorry, Daphne. I can imagine it's all a bit much to adjust to."

"I mean, seeing what I did yesterday . . ." She shuddered. "It was so terrifying, so . . ."

Ben lifted his other hand to stop her from speaking. "Look, Daphne, I wasn't sure if I'd bring this up tonight, but I might as well."

She looked at him. "Bring what up?"

"Sheriff Patterson called me."

"What did he say?"

Ben hesitated. "He spoke with April Flynn, the violinist."

"Did she see the clown?" Daphne asked excitedly.

"Yes," Ben told her. "She did see a clown."

Daphne nearly jumped off the sofa. "So you see! I wasn't hallucinating!"

"Well, actually . . ." Ben was struggling for words. "April said she saw the clown hand some balloons to a couple of kids."

"Right. He did!"

"And then she saw you get up off the bench and walk away quickly. She said you eventually started to run."

"I did! Because the clown was chasing me!"

Ben didn't say anything for a moment. "Actually, Daphne, what April said was very different. She said you were running one way—but the clown was walking off in the complete opposite direction."

ELEVEN

Daphne couldn't sleep after hearing the news Ben had given her.

How was that possible? How could the violinist say the clown had walked the other way? Daphne had been sure that the clown had followed her, chased her down that side street. No, she hadn't actually turned around and seen him, but she had heard the music!

But why would the violinist lie?

The clown had actually walked the other way.

Which meant—Daphne swallowed hard at the realization—that she really *had* hallucinated seeing the creature in the Dumpster.

But it was the very spot where Pete Witherspoon Senior had left one of his victims!

Could it be . . . just a freaky coincidence?

She tossed and turned most of the night, trying to determine what was real, and what was not. Was she losing her mind? Had the shock of leaving the sheltered environment of Our Lady been too much for her? Was she in the midst of some kind of break-down?

Dreams crept stealthily upon her like rats over a decomposing corpse.

Thunder was rumbling. Real—or in her dream? Her consciousness weaved in and out, and Daphne wasn't sure.

But she could hear rain hitting the house. A flicker of lightning crackled by the window. Daphne thought she saw Gregory outside the window, but it wasn't Gregory. It was another man she didn't recognize. She turned on her lamp and got out of bed—was this a dream or was it real?—to peer outside into the rain.

A huge thunderclap made her jump.

"Who is out there?" she called.

There was another loud peal of thunder, and the lamp beside her bed went out.

Daphne didn't want to face whatever might be coming in the dark.

She wasn't, of course, Daphne anymore. She was someone else. Another woman in another house. She stood in the dark and tried to remember her name.

There was a small candle on the table as well, and a book of matches. The candle was little more than a stub. She lit the candle, and it flickered in a sudden breeze.

Daphne, or whoever she was, looked up at the door—and saw a man standing there, a man without a head.

Daphne screamed.

It took her several minutes to calm herself, to realize she'd just had a hallucination. There was no man in the doorway. It was her mind, playing tricks.

Or maybe . . . this was a dream.

A dream, she tried telling herself. *A dream!*

Wake up!

Thunder again, the loudest yet, directly over the house. The candle struggled to stay lit, shivered, and then went out.

Darkness.

How terribly dark it was. Gripping the box of matches in her left hand, Daphne felt around for the candle with her right. The little stub would never last. . . . She moved her hand over the table-top. Where was the candle? It had been sitting right there! The darkness was absolute. Deep and thick. The rain kept up its pummeling of the roof. She prayed for a flash of lightning just to show her the candle. But all she got was a low rumble of thunder.

There!

She felt something in the dark. The candle—

She moved her fingers to grip it.

And whatever it was that she touched—moved!

It was hand! A human hand!

Someone was in the dark with her!

Daphne screamed.

"Who's there? Who is it?"

Finally, a crash of lightning. The room lit up for an instant. Daphne saw she was alone in the room.

And there—there was the candle!

She grabbed it as the darkness settled in again. She fumbled for the matches, her hands trembling so much she worried she wouldn't be able to light one. But she managed, and lit the wick of the candle. A small, flickering circle of light enveloped her. She sat back on the couch, her heart thudding in her ears.

The memory of that hand—

It was real, she told herself. *It moved.*

No! It wasn't real! This is all a dream! Wake up! Wake up!

Daphne lifted the candle and moved into the center of the room. But as she walked, she realized she was stepping in something sticky.

Was rainwater dripping in from the walls?

She lowered the candle.

And she could see plainly that it wasn't water.

It was blood!

Daphne screamed.

Except she wasn't Daphne. She was another woman in another house.

She spun around, just as another bolt of lightning illuminated the room. In her terror and panic, she dropped the candle. She was returned to utter darkness.

Wake up! This is a dream! It is the house playing tricks on you! This woman will die ... but you don't want to die. Wake up, Daphne!

Her shoes made squishy noises in the blood on the floor.

Daphne was paralyzed with fear. Her mind could no longer process what was happening. She simply stood there, trembling, terrified—

Until the door blew open—and she saw the man without a head.

Daphne turned and ran. Her room was small, but suddenly it seemed cavernous. Such a small space—and yet she ran and ran, for many minutes it seemed, down an endless corridor that stretched farther and farther off into the distance. How could this be happening? How could she keep running for so long? What had happened to this room?

Behind her, the headless man's footsteps echoed as he pursued her. Thunder clapped overhead. Daphne just kept on running, down that impossibly long corridor.

The dream went on that way all night.

In the morning, when Daphne finally opened her eyes, the dream fragmented into a million tiny pieces, and all she could remember of it was the terror.

When she looked in the mirror, her eyes were red and puffy. She staggered down for coffee, avoiding everyone, then made her way up to meet Christopher in the upstairs study, which they used as a classroom. Lately he'd been cooperative, and even if Daphne had kept her guard up, suspecting his too-wide smile was inauthentic, she'd at least been pleased that he finished all his assignments. This morning, however, he folded his spindly arms across his chest and told her he hadn't done any of his homework. When Daphne asked him why, he said, "I didn't feel like it."

She told him he'd better feel like it tonight, because she was doubling the amount of work he had to do.

His round little button eyes burned with fury. "Why should I concern myself with petty little arithmetic assignments or reading about Paul Revere when we are all in danger of being slaughtered as we sleep?"

Daphne made a small gasp. "What do you mean?"

A sly smile played with his lips. "Surely you know, Daphne. You know all about my grandfather now. You know about all the little children whose throats he slit."

"What are you talking about, Christopher?"

"I was at the computer late last night. I saw the history. I knew you were the last one to use it, and I saw all the news sites you'd visited, and the stories you'd read." He laughed. "Apparently they didn't teach you how to wipe out your online activity at that prissy little girls' school of yours."

"What I do online is none of your business."

"But I think it would be my father's," Christopher said. "Gee, what would dear old Dad have to say if he knew you were researching his father's nefarious crimes?"

"I suggest we get back to our lesson."

Christopher jumped out of his chair and went over to the window. "I want to go outside. I want to search for the bones of the little children who were never found."

Daphne said nothing.

"Surely you read about that, did you not, Daphne? There were seven little kids whose bodies were never located. Pity their poor parents, never having closure. What do you say you and me go on a hunt to find them?"

"We'll do nothing of the sort."

He pouted extravagantly. "I suppose it doesn't matter. We'll all be dead come winter."

Daphne tried not to react, but the boy was frightening her. "Why do you say such things?"

He let out a whooping kind of laugh. "Because

it's true. My grandfather has returned. He killed that barmaid. And apparently he's been coming after you!"

Daphne gripped the side of a table to steady herself.

"Do you think I don't know what you told the sheriff? Nothing in this house escapes me. There are all sorts of ways to eavesdrop here. I've heard everything you've ever said to anyone!"

She doubted if that was literally true, but clearly the boy had overheard her Saturday night telling Ben, Ashlee, and Abigail what had transpired in the village.

"This house has an evil life of its own," Christopher continued. "It took my mother from me. She jumped off the tower to her death. Who's to say she wasn't forced to do so by the ghost of Pete Witherspoon Senior?"

"That's nonsense, Christopher."

"My mother was not crazy," he said, growing stern and surly. "She wouldn't have jumped without a reason."

"Of course she wasn't crazy. I'm sure she was a lovely woman."

He scowled. "What would you know? You can't compare to her. And neither can that slut my father remarried."

"Christopher, I won't have you speaking of your stepmother that way!"

He made a face at her. "You won't have me? Please, Daphne. As if you could stop me. You— now, *you're* the crazy person."

The boy seemed to know all of the buttons to push this morning.

"Because the way I see it"—Christopher said, striking a pose of mock contemplation—"it's either that my grandfather's ghost is now haunting the village, or that you're cracking up." He smiled, his little black eyes shining. "I wonder which one it is."

"You are being disrespectful, Christopher. I won't stand for—"

"You won't stand for it? My dear Daphne, I'm only speaking what you yourself have surely wondered. After all, you thought that clown had pursued you down the street. Now you find out that a witness saw him casually walking the other way."

He must have been hiding, listening to her conversation with Ben last night.

"So either that clown was a ghost or you're crackers." He let out that whooping laugh again. "Gosh, I can't wait to find out which!"

"Get out of here," Daphne said, seething. "You have your assignment. It's double from last time. If it's not completed tomorrow morning, I will go to your father."

He just kept laughing. "See ya later, Daphne!" He was bounding toward the door. "Sure you don't want to come with me on a hunt to find some bones?"

His laughter echoed down the corridor.

Daphne felt as if she would cry. She felt the tears bubbling up, and she would have broken out into sobs if Ashlee hadn't come in at that moment.

"What's wrong, Daphne?"

Daphne looked over at her. "I can't stay here anymore," she told her friend. "It's just too much."

Ashlee gave her a look of sympathy. "Oh, Daphne,

I don't want you to leave. But . . . I can't say I don't understand."

"Maybe Our Lady will allow me to come back until I find another job," she said. "I can volunteer there, help with the girls, in exchange for board."

"Oh, Daphne." Ashlee looked as if she might cry now.

"Could I use your cell phone? To call Mother Angela?"

"I should really let Pete know what you're thinking. . . ."

Daphne shook her head. "I'll speak with him afterward. After I speak with Mother Angela, I'll go directly to him and explain my decision."

Ashlee hesitated for a moment, then dug into the pocket of the pink hoodie she was wearing and handed over her phone.

"Thank you," Daphne said.

"Reception sucks here," Ashlee said. "The best place . . ."

"I know," Daphne said. "The tower room."

She hurried through the house. Up the winding staircase she went, her footsteps echoing in the emptiness of the tower. Once at the top, she looked out at the estate, the nearly bare trees, the crashing surf beyond. It would be winter soon. Daphne didn't want to be here when winter came.

Surprisingly, the call went through on the first try. By the time Mother Angela came on the line, however, the connection was fading. Mother's voice went in and out. But she understood what Daphne was trying to say.

She wanted to come home.

"Listen, Daphne, my dear," Mother told her. "You must stay where you are. These things you describe . . . they are not real. There are no such things as ghosts. And you are not going crazy. Please, I urge you. Speak to Mr. Witherspoon. He is a good man. I am certain of that. Explain to him all your fears. Be honest with him."

Daphne was crying now. "I don't want to stay here."

"In life, we are given many challenges. You mustn't give up, my dear. I know it is hard. And I would do anything to hold you in my arms and take care of you. But I would not be doing you any favors to encourage you to give up now. Remember, Daphne, this is your destiny."

"Why do you keep saying that?"

"Because I believe it." The phone crackled then, and whatever else Mother said was lost. "Mr. Witherspoon," Mother was saying when the connection cleared. "I feel you can trust him. Go to him."

"All right, Mother."

"Be brave, my dear, beautiful child. God will give you strength. All of these things that frighten you . . . you are stronger than all of them."

"But when I don't know what is real and what is not—"

Daphne stopped in midsentence. She saw the call had been dropped.

She figured it was no use to try calling back. Mother had made her position clear. She did not feel Daphne should give up.

Over the next couple of days, Daphne began to agree with her. Mother was right. She couldn't expect to go running back to the sanctuary of Our

Lady every time she got scared or confused. This was her life now. It was sink or swim, fight or flight. She knew she was not crazy. She had always been a sensible, logical person. All her teachers had commented on Daphne's grace under pressure. She had to believe in herself. Mother Angela had taught her that. She had to believe she would succeed, and then she would.

She took Mother's advice to speak with Pete. She shared with him her concerns about Christopher. She admitted—lest the boy expose her first—that she had done some research on the family tragedy, not for any "prurient reasons," she told Mr. Witherspoon, but because she felt she had to know the full story. She assured him the details would never be shared with anyone, nor, now that she knew everything, did she feel the need to bring any of it up again. He seemed relieved at that. He also said he would speak to Christopher about being more cooperative. Daphne urged him to rethink the idea of a psychotherapist or counselor for the boy. His problems went very deep, she said, far deeper than she was capable of handling. Multiplication tables and American history she could take care of. But his ongoing grief and anger were matters for a very different kind of skilled professional.

Mr. Witherspoon seemed impressed with Daphne's articulate expression of the situation, and indeed, she was quite pleased with herself. Mother Angela's talk, while difficult, had had the desired effect on her. A day before, Daphne had been a crying, frightened child. Now she might still be frightened, but she was no longer crying.

And she no longer felt like a child.

Ashlee had seemed surprised to learn that Daphne wasn't packing back her bags to leave, but then insisted she was delighted she was staying. But, she said, if Daphne stayed, she had to do one thing.

"What's that?" Daphne asked.

"You have to take Gregory Winston up on his offer of a date."

Daphne didn't know if it was a good idea. It would feel as if she was going behind Mr. Witherspoon's back. But Ashlee insisted what Daphne did in her off time was her business. "Besides," Ashlee added, "you have *got* to get out of this house once in a while. Look how upset and jittery you were a day ago. You need some time out of here so you can breathe."

So, when Wednesday night arrived, Ashlee told everyone that she and Daphne were going down to Portland to see a movie. But what she really planned to do was drop Daphne off at Rico's, where she'd meet Gregory. They spent the late afternoon getting ready. Ashlee styled Daphne's hair in a sophisticated sort of updo, and let her borrow a pair of Manolo Blahnik high heels. Of course the polka-dotted skirt from the other day was taken out of the closet. Daphne had thought she'd never have a chance to wear it, but that chance had come. To top it all off, Ashlee let her wear a gorgeous white faux-fur coat. Daphne looked, Ashlee said, like a model.

Then it was off to meet Gregory. That was, if he remembered.

He did. He was waiting for her at a table in the back. A bud vase containing a single red rose sat opposite him at the table.

"You came," he said, with genuine pleasure. The rose, he said, was for her.

She was touched. She sat down, and for a few awkward moments, neither of them said a word. Then Gregory snapped his fingers and a waiter brought over a bottle of what looked like champagne.

"Don't worry," Gregory said. "It's sparkling, but there's no alcohol."

Daphne laughed. She felt her cheeks blush.

"You look . . . amazing," Gregory said. "Hardly the picture of a convent girl any longer."

"Oh, I really still am," she said with a laugh.

Gregory smiled. "And that's why I like you."

They talked about everything other than Witherswood and the events that had gone on there. They talked about the harbor, and the boats Gregory owned. They talked about things to do in Maine in the winter. Did Daphne like to ice-skate? She did. Gregory knew places to go. Did she like to ski? She'd tried just once, she replied, with a group of girls from Our Lady, and had been kind of clumsy. Gregory told her he was, too, which surprised her. He suggested maybe they take skiing lessons together. Daphne laughed. It was a nice idea, she thought to herself, but just what would she tell Mr. Witherspoon?

Their food was delicious. Gregory had had his chef whip up a special wild salmon for them. The bread was homemade, crusty and warm, fresh from the oven. The butternut squash was the sweetest Daphne had ever tasted.

They talked about places Gregory had been—it seemed he'd been everywhere—and places Daphne had always dreamed of seeing. London, Paris, Rome, of course, but also the fjords of Norway, she told him, and the Great Wall of China. Gregory had been to them all. He described the fjords as breathtaking, especially at sunset. And the Great Wall was like a walk into the far, dim reaches of the ancient past. One of the great man-made wonders of the world.

What an exciting man. What hadn't Gregory done? He was a skilled yachtsman and, Daphne learned, a motorcyclist. He'd climbed mountains, dived into the deep sea, and loved spelunking in caves. He'd also built his own house.

"Would you like to see it?" he asked Daphne. "It's nearby."

She hesitated. Was it right to go to a man's house on the first date?

But she trusted Gregory. So she said yes, and they quickly polished off their dessert—a gorgeous chocolate cheesecake—and headed outside.

A damp, cold mist was rolling in from the sea. Daphne was glad for Ashlee's coat.

"Where's the house?" she asked Gregory.

"On the cliff road," he told her, as he quickly popped into a small lean-to attached to the restaurant. He emerged with a helmet in his hands.

"Ever been on a bike?"

"Oh, my, no," Daphne said.

Gregory helped affix the helmet onto her head. "Don't worry, it won't scrunch your hair too much," he said. "And I have plenty of combs and brushes at my place if you want to fix it up when we get there."

Daphne didn't care about her hair. She should have been terrified about the prospect of getting on the back of a motorcycle. The old Daphne would have been. But the new Daphne . . . in her polka-dotted skirt and high heels . . . the new Daphne who had faced down sinister clowns, whether they were real or in her mind . . . she found herself surprisingly excited to get on that bike.

What a ride it was! Her arms wrapped around Gregory's waist, Daphne felt the wind on her face as they zoomed through the center of the village and out onto the cliff road. A sliver of a white moon hung high in the sky. In less than ten minutes they had reached a strange-looking structure built into the side of the cliff. It looked as if it were a house that had sunk. Only a roof and a few small windows were visible. Dismounting the bike, Daphne looked at the place. Gregory gestured for her to follow him through a small, stained-glass door.

As she stepped through, Daphne's jaw dropped. The reason one saw so little of the house from the road was because it had been built into the side of the cliff. The entire other side of the house was made of glass. It was like living in the ocean. The waves crashed all around her, on both sides and even under her feet.

"This is magnificent," she said, her voice wondrous.

Gregory smiled. "Thanks. I designed it and did much of the construction myself."

He gestured for her to have a seat on the sofa that looked out over the roiling sea below.

"I'll make some coffee," he told her.

Daphne sat down. How very, very far away she was from the staid, redbrick, ivy-covered walls of Our Lady's School for Girls.

"Look, Daphne," Gregory said, when he brought over the coffee. "We've talked about everything tonight except Witherswood. I'll admit I'm concerned about you. I spoke with the sheriff yesterday, and he told me what you reported to him."

She accepted the coffee and took a sip. It was good.

"A few days ago," she admitted, "I wanted to leave. I even called Mother Angela, begging to come back. But now . . ."

"Now?" Gregory asked, when it seemed as if she might not finish her thought.

"Now I feel determined to find out what connection I might have to this place." Daphne looked out at the sea, dappled with moonlight. "There is something going on. What I saw . . . I don't believe it was an illusion or a hallucination. Just because that terrible clown walked the other way doesn't mean he couldn't have doubled back and gone around the block to meet me in that parking lot and scare me. If that had been his intent, in fact, then it would have made more sense for him not to follow me in front of a witness." She looked over at Gregory. "The ride over here on the back of your bike confirmed it was possible. I spotted an alley right near the bench where I had been sitting. The clown could have easily hurried down there to catch up with me."

"So you think this person, whoever he is, dressed as a clown, is somehow targeting you?" Gregory sat down beside Daphne.

"It's either that, or it's the ghost of Mr. Wither-spoon's father."

She saw the look that crossed Gregory's face.

Daphne smiled. "I know that sounds crazy. And maybe it is." She leaned forward a bit to make her point. "But I know that *I'm* not crazy."

"Well, that's good at least."

"And I also know that I'm going to find out what's going on. Because I'm starting to believe there's something about myself I'm supposed to find out here." She took a sip of coffee. "My destiny."

"Well, I'm glad you're not leaving," Gregory said. "But it's not just mysterious clowns and the possibility of ghosts that has me worried about you in that house."

"Oh no?" She smiled. "What else then?"

"They are a very dysfunctional clan, Daphne, and that's putting it mildly." Gregory sighed. As he settled back into the couch, his broad, strong shoulder touched Daphne's, and she felt what could only be described as a surge of electricity crackle through her. "How could they not be, after what they've been through?"

"Well, Christopher started acting up again, but

after his father spoke with him, he's once again being cooperative," Daphne told him. "I suspect more outbursts will come in the future though."

"Pete needs to get the boy to a shrink," Gregory said.

"I agree. He said he'd consider it."

"I'll believe it when it happens." Gregory let his shoulder touch Daphne's again. "What about the others?"

"Abigail is still very hostile. It's like she doesn't want me in the house."

"A bitter old woman. I don't she's ever been—" Gregory caught himself. "Well, I think she's been by herself too long."

"Were you about to say she's never been laid?" Daphne asked.

Gregory blushed.

"I might be a convent girl," Daphne said, laughing, "but it's not like I'm completely clueless."

Gregory smiled. "What about Donovan?"

Daphne's smile faded. "He's become . . . more aggressive."

"Watch out for him," Gregory cautioned. "I don't trust him."

"He made a move the other night, and I made it clear he was never to do that again."

"I'll break his neck if he tries anything again," Gregory mumbled. "Isn't his fiancée around?"

"Yes, and I think she thinks I'm the aggressor."

"He probably tells her that you are. He's pathological. Remember, I grew up with all those boys. Donovan, Ben, Gabe. They were my best friends. We did everything together. But even then Donovan was a prick." He looked over at Daphne to see if he'd offended her with the word, but she just nodded for him to go on. "He was always teasing Ben about being gay. Ben was a brave teenager, coming out at a very young age. But Donovan was even worse to Gabe, making him feel like a lesser athlete, a lesser horseman, a lesser everything. And Pete didn't help, always seeming to favor Donovan over his other two nephews. We all believed that Donovan was going to inherit the estate—but I guess that's changed now that Pete actually had a son of his own."

"Is that why they all still live at Witherswood? They hope they're going to inherit it?"

"Well, Pete has them all employed in various, mostly nominal, capacities in the various family businesses. How he'll divide all of that up when he dies is unknown, but I imagine the bulk of it will go to Christopher, which I'm sure burns the rest of them up."

"Ben stays because he feels an obligation to take care of Gabe."

Gregory shrugged. "That might be true. I had left by the time Gabe had his accident. I know he's become quite the recluse now, but he was always bitter. Even before he broke his back. And that's because of that oppressively dysfunctional family."

"But when you were a boy, you were part of that family."

He nodded. "My father and Pete were like brothers. Pete treated me more like a son than a nephew. I said before that Pete seemed to favor Donovan. That was true, as far as Ben and Gabe were concerned. But Pete's true favorite was yours truly. And he was like a second father to me." Gregory's face clouded. "That is, until I was nine years old and left Witherspoon to go live with my aunt and uncle."

Daphne told him how she'd read about the murders. She shared that she knew it must have been so terribly difficult for him. She reached over and touched his hand. He smiled sadly.

"Pete tried to make amends," Gregory said, in a distant-sounding voice. "He gave my aunt and uncle a lot of money. I used it, too, for school, and for investing, buying property. I turned that sum of money into a hundred times its worth. And then do you know what I did?"

"What?" Daphne asked.

"I gave it back to him. I showed up at Withers-wood one day, with cash. It was the amount Pete had given to me, plus interest, for all the years that had gone between. And I plopped it down on the table in the parlor. We were now even."

"What did he say?"

"He was furious. Because he knew I had used the money he'd given me to get rich, and then to try to put him out of business."

Daphne made a face. "But . . . if you put him out of business, you'll put me out of business, too."

Gregory cracked a smile. "I have a feeling, Miss May, you will land on your feet just fine."

"Maybe so," she said, "but I wish you and Mr. Witherspoon didn't have to be enemies. I understand your anger toward him. But maybe someday . . ."

"Someday is never going to happen." Gregory stood abruptly, his mood suddenly sharp and sour. "I'll never forgive him. He discovered his father's

bloody clown suit and realized he was the killer.
Still, he waited a day before taking any action—
and in that delay my parents were slaughtered. I
can never forgive that."

"I wonder if he's ever been able to forgive himself."

Something else seemed to occur to Gregory.
"How's that creepy butler been to you?"

"Boris? All right. Keeps his distance, mostly. He
talks about ghosts a lot."

"Doesn't surprise me. He was extremely loyal to
Pete Senior. Had been with him all his life. And I
think he might have known what was going on,
and out of loyalty, said nothing to the police. He
was there the night my parents died, in fact. His
room was only a few yards from where that monster slit their throats. And he claimed he heard
nothing."

"You think . . . Boris let them die?"

"I have always wondered whether, out of loyalty
to his master, he let my mother and father bleed to
death rather than wake the house and call the police."

Daphne shuddered.

Gregory sighed. "Look. Enough of all this. It's
almost time for us to head back." He smiled.
"Come here. I want to show you something."

He motioned for Daphne to follow him. He
stepped out onto a terrace off the living room, a
dramatic platform of steel and glass that spanned
a break in the cliffs. If you looked straight down,
you looked into the surf. Daphne gasped in awe.

They stood there, looking out over the white-crested, moonlit waves, getting a little damp from the mist blowing off the sea. Daphne suddenly shivered, and Gregory put his arm around her, drawing her in close. How strong he was. How solid he felt.

"I like you, Daphne," he whispered.

She felt too overcome to reply at the moment.

It was getting late. Ashlee was scheduled to pick her back up at the restaurant at eleven. Back in the house, Daphne wrapped herself in the faux fur and thanked Gregory for a truly lovely evening. "I hope there will be more," he told her.

Daphne hoped so, too, though she just smiled in reply.

As they stood beside the bike outside on the driveway, Gregory made a move to secure the helmet once again on Daphne's head. But he paused, and all at once reached down and kissed her. Just a light kiss, on the lips. Daphne responded, and so he kissed her again, deeper this time. Daphne felt as if she might faint right there on the spot. Her head floated off her shoulders and headed out somewhere over the ocean. Never had she known such a feeling. Everything was spinning. Her whole body tingled. Wrapped in Gregory's arms, Daphne wanted to stay right where she was for eternity.

She had never been kissed before in her life.

Gregory smiled at her kindly as they, finally, gently, broke contact. Then he tenderly affixed the helmet to her head.

Mounting the bike, Daphne was glad for the opportunity to once again snake her arms around Gregory's strong torso. "Hang on!" he called. The motorcycle revved into life and took off down the cliff road.

As planned, Ashlee was waiting for her. Gregory dropped Daphne off, then sped back down the road. It wouldn't do for someone to come upon them all together. Once Daphne was in the car, Ashlee pumped her for details. But all Daphne would say was that it had been wonderful. She felt as if she wanted to keep all the details to herself, like precious gems in a jewelry box.

"Sweetie, if I were you, I'd say to hell with Witherswood and bratty little Christopher and take off with Gregory," Ashlee said. "Really, I would not blame you for an instant."

When they got back to the great old house, Daphne was still in kind of a dreamy daze, and told Ashlee she'd be inside in a little bit. She just wanted to walk for a while. Ashlee smiled, seeming to understand. As her friend went into the house, Daphne wandered out toward the stables. She loved coming out here. Even on a cold, damp night like this, there was something warm and comforting in the stables—the smell of hay, the kind, compassionate nickering of the horses. Ben had offered to teach her to ride. She'd like that. Gregory could ride, and wouldn't it be lovely to go riding with him?

She was walking past the horse stalls when she heard a clank of metal.

She looked up.

There was someone in the shadows.

The figure of a man.

Daphne's heart began to race.

The figure was approaching her.

She was about to run when a slice of moonlight revealed the figure to be Donovan. Even at five or six yards away, she could smell he'd been drinking.

"Have fun tonight?" Donovan asked.

Daphne held her ground. "Yes," she replied. "Ashlee and I just got back."

"Gee," Donovan said, drawing closer. "I didn't know Ashlee could drive a motorcycle."

Daphne's blood turned to ice.

Donovan was nearly in front of her now. "Not very discreet of you, doll, to go riding around town on the back of Gregory Winston's Harley-Davidson." His eyes burned with fury. "Wouldn't Uncle Pete like to know how you really spent your evening?"

"How did you—"

"I was in town, having a few pops," he said, and burped in her face. The smell of gin was putrid. "And who do I see go whizzing by but everyone's favorite little virginal governess."

Daphne turned to leave, but Donovan grabbed her wrist. It hurt.

"Let me go!" she shouted.

"You little slut," he seethed. "How dare you refuse me, then go whore yourself out to the man who's trying to destroy this family?"

"Help me!" Daphne screamed, but now Donovan had her in his grip, and he clamped his other hand over her mouth.

"Scream all you want, bitch, but no one can hear you out here," he said into her ear.

With that he pushed her down into a pile of hay, falling on top of her. Pinning her down by the neck with his left hand, he used his right to tear open her blouse.

"I'm going to take what I've wanted from the first day you walked into this house, you lying little tramp," Donovan told her. "And there's nothing you or that fucking asshole Gregory Winston can do to stop me."

TWELVE

"Help me, please!" Daphne screamed, as she felt Donovan begin to tear at her skirt—her new polka-dotted skirt. "Help, someone!"

"Donovan!"

Right away Daphne recognized the voice. It was Suzanne. She seemed to be always on the hunt, looking for her fiancé, and with good reason. Now she walked into the stable with a look of utter horror on her face.

"Donovan!" she shrieked again.

He backed off of Daphne, staggering to his feet, looking away, not making eye contact with Suzanne. She rushed at him, grabbed him by the shoulders, and spun him around to face her. Then she slapped his face. Hard.

Daphne stood, pulling her torn blouse together.

"He tried to rape me," she told Suzanne.

The other woman glared at her, then turned again to Donovan.

"She lured me in here," he said, his eyes still averted from both of them.

Suzanne slapped him again.

Then she spun on Daphne. "If you breathe a word of this, I'll destroy you."

Daphne was so shocked she couldn't answer.

"I mean it," Suzanne said, taking a step closer. "I will say you really did lure him in here, that I caught you very happily engaging in a sexual seduction of my fiancé."

Daphne was aghast. "You'd really do that? No matter that he tried to rape me."

"I would." Suzanne lifted her chin defiantly.

Daphne understood. To lose Donovan meant to lose his money, and the fortune he hoped someday to come into. Suzanne wasn't going to risk that.

"No one would believe you," Daphne said, refusing to cower. "Everyone knows his reputation, and they know I'm just a little girl from a convent." She let her blouse fall open, revealing her bra. "With a torn blouse, which I shall keep for evidence."

"If you're so confident, then go ahead, spill the whole sordid story to Uncle Pete," Suzanne snarled. "Donovan's his favorite nephew. See what his reaction will be. See who he will choose. Him or you."

Daphne said nothing. She just pulled her coat closely around her and took a step toward the door. But then she turned back.

"If he ever comes near me again," she spit, "I swear, he will be sorry."

Then she hurried out of the stable.

She wanted to cry. In fact, she did cry a bit as she walked back up to the house. She felt certain Mr. Witherspoon would believe her if she told him. But what his reaction would be, as Suzanne pointed out, was unknown. For now, Daphne decided to say nothing. She wanted to report Donovan to the sheriff. And she might. She very well might do just that. But for now, she just needed to be by herself and think.

Oh, how easily she could crumble after such an episode. But Daphne resolved she would be strong. Every day, it seemed, brought her a new challenge that she had to meet. She wasn't going to be beaten. Not by Donovan, not by any of the horrors she had encountered in this house and this family. She'd best them all. She'd make Mother Angela proud. She'd survive her challenges. She'd discover why this place was her destiny.

But more than anything, Daphne wanted to be in Gregory's arms. She had felt safe there. Safe in a way she had never felt safe before.

Despite the trauma she'd undergone in the stable, Daphne fell quickly to sleep, and her rest was not fractured by nightmares. She slept soundly, and when she woke up in the morning, it was Gregory she thought of first, Donovan second.

She still hadn't decided what she would do when she headed down for breakfast. And by then her decision had been made for her.

Pete was waiting for her, his yellow, weary eyes blazing in his head. He told her he wanted to speak with her immediately in the study.

Once there, Daphne noticed Ashlee was sitting in a chair waiting. She looked upset.

"I understand you did not go to the movies with my wife last night," Pete said, his lips trembling with rage. "I understand, instead, that you went off riding with Gregory Winston on his motorcycle."

"I—I—" Daphne stammered. She had not been prepared for this.

"I forced Ashlee to tell me the truth," Pete said, "so don't try to deny it."

"I'm sorry, Daphne," Ashlee said in a small voice.

"Mr. Witherspoon," Daphne said, aware that her own voice was shaking, "Gregory has been very kind to me. But I can assure you that I've told him that I think his vendetta against you is wrong, and that he should really—"

"I have no interest in hearing your excuses." He turned away from her, needing to steady himself against a chair. "Don't you see that man is using you to get to me? He has vowed to destroy me and my entire family."

"I don't think he really wants to do that, not deep down," Daphne said. "It's just the terrible grief he carries. . . ."

"How dare you stand there and defend him? Do you know how many businesses and employees he's stolen from me? How he's devalued my properties?"

"I'm sorry, sir. I never wanted to offend you."

Pete's pulsing red face seemed ready to burst with anger. "Well, you have! And thanks to Donovan, I now know you to be ungrateful and unreliable."

"Donovan?" Daphne asked, the name bitter on her tongue.

Mr. Witherspoon nodded. "He and Suzanne were out last night. They got back together here very late. Both of them saw you on Winston's motorcycle."

All at once Daphne understood their strategy.

They would claim to have been together all night, so that gave Donovan an alibi for what happened in the stable. And by beating her to the punch, by going to Pete accusing her before she could accuse Donovan, they had ensured that anything Daphne might now say about the attempted rape would look like an attempt merely to discredit Donovan, or at least, to shift the focus off her own transgression. It was a brilliant, devious move, and Daphne was stunned into silence.

"Pete," Ashlee was saying, "it was just a simple motorcycle ride. Nothing more than that happened. It wasn't premeditated. Daphne and I were out, and we ran into Gregory. He offered to give us both rides. I declined, of course, but it's true I encouraged Daphne to give it a whirl. After all, she's been cooped up here, and things have been tough for her, with Christopher acting out and all. . . ."

Pete said nothing, just turned away from them both to stare out the window. "I may have to consider terminating your employment here," he said to Daphne.

"Mr. Witherspoon, I assure you I have not been disloyal to you," she replied.

"By going out with that man, even just accepting a ride on his motorcycle, you have been disloyal."

"Don't worry, sweetie," Ashlee said. "We'll give you a terrific settlement and help you find a place of your own in Boston. We won't leave you without resources."

Daphne blinked in surprise. Ashlee seemed to be accepting rather too quickly a decision that her husband hadn't even made yet. But maybe she knew more than Daphne did. Maybe Pete's mind was already made up.

But it appeared there was still some reason for hope. "I will need to think about this," Pete said, his back still turned. "That's all for now, Daphne. You'd best begin Christopher's lessons."

With great difficulty, Daphne got through the day. Christopher was back to being super-cooperative and excruciatingly polite. His governess, however, remained wary, on the alert, waiting for his next move, because she was sure it was coming.

That afternoon, sitting in the glass sunroom, Daphne drank some chamomile tea cook had prepared for her and tried to calm herself. What extremes of emotions she'd felt in less than twenty-four hours. Happiness, anxiety, terror, confidence, confusion. What if Mr. Witherspoon asked her to leave? She longed to talk with Gregory, but knew that, for now at least, any communication with him would have to wait.

Outside, the trees were all bare now, gray skeletal arms etched against a sky almost as dark and gray. Winter was coming. The sky looked heavy, as if it were holding the snow it planned to dump on them soon.

Daphne was suddenly startled by voices coming into the room behind her. They belonged to Abigail and Louella, and the sisters were bickering. Abigail was complaining about the housekeepers, who, it seemed, were Louella's responsibility. The forthright, strict Abigail was scolding the dithery, easily befuddled Louella, insisting she needed to take a firmer hand with the help. When the sisters noticed Daphne sitting there, their conversation ceased.

"Oh, I'm sorry, Daphne," Louella said. "We didn't mean to disturb you if you were doing any lesson plans."

"Does it look as if she's doing lesson plans, Louella?" Abigail snapped. "She's only sitting there mooning over that traitor, Gregory Winston."

Apparently Donovan's announcement had made its way through the house.

"Oh, Gregory," Louella said, dimwitted as always. "Are you friendly with Gregory, Daphne? He was such a nice little boy when he lived here."

"Nice little boy!" Abigail huffed. "That nice little boy has plans to ruin this family! He wants to drive Pete out of business!"

"Oh, that's right," Louella said, making a face, revealing not only a double chin but a triple. "I forgot that."

"And *your* son, Louella, saw *this* young woman cavorting around town with him last night on a motorcycle!"

"Oh, I've always wanted to ride on a motorcycle!" Louella exclaimed.

The image of chubby little Louella on a motorcycle was enough to almost make Daphne laugh, and she decided she'd had enough. She turned around to look at the sisters. "I was not cavorting around town," she said. She figured she'd stick to the story Ashlee had put forward. "He offered rides to both Ashlee and me. I accepted. I shouldn't have, for which I've apologized to Mr. Witherspoon."

Abigail harrumphed. "It's not surprising that Ashlee was part of it all."

"Oh, Ashlee's a sweet little girl," Louella said in her squeaky voice.

Abigail shook her head as she poured herself a cup of tea. "The way Pete dotes on her . . . gives her anything she wants. That car. Those clothes and shoes. He never treated poor dear Peggy so well."

Daphne knew that was because Pete had never gotten over his childhood sweetheart, a girl named Maria. She wondered if Pete doted on Ashlee now to make up for the fact that he could never love her as much as he loved Maria? Daphne felt quite certain that the photograph she'd seen Pete holding that day, the one he'd so quickly hidden, was not Peggy, after all. It was also not Ashlee. It was, almost certainly, Maria. He still carried a torch for a girl he had loved more than two decades ago.

At that moment, the sound of the heavy knocker on the front door reverberated through the house. It always made Daphne jump. And for some reason, it made her especially anxious this time.

She stood, scooting past Abigail and Louella, who followed her like curious cats. She saw Boris come out of his room and stride across the marble foyer toward the door. The butler looked ghoulish as ever, tall and hulking. He was ancient—he had to be in his seventies—but he was still as strong as an ox, and swift on his feet. He reached the door and pulled it open.

Peering from the corridor, Daphne gasped when she saw who the visitor was.

Gregory!

"Hello, Boris, long time no see," Gregory said,

his voice echoing across the marble in the quiet house. He looked so handsome in the frame of the doorway, the sun reflecting in his reddish-gold hair, his green eyes sparkling.

Behind her, Daphne heard Abigail huffing. She and Louella were scoping out the scene from over Daphne's shoulder. "How dare that man come here?" Abigail whispered; then she lowered her voice even more. "I imagine he's here to see you," she said, her voice dripping like poisoned honey over Daphne's ear.

Boris had said nothing in reply to Gregory. The butler just stood there looking at him.

"I'm here to see Pete, Boris," Gregory said cheerfully. "Would you please tell him I'm here?"

Boris hesitated, then nodded.

"Maybe he's come to make up with Mr. Witherspoon," Daphne whispered.

"Oh, that would be nice," Louella said.

"That would as likely as the sun falling out of the sky," Abigail snarled.

Boris was about to close the door on Gregory while he went to get the master of the house, but Gregory placed his hand on the door to stop him.

"Oh, come on, Boris, might I at least wait in the foyer?" Gregory asked. "This used to be my home, after all. And it's rather cold out here."

"I'm not sure if Mr. Witherspoon would want you to come inside," Boris said, in that odd, high-pitched voice of his.

"Oh, now, really Boris, what do you expect me to do, set the place on fire?"

"I wouldn't know, sir," the butler replied.

Suddenly Daphne's attention was drawn by footsteps coming from the direction of the study.

"Never mind, Boris," a voice echoed from the corridor. "I'll see him right here in the foyer. Step inside and state your business, Winston."

It was Pete. He strode out to meet Gregory, who entered the house and walked toward him. They met in the middle of the room. Daphne and the two older ladies held their breaths.

"What possible reason could you have for coming here?" Pete demanded.

Daphne saw the way the two men looked at each other. There was an obvious, visceral hatred. But . . . there was also something more.

Pete had once been a second father to Gregory.

Gregory had been the son he had never had, up to that time.

They glared at each other.

"I've come to apologize, Pete," Gregory said.

Daphne's heart leapt. "You see?" she whispered over her shoulder to Abigail and Louella.

"I've come to apologize," Gregory repeated to a stunned Pete, "for asking your wife and your son's governess to accompany me on a motorcycle ride. It was inappropriate, and I apologize. I just don't want you blaming them for my lack of thinking, and especially Miss May, who only accepted the offer after I pressured her into doing so. I take full responsibility."

Pete considered him, his yellow eyes taking Gregory in carefully.

"That is what you came up here to say?" he asked finally.

"I had to come up in person, since you don't have a phone, and sure can't get you on Facebook or Twitter." Gregory smirked. "Other than that, everything else between us remains exactly the same."

"Then get the hell out of my house," Pete growled.

"With pleasure," Gregory said, turning on his heel.

"And never come here again!" Pete shouted after him.

"Oh, I'll be back"—Gregory spoke over his shoulder as he passed through the door Boris held open for him—"when I come here to take owner-ship of Witherswood!"

"Get out!" Pete rasped.

Gregory laughed, and was gone.

Behind Daphne, Abigail sniffed. "Coming to make up, was he?" The older woman huffed off, Louella following her, seeming unsure of what she had just witnessed.

Pete stormed back to the study. Daphne, full of despair, hurried upstairs to her room. She under-stood what Gregory was trying to do: absolve her from any responsibility for being seen with him. But his anger was so deep . . . how could she possi-bly now continue to see him and work in this house? It was impossible. She wanted very much to see Gregory again, but she couldn't go behind Pete's back another time. She would have to make a choice at some point. She threw herself on her bed and closed her eyes.

She must have drifted off to sleep because when she opened her eyes again it was dark. Pitch dark. The wind had kicked up, too, and was howling through the eaves. Daphne flicked on the light. It was 9:49. Her stomach rumbled. She was hungry.

She was sitting on the edge of her bed, trying to work up the will to go downstairs and eat some dinner, when there was a light rapping on her door.

It was Ashlee.

"Did you catch Gregory's performance?" the young mistress of the house asked, delightedly, as she came rushing into Daphne's room. "Abigail, that miserable old bitch, told me you watched it with her from the corridor. How did he do?"

"You knew he was coming?"

"Of course I did! I called him. I explained what Donovan had done and we came up with the plan. Gregory was only too happy to do it, even if it meant seeming to humble himself in front of Pete, if it could in some way help you out." She looked at Daphne deliberately. "He really cares about you."

Daphne didn't know what to say.

"Well, I'm happy to report it worked," Ashlee said. "Pete came to me and said he forgave me—and he forgave you!"

"But don't you see?" Daphne cried. "How can I possibly see Gregory again now?"

Ashlee looked at her kindly. "I think you should go to him. Leave here, sweetie, and go to Gregory. He'd take much better care of you than we can!"

Daphne laughed. "I've just met him! What are you talking about? You don't just meet some guy and move in with him."

Ashlee smirked. "Why not? I did."

Daphne shook her head. "Well, I'm not you."

She sighed. "Look, I'm hungry. I missed dinner. Come downstairs with me and get a snack?"

"Sure," Ashlee said. "Pete's sound asleep. Usually is by eight thirty." She winked at Daphne. "I'll put it to you this way, sweetie. I think I might have to give up on the idea of Christopher ever having a baby brother or sister."

They headed downstairs. The house was, as usual, as quiet as a tomb. Daphne knew Ben was out—back in Portland again. She suspected he may have met someone, and she hoped to hear the details soon. Pete, Abigail, and Louella were all in their rooms, as were Boris and Axel. Christopher was supposed to be in his room, but Daphne knew she could never be sure about Christopher. She had no idea where Donovan and Suzanne were, nor did she much care.

In the kitchen, they found some wrapped chicken-salad sandwiches in the refrigerator. Cook had prepared them before she'd left for the day in case anyone wanted a late-night snack.

"Listen," Daphne said, after she took her first bite. "I need to tell you something."

"Shoot," Ashlee said.

"Donovan . . ." She wasn't sure how to say it. "Well, last night . . . in the stable . . ."

"Oh my God, Daphne," Ashlee said, as if reading her mind. "Did he try something with you?"

She nodded. "Pushed me down into a haystack. Ripped my blouse and was going for my skirt when Suzanne walked in."

Ashlee was horrified. Daphne related the whole sordid tale, including Suzanne's threat. All the while, Ashlee was shaking her head.

"Now it all makes sense, why they said what they did to Pete." Her eyes blazed with a rage that surprised Daphne. "Those dirty bastards."

"I'm not sure what to do," Daphne said. "I feel like reporting him to the sheriff, but after all that has happened. . . ."

"Of course, you should report him," Ashlee said. "He tried to rape you. But sweetie, you know as well as I do, it would do no good. Their word against yours. And after what Pete's just been through . . ."

"I know." Daphne had finished half of the sandwich and now felt full. "It just galls me that a man like that can get away with assaulting me."

"Oh, he won't get away," Ashlee said.

"What do you mean?"

Ashlee grinned. "A guy like that always gets caught eventually. It catches up with him. Eventually he'll be on the other end, getting what he deserves."

"You sound so certain."

"You forget I've been around a little more than you have. I've seen his type all my life. And I've seen what happens to guys like him."

Daphne shuddered.

That's when she heard the music.

From somewhere off in the distance . . . a tinny sound. Far away, somewhere in the house, but it seemed to be coming closer.

All around the mulberry bush, the monkey chased the weasel. . . .

"Oh my God," Daphne muttered.

"What is it, honey?"

"Listen. Do you hear that?"

Ashlee listened. "Music," she said. "It's like . . . a kid's song."

" 'Pop Goes the Weasel,' " Daphne breathed, and a terrible paroxysm of terror shook her to her core. "It's what I heard that day in the village! When I saw the clown!"

"Maybe it's Christopher. . . ."

"Believe me, Ashlee, that's not the kind of music he listens to."

The tune continued to lilt through the darkness, but just where it was coming from, they couldn't tell.

"Maybe we should wake Mr. Witherspoon," Daphne suggested.

"No," Ashlee said. "I don't want to disturb him. It's probably nothing Daphne. It's probably just a radio . . . or a toy. . . ."

Daphne knew it was no such thing. She stepped out into the parlor. As far as she could tell, it was coming from across the foyer.

"The tower room," she whispered to Daphne. "I can't be sure, but I think it's coming from behind the door that leads up to the tower room."

"Well, let's go see," Ashlee said, grabbing a flashlight. "It's dark going up those stairs."

"You're crazy," Daphne said, grabbing her arm and stopping her. "I'm telling you, that's the music that clown was playing that day on the street."

"And I'm telling *you*, sweetie, that you imagined what you saw that day. Look, Daphne, this house has a foolproof security system. Nobody's going to be able to get in here. That music we hear . . . it's no murderous clown ghost or whatever you think you saw." Ashlee's lips tightened. "But it just might be my stepson trying to scare us."

"You . . . you think it might be Christopher?"

"You said he overheard us talking the other day. This would be just like him."

With that, Ashlee forged ahead toward the door to the tower room. Daphne followed, a few steps behind.

When they pulled open the door, however, the music stopped.

"Now I can't be sure if it was coming from in here," Ashlee said. "Damn it."

"Let's go back," Daphne said.

"No way," Ashlee said. "If Christopher is up there, there's no way he can get back down and nowhere for him to hide. I'm going up." She turned to look at Daphne. "Coming with me?"

"I . . . I don't know."

"Come on, Daphne. I want to prove to you these things you think you see aren't real, or that there are logical explanations. Besides, you're Christopher's governess, so you really should take charge of the situation."

Daphne hesitated, then agreed to follow Ashlee up the iron stairs.

Their footsteps echoed in the darkness of the tower as they climbed. At the top, the little round room was in darkness. The light switch failed to illuminate the lamp. Either the bulb was out, or someone had taken it out.

"Christopher?" Ashlee called, swinging her flashlight through the darkness.

They both took a couple of tentative steps into the room.

Then the music started again.

All around the mulberry bush . . .

They both gasped out loud. Ashlee swung the flashlight around to her right, and its beam spotlighted the laughing face of a clown—white face, red nose, blue mouth, sharp yellow teeth.

They screamed, but as they turned to run, they fell—tripping over a body on the floor. The flashlight's beam provided enough illumination before it smashed on the floor to reveal who it was.

The body was Donovan—and his throat had been slit.

THIRTEEN

Screaming at the top of their lungs, Ashlee and Daphne practically leapt onto the stairs, tripping and falling over each other on the way down.

As they stumbled into the foyer, Ashlee had the sense to turn immediately around and bolt the door behind them, so the murderer couldn't get out. Daphne was shuddering with terror. "He's dead!" she kept screaming. "Donovan's dead!"

Their screams awoke the house. Lights went on all around them, including the chandelier that hung in the center of the foyer's ceiling. Once there was light, Daphne saw the bloody footprints she and Ashlee had tracked all across the marble floor.

Donovan's blood.

"Oh, God, he's dead!" Daphne screamed again, her hands in her hair. "Donovan's dead!"

Boris was the first one on the scene, in his nightgown and nightcap, looking like a walking corpse. Then Axel came out of his room, rubbing his eyes. At the same time Abigail, her gray hair falling loose around her shoulders, came darting down the stairs, nose first, her eyes flashing. Behind her, Louella waddled uncertainly. On the landing, Christopher appeared, staring over the banister, proving once and for all that it had not been him in the tower. With some difficulty, Pete came down the stairs behind his sisters, puzzlement and fear appearing alternately on his face.

And finally, from the side hallway, Suzanne emerged, in a black nightgown. "Donovan?" she asked. "What are you saying about Donovan?"

"He's dead!" Daphne screamed. "And that thing—that clown—is still up there!"

"Don't be absurd—" Pete started to say.

"Pete, it's true!" Ashlee shrieked. "I saw it, too! Oh, God, it's terrible!"

"Donovan," came the timid little voice of Louella, coming around Pete. "What do you mean that Donovan is dead?"

Daphne looked at her. Louella was Donovan's mother. Her heart broke for the poor, confused woman.

"Well, if something's happened to Donovan," Suzanne said, "I'm going to find out." She turned and pulled open the door to the tower room, ready to bolt up the stairs.

"No!" Ashlee shouted, jumping ahead of her and slamming the door shut again. "That thing is still up there! We need to keep the door bolted!"

"Why do we need to keep the door bolted?"

They all turned. This was a new voice. Gabriel was wheeling his chair into the foyer from the corridor, his eyes bleary from sleep. "All this commotion. What's going on here?"

"It's Donovan," Daphne told him. "He's . . . he's dead!"

On hearing this again, what they were saying seemed finally to sink in for Louella, and she began to cry. Abigail put her arm around her sister, though she seemed loath to do it.

"Where the hell is Ben?" Pete asked, looking around.

"He's . . . he's in Portland," Daphne managed to say.

"Well, we can't just stand here!" Pete blustered.

"We've got to keep that door bolted and go get the sheriff," Ashlee said, trying to keep her wits and act logically. "Axel, get in the car and speed like the devil into the village, tell the cops to get up here as fast as they can. And have them call Sheriff Patterson."

"This is why we need a goddamn telephone in this place," Gabriel grumbled under his breath, looking down as usual, shaking his head.

Daphne had backed up as far away from the tower entrance as possible. "There's no way out of there except through that door?" she asked in a small voice.

Only Gabriel seemed to hear her. "None," he assured her, and she caught a flash of his eyes as he shyly looked up at her. "Don't worry, Daphne. You're safe here."

It was the first time the young man in the wheelchair had ever addressed her directly, and the first time he'd ever spoken her name. Daphne was touched that, even in a moment of crisis such as this, Gabriel would try to reassure her. Maybe he wasn't so far gone in bitterness as she'd thought.

They all retreated into the parlor to wait for Axel to bring the police. Pete stood holding his hunting rifle, though the way his hands shook didn't inspire much confidence. Louella sat in a chair looking dazed. Suzanne paced back and forth, insisting that Donovan might just have been wounded, and they were wasting valuable time in not going up to check on him. Ashlee told her to go into the tower would be to risk getting killed herself.

Christopher sat watching everyone, not saying a word. Daphne couldn't tell if the boy was frightened or excited. Probably a mix of both. But Christopher wasn't the only one who was silent. Except for Suzanne, who kept muttering and swearing, no one spoke much as they waited. The eleven minutes it took to hear sirens in the distance seemed to stretch into an eternity.

But then the flashing lights of police cars came shining through the windows, turning the night air electric blue. Abigail rushed to let the police in. They immediately ordered the family to stay in the parlor while a team of ten heavily armed men surrounded the door to the tower room. They shouted to whoever was inside to come out with his hands up. When no one emerged, they moved in, unbolting the door, and with guns pointing forward, moved nearly as one up the stairs. Sheriff Patterson followed.

Except for the echo of their boots, there was no sound.

After about five minutes the police came back down. Sheriff Patterson walked into the parlor with a somber face.

"I'm sorry, Louella, Suzanne," he said. "But it's true that Donovan is dead."

"No!" Suzanne screamed.

Louella just wept silently in her chair.

"His killer?" Pete asked.

The sheriff looked at him, then moved his eyes over to Ashlee and Daphne, who stood closely together behind Pete.

"Did you girls say you saw someone up there?" the sheriff asked.

"It was a clown," Daphne said. "It was the same clown I saw in the village! You see, I'm not crazy!"

"It's true, Sheriff," Ashlee said. "I saw a clown up there too."

Sheriff Patterson's mustache was doing its usual twitching. "Well, there's no one up there now, no clown, nobody, except Donovan's body. And there's nowhere to hide. It's practically an empty room." He looked back at Pete. "Is there any other means of egress from the tower except those stairs?"

"There's a hatch in the ceiling that leads to the roof, but I had that sealed over decades ago, because squirrels kept getting in," Pete said.

The sheriff shouted to one of his deputies to get up on the roof and check the hatch. Meanwhile, Daphne could hear the squawk of the police-car radios. The coroner was on his way. For now, Donovan's body would remain where it was, the sheriff insisted. Even Suzanne, despite her shrill demands, was not allowed up into the tower until the coroner could arrive.

Both Daphne and Ashlee gave statements. When the sheriff asked them how they could be sure it was someone dressed as a clown, they said the flashlight clearly revealed its features, and both described the clown exactly the same way. "Its teeth are the worst part," Daphne said, shivering. "Pointed and yellow."

Overhearing this, Pete grew distraught and had to sit down. Ashlee rushed over to console him. Abigail lamented how this was dredging up all the terrible past tragedies.

"Yes, indeed, it is," the sheriff agreed, "and I'm afraid I can't keep it from the press. They'll be here soon, and there's no way I can prevent the statements made by these young ladies from going public. We need to inform the community that we have a copycat killer on the loose. Someone obsessed with the case, or with your father, Pete."

"But how could anyone get in here?" Abigail asked. "I set the security system myself."

"Who knows the code to turn it off?" the sheriff asked.

"Only the family, and Boris," Abigail replied.

"Even I don't know it," Daphne said.

"Is everyone in the family accounted for?" the sheriff asked. "Wait a minute. I don't see Ben."

"He's in Portland tonight," Daphne said. "But he'll be home soon, I'd imagine."

The sheriff made a note of it. "Any hostility between Ben and Donovan?"

"Are you accusing my brother of being the murderer?" Gabriel suddenly spoke up.

"I just have to ask questions, Gabe."

"Well, to be honest, they were never the best of friends," Gabriel said. "But then, I never liked him much either. He didn't have many friends."

"Shut up, you miserable cripple!" Suzanne bellowed from across the room. "Donovan had hundreds of friends."

"So long as he was picking up the tab, I suppose everyone in the bars he frequented in town loved him," Gabriel said. It was the most Daphne had ever heard him speak in the entire time she had been at Witherswood.

"Stop it, both of you," Pete croaked. "I can't stand bickering at the moment."

"Sorry, Uncle Pete," Gabriel said.

Daphne looked over at Louella. She seemed in a daze, hearing nothing, comprehending nothing.

A deputy came in to report that the hatch on the roof was secure. The boards nailed over it were still in place.

"Then how the hell did the killer get out?" the sheriff wondered.

"Maybe it was a ghost," Christopher piped up, his round button eyes dancing.

Daphne saw the look that crossed Boris's sunken face at the boy's words. "He has returned," he whispered. "The master . . ."

"Stop it!" Pete shouted. "I won't have such nonsense spoken in my house."

"There has to be another way out of there," the sheriff said, "or you girls were hallucinating when you thought you saw a clown."

"Or maybe *she* killed him," Suzanne charged, pointing at Daphne. "Maybe she killed Donovan, and Ashlee's covering up for her."

"How *dare* you?" Ashlee barked.

"You think *I* killed Donovan?" Daphne asked.

"She has a motive, Sheriff," Suzanne said, talking fast and furious. "Last night, in the stable, Donovan made a pass at her. She resented it. She said she'd get even!"

"Is this true, Miss May?" Sheriff Patterson asked.

Daphne could barely speak, she was so outraged. "He didn't just make a pass at me. He tried to *rape* me!" She felt the anger surge past any fear she might have been feeling. "Sure, I had a motive for killing him, and I don't think any woman would blame me!" She glared over at Suzanne. "Any woman with a conscience and an ounce of self-respect, that is."

"You little—"

"Ladies!" the sheriff shouted. "Okay, Miss May, you say you had a motive to kill him. Did you?"

"No," Daphne said, horrified at the notion. "Of course not. It's just as Ashlee and I told you. We went up there when we heard the music. We saw the clown and we found Donovan's body."

"Dear God, this is all too much," Pete groaned, sitting in his chair, his face in his hands. Ashlee once again went over to stand beside him.

The coroner finally arrived and trooped up the tower stairs to examine the body. An hour later, it was brought downstairs on a stretcher, and Suzanne and Louella were allowed to see it. The body was draped with a sheet, so only Donovan's face was showing; his slit throat was concealed. Suzanne collapsed in tears. "Is he just sleeping?" the dreamy-eyed Louella asked. "Wake up, Donovan. Wake up!"

As the corpse was being carried out the front door, Ben was walking in.

"What the hell is going on here?" he asked.

The sheriff told him, and asked if he could provide an alibi for his whereabouts tonight. He said of course he could. Did the sheriff suspect a family member of doing this? Only a family member knew the code to disarm the security system, the sheriff said. But the system was never disarmed, Abigail reminded the sheriff. Then, the law enforcer surmised, perhaps the killer had hidden himself in the house before the alarm was set. Perhaps, Sheriff Patterson realized with growing alarm, he was still in the house.

At one o'clock in the morning, cops and bloodhounds combed through every square foot of Witherswood.

No one was found.

Daphne saw the small, almost indiscernible smile of satisfaction that bloomed on Boris's ghoulish face.

He believes Donovan's murder is the work of a ghost, she understood.

And at the moment, the theory seemed to fit better than any other.

By then, the press had arrived, though the police kept them well down the hill, away from the house, or else Pete would have them arrested for trespassing. But the lights of the television cameras could be seen from the windows.

"Dear God," Pete groaned. He looked over at his son. "I tried to spare you all of this, Christopher, the horrors of your birthright."

The boy only grinned. "I think it's rather exciting."

His father only shook his head, apparently defeated. Ashlee asked the sheriff if she couldn't possibly take Pete upstairs to bed. The sheriff agreed.

But no one got any sleep that night. When Sheriff Patterson and his men were finally finished inspecting the house, they sealed off the tower as a crime scene, and finally withdrew outside. Daphne noticed Christopher nodding off on the couch, and nudged him awake, getting him to follow her upstairs. She put him into bed and asked him if he needed to talk, but he just looked at her and said, "I agree with Suzanne. I think you killed Donovan."

Daphne told him to go to sleep, and left the room.

She lay awake, staring at the ceiling. She admitted she wasn't sorry that Donovan was dead. But it was an awful thing, nonetheless. She hoped he hadn't suffered. Did one die slowly or quickly when one's throat was slashed?

What did it mean? If it was a copycat killer, someone obsessed with the original crimes, then how did he get in here? And how did he get out of the tower?

And if it was the ghost of Pete Witherspoon Senior . . . then were any of them safe?

In the morning, bleary-eyed, they all ate breakfast together, except for Louella, who remained sedated in her room, and Suzanne, who had gone into town to make arrangements for Donovan's funeral. It was unusual that the clan all ate together, but an unspoken bond seemed to unite them now. No one spoke much, but Daphne had recalled something as the dawn broke, and she turned to remind Ben of it now.

"That day in the study, do you remember?" Daphne whispered, so the others wouldn't hear. "I saw a man, a man who looked like Mr. Witherspoon, only it wasn't."

"I remember," Ben said quietly.

"You tried to tell me it was one of the stable hands, but then you showed me the photograph of Mr. Witherspoon's father. That's who the man I saw looked like. And he was covered in blood."

"Daphne," Ben said, but he seemed to have no argument left.

"You can't say I hallucinated that, not when my other so-called hallucinations have turned out to be true. I believe I saw the ghost of Pete Witherspoon Senior that day. And maybe the first day I was here as well, at the inn and again in Christopher's room!"

"So you think my grandfather came back from his grave to kill Maggie and Donovan?"

"How could someone flesh and blood get out of the tower?"

"Daphne, it's very possible that what you thought you saw in the darkness in the tower was not a clown—"

"Then what was it? Ashlee saw the exact same thing!"

"I don't know." He sighed. "But I'm sorry. I just don't believe in ghosts."

"I'm not sure I do, either," Daphne admitted, sitting back in her chair. "But I just don't know what else to think."

The murder headlined the newspapers, as everyone expected. CLOWN KILLINGS RESUME IN POINT WOEBEGONE. COPYCAT KILLER STRIKES AT ORIGINAL KILLER'S FAMILY. Helicopters flew over the estate, snapping photographs. A couple of reporters snuck past security forces and banged on the door of Witherswood. Pete had them arrested. There were no televisions in the house, of course, but Ben showed Daphne on his computer how sensationally the story was being picked up by all the media outlets.

Late in the afternoon, Sheriff Patterson came by with a request he'd received from Boston. Mother Angela, unable to telephone Daphne at Witherswood, had phoned the local police. She was worried. The sheriff told Daphne she could use the radio phone in his car out front to call her.

"Maybe I was too rigid last time we spoke," Mother said, after Daphne had settled into the cruiser's front seat and a deputy had placed the call to Boston. "Maybe, at least until the person who committed this horrible deed is apprehended, you could come back to us."

"No, Mother," Daphne replied calmly. "I'm not leaving here."

"What? Last time we spoke you were desperate to get out!"

"Correct. And you told me that I needed to face the challenges that were given to me."

"Daphne, dear, but I had no idea there was a murderer at large. . . ."

Daphne was firm. "My destiny is here in Point Woebegone. I could not leave now even if I wanted to. To abandon Christopher at this point would be irresponsible on my part. He might still fight me, but in fact, I'm all he has. Besides, I want to know what's really going on. Who killed Donovan? And what connection does it have to me?"

"Why do you think there's a connection to you?"

"Because whoever the killer is—or *what*ever the killer is—he has shown himself now to me four times. I'm part of this, Mother, whether I like it or not. And I intend to find out exactly *what* part."

As she stepped out of the sheriff's car, Daphne's arm was taken by someone from behind. She expected it to be a policeman, helping her out of the car, but to her great surprise—and delight—it was Gregory.

"I figured I shouldn't show my face at the house again so soon, but I had to see you," he said, slightly out of breath. He wore faded jeans and a black leather jacket over a white T-shirt. "The sheriff understood my dilemma and so he just called me, telling me if I hurried, I could make it up here and catch you before you went back into the house."

Behind him, Daphne saw his motorcycle.

"You're fast, Mr. Winston," she said.

"I can be, when I want something."

She smiled. "And what is that you want?"

"To know that you're all right."

Daphne's heart melted.

"The sheriff told me that Donovan assaulted you," Gregory said.

Daphne looked past him toward the house. From this angle, bushes blocked the view from any window at Witherswood. She supposed she had to be grateful to Sheriff Patterson for his strategic parking.

"He tried," she admitted to Gregory, "but he didn't get very far."

"Are you okay?"

"Yes."

"Are you sure?"

Daphne reached up and touched Gregory's cheek. He hadn't shaved today. His skin was rough like sandpaper. Daphne loved how it felt. She could have caressed Gregory's cheek all day long.

"Yes, I'm sure," she told him.

"Well, he got what he deserved then," Gregory said.

Daphne removed her hand. She thought it was cold of Gregory to say such a thing. Yes, he was trying to be supportive of her, defending her against the horror of Donovan's assault. But while Daphne wasn't unhappy that Donovan was dead, no one deserved to die like that, and she told Gregory so.

"Once again, you are the sensitive, compassionate one," he told her, laughing a little. "You're really too good to walk this earth, Daphne, too gentle to live among us wolves."

"I'll take my chances," she said.

"Any idea who did it?" Gregory asked.

"The sheriff's saying a copycat killer, someone obsessed with the original murders. But inside, some of us are starting to think it's a ghost."

"You're not serious."

"How else could the killer have gotten out of the tower?"

"The ceiling hatch. As a kid, I climbed in and out of there all the time."

"That must have been before Mr. Witherspoon sealed it shut."

"No, it wasn't. It was sealed as long as I can remember. Or at least the adults thought it was sealed. But I discovered it was easy to jimmy the boards up, keeping the nails in place as I did it, and then climb out and press it back into place." He grinned. "That way no one knew I'd ever been there. And in those days, Pete was spry enough to get up on the roof and check."

"Then do you think that's how the killer got out?"

"Who knows?" He took her in his arms. "Maybe the killer was just trying to protect you from a very bad man."

"Stop, Gregory, don't tease," she said. "I don't know what to think anymore."

"I do. I think I want you out of that house."

"No," Daphne said, repeating what she had just told Mother Angela. "I'm not running away."

The sheriff had come up behind them. "Sorry, lovebirds, but I'm going to have the move the car. Another officer's coming up to relieve me, don't worry. We're keeping a twenty-four-hour watch on the house."

Gregory and Daphne broke their embrace.

"When will you be able to get away?" Gregory asked her.

"I don't know. Not for a while. There's going to be a funeral and then . . . well, I just don't know."

"Have Ashlee call me. I'll go crazy if I don't know you're okay."

Daphne smiled, then hurried back up to the house.

That night, when Daphne told Ashlee how Mother Angela had called, pleading with her to come back to Our Lady, her friend told her she was being foolhardy to refuse.

"You should get out of here now, Daphne, while you still can," Ashlee said, grabbing hold of her by the wrists.

"What do you mean, while I still can?"

"I'm terrified that Donovan won't be the killer's only victim. Whoever the killer is, some copycat nut job or an avenging spirit, it is targeting this house. Why stay here and be in danger? I'm already trying to convince Pete we should leave. He owns a condo in Florida. We could go there. You should go back to Boston, where it's safe."

"I'm not going anywhere," Daphne replied. "The sheriff has men posted outside. We're safe here." She looked Ashlee squarely in the eye. "And I'm not sure it's just this house the killer has targeted. He killed Maggie, too, remember? And she had no connection to the Witherspoon family."

Even though the sheriff said he wasn't drawing any conclusion that the same person had killed both Maggie and Donovan, Daphne was certain they were indeed the same. After all, she had seen the same clown both times.

"Well," Ashlee said, considering this, "Maggie did *sort of* have a connection to the family. She was an old friend of mine. So maybe this monster is going to try killing all of us and everyone we know."

"Well, that's a rather big order," Daphne countered. "Really, Ashlee, I feel I belong here now. I'm going to stick this out, see it to the end."

Her friend just glared at her. "Have it your way then." She seemed near tears. "I just hope I never have to say that I warned you."

Another night passed without Daphne getting much sleep. Gregory's words had come back to haunt her. What was more frightening? A ghost or a real-live killer? Because now it seemed as if it could be the latter, if a real-live killer had known the secret of getting out of the tower room without being noticed.

And who would know that? Someone who had lived here. Someone who had played in the tower room with Gregory.

Someone like . . . Ben.

Daphne sat up in bed. What she was thinking was crazy!

Could Ben have killed Donovan? Dressed like a clown, to throw everyone off the track?

But Ben was in Portland at the time of the murder.

Or so he said.

Ben was the only one in the family not present and accounted for that night.

But Ben had no motive to kill Donovan.

Then who did?

The answer came to Daphne even as she tried to push it away.

Gregory.

Gregory had the motive. Even if he hadn't known at that point that Donovan had assaulted her, Gregory had come up to Witherswood, raging with anger, to defend Daphne's honor after hearing how Donovan had lied about her. In his rage, had he decided to kill him?

Well, he got what he deserved then.

Gregory's own words.

Maybe the killer was just trying to protect you from a very bad man.

Daphne suddenly felt sick to her stomach.

Had he been confessing the crime to her?

Was all this part of Gregory's vendetta against the Witherspoon family? The sheriff had said a copycat killer would have an obsessive interest in the original case. That certainly described Gregory.

But why would Gregory kill Maggie then? And he *couldn't* have killed Maggie that night—he'd been with Daphne!

Except . . . not the whole time. He'd left and gone into the kitchen. During the time he was gone, Daphne had spotted the clown. And when Gregory came back, the clown was gone.

What she was thinking made no sense.

But it did make sense, too.

This is crazy, Daphne thought, near tears. *I'm suspecting the two men I care most about!*

She fell asleep as the sun was beginning to edge the horizon. She dreamt strange and twisting dreams in which nothing made sense; she was lost in a long corridor of doors that, when she opened them, had nothing but dark empty space behind them.

For the time being, Christopher's lessons were halted. Ben appealed to his uncle to let the boy see a counselor. There was a good one in town, a Dr. Duane, recommended to him by friends in Portland. After Donovan's murder, it was imperative that the boy get some professional help. Once again, Pete said he'd consider it, but made no decision.

Two days later, on a cold, dark day that saw the season's first light dusting of snow, Donovan was laid to rest in the family crypt.

A small, private service was held at the cemetery chapel. A minister blessed the coffin, and then Ben, Boris, Axel, and the cemetery's caretaker carried it over to the Witherspoon crypt. Daphne looked around at the names on the plaques lining the wall. AMELIA WITHERSPOON, mother to Pete, Abigail, and Louella, and the wife of the infamous serial killer, who had thankfully died many years before his reign of terror began. JOHN WITHERSPOON, Ben's father, who had been killed at the hand of the crazed family patriarch. And finally MARGARET WITHERSPOON—Peggy—Christopher's mother. Daphne saw the little boy place his hand on his mother's plaque, and her heart broke for him.

There was, however, no plaque for Peter Witherspoon Senior. Daphne wondered where the madman had been buried.

Suzanne sobbed as the coffin was lowered into the ground. Louella stood, glassy-eyed. The minister said a last prayer. Pete looked so frail, so broken, that he might have toppled into the grave after his nephew's coffin if Ashlee hadn't been standing beside him, holding his arm.

Leaving the cemetery, which was located near the cliffs just beyond the town, they confronted a gathering of curious townspeople, as well as a mob of photographers and newspapermen, who were snapping photographs and calling out questions.

"Do you think it's a copycat killer?" someone shouted.

"Are you taking any extra precautions at Witherswood?" another barked. Pete had given strict orders that none of them say a word to the press, so they all just got back into the limousines that had brought them to the cemetery. The police pushed the crowd back, telling them to respect the family's privacy.

Back home, Ben gazed out the window at the falling snow and reflected on being a child growing up in such a mysterious old house.

"It wasn't easy," he told Daphne, who, with Gabriel, sat in the parlor behind him as fire roared in the fireplace. "Uncle Pete tried to keep the knowledge of Grandfather's killing spree from us, but we learned about it, eventually, in bits and pieces. Whispers from the servants, overheard conversations from the adults, the comments of strangers on the few occasions we were brought into town. I remember after first understanding the nature of the crimes that had been committed, I worried that Grandfather's ghost would come back and kill me, too. I told Donovan my fear. He laughed at me, called me a sissy for being afraid of ghosts."

"You got off easy with him," Gabriel said. "He only taunted you. He was always trying to beat me up, because I was the youngest. He was brutal, and cruel, and seemed to take delight in always making me feel worthless."

"It's true that Donovan wasn't a very nice person, even as a child," Ben said, turning around to look at them. "But I think it was due to the fact that his father left Aunt Louella after the murders were publicized. He didn't want any association with the family. And Donovan felt abandoned."

"Donovan's father was a hopeless drunk," Gabriel said.

"That, too," Ben said. "So I guess we ought to be a bit more compassionate when we think of his unpleasantness."

"Absolutely," Gabriel said.

Ben seemed surprised. "You agree with me, Gabe? I thought if anyone would hold a grudge against Donovan, it would be you."

"I think it's pointless to hold a grudge past the grave, don't you?" Gabriel shrugged. "He's dead now. Whatever he did in the past is irrelevant. He's paid the ultimate price. To go on hating him would be unjust, I think." He lifted his head just a little, and Daphne caught the flicker of a smile. "Rest in peace, Donovan."

Ben smiled. "I commend you, Gabe. That's generous of you."

The young man in the wheelchair fell quiet again, as if embarrassed by too much conversation.

"You know," Daphne said, breaking the silence, "I've been thinking."

"Uh-oh," Ben joked.

She smiled. "I'm wondering again how the killer could have gotten out of the tower room after he killed Donovan."

"I'm convinced that he killed him earlier, and got out before you and Ashlee went up there, and I believe that's the theory the sheriff is leaning toward as well," Ben said,

Daphne frowned. "But that's presuming Ashlee and I didn't see that clown."

Ben nodded. "Daphne, you were both very frightened. . . ."

"We did not hallucinate!" she insisted, looking over at Gabriel, to see if their new friendship might generate some sympathy for her position. But Gabriel just shrugged, seeming to share his brother's skepticism.

"Well," Daphne said, "maybe, at least, you two could answer a question for me."

"Happy to try," Ben said.

She looked at him intently. "I know that Mr. Witherspoon said he sealed the hatch in the ceiling of the tower room a very long time ago. But . . . is there any way through it regardless?"

"Not that I know of," Ben said.

"I don't know any way either," Gabriel added.

"Are you sure? You said you played up there as a boy, Ben. You never figured out a way to—I don't know—jimmy the boards that were nailed over it and get them to move, and then replace them, nails intact, so no one knew you had ever been there?"

Ben laughed. "Well, that certainly is imaginative! No, Daphne, I was never good at jimmying things! How about you, Gabe?"

He shook his head. "Interesting theory, though."

Daphne held Ben's gaze. Either he had never

played that particular game with Gregory, or he was lying.

If he was lying, he might be the killer.

If he wasn't lying, then—Daphne had to look away from him—then Gregory might be the killer.

She couldn't believe she was thinking such thoughts.

"I'm not sure why you all keep trying to come up with a logical explanation for it," came a high-pitched voice.

They turned. Boris had entered the room, carrying a tray with a pot of tea and three cups. As he poured tea for each of them, he shared his own thoughts about Donovan's murder.

"I have seen the ghost of the original master of this house many times," Boris said, handing Daphne her tea, which she took but did not drink. "I know the current master does not wish me to say such things, but at the risk of being disloyal, I must say what I think. For only if we understand what is happening can we protect ourselves."

"Boris, I've heard you talk about ghosts all my life," Ben said, accepting his own cup of tea. "But I've lived here a little more than thirty years myself, and I've never seen a thing."

"Perhaps that is because your eyes are not fully open to it." He turned to look at Daphne after giving Gabriel his cup. "You have seen him, haven't you, my dear?"

"I've seen things," Daphne admitted. "But I'm not sure what they were."

"I believe only those of us who see him and recognize him are safe from his wrath." Boris looked sternly at each of them, his sunken eyes and thin lips giving his head the appearance of a skull. "He did not give up mastership of this house willingly. He was a proud man, and for all his terrible crimes, I daresay, a noble one, too."

"Noble?" Ben asked. "You call slaughtering children noble?"

"I say he was a noble man," the butler said, removing the teapot and placing it on a table, and carrying the now-empty tray back with him toward the door. "And I say to everyone in this house, if you value your lives, see him—and recognize him."

He laughed then, a horrible, grinding sort of sound.

But it wasn't what she heard that terrified Daphne as much as what she saw.

As he laughed, Boris exposed his teeth—teeth she had seen before, only not on him. The butler's teeth were surprisingly sharp, and very yellow.

They were the teeth of the clown.

FOURTEEN

Daphne didn't know what to think, believe, hope, or fear.

She suspected nearly everyone. Both the living and the dead.

And, somehow, what was happening in this house involved her.

Late at night, sitting in her room, staring out the window at the crashing waves below, lit by a winter moon, she wondered if she'd ever understand why this place was her destiny.

She was crazy to think Gregory or Ben was the killer.

But Boris . . .

He had repeated his tale of Pete Witherspoon Senior's ghost to Ashlee and to Axel, though he seemed too cautious to say it in front of Pete Junior or Abigail. Louella, of course, remained confined to her room. But to those he felt were open to listening, Boris insisted they needed to recognize the power the "old master" still had over this house. In effect, he wanted people to recognize the "nobility" of a man who had been so demonized by his evil deeds. Daphne thought the butler was crazy.

Crazy enough, in fact, to have committed murder.

"Think about it," she said to Ashlee one day, when another light snowfall was in the process of turning the fields around the house white. "If Boris killed Donovan, he'd want to throw us off by insisting it was a ghost. Or maybe he's so obsessed with Pete Senior that he actually thinks he *is* him when he commits the murders."

"So you think Boris killed Maggie, too?"

"He could have. Remember, he and Axel weren't around that night. You had given Axel the assignment to pick me up, but both he and Boris claimed not to have seen it and took off that night."

Ashlee had to admit that was true. "So do you think Axel is in on it?"

"Who knows? I think anything's possible. And after all, he was in the house the night Donovan was killed. No need to turn off the alarm. He was already inside."

"But wait. Boris was the first one to show up after we found Donovan's body. Like in a matter of minutes."

Daphne had already considered this. "If he knows how to get out of the ceiling hatch, then his room is directly beneath the tower. He's the closest one to it, in fact. And you and I took a while getting down those stairs, screaming and falling. Meanwhile, he's out the hatch, shimmying down the trellis, hopping into his room through the window, doffing the clown suit, wiping off all that makeup, and then coming out his door to find us in the foyer."

"But he's an old man, Daphne."

"But strong. And fast. You see how quickly—and how stealthily—he moves around here."

"That's true, too." Ashlee seemed to be considering the idea. "And you sure are right about the teeth."

"Think we should go to the sheriff with this?"

Ashlee shook her head. "Not yet. I think the sheriff feels we're a couple of excitable little girls. We need more proof to bring to him than this."

Daphne agreed. For now, both of them would keep watch on the butler for a sign of anything suspicious.

Thanksgiving came and went, without any kind of family celebration. Cook made a turkey and carved it in the kitchen, and one by one, the members of the clan came by and made plates for themselves. Most took their plates back to their rooms. Daphne fixed two plates and brought one to Louella. They ate together in Louella's room, but the older woman said very little, despite Daphne's attempts to engage her in conversation.

The house had grown even quieter than usual. Suzanne had left to spend time with her family in Bangor, but had informed Pete she would be back in a few days to gather her things. Because she and Donovan had never had a chance to marry, she had no legal claim to any part of the estate. Ashlee said Pete wasn't sorry to see her go.

Ben, too, was gone much of the time. He'd met a great guy in Portland, he told Daphne, a fellow named Charlie. A regular sort of guy, Ben said. An electrician who played touch football and cheered on the Patriots. Spending time with Charlie in his small loft apartment in downtown Portland was far preferable at the moment, Ben explained, to living in the morgue that Witherswood had become.

But in the midst of the bleakness there was a bit of good news. Pete had agreed to let Christopher see Dr. Duane. On the appointed morning, Daphne explained to the boy he was going to see "someone he could talk to." Christopher exploded.

"You're sending me to a shrink?"

"He's a psychologist, Christopher. He has a wonderful reputation for working with young people going through grief."

The boy folded his arms across his chest. "I'm not going to talk about my mother."

"You can talk about anything you like," Daphne said.

"I'm going to talk about how you killed Donovan."

"Go ahead. Talk about that if you want."

Daphne could see it irked the boy that he wasn't getting a rise out of her. "I'm going to tell him that I think you killed that barmaid too," he spit at her. "All of this started the night you arrived in town."

"Yes, you're right, it did. I think that would be an excellent thing for you to talk to Dr. Duane about. Now get dressed. Axel is bringing the car around to meet us out front."

Daphne slung her purse over her shoulder and they headed downstairs. Axel waited for them in the Lincoln Town Car the family used for "official" family business. Daphne and Christopher climbed into the back. The boy slunk far down in the seat, his arms crossed across his chest, his bottom lip protruding, the cords of his iPod firmly planted in his ears.

Daphne reached over the seat to hand Axel the address of Dr. Duane's office. "Do you know where it is?" she asked.

"I know every street in Point Woebegone, Miss May," Axel boasted. "I know practically every house, where everyone lives."

He steered the car down the winding road toward the village.

Daphne noticed the round-the-clock police protection had ended. Sheriff Patterson was convinced she and Ashlee had imagined that clown and that the killer had come and gone some time before they discovered Donovan's body. The coroner's estimation of time of death suggested that Donovan had been lying there for at least a couple of hours, so the sheriff felt he was justified in thinking as he did. They were looking into employees of the Witherspoons' various businesses who had had run-ins with Donovan, and a guy he apparently offended a few nights before his murder at the inn, for—what else?—making a play for his girlfriend.

So the comfort of a twenty-four-hour police presence was no more. After all, Witherswood had a first-rate security system, the sheriff told Pete.

Daphne laughed to herself. First-rate. Right. What a joke. It hadn't kept Donovan's murderer from getting in to perform his grisly task.

Of course, if the killer was Boris, he'd already been in the house.

Daphne noticed that Axel wasn't taking the usual road into town. "Why are you turning this way?" she asked.

"Driving along the ocean is quicker, Miss May, especially if we are heading to the part of town where this Dr. Duane has his office," Axel replied.

"Oh, all right." Daphne settled back in her seat, looking at the back of Axel's round head. The squat little man barely rose to steering-wheel height. He had to sit on a cushion just to get this high. What an odd choice he was for a chauffeur. Then again, what wasn't odd about the Witherspoons?

"So you'd consider yourself an expert on the town, huh, Axel?" Daphne asked.

"Well," he said, "I know my way around."

"How long have you lived here?"

"Thirty-three years," he said proudly.

"And how many of those at Witherswood?"

"All of them, miss. Boris got me the job by recommending me to . . ." His voice faded off. "The family at the time."

He didn't want to say Pete Senior.

"I see," Daphne said. "So you've known Boris a long time."

Axel lifted his squinty blue eyes to her in the mirror. "Oh, yes, miss. We grew up in the same town in Minnesota."

"Boris has been with the family even longer than you have, I understand."

"Indeed he has. Forty years, I think, this winter. He saw all those boys born. . . ." His voice became sad. "Including Mr. Donovan."

"The family's had so much tragedy," Daphne said.

"Indeed it has, miss."

"But you and Boris have always stayed loyal."

"Of course. I'd do anything for Mr. Witherspoon."

"I'm sure Boris feels the same way."

"Oh, yes, he does, miss."

They were passing by a place where the cliffs dropped dramatically into the sea. A flurry of seagulls circled in the sky.

"Even when the first master of the house committed his crimes," Daphne observed, "you both remained loyal. That must have been terribly difficult for you."

"Well, yes, miss, for me it was terribly difficult. But I wanted to stay on and help the family recover from such a terrible shock."

"It must have been difficult for Boris, too."

Axel was quiet.

"Wasn't it?" Daphne asked. "I mean, he was so close to the first Mr. Witherspoon. It must have been extremely difficult for him."

Still Axel was silent.

"I only mention it because, as you know, Boris is always talking about the first Mr. Witherspoon's ghost. It's rather peculiar, don't you think? I worry about him sometimes, because . . . well, who believes in ghosts?"

Finally Axel spoke again. "I am glad to hear you say that, miss, because I worry about him, too. He does indeed go on and on about the ghosts haunting Witherswood. You see, Miss May, Boris was tremendously fond of the first Mr. Witherspoon. I think even when it became clear that he committed all those heinous crimes, Boris didn't believe it. On some level, I think he still won't believe anything bad about his old master."

"That's very odd," Daphne said, "since even his own family acknowledges the man's guilt."

"Indeed, it is very odd. There are times when all Boris does is talk about Peter Witherspoon Senior. I'll come in, and he'll actually be talking in the old master's voice! He'll be acting like the old master is still here, giving orders."

A sudden, terrible, freezing chill shot down Daphne's spine.

"Of course, Boris is getting up there in age. He'll be seventy this year. They say seventy isn't so old anymore, but nonetheless, sometimes I do worry that Boris is getting a bit strange in the head."

He suddenly spun around in his seat to look at Daphne.

"Oh, but you won't say what I've told you? You won't tell anyone? I'd hate to get Boris in trouble. He still does his job to perfection."

"I won't say anything," Daphne assured him.

Axel turned back around to keep his eyes on the road. "It's just that I worry about him. He's my oldest friend. I'd do anything for Boris. Anything."

They were quiet for a while as the car glided into the village, past the inn, past the shops, past the place where Daphne had seen the clown, past Rico's. Daphne noticed Gregory's motorcycle out front, and her heart beat a little bit faster.

"I think the address you gave me should be right

up this road," Axel was saying, peering out his side window, checking for numbers. "Ah, there it is."

He pulled up in front of a small white clapboard house with blue shutters. A shingle out front bore the name TIMOTHY H. DUANE, PHD.

She noticed that the cemetery where so recently they had entombed Donovan was directly across the street. She wondered if Christopher noticed, and if he thought about his mother. But the boy never glanced in that direction. In fact, he wasn't stirring at all.

"Come on, Christopher," Daphne said, grabbing her purse. "We're here."

She nudged the boy to get out of the car. He remained resolutely listening to his iPod. It took three nudges for him to finally open the door and step out.

Daphne followed, but leaned back into the car for a moment. "Axel, just a quick thought. Since you know so much about Point Woebegone, do you remember a couple, say twenty-two, twenty-three years ago, who had a baby girl but gave her up for adoption? Or maybe, more likely, a single mother who had a baby she couldn't keep?"

"Well, I'll have to give that one some thought, Miss May," Axel replied.

"Please do," she said.

"Be back out front here in a couple of hours, right?"

"Yes," she said. "Thanks."

She closed the door and Axel drove away.

She stood beside Christopher looking up at the house in front of them.

"You sure asked him a lot of questions about Boris," Christopher observed.

"I thought you were listening to music," Daphne said.

Christopher gave her a sly look. "You thinking of pinning Donovan's murder on Boris so you can get away scot-free?"

"Yes, that's exactly what I'm thinking of doing, Christopher," Daphne said. "Now come on. Dr. Duane is expecting us."

She was surprised when he grabbed her hand, like a frightened little kid, as they walked up the steps to the psychologist's office.

Inside the house, a pleasant-looking woman behind a desk told them to have a seat. Daphne flipped through a couple of *People* magazines, but Christopher just sat in the chair, arms still crossed, lips still in a pout, earphones in place, iPod in his hands.

Soon Dr. Duane came out and introduced himself. He was a handsome man, blond, and younger than Daphne had expected. He greeted them warmly, then remarked on Christopher's iPod. "Hey, maybe you can show me how to get mine working," he said. "It seems to have gotten stuck."

Daphne thought it was a brilliant move. Christopher eyed the doctor, then nodded that he would try to help. It balanced things out between them, which would make the boy less averse about meeting with the doctor. Christopher stood from his seat and followed Dr. Duane down the hall. Daphne figured he was in good hands.

The session would last for ninety minutes, so Daphne decided to take a walk. The day was sunny, if still pretty cold. She figured on walking back toward town. Rico's wasn't very far, after all. She wouldn't go in. She'd just walk by.

She slung her purse over her shoulder and started to walk. But before she could get even a few feet down the road, she heard the sound of a motorcycle. She turned. Gregory pulled up alongside her.

"Out for a stroll?" he asked.

He looked so handsome with his hair blowing in the wind.

"How did you find me?" Daphne asked, smiling.

"I saw the official Witherspoon car go by, with that little gnome at the wheel," he told her. "And I thought I saw you and the boy in the backseat. So I hopped on the bike and went out on a hunt."

Daphne explained that Christopher was seeing Dr. Duane, which Gregory said was a good thing. He knew the doctor, casually, from the restaurant. He parked the bike at the curb and hopped off.

"Mind if I walk with you?"

"Gregory, if we're seen together again . . ."

"Then let's go in here." He gestured to a little coffee shop. "I know the owner. She'll give us the room in back, where we can be alone."

So for the next hour, Daphne and Gregory enjoyed a rare interlude of peace and quiet and privacy. Under the table, they held hands. It was exactly the kind of dream date Daphne had imagined as a girl. They shared a large chocolate chip cookie and Gregory made her laugh by putting whipped cream on his half. But there was seriousness, too. He was worried about her. He was afraid that Donovan's killer might strike again.

Daphne's cheeks burned as she remembered how she'd allowed herself to suspect Gregory, even for a few minutes. That was absurd. This kind, compassionate man could never hurt anyone. She did her best to forget his angry words to Mr. Witherspoon.

"What do you think about Boris?" she asked. "He has teeth—horrible teeth—that remind me of the teeth of the clown I've seen."

Gregory frowned. "You mean to say you think Boris dresses up in a clown suit and runs around slitting people's throats?"

"It's crossed my mind."

Gregory considered the idea. "Well, he was unnaturally close to the first Mr. Witherspoon. Worshipped the ground he walked on."

"Axel said sometimes he hears Boris speaking in that horrible man's voice."

"Now that's pretty creepy," Gregory admitted.

He told her he wanted her out of the house.

"Quit your job, Daphne," he said. "I'll—I'll make sure you're taken care of until you can find a new position."

"You're very gallant," she said, and squeezed his hand. "But strange as it sounds, I feel a responsibility to that young boy I just left at Dr. Duane's. Everyone has failed him. I don't want to be one more person who doesn't do right by him."

Gregory took her hand out from under the table and pressed it to his lips.

He walked her back to the doctor's office. Just as they arrived, Dr. Duane was walking Christopher down the front steps.

"Oh, hello, Gregory," Dr. Duane said.

"Hi, Doc, how are you?"

Daphne saw Christopher's eyes fix on Gregory. So this was the man his father hated so much. Daphne noticed the gleam that lit up in the boy's gaze.

"Hello, young Master Witherspoon," Gregory said, bending down to offer the boy his hand. Christopher shook it. "I just happened to be walking by this moment and saw your pretty governess waiting for you."

"How did he do, Doctor?" Daphne asked.

"I think we made some progress." The doctor smiled. "Of course, everything we discussed is just between Christopher and me. I hope next time he trusts me to open up even more." He tousled the child's hair.

Daphne wasn't sure if they had made any progress at all. She also wasn't sure if Christopher liked Dr. Duane. All she could observe was the way the boy kept staring at Gregory.

After Dr. Duane had left, Christopher finally spoke.

"Is that your bike?" he asked, gesturing to Gregory's motorcycle.

"Indeed it is. Want a ride?"

"Yes!" Christopher blurted, and for the first time all day a genuine smile bloomed on his face.

"No, no, no," Daphne said. "Your father wouldn't approve. Besides Axel will be here to pick us up in about fifteen minutes."

"My father," Christopher spit, bitterly.

"Another time, pal," Gregory said. "Well, nice seeing you both."

And without another look at Daphne—he was

so discreet—he gave them both a jaunty salute and sauntered over to his motorcycle. Hopping on, he gave them a cheery wave. Christopher waved back. Then Gregory revved the motor and sped off.

"He's cool," Christopher said, watching him go.

Daphne thought of asking him to not mention seeing Gregory to his father, but figured the boy might do so just to spite her. But she suspected Gregory had made a positive impression on Christopher, so maybe he wouldn't say anything after all.

"Could I ask you a favor, Daphne?" the boy suddenly inquired.

"What is it?"

"Could we go across the street so I can visit my mother's grave?"

"Oh, Christopher, I don't know if we have time. Axel will be here soon and . . ."

He looked as if he might cry. "Please! She's all I talked about with Dr. Duane! I want to see her! The cemetery is just across the street!"

"Oh, all right," Daphne said, melting. "Of course we can go to your mother's grave."

They hurried across the street and into the cemetery. The recent snowfalls had left the ground wet and muddy. Daphne's feet sunk into a quicksand of wet grass and mud. She had to pull them back out with little "pops." Christopher was marching on ahead, toward the Witherspoon crypt, as Daphne tried to keep up. She passed the crooked old gravestones, some marble, some faded brownstone, many dating back to the nineteenth century. Engravings of skulls and winged angels stared out at her.

"Wait for me, Christopher," Daphne called as she noticed the boy enter the crypt.

Yet as she stepped inside herself, she noticed the boy was not standing beside his mother's plaque but was, instead, standing in a small stairwell that led down to a lower floor of the crypt.

"Have you ever been down here?" he asked Daphne.

"I thought you came to pay your respects to your mother."

"I will. But I want to show you the graves down there. They're from a really long time ago. Like my father's great-great-a-million-great grandparents."

"I don't want to go down there, Christopher," Daphne said.

The crypt was a dark, dank place, and Daphne shuddered. Here the sun was completely blotted out, the only half-light that penetrated the cold stone walls coming from a series of small, stained-glass circular windows. In the walls of this place lay the bones and decaying flesh of dead people. Daphne wanted out as soon as possible.

"Please, Daphne! I want to show you something! Please, it's something I told Dr. Duane about. Something that means a lot to me!"

He disappeared down the steps to the level below.

"Christopher!"

Daphne hesitated, then, clutching her purse tightly, followed the boy down the stairs.

The light in this lower room was even dimmer than the one upstairs. Daphne stepped inside, shivering. Her eyes were blinking, trying to adjust.

"Christopher?"

From behind her she heard the low, scraping sound of metal against stone.

"Good-bye, Daphne!" Christopher suddenly sang out. "You will rot in here with the bones of my ancestors!"

He laughed, a hideous, high-pitched cackle.

Daphne spun around to see the boy pulling a large iron door behind him, sealing her inside.

"Christopher!" she screamed.

"No one will know where you are," he said gleefully, as she caught a last glimpse of his crazed, ecstatic face before the door closed. "I'll tell them you rode off on Gregory Winston's bike, leaving me all alone! No one will think of looking for you in here. No one can hear you scream from down here either! And there's a big snowstorm coming tomorrow. It will cover the crypt. So you'll die down here!"

He laughed again.

"No, Christopher, please don't!"

The door thudded shut.

Daphne was left in the dark.

With the dead.

FIFTEEN

It had to be a joke. He'd open the door.

"Christopher!"

But from the other side, there was only silence.

"Christopher, please! Open the door!"

She began to panic.

"Christopher!" she screamed. "For God's sake, don't leave me here!"

Was he standing on the other side, laughing at her?

If that were the case, Daphne didn't want to panic. If he planned on opening the door, laughing hysterically, revealing it all to be a prank, then Daphne had best keep her cool. If she freaked out, he'd have the upper hand. He'd use it against her.

"Okay, Christopher," she said, keeping her voice steady, "your father is not going to be pleased when he hears about this. Open the door now and I'll let it go. But if you keep up this prank for much longer, I won't be as forgiving."

Nothing. There was no sound at all.

Daphne suddenly suspected that even if the boy was on the other side of the door, he couldn't hear her. The door was thick, heavy metal. He had warned her that no one could hear her scream, hadn't he?

"Dear God," Daphne whispered to herself, and stepped away from the door.

The reality of her situation struck her.

This wasn't a prank.

He wasn't going to be opening that door.

He had really locked her in here, intending for her to die.

Christopher was even more deranged than she'd imagined.

"Oh, dear God," Daphne said again, suddenly shaking all over.

She looked around the room. Most of it was submerged into the ground, but on one wall, the upper part of which was clearly aboveground, there was a line of four round stained-glass windows. The windows were too high for Daphne to reach, and even if she could, they were much too small for her to crawl through, being only about eight inches in diameter. But it was the dim light that came through them that gave the chamber its only illumination. Daphne's eyes had adjusted by now, but it was still very difficult to see around her. And when the sun set, she realized, even that minimal light would be gone.

Panic threatened to overtake her. She did not want to be trapped down here in total darkness.

"Christopher!" she called once more in desperation, no longer caring if she was giving him the upper hand. "Oh, Christopher, please! Let me out of here!"

But nothing.

The boy was gone. She was sure of it.

In her mind's eye, Daphne could see him returning to the place where Axel was to meet them, and telling the chauffeur that his governess had abandoned him, taking off with Gregory on his motorcycle. Axel would be aghast, and they'd report back to Mr. Witherspoon, who'd be irate. Of course, when Gregory was called, he'd tell them it wasn't true, but no one would believe him, at least not right away. Dr. Duane would even confirm that he'd seen them together.

"The sheriff will investigate," Daphne reasoned out loud. "He'll have a search party to look for me." She brightened, momentarily. "Gregory will come looking for me!"

But would anyone think to look for her here? In a snowstorm?

Her hopes sank.

Christopher was right. There was indeed a big storm on the way. Daphne had seen the weather report in the newspaper this morning. A big storm like that might mean a delay of looking for her for several days. And Daphne didn't think she could survive that long in this place—this place of the dead.

She felt something tickle her ankle. Unable to see clearly, she whacked at it, and her hand came into contact with something fuzzy. She gasped out loud. A mouse? A rat? A giant spider?

"Oh, dear God," she cried, and moved toward the far wall.

Was it her imagination, or was the light already changing? The sun set so early now. How many more hours before she was plunged into blackness?

And suddenly, she thought of something.

Her first night at Witherswood, Ben had given her a gift. A tiny flashlight. He had said the power went out frequently. It was a good tool to have.

"Don't want you to find yourself alone in the dark," he had said.

Did she still have it? Had she put it in her purse?

Her purse was still slung over her shoulder. She opened it quickly, rummaging through the contents. There wasn't much inside. A date book. A compact. A lipstick and a ChapStick. A couple of sanitary napkins. A package of crackers. And . . . yes! The flashlight!

"Thank you, Ben!" Daphne exulted, pulling out the flashlight and flicking it on.

Its small beam of light comforted her. She used it to survey the room.

It was maybe fifteen feet by twenty, made of solid stone—brownstone, she thought, and concrete. Plaques like the ones in the upper chamber adorned two of the walls, although these were much older and more worn. Daphne took a few steps closer, shining the light onto the plaques. The names were unknown to her.

ROSCOE WITHERSPOON
1915 – 1967

MABEL WITHERSPOON
1918 – 1972

And then, in the corner, a plaque with no name, just a date.

A date that was twenty-three years earlier than the present one.

Who would be buried down here with just a date and no name?

The answer came to Daphne right away.

"Pete Witherspoon Senior," she whispered. It had been twenty-three years ago that he had taken his life in that jail cell.

She stifled a scream as she stared at the plaque.

His crimes had damned him to an unmarked grave.

It had to be him. Roscoe and Mabel were probably his father and mother.

Daphne stepped back. The thought of being in such close proximity to the madman's grave unnerved her.

Not just his grave.

But his remains. His skeleton lay behind that wall.

Now she understood why Christopher had chosen this particular place to torment her.

She flicked off the flashlight. As long as there was still a little light left coming in from the windows, she figured she ought to conserve the battery. She had no idea how long she might be a prisoner in this terrible place.

She closed her eyes, trying to zone out. Mother Angela had taught the girls relaxation exercises, akin to meditation. Daphne tried that now. She pushed from her mind all thoughts, all awareness of her body and surroundings. She must have been successful, at least for a while—a half an hour? forty minutes?—because when she opened her eyes it was clearly darker in the chamber. The light from outside was fading.

Pressing her back up against the wall beneath the small windows above, Daphne took several deep breaths. She could smell the rancid odor of decay. Leaves and roots and earth, and underneath all of that, the disgustingly sweet fragrance of rotting bones. She wanted to cover her nose with her hand, but she was also aware that the amount of oxygen in this chamber was limited. She did not want to pass out. If she did, she thought she'd never awaken.

It was getting more difficult to see. The sun was indeed setting. Gripping the flashlight in her hand, she suddenly replaced it in her purse. What if she dropped it? Broke it? That flashlight had become her totem, her key to survival.

They'll find me, she kept repeating to herself. *There's no need to panic. A search will go out. . . .*

Unless Mr. Witherspoon is so outraged he does nothing.

In that case, it might be days before the sheriff or Gregory gets word that I'm missing.

She ordered herself to stop thinking the worst. She could get through this. A few hours . . . maybe the night. Surely by tomorrow . . .

When it was snowing. And when the whole town was under two feet of snow.

The snow would cover those windows, Daphne realized. And then she might be in complete darkness 24-7.

"Oh, dear God," she muttered, feeling panic brewing in her belly again.

So many times over the last few months she'd wished she were back at Our Lady, but never more than this very moment. Back in her old room, on the bottom bunk, laughing with Katie, in the upper bunk, watching some silly show on Bravo, maybe *Project Runway* or one of the cooking shows. Back then Daphne had never seen a dead body, or worried about murderers, or wondered if there might be such things as ghosts. Now here she was, trapped in an underground crypt in a cemetery.

Where she might, in fact, die.

That was the worst-case scenario. But just because it was worst case didn't mean it couldn't come true.

Her mind began playing tricks on her. She had been standing with her back against the wall, under the windows, but now suddenly she realized she was squatting in the opposite corner, looking up at the windows. It felt as if a good chunk of time had elapsed, slipped by without her noticing. Only the faintest glow remained.

How long had she been in this place now? An hour? No, more than that. Two? She thought maybe it was getting closer to three. . . .

The light from the windows was suddenly extinguished like the flame on a candle.

Daphne took a deep breath and felt inside her purse. Her fingers closed around the flashlight and she let out a breath in relief. She removed the flashlight from her purse and switched it on. Its tiny spotlight illuminated no more than a few inches immediately around her. But it was enough to keep her from panicking.

Her stomach rumbled, so she took one of the two crackers out of the cellophane wrapper in her purse and forced herself to eat half. The cracker was stale and a little soft. Still, it was sustenance. After she had finished chewing, she turned off the flashlight. Conserve, conserve, conserve.

She wished she wore a watch. She never had. There had been clocks all over the Our Lady campus, so she'd never needed one. And now the tall grandfather's clock in the foyer of Witherswood allowed her to keep track of the time. But here, in the darkness, time was meaningless. She was no longer sure if she'd been trapped for three hours or five. Or maybe it was even more.

Her mind faded out on her again.

When she became conscious of herself again, she suspected it must be the middle of the night. She could the sounds of scurrying. Mice and rats, no doubt. She realized she still held the flashlight tightly in her fist. Even as she had slept—or experienced what passed for sleep—she hadn't let go of it. The flashlight was her talisman, her protection, her comfort—she was like a little girl sleeping with her doll.

The scurrying and scratching only got louder, and seemed to be coming closer. Daphne lifted the flashlight and flicked on the switch, aiming the light in the direction of the noise. Its spotlight picked out a gray face with pink eyes staring at her. Daphne gasped.

She knew what it was. To her, it was worse than any rat.

It was a possum.

She'd stumbled on a possum once, late at night, at Our Lady, as she took out the trash. Its unearthly eyes had terrified her then. Now, sitting in the dark with one of them—or maybe there were many—Daphne's skin crawled.

"Go!" she shouted. "Get out of here!" Anything to keep it away, to prevent its slimy, rubbery paws from touching her.

But as she shouted at the possum, a thought came to her. Steadying her trembling hand, she used the light of the flashlight to pick out the creature from the darkness again. It was a big fat one, all right, with a long, wormy tail that curled under its blubbery body. The possum was so big, in fact, that Daphne realized it couldn't have gotten into the crypt through the little burrow holes made by rats and mice. There must be a larger passageway that it came through—and if a big fat possum could get through it, maybe a small, slender Daphne could get through it, too.

She followed the waddling possum with the flashlight, shouting at it to keep it moving. "Show me how you got in here," she told it loudly, and the creature seemed to be obeying her command.

For a second she lost it in the darkness, but then she saw it again, and indeed, it did appear to be entering some kind of passage. At the far corner of the room, the possum seemed to be disappearing into the floor. As Daphne moved the flashlight closer, she saw the creature's back legs and slimy tail pushing through a grate of some kind. She knelt down and brought the flashlight close. It wasn't a grate. It was a trap door in the floor, and it had been dislodged from its hinges by decades of nocturnal mammals like her friend the possum.

Gripping the edge of the trap door, Daphne gave it a pull. It opened easily. Aiming the flashlight inside, she saw to her utter surprise that a set of steep stairs descended into the darkness below. How far the stairs went down, she couldn't tell, as the beam of light was not strong enough to penetrate the inky blackness more than a few inches. But the stairs obviously went somewhere.

Daphne was unsure what to do. Going down, deeper into the ground, hardly seemed like a way out. It seemed like a way of becoming more trapped, in fact.

What could the stairs possibly lead to? A cellar under the crypt? Why would there be a need for such a thing?

She could stand there and wonder, or she could find out.

She decided to take a few steps down, shine her flashlight, see what she could see, and if nothing looked promising, get out of there.

"Dear God, be with me," she breathed.

Daphne took the first step down.

The stairs were made of wood, and she could feel them sag under her feet. The wood had grown moist and fragile sitting so long in the dark earth, and could easily snap under her weight. The stairwell was extremely narrow. No more than one person would be able to fit through at one time. It was also short, Daphne discovered, when her foot moved off the last step and felt solid earth, her head still only inches from the trap door.

The space under the crypt was no more than six

feet; a tall man would have to walk with his head bent. As it was Daphne could easily touch the ceiling—solid stone—with her hand. The darkness down here was absolute, and her little flashlight did very little to illuminate it. But from what it did reveal it seemed that this strange cellar was empty—just a rectangle cut into the earth under the crypt, for reasons she couldn't possible imagine.

She swung the flashlight across the space a few times, seeing nothing but earth and earthworms and cobwebs. She was about to go back upstairs when the flashlight passed over a bit of color. Red, she thought, but it was hard to tell in such darkness. She moved the light back in search of it.

There it was.

She gasped.

On one of the wooden beams that defined the four corners of the space, something was written, it seemed, in red spray paint.

She approached.

And made a sound of terror in her throat.

WELCOME TO HELL, DAPHNE was written on the beam.

"Oh, dear God," she rasped.

Who had written it? It must have been Christopher. He must have been down here. He must have been planning this for some time.

But there was something else on the beam.

An arrow.

Underneath the grisly message an arrow had been spray-painted, pointing down. With the beam of the flashlight, Daphne followed the arrow. It seemed to point to nothing, just earth.

Maybe it just meant hell was below them.

But she ran the flashlight beam along the floor, just to be certain.

The beam picked out something embedded in the earth.

She bent down to look closer.

"Oh, no!" she screamed, standing up suddenly, and in her terror, she dropped the flashlight. She watched as it flew from her hand and fell onto the earthen floor, rolling a few feet away from her, sending its light off in a wayward direction.

Did she really see what she thought she just saw?

With careful steps she moved across the space and closed her fingers around the flashlight, taking comfort once again in the coolness of its metal body in her hand. She lifted it and pointed it back to the area where the arrow was pointing. Holding on to the flashlight more steadily this time, she moved in as close as she dared.

Yes, she was right.

Protruding from the earth was a human skull.

It was partially buried, but its empty eye sockets stared up at her, its death grin seeming to mock her. Daphne forced herself to move the beam the length of the floor. There were more bones poking up from the earth at various points. An arm. A foot with the toes broken off it. And, to her surprise, two more skulls.

Her first thought was that these were the bones of Witherspoon ancestors. But those had all been carefully entombed in stone vaults. No, these were the remains of others.

She moved the flashlight back over to the first

skull she had seen, and she understood in an instant just whose bones these were.

The skull was small.

A child's.

These were the remains of the seven victims of Pete Witherspoon Senior who had never been found.

The monster had put them here, under his family's crypt.

And his body reposed right above them.

Daphne felt as if she might get sick on the spot.

But she had no time to. In the very moment she realized the identity of the bones, she also heard a faint sound.

It grew louder.

"Oh, dear God, no . . ."

All around the mulberry bush, the monkey chased the weasel. . . .

"No," Daphne cried, turning to face the little wooden staircase that led back into the crypt.

The monkey thought it was all in fun. . . .

She held the little flashlight out in front of her, like a weapon.

Pop! goes the weasel!

The tune started again, over and over, just like before.

And from the trap door, a foot appeared. A foot wearing a purple, flapping, rubber shoe. A second, identical foot appeared.

Clown's feet.

Daphne watched in mute, unthinking horror as the clown descended the stairs into the tiny, enclosed space. His puffy pants were yellow, covered in green and red polka dots. Soon its torso was in evidence, the same bright colors, with big buttons on its shirt. Then, finally, the ultimate horror: its grinning stark white face. Red nose, blue mouth, orange hair.

And the teeth. The snarling, gnashing yellow teeth.

From the wooden staircase the clown stepped off onto the earthen floor.

And it laughed.

From its shirt the creature produced a long, sharp razor. It ran it through its gloved fingers as if to polish it. The beam from Daphne's flashlight reflected off of the blade.

The clown laughed again, and took a step toward her.

"No!" Daphne screamed.

But the beast was on her.

She felt the cold sting of metal puncture her neck.

SIXTEEN

From somewhere on the other side of her pain and terror she heard someone calling her name.

"Daphne! Daphne!"

It was Gregory.

A hallucination. A last wish, a burst of hope, before she died.

But he kept calling her name, over and over.

And suddenly he was there, kneeling over her, lifting her from the ground.

The clown was gone.

"Are you all right?" Gregory was asking her.

He held a light—a flashlight a thousand times stronger than her puny one. Daphne began to sob uncontrollably.

"It's all right, baby. I'm here. You're safe now."

He lifted her in his arms and carefully made his way up the stairs with her. It was an extremely tight fit, but he managed.

It was then that Daphne passed out.

She woke up in Gregory's car.

"Help! Help! Help!" she began to scream.

Gregory reached over and stroked her hair. "It's okay, Daphne. You're with me. I'm taking you home."

She could see it was lightly snowing. The wipers kept the snow from the windshield.

"The clown," she muttered. "It attacked me."

She felt her neck. It was sticky with blood.

"I examined your wound," Gregory told her. "It's pretty superficial. It looks as if you may have scraped yourself when you fell."

"No!" she shouted. "The clown did it! Didn't you see the clown?"

"Baby, all I saw was you on the ground."

Daphne tried to think. "How . . . how did you find me?"

"Sheer luck. I got a call a few hours ago from Pete. He was demanding to know what I knew of your whereabouts."

"Christopher locked me in there!"

"That's what I gathered. Pete told me Christopher said we'd gone off together. To Pete's credit, he didn't seem to believe the kid. But he was still pretty pissed off."

"Did he call the sheriff?"

"Oh, yes. But you know, it takes twenty-four hours before a person is considered missing. So I went out on my own. Christopher stuck to his story, refusing to give any clues as to where you might be, but I figured it had to be near to where I'd last seen you. The cemetery seemed a likely bet. It was hard to see anything, given how dark it was, but we can be glad that the ground was muddy, because I found footsteps in the mud . . . and we can also be thankful that the snow has only just started. An hour later and all the footprints in the mud would have been covered. I'd never have thought to look in the chamber under the crypt."

Daphne shivered. That was what Christopher had been counting on.

"The footprints led inside the crypt," Gregory continued, "and then down the steps to a closed metal door. I was able to pull the door open, and that's when I heard you screaming . . . from that strange little cellar."

Daphne could barely speak. "Did you . . . did you see what else was down there?"

"The bones?"

Daphne nodded.

"I did see them." Gregory let out a long, anguished breath. "I think they may be Pete Senior's undiscovered victims."

Daphne shuddered. "That's exactly what they are! Don't you see? Christopher wanted me to die down there with them. He must have had this in his plans for some time. He must have discovered the bones at some point, and told no one. But I remember now how one time he tried to coax me to go with him on a hunt to find the children's remains. He would have done this to me then if I had agreed."

"The kid is way sicker than any of us thought," Gregory said. "He needs to be locked up."

Daphne said nothing. Maybe Gregory was right.

They turned up the winding road that led to Witherswood.

"If I had my way, I'd be taking you back to my place," Gregory said. "But Pete insisted that I bring you back to Witherswood if I found you, so that he could confront Christopher." He turned to look at her. "But I mean this, Daphne. I want you out of that house tomorrow."

"I appreciate your concern," she told him, her hand on her wounded neck. "But only I can decide that."

He sighed. "Sorry. Of course. Didn't mean to sound like a male chauvinist."

"It's okay." She looked up at the great house they were approaching. All the lights were on, even as the eastern sky was starting to turn pink. "I may make that very same decision myself. After what happened today, I know things are only going to get worse."

They parked in front of the house, and Gregory escorted her inside.

"Daphne! Thank God!"

It was Ben who rushed across the foyer to greet her. Behind him, Gabriel rolled forward in his wheelchair, and Daphne caught a smile on his face as well.

They're actually glad to see me, she thought to herself. This house is not completely bad.

Ben was embracing her, and now Ashlee was approaching as well.

"Thank God indeed," Ashlee said, putting her arms around Daphne after Ben let her go. "Where were you, sweetie?"

"I think Daphne should sit down before she tells her story," Gregory said, "and maybe someone could get her some tea. She's chilled to the bone."

"I will determine how and where and when Daphne tells her story," came Pete's voice, as the old man strode out of the parlor. "Your services are no longer needed here, Winston. Thank you for bringing Daphne back to us. Good night."

"Not so fast, Pete," Gregory said angrily. "I'm not just your errand boy, someone you send out find your son's governess and then summarily dismiss. Your son attempted to kill Daphne—and I want guarantees this will never happen again."

"Why don't we all go in the parlor and let Daphne tell us what exactly happened," Ben suggested. When no one objected, they all proceeded through the parlor doors.

Daphne saw that Christopher was nowhere to be seen. He had probably been ordered to stay in his room. But other than the boy—and Louella, who hadn't emerged from her room since Donovan's death—the entire household was present, including Suzanne, who had come for her things and had stayed the night due to the approaching storm.

Standing to one side, Daphne noticed with some revulsion, was Boris. She made eye contact with the butler. Had that been him in the crypt, terrorizing her? But if so, how had he gotten out without Gregory seeing him?

In soft, measured tones, Daphne explained everything that had happened. When she told the part about Christopher closing the door on her, she saw Pete stand and cover his face with his old, gnarled hands.

For the moment, she left out telling them about the clown. She described finding the secret cellar, but said her screams that lured Gregory into finding her were produced when she discovered the bones. There was general astonishment from everyone present that the undiscovered victims had finally been found, and Ben said he would call the sheriff and let him know.

"What a relief for their families this will be," he said.

When Daphne was finished speaking, there was a kind of stunned silence in the room. Even Suzanne seemed horrified, and a trace sympathetic. Finally Pete spoke.

"Christopher will be sent away," he announced.

"I think," Daphne said, before Pete could say anything else, "that we ought to allow Dr. Duane to weigh in on this. I think too often in the past Christopher has suffered because professional opinions were not taken into account when decisions were made concerning him."

"Daphne's right," Ben said. "We should get Duane up here as soon as possible this morning."

Pete sighed his assent. He seemed beaten.

"All that is well and good," Gregory said, "but I think Daphne is owed some assurances that such a terrible thing, or anything like it, can never happen in the future."

"We'll all be vigilant," Ben promised.

"And might I just raise the possibility," Gregory said, "that if the boy was capable of the attempted murder of Daphne, he might be capable of the real thing?"

"Are you suggesting," Gabriel asked, sitting forward in his wheelchair, "Christopher may have killed Donovan?"

Suzanne gasped at the idea.

"I'm just asking if he is capable of such a thing."

"He's just a child," sniffed Abigail.

But no one else raised much objection to the idea.

Except Daphne. "Christopher didn't kill Donovan," she said. "I can't believe that much. He is not a bad child, deep down."

"After what he did to you, sweetie?" Ashlee asked. "How can you say that?"

Daphne didn't reply. But in her mind, she was remembering the clown she had seen in the crypt—the same she had seen in the tower and on the street and at the inn. That was no little boy playing dress-up.

She felt terribly and utterly exhausted then. All she wanted to do was sleep. Everyone in the room agreed that was probably for the best. Gregory kissed her hand, and said, in front of everyone, that he would return sometime that afternoon to check on her. "And if she wants to leave here," he announced, "I will take her away."

No one dared object.

After Gregory had left, Ashlee escorted Daphne upstairs.

"When Dr. Duane comes," Daphne said, "please wake me. I want to be present when any decisions are made regarding Christopher."

"Of course, sweetie," Ashlee assured her.

First, a hot, vigorous shower. Daphne was tired enough, however, that while it removed the mud and grime, it did not rouse her. Gratefully, she climbed into bed. Once more she touched the wound on her neck. Had the clown only meant to scare her, and not kill her? Or had Gregory really scared it away in the nick of time?

Or had she, as Gregory suggested, only scratched herself as she fell?

Was the clown real, or her imagination?

Was it a ghost? Was it Boris? Or was it someone else?

A ghost wouldn't have been frightened off by Gregory's arrival.

Or would it have been?

She drifted off to a deep sleep that, thankfully, for once, wasn't plagued by dreams.

When Daphne awoke, the light seemed unchanged. A glance at her clock told her the reason why. She had fallen asleep at dawn; it was now dusk. She had missed Dr. Duane! She leapt out of bed, wrapping her robe around her. Outside, the snow had continued falling all day. The grounds were now covered in a deep blanket of white, and it was still coming down.

Once again she gave thanks to God that Gregory had found her when he did.

Otherwise, I'd still be down there . . . in that place.

And I might be dead.

She hurried down the hall to Christopher's room. The door was open, and the room was empty.

"Oh, dear," Daphne mumbled to herself.

Had they taken the boy away? Committed him to some institution? Without allowing her to talk with Christopher, confront him about what he had done, and ask him why?

Daphne hurried down the marble stairs into the foyer.

Boris was standing there at the bottom, looking up at her. Daphne recoiled, slowing her descent.

"Good evening, Miss May," the butler said in that terrible high voice of his. "Axel told me you were very interested in our past here at Witherswood. I'd be glad to tell you all about it some time."

He smiled, exposing those horrible sharp teeth.

Daphne said nothing as he moved away, a surprisingly agile corpse.

She saw no one else. Cook had taped a note to the refrigerator in the kitchen. She was leaving due to the storm, she wrote, but she'd made sandwiches and salads for them all to eat for dinner. Daphne was suddenly ravenous, having not eaten since early the day before, and helped herself to a ham-and-cheese on a bulky roll and a tossed salad. She felt better after she'd eaten.

But where was everyone? And most particularly, where was Christopher?

Daphne was surprised at how little enmity she felt for the boy. Oh, she wanted there to be repercussions for him, and she wanted him to see the seriousness of what he had done. But she also wanted Christopher to get the help he needed. It would do no good to simply rant at him and leave him even more disturbed than he was before.

This was the conversation she'd wanted to have with Mr. Witherspoon and Dr. Duane. What could they do that would help him, and not just punish him? She would be very upset if they'd shipped him off somewhere without any input from her.

She could hear the wind whipping outside the house. Peering from the window over the estate, she could see that the snow was already a couple of feet on the terrace, and it was drifting. Once again she said a silent prayer of thanks that Gregory had found her when he did.

"Hello?" she called, heading down to the study. No one there either.

It was starting to feel as if she was in the house alone . . . alone with Boris, that was. Daphne shuddered.

She turned down the hallway when suddenly she was startled by someone coming around the corner.

It was Abigail, looking down her nose at her, as usual.

"I assume you're looking for him, too?" the older woman asked.

"Looking for who?"

"Christopher. He's disappeared."

"What do you mean, disappeared?"

"I mean precisely that. Do you think I play word games?"

Daphne frowned. "How long has he been gone?"

Her question was answered by Ben, who at that moment came from the other direction of the corridor. "For about four hours," he said. "When Dr. Duane arrived, Christopher wasn't in his room. We've all been searching ever since."

"Well, what makes you think he's still in the house? He could have left."

"I don't think so," Ben said. "The snow is pretty deep out there. There were no tracks outside any door or window. Even still, I did manage to get over to the stable, and he's not there."

"There are dozens of places he could hide in this house," Abigail said. "But I've looked in all of them, and I'm beginning to run out of ideas."

Daphne sighed. "Has anyone looked in the tower room?"

"First place I checked," Ben said. "Nobody there."

"Well, I'll help look," Daphne said.

"You sure? After what happened?"

She smiled at him. "Especially after what happened."

Daphne made her way up to Christopher's room, looking for any clues. She thought it was odd that wherever he'd gone, he'd left his iPod behind. That thing seemed permanently affixed to his ears. She looked in his closet, the place where she had first seen the clown in this house. It had been no toy, she was convinced now. It was the clown. Ghost or human, it had been a clown to look back at her, no child's toy.

And had Christopher known she'd see it there?

Daphne had started to wonder if somehow Christopher was in on this. Gregory's question wasn't unreasonable. That first day, Christopher, Daphne was sure, had lured her into his room by calling her name. Then she had seen the clown in his closet. Yesterday, he'd lured her into the crypt, where she had seen the clown again. The boy hadn't been involved in the other episodes, but twice was enough to get her to consider the possibility that he was somehow a part of all this.

After searching the boy's room, Daphne headed back downstairs. She found Ashlee and Gabriel in the parlor.

"Any luck finding Christopher?" she asked.

Ashlee shook her head. "He's just vanished."

"There are lots of hiding places in this house,"

Gabriel said. "I know when I was a kid, if I didn't want to be found, then no one could find me."

"Like where?" Daphne asked. "Ben's looked in all places he used to hide in."

"Oh, there's lots and lots," Gabriel told her. "There's the crawl space under the front staircase, the old cedar closet in the attic, the storage room in the basement . . . I mean, I can't even think of them all." He smiled sadly. "I wish I could help you all look."

Ashlee was looking out the window. "This storm is only getting worse." She turned around to look at them and shivered. "I was just reading online that it's expected to dump up to five feet of snow by the end of it tomorrow afternoon. Five feet! I mean, that's like as tall as me!" She laughed. "I've never seen so much snow. Remember I'm from Florida!"

"The roads are going to be impassable," Gabriel commented. "Especially the road up to Witherswood."

"Let's just hope we don't lose power," Ashlee said, shivering again.

Daphne thought of her trusty little flashlight. It wasn't in her purse when she'd looked inside after she'd gotten back home. No doubt it was still on the floor of that terrible underground chamber.

"Well, I'm going to keep looking for Christopher," Daphne said.

"I admire you, sweetie," Ashlee said, smirking. "Between you and me, I'd send the brat to the funny farm if I had the chance."

"I understand why you feel that way," Daphne said, "but it's exactly that attitude that has made him so disturbed today."

Ashlee smiled. "You're a better person than I am, sweetie."

"Daphne," Gabriel said.

She turned to look at him. He seemed to be struggling with what he wanted to say to her.

"Listen," he said at last. "Be careful. There's something going on in this house. It's not just Christopher. I think you know what I mean."

"I do know," Daphne replied. "Something— someone—some force . . ."

"Yes," Gabe said. "And I just wanted to say, be careful."

She smiled at him. "I will. Thank you."

She decided she'd start looking for Christopher in the basement and work her way up. She might look in places the others had already searched, but maybe she'd see something they didn't. Maybe, in fact, Christopher would show himself to her when he wouldn't show himself to others.

The basement was a cobwebby collection of old furniture, boxes, and books. The boy could be hiding under any one of the overturned sofas or inside an empty cabinet.

"Christopher," Daphne spoke in a calm voice. "If you're here, come out. We have some talking to do, don't we? I'm not going to flip out on you. Don't worry about that. I just want to know why you did it. And I'd like to help you, too."

No sound, no movement.

She moved deeper into the basement. She could hear the wind rising in pitch and strength, whistling through the wooden beams of the old house. The snow had piled up against the narrow windows that were carved high in the walls of the basement, casting an eerie white glow over the dim interior.

"Christopher?" Daphne called.

The basement was mostly open space—cluttered, packed open space, but not broken off into separate rooms. Yet Gabriel had mentioned a storage room down there. Daphne looked around, but saw nothing that seemed to lead to any storage room.

"Christopher, come out, please," she called again. "Let's talk."

As she passed the massive, trembling furnace, hissing and shaking as it struggled to heat the enormous house, Daphne noticed a door. Could that be the storage room? She opened the door and found herself in a long dark corridor. This part of the basement must be under one of the house's wings. She took a couple of steps inside, grateful to find a string hanging from a single bulb overhead. She pulled the string and the bulb came to life, casting the dusty corridor in a dim, amber light.

At the far end of the corridor was another door— a big, iron door.

She approached it, fully expecting the door to be locked. But although there was a keyhole, indicating it could be locked with a key, the door was unlocked at present. Pulling it open—no easy task, given the weight of the iron door—Daphne peered inside. Another string dangled from a bulb on the ceiling, and she pulled it, filling the small room with light. Right away she noticed that the door had a heavy bolt on the inside, meaning whoever came into this room could keep others out. What business did someone have in a storage room, Daphne wondered, that they'd want to keep so private? Why would a storage room have locks on both the inside and out?

A room that held important secrets, she told herself.

The room was indeed used for storage, but not for furniture or boxes, as Daphne had assumed. Instead, it was used to store records and documents. In the center of the room was a large wooden chest, so heavy that Daphne couldn't budge it. All around her, shelves held long cardboard file boxes, all carefully labeled. Daphne glanced at some of them. Most were inscribed only with dates: 1951–1955. 1956–1960. 1961–1965. And so on. Some had descriptions written on them: TERRACE CONSTRUCTION. EAST WING ADDITION. But one box, on the lowest shelf, near the floor, caught her eye more than any of the others. On its front was written just one letter: M.

A box marked M would not normally have made Daphne look twice, but this one did, because of what was sticking out of the top.

A blanket.

Purple brocade.

She withdrew from her blouse the locket she always wore around her neck. It never left her. She opened the locket and removed the small piece of fabric she kept inside. The fabric of the blanket she had been wrapped in as a baby.

It matched the blanket sticking out of the box marked M. Perfectly.

Daphne lifted the box off the shelf and set it on the chest in the center of the room. Carefully she looked inside.

Under the blanket were letters. Dozens of them. Maybe hundreds. They were all addressed to Peter Witherspoon Junior, and sent to a post office box. The postmark on every envelope Daphne checked was Boston. And the dates—she looked closer in the dim light—twenty-two years ago, she determined, some twenty-three.

She opened one letter and read. It was brief. No salutation.

> *She has taken her first steps. Thought you would want to know. She is already a very smart girl.*

It was signed merely *M.*
A second letter was equally perplexing.

> *Just a fever. Doctor says not to worry. Common at this age.*

Again signed *M.*
Another was even more terse.

> *Donation received with thanks.*

No *M* even this time.
Finally, a longer message.

> *She has your smile. It breaks my heart to see it. I know we vowed to put all of the feeling behind us, but sometimes it breaks through. I hold her in my arms, I watch her as she plays, and I cannot help but think of you.*

There was no signature on this letter either.

Daphne looked again at the blanket. Where it was folded underneath, she noticed a pin. And the pin held a photograph. She looked at it. A baby, in someone's arms. She couldn't see who held the baby, but she could tell that the photograph had been taken outside the front door of Witherswood. She recognized the swallowtail engravings.

Did *M* stand for Maria? Mr. Witherspoon's long-lost love?

Yet before she had a chance to consider what she had found any further, Daphne was distracted by a sound.

"Daphne."

Someone was calling her name, very quietly, from some place nearby.

"Daphne."

She stood and peered out of the storage room. It seemed to come from beyond the corridor, from back in the main part of the basement.

"Daphne. Daphne. Daphneee."

She recognized the voice.

It was like the voice she had heard her first day here.

"Christopher?" she called.

"Daphneee . . ."

She stood, turning off the light in the storage room but leaving the box out so she could finish her investigation later.

"Daphneeeeeee . . ."

She was certain it was Christopher, taunting her the way he had done her first day in this house. She headed out of the storage room, back into the corridor, but as she did so, she heard—and felt—a huge gust of wind hit the upper part of the house, and the little bulb lighting her way was snuffed out.

Daphne was left in darkness. Maybe it was just that one bulb, but she had a feeling the entire house had lost power.

Suddenly she felt something run past her. A small bundle of energy that she was certain was Christopher. He scooted around her and toward the storage room behind her.

"Christopher!" she called after him.

She could hear his footsteps running away from her, across the concrete floor of the corridor. Then, suddenly, the footsteps ceased—followed by the scream of a little boy.

"Christopher!" Daphne shouted, rushing forward in the dark, back toward the storage room. Had he tripped over the chest in the middle of the room?

But the scream hadn't been one of pain.

It had been one of fear.

At that moment, the lightbulb above her came back to life.

And there, in front of her, stepping out of the storage room she had just left, was the clown— grinning, laughing, and moving toward Daphne.

But worst of all, in its arms, it carried what seemed an offering to her: a terrified, immobilized Christopher, the boy's face as white as his captor's.

SEVENTEEN

"Let him go," Daphne said, in a meek, almost inaudible, voice.

Christopher was silently crying, too terrified even to struggle.

The clown winked at her. Jostling the boy in one arm, it reached inside its shirt with its free hand, and withdrew the long blade, much as it had in the crypt.

"Let him go!" Daphne demanded again. "Look, it's me you want! I've been the one you've been chasing for weeks. Come get me!"

The clown put its head back and laughed, as if Daphne had just made a really funny joke, and exposed those awful teeth. Christopher whimpered in fear.

"Let him go!" Daphne demanded for a third time, in a loud voice now, fearless and defiant. "You monster! You child-killer! Come after me, you bastard!"

And without even stopping to think about what she was doing, Daphne charged the creature. Its eyes widened, its teeth gnashed. It dropped Christopher just before Daphne made contact with it.

"Run, Christopher!" Daphne shouted. "Lock yourself in the storage room!"

The boy did as she said, bolting into the storage room and pulling the heavy iron door shut behind him. Daphne had no idea if there was a lock on the door, or even if there was, if a locked door could keep this creature out. After all, she'd just been in that room. It had not been in there with her. There was no place it could have hidden. How did it appear in there—unless it really was a ghost?

The clown hissed at her, gnashing those teeth.

And the power went out again, leaving them in blackness.

Daphne turned to run, braced for the creature to lunge at her. But it never did. She ran out into the main part of the basement, calling for help.

"Daphne!" came Ben's voice, flashlight swinging through the dark. "Daphne, where are you? Are you okay?"

"Over here, Ben!"

He found her.

"The storage room," she managed to gasp, and Ben turned his light toward it. The door was now open. Christopher was on the floor, crying and covering his hands with his eyes.

"I told you to lock the door!" Daphne shouted.

"I couldn't reach it!" the boy sobbed. "He came in here after me! I thought he was going to kill me."

"Who came in here?" Ben asked, hurrying to his cousin.

"The clown!"

Ben exchanged a look with Daphne, who nodded solemnly.

"The clown came back in here?" Daphne asked Christopher. "Then where did it go? It's not in here now."

"I don't know," the boy cried. "I was too scared to look!"

Daphne looked around the room. No windows, no second door. Just the shelves with all the file boxes.

Suddenly Christopher was leaping onto her. At first she was ready to push him back, not trusting the boy. But then she realized he was clinging to her neck, sobbing.

"Daphne saved me! Daphne saved me from that clown!"

She could feel his small frame heaving with sobs.

"I'm sorry I locked you in the crypt, Daphne! I'm so, so, so sorry!"

He cried even harder.

"It's okay, Christopher," she said quietly.

Ben attempted to peel the boy off of her. "Come on, buddy, let's go upstairs."

"I want to go with Daphne!" he shouted.

"I'll stay right next to you," she promised.

She held his hand as they walked through the basement back upstairs, Ben leading the way with his flashlight.

They found Abigail, Suzanne, and Axel sitting by candlelight in the parlor. Although it was now dark outside, it was clear from the drifts along the windows that the snow was still falling, and heavily.

After Daphne and Christopher related their account of what had happened downstairs, the three who sat listening to them reacted with some skepticism.

"You've been seeing clowns since the day you got here," said Abigail. "Now you've got the child seeing them, too."

"Really, Aunt Abigail, it's true," Christopher insisted.

"Ashlee saw the clown as well last time," Daphne pointed out.

"Well, *Ashlee*," Abigail sniffed, turning her face away and rolling her eyes, as if that was all that was needed to prove her point.

Suzanne sidled over toward her. Daphne felt she still somehow blamed her for Donovan's death. "It does seem odd that none of us has ever seen anything unusual," Suzanne said. "Don't you think it's odd?"

"I can't explain it," Daphne said. She looked around the room. "Where's Boris?"

"He must be rustling up some more candles," Axel suggested.

Either that, Daphne thought, *or changing out of his clown suit.*

"Ben," she said suddenly, turning to her friend as a thought came to her, "there was a secret way out of the tower room. Might there be a secret way out of that storage room downstairs as well?"

"There are secret doors and passages all through this house," Ben replied. "A whole labyrinth really. I used to explore some of them as a kid, but I wouldn't know about the storage room. That's been largely Uncle Pete's territory. Before today, I don't think I had been down there for years."

Someone came into the parlor behind them.

"Did I hear you asking for me, Miss May?"

It was Boris. In his hands, the butler carried a small portable radio. It was buzzing and wheezing with static.

"I was searching for this," Boris said, as Daphne watched him closely. "I thought we might get an update on the blizzard."

He set the radio on the coffee table in front of the fireplace and began fiddling with the knobs. "It's an old radio, probably dates from the nineteen eighties," Boris said, as the crackling static filled the room. "As you know, Mr. Witherspoon has preferred to keep all televisions and radios out of the house, but I thought I remembered this was still down in the basement somewhere."

"Were you just in the basement?" Daphne asked.

He looked at her and gave her a half-smile. "Yes, miss," he said, "I was."

The butler turned back to the radio and kept adjusting the knobs. Finally, a voice broke through the static.

"Ah, here we are," Boris said, pleased with himself.

"Severe storm alert," came the voice of a man from the radio. "The National Weather Service reports power and telephone lines down all across the northeast United States. Reports of snow, hail, sleet, and ice are coming in from New York, Connecticut, Massachusetts, Rhode Island, New Hampshire, Vermont, and Maine. Roads are closed throughout the region. The Coast Guard is advising any small craft on the water to make for safe port until the storm passes. Maine state officials are urging residents to stay off the roads and stay indoors until further notice. Temperatures will continue to drop throughout the night, which will freeze any water on the ground. We will keep you updated on conditions of this dangerous storm— the worst nor'easter, according to meteorologists, in more than a decade."

"Gee, and here I was thinking I might take a drive down to the beach," Ben joked.

"We won't get power back for a few days," Abigail predicted. "I've been through enough nor'easters to know what we're facing."

"Jesus Christ," Suzanne grumbled. "Why did I have to pick this week to come back to this godforsaken house?"

"You didn't find it so godforsaken when you thought you might be marrying into it and getting a piece of it," Abigail snarled.

Suzanne ignored her and went over to sit by the fire, sighing dramatically in frustration.

"Where's Mr. Witherspoon?" Daphne asked.

"I believe he's in his study," Abigail told her. "Being sensible, as Pete always is, staying put during this blackout and not running all around the house."

"Well, we ought to at least let him know that his son has been found, don't you think?" Daphne asked, looking around at the group.

Ben told her that was a good idea.

Of course, Daphne also intended to ask Pete for blueprints of the house. She wanted to see just what secret passageways there might be that would make it easy for a killer to move around from one part of Witherswood to another.

She glanced over at Boris. She was certain he knew all the passages like the back of his hand.

Daphne started to leave the parlor when Christopher jumped up and latched on to her arm. "Don't leave me, Daphne!" he begged. "That thing might come back!"

She smiled, gently removing the boy's fingers from her arm. "I'll be back, Christopher. You just wait here with Ben. Don't worry about anything. Everything will be fine. I just have a couple questions I want to ask your father."

She headed out of the parlor into the foyer, carrying a small candle to light her way. It flickered against the wall, casting strange, eerie shapes that Daphne preferred not to look at for very long. No need to further enflame that imagination of hers.

But she hadn't imagined what she had seen downstairs. She was certain of that now. Nor had she imagined anything else since coming to this house. There was a lunatic loose, a real live flesh-and-blood lunatic. And the reason he seemed to appear and disappear was because there were secret passages that gave him the power to do so. There may have been one in the crypt that they had yet to discover. Their menacing clown wasn't a ghost. He was someone who knew this house and its secrets very well.

More than ever, Daphne thought Boris was the culprit. Proving it, however, was going to take some work.

She heard whispering as she approached the study, and saw the soft glow of candlelight spilling from the room into the hallway.

"Darling," she heard Ashlee say.

Daphne paused before turning into the doorway. Through the shadows, she caught a glimpse of Mr. Witherspoon sitting in his chair. It appeared that Ashlee was sitting on his lap, facing him, giving him a series of quick kisses. Daphne backed up, not wanting to intrude on their moment of intimacy.

But as she backed up, she saw Mr. Witherspoon stand. He was gently urging Ashlee to get off his lap. "Come on," he whispered, "not now."

And Daphne knew from his voice it was not Mr. Witherspoon.

Watching from the slit in the doorframe, Daphne saw the man, whoever it was, take Ashlee in his arms and kiss her. They were both obscured by shadows, with only a small candle on a nearby table casting any light. But it was obvious the man Ashlee was kissing was not her husband. He was much taller than Mr. Witherspoon, and clearly more strong and vital.

Daphne, shocked, turned to hurry away. But as she did so, she dropped her candle. It snuffed out once it hit the marble floor.

It also made a sound. Before she get away, Daphne's arm was being gripped by Ashlee.

"Daphne! What are you doing?"

"I dropped my candle. . . ." She tried to stoop down to retrieve it, but Ashlee, holding another candle in her free hand, kept her grip tight on Daphne's arm.

"Were you spying on me?" Ashlee asked.

Daphne faced her. "Who is that in there?"

Ashlee's face tightened in the glow of the candle. "Come with me!" she demanded, and pulled Daphne down the corridor toward the library, which she practically pushed her inside. Still, her fingers dug into Daphne's arm.

"Ow," Daphne said. "You're hurting me!"

Ashlee let her go. She closed the door behind them, then turned to face Daphne. Her face had softened.

"Oh, Daphne," Ashlee cried, "please don't judge me!"

"Who is that man you were kissing?"

"He's . . . a friend of mine."

"How did he get up here?" Daphne asked. "In this storm?"

"He has a snowmobile," Ashlee explained. "He brought us up some rations. Some bread and canned goods. He was afraid we wouldn't be able to get out to get food."

"You were kissing him," Daphne said again.

Ashlee looked as if she might cry. "Yes, I was. Oh, Daphne, please try to understand and don't pass judgment on me. Try as I have to be a good wife, Pete has never really loved me. . . ." The tears started flowing then. "He's never gotten over his first love. She's who he thinks about. Soon after we were married, I found that he still kept her photograph. It broke my heart."

"Her name is Maria," Daphne said.

"How did you know?"

"I heard stories." She smiled sadly at her friend. "I'm sorry, Ashlee. I really am. But to kiss another man in your husband's house . . ."

"I know, I know, it was wrong." Ashlee ran her fingers through her hair. In the dim light of the candle, which now sat on the table, all the pain and heartbreak was clear on Ashlee's face. "I put up a good front of saying that Pete loved me. I think I was trying to convince myself. But it was always Maria. It got so that he wouldn't even kiss me, wouldn't even hold me. He married me because he wanted a mother for Christopher. But Christopher rejected me, too."

Daphne nodded.

"I have been so lonely in this house," Ashlee said. "I know it's wrong, but when . . . my friend . . . kisses me, I feel like a woman again."

"What's his name?"

There was the slightest hesitation on Ashlee's part. "John," she said.

"And he lives in the village?"

"Yes," Ashlee told her, "he does."

"How did you meet him?"

"He knew who I was. He came over and introduced himself. 'Hello, Mrs. Witherspoon, my name is . . . John.' " Ashlee smiled. "And so we became friends."

Daphne just sighed.

"Please, you must understand. . . ." Ashlee pleaded.

"I know how hard it must be, with your husband always thinking about someone else. It's what his first wife went through, as well. Peggy. She killed herself because of it. Gregory told me."

"I know," Ashlee said. "I didn't tell you because . . . well, I thought you might start asking questions why, and that just got too close to my own situation. I pretended I resented Peggy, because she's the one Abigail and Louella always talked about so fondly. But in reality, it was this Maria who I really resented."

"Ashlee," Daphne asked, "was it possible that . . . Pete and Maria had a child?"

Ashlee looked at her intensely. "Why do you ask that?"

"I found some letters downstairs, written to Mr. Witherspoon from someone who signed themselves 'M.' The person writing the letters seemed to be giving him updates about a child. And in the box there was a photograph of a baby."

Ashlee was quiet. "I don't know anything about that."

"I'm sorry if I've upset you further."

They were quiet for a few seconds. The candle flickered.

"Has he left?" Daphne asked.

"Has who left?"

"John." She paused. "Your friend."

"Oh, yes," Ashlee said. "He just came to bring the food. I told him we were fine, that we had a fully stocked pantry. But bless his heart, he just wanted to make sure."

Daphne looked out the window. "I didn't hear his snowmobile, or see any light," she said.

"Of course not," Ashlee replied. "He didn't want Pete, or anyone else, to know he was here. He'll walk the snowmobile down the hill a bit before starting it."

Daphne nodded.

"Anyway," Ashlee said, "you really don't think any less of me?"

Daphne looked at her. "It's not my place to judge anyone else."

"Thank you, Daphne," Ashlee said, and embraced her.

"Maybe," Daphne told her, "your friend should have taken us all out of here, one by one, on his snowmobile."

Ashlee let her go, looking into her eyes. "What do you mean?"

Daphne told her she suspected Boris was the clown, and filled her in on what had happened in the basement. A look of terror crossed Ashlee's face.

"If that's the case," she breathed, "we're all trapped with a killer in the house."

Daphne took a deep breath. "I need to find Mr. Witherspoon. I want to find out about any secret passageways through the house. I'm convinced that whoever was dressed as that clown got out of the storage room by some means as yet unknown. It's the only way to explain it."

"The only way to explain it if it's a living person," Ashlee reminded her. "If it's a ghost, then I don't think we need secret passageways to explain anything."

Her observation was punctuated by a derisive laugh.

"I should have known coming on the two of you I'd stumble in on a conversation about ghosts."

They looked up. Suzanne had opened the door of the library and now stood looking at them, holding a candle in her free hand.

"Hello, Suzanne," Ashlee said.

"I just wanted to let you know, Little Miss Governess, that your charge is sitting back in the parlor crying his eyes out for you." Suzanne frowned.

"It wasn't very wise of you to fill his head with stories of murderous clowns."

"I didn't fill his head with it, Suzanne," Daphne told her. "He experienced it himself."

"Oh, please," Suzanne spit. "I'm disgusted by the both of you. Look at you. Grown women in here talking about ghosts."

"For your information, Suzanne," Ashlee said, and Daphne could hear the anger surging in her friend's voice, "what Daphne and I talk about is our own goddamn business. You had no right to come barging in on our private conversation."

Suzanne laughed at her. "In case you hadn't noticed, Miss High and Mighty White Trash, we are in the midst of a blizzard. The power is out. There are things that need to be done. We don't have time to be hiding behind doors telling ghost stories."

"Who's calling who white trash? What are you, sugarplum, Korean trash? Because let me tell you, I know very well that the main reason you're shedding tears over poor, dear Donovan is because you're never going to be his rich bride now."

"Ashlee, don't," Daphne said. She didn't like Suzanne either, but that was no reason to claim her grief over her fiancé wasn't authentic.

Suzanne seemed to take no offense, however. She just got up close in Ashlee's face and started in on her. "Well, looky here, bitch. Takes one gold digger to know one, I guess. Like you married old Pete out of love and affection!"

"Suzanne!" Daphne scolded. "Stop that!"

"Oh, don't get me started on you, baby." Suzanne turned her venom on Daphne. "If not for you,

Donovan would still be alive. Don't start talking to me about ghosts and whatever crazy killers you've got running around through the secret passage-ways of your mind. I know you got Donovan killed, and someday I hope to prove it!"

"Me? How did I get Donovan killed?"

"You decided he was a goner that night in the stable," Suzanne barked at her. "I heard it in your voice, saw it in your eyes! And you got someone to do the dirty deed for you!"

"And who did I get, Suzanne?"

"Your sweet little boyfriend, Gregory Winston!"

"You think Gregory killed Donovan?"

Suzanne put her chin in the air and looked down her nose at her. "I most certainly do. I saw the way he came rolling in here, all Mr. Good and Noble. I know what men like that do. They kill any-thing they think has offended their sweet little lady's honor."

"You are crazy," Daphne told her.

Suzanne turned to Ashlee. "And you were in on it, too, bitch. The two of you just happen to wan-der into the tower and come across Donovan's body! You probably had just let Winston out of the door before you did so."

Ashlee was smiling. Her anger was gone. She seemed genuinely amused by Suzanne's paranoid imagination.

"Well, it wasn't right after we let Gregory out that we went into the tower," Ashlee told her. "We let him get away on his motorcycle first, didn't we, Daphne?"

"Oh, Ashlee, don't joke about such things," Daphne said.

"I'll prove it!" Suzanne ranted. "You just wait! I'll prove you were both involved in Donovan's death! I'll make you both pay!"

"Eat me, Suzanne," Ashlee said, turning away.

Suzanne huffed back out into the dark corridor. Daphne watched her. Almost as if in slow motion, she saw Suzanne turn away from them, and in that very same moment, her candle was snuffed out by a gust of air. In the instant before all light was gone, Daphne saw a shadow descend upon Suzanne, a shadow that possessed both substance and speed. Then a scream punctured the darkness.

Daphne snatched the candle from the table and rushed forward. She held the candle out into the hallway.

Suzanne lay at their feet, her body twitching in its death throes.

Her throat had been sliced clear through.

And in the distance Daphne could hear the tune she had come to dread:

All around the mulberry bush . . .

EIGHTEEN

The whole family was gathered in the parlor, white-faced with terror.

"It would seem," Pete announced, his voice trembling, "there is a killer in the house. How he got in here is unknown, but after what happened to Suzanne we can no longer deny that we are facing a very serious threat."

In his quivering hands, he held his hunting rifle.

"We've got to get out of here!" Abigail shrilled. "Out of the house!"

"And how would you suggest we do that, Abigail?" Pete asked. "There is a monster storm raging outside. We can barely get out the front door, let alone down that long, narrow, twisting, treacherous road into the village."

Daphne glanced out the window. The snow had already reached the center of the glass panes. Ben had forged outside, and reported the drifts were nearly as tall as he was. All he could see of the stable was its roof. The view of the sea was obliterated in a swirling whiteout of snow.

"We could get out with snowmobiles," Daphne said, looking over at Ashlee.

"I wish we had one," Ben said.

Daphne kept her gaze on Ashlee. "Maybe someone who has one could come up for us. Or several people. Take us all out of here."

"That's a brilliant suggestion, Daphne," Ashlee told her. "Only problem is, how do we contact said persons with snowmobiles?"

"None of the cell phones will work?" Gabe asked anxiously, clenching and unclenching his fists in his wheelchair.

"Nope," Ben told his brother. "I took my phone up to the tower room to try to call the sheriff, but I couldn't get a signal."

"And with the power out," Ashlee said, "our modems are down. We can't connect to the Internet to even send an e-mail."

"Why does everyone want to leave?" Louella asked, sitting off to the side in a wingback chair. Pete had insisted she be brought down to join them in the parlor. There was safety in numbers, he said. But Louella was just as dazed and confused as ever, the result of the medications she'd been taking since Donovan's death. "Why should we want to leave Witherswood?"

"Hush, Louella," Abigail snapped at her.

"It's for the best, Aunt Louella," Ben told her. "And it will just be temporary."

"Will Donovan be leaving, too?"

No one replied.

Daphne noticed that neither Boris nor Axel were in the room, and she inquired about the servants' whereabouts.

"They've gone to get more candles and search for some kerosene lamps," Pete told her. "As you can see, our supply is running out, and we have a long night ahead of us."

"Are there any more guns in the house?" Ben asked.

"This is it," Pete said, gripping his rifle tightly.

Ben made a face of concern. "Uncle Pete, I appreciate your desire to protect us, but with the way your hands shake, maybe I ought to take the rifle."

Pete scowled. "You? You don't know how to shoot. Only Donovan took the lessons I requested. You said you didn't like guns."

"Uncle Pete," Gabriel interjected. "*I* know how to shoot. *I* took the lessons. Why do you always refuse to acknowledge that *I* did what you wanted? Not only on the rifle lessons, but so much else. Why do you only remember Donovan, and never me?"

The old man looked over at him, then looked away. "You're right, Gabe. You know how to handle a gun."

"Then give it to me," Gabe said.

"You?" Pete made a face. "I can't give it to you!"

"Why not?"

"Because you're in that . . . chair!"

Gabe frowned. "This chair has no bearing on my trigger finger."

"But still . . ."

"Goddamn it, Uncle Pete! This whole family has

never seen me as worth anything! Even before I was in this chair! But I am just as good as Donovan or Ben or anyone else!"

The room was silent.

"Give me the rifle, Uncle Pete," Gabe said. "I will keep it trained on the parlor doors. If anyone comes in, I'll shoot him through the heart. I'm a good shot. You'll see."

Abigail wasn't happy with the idea. "I'm not comfortable being protected by a cripple. What if the killer moves around and you can't follow him?"

"Then I'll throw the rifle to you, dear Aunt Abigail."

"Really, the disrespect!" the old woman sniffed.

"Give him the rifle, Uncle Pete," Ben said. "I'll be at his side. If needs be, I can get it from him and use it myself, or toss it to you."

The old man hesitated.

"No," he finally said. "The rifle stays in my hands."

Daphne saw Gabe's eyes fill with tears, but he bit them back. His lips curled in a furious scowl.

From outside the parlor doors came a short series of four raps, the signal that it was Boris or Axel and not the killer—though Daphne was still convinced the butler was the one they had to fear. Ben let Boris into the room. The butler carried a large kerosene lamp.

"You found one!" Ashlee exclaimed.

"Yes," Boris said in his high voice. "There are so many treasures down in that basement."

"Is there enough keroscne?" Pete asked.

"Enough for a few hours, I think," Boris said.

Once the lamp was burning, they snuffed out all the candles to conserve for future use. This blackout could go on for days, after all.

Daphne was sitting on the sofa, Christopher at her side. He rested his head against her shoulder. "You smell like my mother," the boy whispered, dreamily, as he fought off sleep. Daphne put her arm around him and pulled him in for a hug.

She knew Gregory must be worried about her, but even someone as resourceful as Gregory couldn't overpower a storm like this. There was no way he could reach her. It was too bad that he didn't own a snowmobile like Ashlee's paramour.

She hadn't had much time to reflect on the discovery that her friend was cheating on her husband. Maybe it was just a kiss from time to time, but Daphne doubted it. Besides, even if it was just a kiss, it was still cheating. It was wrong. No question about it. Yet Daphne really didn't blame Ashlee. Pete's undying love for Maria had led poor Peggy to take her own life. Daphne supposed having an affair was a healthier way to deal with the heartbreak and rejection.

As they sat there in the parlor, not speaking much, listening to the wild whooping of the blizzard outside, Daphne speculated that this Maria must have been quite the woman to have held Pete's heart for so long. How tragic that the actions of Pete's nefarious father had prevented the couple from ever being together.

But . . . might they have been together, at least once?

Daphne tried to make sense of the box marked M that she had found in the storage room. Had

Pete and Maria had a child? A daughter? Did Maria write to him, anonymously so no one would ever find out, giving him updates on the little girl?

And if so, where was that child now?

The blanket, of course, had given Daphne pause. It was exactly like the one she had been wrapped in when she had been left at the door of Our Lady. In her romantic imagination, Daphne imagined that she was the little girl Maria was writing about, that she was Pete's daughter. It would make sense on some level, would explain why he had sent for her to come live at Witherswood. But there was a catch to the theory.

Maria, as reported in her letters, had kept her child. She watched her grow. Daphne had been raised by nuns.

But the blanket seemed to confirm that somewhere in this house, somewhere among all its many, many secrets, was the story of Daphne's own origins.

Whether she'd survive this night to discover the truth, however, remained to be seen.

Suddenly, without warning, one of the windows that overlooked the cliffs came flying open, and a ferocious gust of wind and snow and freezing air blew into the room. Louella screamed and Christopher yelped in Daphne's arms, and in the melee, the kerosene lamp fell over on its side. They were plunged into darkness amid a cyclone of swirling snow.

"Everyone stay calm!" Ben yelled, though Daphne couldn't see him through the blinding wall of snow. She could barely hear him either, over the terrible shrieking of the wind. In that single instant, the blizzard had rushed in to fill the entire room. Christopher clung to her tightly.

"It's okay, Christopher," Daphne shouted over the wind. "It will be okay."

All around them was a sense of confusion as several people—Ben, Ashlee, maybe Pete, maybe Abigail—struggled against the elements toward the window. Daphne remained on the couch holding Christopher. The snow swirled furiously around them. It was almost as if they were outside.

"Push!" she heard Ben command, and finally she heard the window bang shut.

Silence suddenly replaced the shrieking of the wind.

"Dear God," Daphne uttered, looking around.

Snow was everywhere. On the tables, chairs, bookcases, crusted around the frames of family portraits. The fireplace had been nearly extinguished. Daphne and Christopher were covered in a layer of white stuff, as was Louella, opposite them in her chair. Gabe, however, seemed to have escaped getting a snow bath, though he sat huffing and puffing, completely out of breath, in his wheelchair.

"Look at this room!" Ashlee exclaimed, after she'd gotten the kerosene lamp lit again. "This is all going to melt and we'll be sitting in a cold mess. We're going to have to move to a different room."

Pete was still standing at the window. "How did that damn thing fly open?" he groused, snow and ice on his wrinkled old face making him look like a cartoon character. "I latched those windows myself. They should have been secure!"

"I don't know how it happened, Uncle Pete,"

Ben said, "but it did, and Ashlee's right. We need to move down to the study."

They were all shaking snow off themselves when Daphne noticed Boris wasn't in the room. When had he left? Before or after the window blew open? And where was he now?

"Are we all going to die?" Christopher asked her suddenly.

"No, we are not," Daphne told him forcefully. "I promise you that."

They were startled by four knocks on the door. Abigail went to open it.

As she did so, she screamed.

The dead body of Axel came tumbling in, his throat slit.

Pete immediately rushed through the doors, brandishing his rifle, but he saw no one.

Ben stooped to inspect the body. Axel lay on the ground, faceup, eyes open, blood pouring from his throat, staining the snow on the carpet a bright pink. "It's a fresh wound," Ben said. "This just happened."

"It's Boris," Daphne said, standing. "Don't you all see? Where is he? It must be Boris!"

No one said anything. The butler's absence did seem to implicate him.

"Axel told me that Boris talked about the first Mr. Witherspoon all the time, even sometimes spoke in his voice," Daphne said. "Don't you see? He's trying to re-create his killing spree."

"Dear God," Pete groaned.

Louella had stood from her chair, and was now walking around Axel's body on the floor. The fat little woman had shaken off none of the snow that had accumulated on her, and she looked like a snow creature come to life.

"Father's ghost," she said dreamily. "Father's ghost."

"Not a ghost," Daphne told her. "The killer is all too real."

"Father's ghost," Louella insisted. "He said he would come back. I went to see him in the jail cell, and he told me what he was going to do."

"He told you he planned on killing himself?" Pete demanded to know.

Louella smiled. "Yes, he did. I was his favorite, you know."

"And you didn't notify the authorities?" Pete was horrified. "They could have stopped him! Forced him to stand trial for everything he did— for all the pain and suffering he caused—for all the shame he left us with!"

Louella seemed not to hear him. "He told me he was going to die that night," she said, looking down at Axel's body. "And he also told me that he would come back to us." She looked up and smiled at the group. "He said he'd come back to us when we least expected him."

"Enough of this, Louella," Abigail snapped, gripping her sister by the arm. "Well, are we moving to the study or not?"

"Yes," Pete said, "go along. I'll follow with the rifle."

"As if he can actually shoot that damn thing," Gabe snarled under his breath so only Daphne could hear him.

She walked alongside his wheelchair, holding

hands with Christopher, as they scooted around Axel's body out into the corridor.

"Poor man," Daphne said, looking down at his dead eyes.

"He was with our family a long time," Gabe said. "But I used to see him cheering on Donovan in our relay races. They all preferred Donovan over me. Even the servants."

Daphne thought it was odd that Gabe should cling on to such bitterness even at a time like this.

They had moved out into the dark corridor, passing in single file down the hall, Ashlee leading the way with the kerosene lamp, Pete hobbling alongside them with his rifle.

"Donovan always liked to play the man of the house," Gabe whispered to Daphne. "He had father issues." He chortled. "I guess I can understand why!"

Up ahead, the kerosene lamp went out, and they were left in total darkness in the corridor.

"Hang on!" Ashlee called, a voice out of the blackness. "It must have gotten wet. Let me try to relight it."

There was the sound of striking matches, but no flame appeared.

Christopher gripped Daphne's hand. "Here is where we all die," he said, shivering.

"Christopher, stop it," she scolded. "We are not going to die."

But in the darkness, from not far away, came the tinny little tune.

All around the mulberry bush, the monkey chased the weasel. . . .

Abigail screamed.

"Everyone stay calm!" Ben shouted, and he lifted his cell phone. It might not have any service, but the light still worked. A small golden glow lit his face. "Let's get into the study! Hurry!"

He held the cell phone aloft so people could follow, but the music was nearly upon them now. Daphne squeezed Christopher's hand tighter. "Run!" she ordered the boy, and he obeyed.

The music was louder and closer than ever. *The monkey thought it was all in fun. . . .*

Around Daphne, the others were running, too. They were halfway to the study when suddenly they were all stopped in their tracks by the sound of a scream. Daphne turned, for the scream had come from her immediate left, and all at once she felt a large body falling into her. She would have been crushed under it, knocked off her feet by its tremendous weight, if she hadn't managed to jump out of the way in time, clinging to Christopher's hand all the while. A terrible thud hit the floor beside her.

Ashlee succeeded in relighting the lamp and came running toward Daphne. She held the lamp aloft over the body.

It was Louella. Splayed out on the floor, a hideous circle of blood had been knifed across her neck.

Daphne screamed.

"I told you this was where we all die," Christopher shouted.

The music continued, though it was moving away. *Pop! goes the weasel!*

Ashlee turned the lamp toward the sound.

And there, only its face visible in the lamplight, was the clown, a few feet away and laughing at them, baring its awful teeth.

Suddenly, from behind them, Pete's rifle boomed through the darkness.

There was a scream.

But it hadn't been the clown Pete had hit. The clown danced out of the spotlight into the darkness, still laughing at them.

Ashlee moved the lamp toward the floor.

It was Ben who lay at their feet. He was bleeding from his chest.

NINETEEN

"Oh, my God, Ben!" Daphne cried, dropping to her knees and checking on her friend. "Ben, can you hear me?"

"Yeah," he managed to say, though it was obvious he was in great pain. "I think he hit my shoulder, that's all. . . ."

Daphne had learned a little first aid at Our Lady, and she tried to inspect his wound, with the pitiful amount of light coming from Ashlee's lamp. Meanwhile, she could hear Pete blustering, "What? What? What?" in disbelief over what he had done.

"Damn fool," Gabe's voice came from the dark. "I knew the old man shouldn't have that gun."

Daphne heard the sound of ripping fabric, and suddenly she felt the wheels of Gabriel's chair beside her. He handed her a piece of his shirt. "Wrap Ben's wound in this," he told her.

She accepted the shirt and got to work. "I can't see it very well, Ben, but we can keep it wrapped tight to stop the bleeding," she told him.

"We're all going to die!" Christopher keened behind her.

"Shut that child up," Abigail's voice snapped from the dark.

"You all need to get to the study," Ben said. "That maniac is going to come back."

"We're not leaving you here," Daphne told him. "Can you walk?"

"I can try," Ben said, and as soon as Daphne had tied a knot in the makeshift bandage across his shoulder, he got to his feet. He managed to stand up, though he seemed dizzy.

"Come on," Daphne said, "hang on to me."

He did so, with Christopher clinging to Daphne's other side.

They had to walk around Louella's dead body. She was so large that she took up most of the corridor. Ashlee actually had to lift the dead woman's arm so that Gabriel could get his wheelchair through.

"We just need to barricade ourselves in the study," Ben said, gritting his teeth through his pain. "Then we can wait out this storm."

Gabriel had rolled ahead of them. The light from Ashlee's lamp reflected off the chrome of his wheelchair as he got up close to Pete.

"I think you really ought to give me the rifle now, Uncle Pete, before you do any more damage," Gabriel said.

The old man handed it over without any further protest.

Gabe accepted it, and held it in both his hands. "Looks like I'm in charge now, with Ben wounded and Uncle Pete admitting he's incapable."

Ashlee had stopped walking and looked down at Gabe. "Well, I wouldn't necessarily say you were in charge, Gabriel. After all, I'm still fully functional. And so are Daphne and Abigail for that matter."

"Women," Gabe said dismissively, rolling on ahead of them into the darkness of the corridor.

Daphne could see the annoyed look on Ashlee's face in the backlight of her lamp.

"Where's Boris?" Daphne whispered to Ben. "Any clue?"

"None." He made a sound in pain. "I guess you're right. I guess he's the one in the clown suit."

They had reached the study. Gabriel had positioned himself out front in his wheelchair, holding the rifle across his lap.

"Everyone go inside," he ordered.

"My brother seems to have finally gotten what he's always wanted," Ben said softly to Daphne. "Power over the rest of us."

"Are there any candles in the study?" Ashlee was asking, as she turned into the room, carrying the lamp. "This lamp is sputtering again. We need backup."

Abigail rushed over to the cabinets and began pulling drawers. Ben handed his phone to Christopher and told him to hold up the light. "That's a good man," he said, giving his young cousin an encouraging smile as the boy did as he was instructed.

"I don't see any candles," Abigail said, in despair.

"Here's one," Daphne said, withdrawing one from a bookcase. "But we have no matches. They all got wet in the parlor."

Outside the snow and wind whooped against the windows. Daphne prayed another one wouldn't blow open.

Ashlee had set the lamp down on the center table. It gave off a weak glow, but it was enough for them all to see their way. Daphne helped Ben settle down on the sofa, and made sure his wound was wrapped tightly. Christopher stayed close by her. Pete sat in the chair that was usually reserved for him, a great wingback. He seemed beaten by all this, and was breathing heavily. Daphne noticed that Ashlee wasn't as attentive to him as she usually was, not nearly so solicitous. She just stood looking out at the storm. Daphne wondered if she was hoping her lover might return and save them.

She had the same wish about Gregory, she had to admit. She kept hoping somehow that Gregory could arrive, like the cavalry in all those western movies they used to watch at Our Lady. Just in the nick of time, the cavalry would arrive to save the day. But Gregory was just one man. How could he get through this storm and make his way to her? And even if he could, what then? How did anyone fight a madman in the dark?

On the table, the lamp sputtered and died.

"Oh, no!" shouted Abigail.

"Don't anybody panic," Ashlee said. "I got it working before, I'll do it again now."

Daphne heard her moving across the carpet

and discerned the sound of the lamp's lid being removed.

"Everybody okay in there?" Gabe shouted in from the doorway.

"Yes," Daphne replied. "But I really think you should come in and close the door behind you now."

"I can't see a thing," Gabe said. "When Ashlee gets the lamp fixed I'll—"

The sound of his voice ended abruptly.

"Gabriel?" Daphne called.

No reply.

"Gabe?" Ben shouted.

Total silence, except for the howling wind outside.

Christopher began to moan in fear.

It was utterly black. The only things Daphne could make out even in the slightest were the windows, but even these seemed to fade into the blackness of the night. Still, she stood, and took a few steps in the direction of the door.

"Gabriel?" she whispered.

"Daphne, get back here!" Ben called.

"Daphne!" Christopher cried.

Suddenly there was light. Ashlee had succeeded in relighting the lamp.

And in the doorway of the study they saw Gabriel's overturned wheelchair. From the darkness of the corridor protruded one foot in a puddle of blood.

"Gabriel!" Daphne exclaimed, and rushed to help the fallen young man.

But as she did so, something else appeared in the doorway.

The clown.

Daphne recoiled.

It laughed, gnashing those sharp teeth. In the dim golden glow of the lamp, Daphne saw the terror that bloomed on the faces of everyone who had doubted her in the room. Abigail, Pete, even Ben.

The clown observed them all, rubbing its big mittened hands. Its red nose twitched, as if smelling their blood.

They were trapped. Backed into a small room, the clown blocking their own means of escape.

But together, Daphne realized, they could overpower him. He was just one old man, after all.

It was with that thought in her mind that Daphne watched events unfold over the next few seconds—events that she couldn't quite fathom at first.

Suddenly, behind the clown, she saw the face of Boris.

Boris.

The butler.

The butler with the sharp yellow teeth.

Boris stood behind the clown, and he was raising something in his hands.

But how could that be possible? Boris *was* the clown!

Yet there was Boris, with a fireplace poker in his hands, and he was bringing it down now on the clown's head!

"Boris!" Ashlee screamed.

Her outburst gave the clown just enough time to react. It spun around, grabbing a hold of the poker before it could hit him, and using it instead to knock the butler to his feet. Then, quick as a flash, the clown produced its razor blade, and—slash, slash!—cut Boris's throat so deep that Daphne heard it scrape bone.

Ashlee screamed again as Boris's blood shot up like geysers.

The music started playing then, and the clown jumped up in the air in a kind of giddy celebration, laughing and chomping its teeth, before it vanished in the dark down the corridor.

Daphne leapt forward and pulled the door to the study shut.

"That door stays locked now," she shouted, "so that monster can't get back in to get any more of us!"

She looked around. Where there had been twelve of them, now there was just six.

"Why did you scream?" she demanded, rushing up to Ashlee. "It gave the clown a chance to react."

"I'm sorry," Ashlee said, shaking. "I was so scared. I thought you said Boris was the killer."

"It doesn't matter," Pete said, hunched down in his chair. "Boris wouldn't have been able to hurt it. How could he hurt something that isn't alive?"

Abigail shuddered. "Pete, what are you saying?"

The old man looked up at Daphne. "I owe you an apology, my dear. All your talk of ghosts . . . I was too stubborn to listen."

Abigail looked as if she might faint. "You really think . . . that clown is the ghost of our father?"

"What else can I believe now?" Pete seemed to be shrinking in size in that large chair. "He told Louella that he would come back. Oh, I've always known the horrors weren't over. That creature who called *itself* our father ruined all of our lives." He looked over at Daphne and suddenly reached out and gripped her hand in his own. "All of our lives, Daphne. Do you understand? All of our lives."

Christopher was sitting on the sofa, staring ahead, unblinking. He was almost catatonic in his fear. Daphne let go of the father's hand to tend to the son.

"It's okay, Christopher," she said, kneeling down in front of him. "We're safe here now. It's gone."

"But it will come back," he told her plainly.

Ben was struggling to stand, but the pain now seemed to be overwhelming him. "I need to check on Gabe," he mumbled. "He might not be dead."

"That thing has killed everything it's touched," Pete said. "There's no reason to believe he failed with Gabriel."

"But we don't know for sure," Ben said, making it to his feet.

Ashlee positioned herself between him and the door. "If you open that door," she told him forcefully, "that monster will lunge right back in here, and kill us all."

"But the rifle is out there, too," Ben argued, his voice getting weaker.

"It's not worth it," Ashlee insisted.

"No rifle can stop something that isn't alive," Pete groaned.

Ben clutched his shoulder. The wound was bad. Daphne saw how much blood he was losing. His whole shirt was sopped in it. She hoped he wouldn't pass out from the loss of blood. Ben took one more step toward the door, then flopped back down onto the couch.

They were all silent for a few minutes, conscious only of their breathing and the gusts of wind and sleet and snow that were hitting the house. Daphne tried to think. The clown was not Boris. That much was obvious now. So it had to be the ghost of Pete Witherspoon Senior.

She hadn't wanted to believe in a supernatural solution to this mystery. She hadn't been raised by Mother Angela to believe in ghosts and the possibility of the occult. But what other answer now made sense? She had seen the ghost close up, right outside that window, soon after she had come here. That should have been proof enough. But if she needed more, all she had to remember was the crypt. Only something undead could have gotten out of that room without Gregory seeing it.

Again she longed for Gregory. Would she make it out of here? She had promised Christopher that they would live, but did she really believe that now, after seeing Axel, Louella, Gabriel, and Boris struck down, one by one? Would she really live to see the sun again? Would she really once again be in Gregory's arms?

If only they had all left Witherswood with Ashlee's lover . . . piled on the back of his snowmobile, as many as could fit. Or at least given him a message to bring back help. Might he even come back, and rescue them yet?

But of course Ashlee's lover—John was his name—had left without knowing the danger they were all in. He had thought the only danger they faced was running out of food during this storm. . . .

All of this terror had begun right after Ashlee's lover left, Daphne thought. From that moment on, the killings began. . . .

"Well, I don't know about everybody else," Abigail suddenly announced, her shrill voice shattering the silence, "but I am not going to just sit here and wait for that killer to come back."

"What other choice do we have?" Daphne asked her.

"We might be trapped here for days!" Abigail insisted loudly, her hands waving in the air. "The storm might finally let up by morning, but it can take weeks to get the power back sometimes. And it will be at least several days for the plows to get this high up the hill. We could be prisoners of this madman for a very long time!"

She spoke the truth, Daphne realized, but still she saw no other option.

"I'm getting out of here," Abigail said, standing up all at once. "I'd rather face this storm than that lunatic clown!"

"You mean, you're going *outside?*" Daphne asked in bewilderment.

"I most certainly am," she replied. "I'll make it down the hill to get help, or I'll die in the process. At least it will be the cold and snow that kills me, and not some maniac's razor."

"That's lunacy, Abigail," Pete said, finding it difficult to speak. "As Ashlee said, you open that door and that beast is back in here."

"If it's a ghost," his sister snarled at him, "can't it just walk through the wall?"

Daphne had to admit Abigail had another good point. Why did they think they were safe behind a locked door if the adversary they faced was undead?

"I'm not going out through the door anyway," Abigail said. "I'm going out through the window. So everyone brace for the wind."

"I can't let you do this, Abigail," Pete said.

She looked down at him, arms akimbo. "All my life I've had to defer to your decisions, brother. Well, not tonight."

"Leaving this room to go into that storm is insanity!" Pete insisted, trying to raise his voice, but realizing he didn't have the strength. "You cannot go, Abigail."

"Are you going to stop me? Is Ben?"

She looked back over at her nephew, who seemed to be falling unconscious on the couch.

"Or maybe your silly little wife will keep me here," Abigail sniffed.

Ashlee glared at her, the years of resentment bubbling to the surface. "Oh, no, be my guest, Abigail," she said. "Here, I'll even open the window for you."

Walking over to the window, Ashlee lifted the latch and carefully pulled the glass pane open so that a minimum of snow and sleet would get into the room. Even still, a huge gust barreled inside, filling the room with cold air and shrieking wind. "Go ahead," Ashlee shouted over the noise. "Climb out, Abigail."

Abigail didn't hesitate. Pulling her wool sweater closer around her, she stepped over the ledge. The ground was only a couple of feet below the window, but since the snow had drifted so high, Abigail actually had to step *up* as she left the house. Pete wouldn't watch. He just covered his face with his hands again.

Daphne couldn't believe Abigail had really left them. But maybe she was right. Maybe it *was* the only way.

"Good riddance," Ashlee grumbled as she latched the window shut.

A few seconds later, they heard a thud.

Abigail hadn't gotten very far. All at once, she was pressed against the window, her face splayed against the glass. Had she fallen? The swirling snow and pitch-black night air prevented anyone from seeing clearly what was happening out there.

But they could hear Abigail screaming. With tightly clenched fists, she banged on the windows, her eyes looking into the room blazing with fear and pain. From the front of her sweater, blood suddenly blossomed, oozing onto the glass of the windows and running down in rivulets that quickly hardened in the freezing air. The way Abigail's body was thrusting against the glass told the story. Something behind her was stabbing her to death.

In mute horror, the whole room watched as Abigail struggled for her life. Her body jerked and convulsed against the glass. Finally there was no struggle left, and Abigail's lifeless body slunk down into the snow, leaving a trail of blood along the glass. All that was left of her was a bloody clump right outside the window.

Underneath the wind and the sleet, the tinny music soared:

All around the mulberry bush, the monkey chased the weasel. . . .

For the first time, Daphne thought Christopher was right.

They were all going to do die this night.

TWENTY

"I told her not to leave," Pete gasped, and suddenly he grabbed his chest and slunk down in his chair.

Still standing by the window, Ashlee watched him closely. "Pete?" she whispered.

The old man did not move.

Daphne rushed over to him, dropping to her knees in front of his chair.

"Mr. Witherspoon!" she cried. "Mr. Witherspoon, are you all right?"

She grabbed his wrist and felt his pulse. He was alive, though the twist of his lips and droop of his eyes worried Daphne.

"I think he's had a stroke," she told Ashlee.

Ashlee walked over to her husband calmly and stroked his hair. "Poor Pete," she said, almost distractedly.

She's losing touch with reality, Daphne thought. That wasn't hard to understand given the situation. After watching all this mayhem and bloodletting, how could anyone stay sane?

But Daphne was determined to keep her wits.

She gripped Pete's hands and squeezed. "Mr. Witherspoon, can you hear me? Squeeze my hand if you can. Or open your eyes. Give me a sign that you can hear me and understand me."

She felt a soft squeeze of her fingers and his eyelids fluttered.

"Can you speak?" she asked.

"Yes," he said, though he was barely audible.

"I need to ask you something," Daphne said. "Can you try to answer me?"

She felt the weak press of his fingers into hers again.

"Is there a secret passageway in this room? I was told there were passageways all through the house. I'm looking for some way to get out of here, and also perhaps to hide in for safety?"

"The desk," he whispered.

"The desk?"

He squeezed her hand.

"There's a secret passageway behind the desk?"

She didn't wait for confirmation now, just flew over to the desk and pulled it away from the wall. There seemed to be nothing there, just paneling.

"Where is it?" Daphne asked, returning to her place kneeling in front of Pete. "How do I access the passageway?"

"Feel . . ." he whispered with difficulty. "Lever."

She moved back over to the wall and moved her hand across the entire area. She was about to give up when she felt a bump, a small rise in the paneling. She pushed it. A low hum reached her ears as the paneling began to slide, revealing a rectangular opening about three feet wide by four feet tall.

"Where does it take us?" Daphne asked.

"Storage . . . room . . ."

"The storage room in the basement?" Daphne asked.

Pete nodded his head slightly.

"Where exactly does the passage bring us out in the storage room?" she asked. "Where is the secret panel found there?"

His sunken eyes, with life seeming to fade away from them every second, locked on to hers.

"Behind . . ." He struggled to speak the words. "Box marked M."

The box marked M.

Daphne knew this wasn't exactly the best time to bring up unrelated topics, but it was very possible that she'd never have the chance again, she realized. Mr. Witherspoon might not make it through the night. She might not either, and if she was going to die, she wanted to know a few things first.

"I was in the storage room earlier," she told him. "I found the box marked M."

There was no reaction from Pete, at least none that she could discern.

"M stands for Maria, doesn't it?"

She took his hands again. He managed to squeeze hers, replying in the affirmative.

"Did you and Maria have a child together?"

"What are you asking, Daphne?" Ashlee inquired, standing over her.

Daphne ignored her. "Mr. Witherspoon, did you and Maria have a daughter?"

"You're harassing him!" Ashlee said, some of

the fire back in her voice. "Leave Pete alone! Can't you see he's weak?"

"Yes," the old man managed to whisper, his eyes opening and staring directly into Daphne's.

That's when the blade of the ax smashed through the door.

Christopher screamed.

The blade twisted and turned, as the thing wielding it extricated it from the wood. A second later it came crashing down again, slicing through another part of the door.

"Christopher!" Daphne shouted. "Quick! Into the passageway!"

The little boy scrambled across the room and hopped into the opening on the wall.

"Can you walk at all?" Daphne asked Pete. "Do you think you could pull him through?" she asked Ashlee.

But Ashlee just stood there, looking at her as if in a daze.

Daphne hurried over to Ben. She shook him. "Ben! Can you hear me?"

Ben didn't move. The couch where he sat was now drenched in blood. The makeshift tourniquet Daphne had applied to his shoulder hadn't sufficiently stopped the bleeding. Ben's hands were cold. He didn't stir.

Daphne realized the truth.

He had bled to death.

"Oh, God, Ben," Daphne cried, lifting his hand to her mouth and kissing it.

Another blow to the door from the ax.

"Daphne!" Christopher cried from the passageway.

She ran back to Ashlee. "We've got to get out of here," she said to Ashlee, who stood looking down at Pete in his chair. "Ben's dead. And if we can't save Pete, then you've got to come along with us now, Ashlee, and save yourself!"

Ashlee looked up at her with the strangest look in her eyes that Daphne had ever seen. "Why leave so soon?" she asked in a singsong voice. "The party's just begun. . . ."

She's gone crazy, Daphne thought to herself.

The ax slammed into the door again, breaking open a hole that allowed Daphne to catch a glimpse of green and red polka dots.

"Mr. Witherspoon!" Daphne cried. "Can you walk? Can you come with us?"

He made no sound, no move. Even when she grabbed his hands, there was no indication from him. Had he died too?

The music started then, and Daphne knew she had only seconds.

She looked over at Ashlee, who just stared at her crazily.

With a heavy heart, she left them behind. She grabbed the lamp and bolted for the passageway. Leaping through, she immediately turned with difficulty in the small space to pull the panel shut. But in the split second before she did so, she saw the door finally splinter into pieces and the clown's big rubber purple foot step inside the study. Daphne began to cry, thinking what that monster would do to Ashlee and Pete.

Thankfully, there was a small locking latch on this side of the panel—nothing that could hold back an ax, Daphne knew, but it might give them a little time.

"Move!" she whispered to Christopher, who obeyed instantly.

Once into the passageway, the ceiling above them was higher, and they were able to stand. But the width was extremely narrow, no more than three feet and sometimes only two. The passageway, Daphne discerned, had literally been built between the walls of the house. She held the lamp aloft to allow them to see where they were going.

After they had walked a few yards, they came to a set of very narrow stairs leading down. Mr. Witherspoon had said the passage led to the storage room, so this would be the way into the basement. Daphne held up the lamp, and they started down the stairs.

Daphne's plan was to make it to the storage room and barricade themselves in there. That heavy iron door would resist the maniac's ax. What Daphne did *not* want was to meet up with the clown here, in this narrow passageway. There would be no escape then.

As they made their way down the narrow steps, cobwebs sticking to their faces, Daphne held the lamp in her right hand and Christopher's hand in her left. How very different their relationship had become in such a short time. She was all the boy had now, literally. If for nothing else, Daphne vowed she would survive this night for Christopher's sake. No doubt his father was now dead in the study, a victim of the clown's razor—or maybe his ax. Daphne shuddered. What a horrible way to die. Ashlee, too—sweet, funny Ashlee, who'd been her first friend in this house.

Everyone was dead.

Everyone but her and Christopher.

Daphne vowed to keep it that way.

As they reached the end of the stairs, the passageway veered off in two directions. Daphne had no idea which way led to the storage room.

"What do we do now?" Christopher wailed.

"I'm not sure," Daphne said. "Let me think."

She tried to visualize the layout of the house. They had come from the study. Where did that leave them in relation to the storage room? Was it to their right or to their left?

For some reason, she staked their very survival on getting to the storage room. She wasn't sure why. Yes, its iron door protected them from the danger of an ax. But if their adversary was undead . . . a ghost . . . then nothing could keep them safe.

But ghosts didn't need axes to break down doors.

"Which way, Daphne?" Christopher urged.

She had to make a decision. "This way," she said, knowing she had a fifty–fifty chance of being correct, and pushed Christopher along to the right.

At the end of the narrow passageway, there was another sliding panel as there had been in the study. With trembling fingers, Daphne pushed it open. Bending down, she peered through. They were in the basement, but not the storage room. Ahead of them stood the furnace, silent now. Daphne realized that with the power out, the heat was also off. The temperatures would keep dropping. It was already bracingly cold, she suddenly realized. The rest of the night's dangers hadn't given her much time to think about the temperature. But, in fact, she was starting to be able to see her breath in front of her face.

They had a choice. They could either go back along the passageway, expecting it to lead them directly to the storage room, or they could exit here. The storage room wasn't far away from this point, Daphne realized. She figured this was the better choice. Who knew how long the passageway would continue winding its way through the walls before depositing them in the storage room?

So she stepped gingerly through the opening, lamp first, then turned around to give Christopher a hand as he stepped through as well.

Carefully they moved across the basement, wary of making any sound. If even one of the old boxes stacked all around them was sent clattering to the floor, the clown would hear, and would make a beeline to the basement, razor in one hand, ax in the other. So it was with deliberate, cautious steps that Daphne and Christopher made their way through the clutter of the Witherswood basement, guided by the kerosene lamp, which was once again beginning to flicker.

Just stay lit until we get to the storage room, Daphne prayed.

Something up ahead caught her eye.

Something on the ground.

Something that looked very strange sitting on the floor.

She squeezed Christopher's hand as an indication that he should stop walking. He looked up at her, and Daphne lifted a finger, a sign to wait a moment.

Stealthily she took a few steps forward on her own.

The thing on the ground seemed to grin up at her.

She held the lamp over it.

It was a set of teeth.

Long, sharp, yellow teeth.

TWENTY-ONE

Daphne was loath to pick them up, as the teeth were covered with saliva. But as near as she could tell, they were plastic.

"Plastic teeth," she breathed.

Christopher had come to stand beside her. "You mean," he said, looking down, "that clown isn't real?"

"Oh, it's real all right," she said. "That's just the thing. It's very real. As real as you or I."

Daphne realized she had been right to doubt the supernatural explanation. They didn't face a ghost. She was now convinced, yet again, that their foe was very human.

Who it was, she didn't know.

But clearly it was someone who, as the sheriff had speculated, was obsessed with the original killings, and who, for reasons they couldn't fathom, was trying to re-create them. Someone, perhaps, who had a vendetta against the Witherspoons . . .

No, Daphne told herself as the thought crept back into her mind.

It is not Gregory.

But the clown had, so far, spared her. Was that a twisted, perverse message that he cared about her, that his grudge didn't extend to her, that he'd spare her—even if he forced her to witness the carnage all around her?

No, that's crazy, Daphne told herself.

Gregory saved me from the crypt! The clown—

She stopped in her tracks as she thought of something terrible.

She had passed out when the clown entered the chamber. And when she'd awakened, Gregory was there. If he was the clown, then that would have given him time enough to change out of the suit, wipe off the makeup, and appear to be Daphne's savior, and not her tormentor.

But why would he scare her at all in the crypt, if that was the case? What purpose would that serve if his mission was to get revenge on the Witherspoons?

It could give him the beginnings of an alibi. . . . Daphne would tell the police of the clown, and that Gregory had saved her, and then the clown had come and killed the family. . . .

This is absurd! Gregory would never do any of this, no matter how much anger and resentment he held against Pete Witherspoon!

Was she sure? She hadn't known him very long, after all.

"Come on," she whispered to Christopher, pushing the thoughts out of her mind and grabbing the boy's hand.

Daphne and Christopher took another few steps and discovered something else on the floor.

A clown suit.

Not just *a* clown suit. *The* clown suit.

In the lamp's glow, Daphne saw dried blood covering the suit's red and green polka dots. Crumpled cloths were covered with gooey white makeup. Off to the side she spotted the white mittens and purple shoes and wild orange wig. And beside the shoes . . . a tiny tape recorder.

Daphne didn't need to turn it on to know the only thing that recorder played was "Pop Goes the Weasel."

The killer had come down here to change out of his costume. Perhaps that meant he was done with his reign of terror. Maybe he assumed Daphne and Christopher had escaped and so had given up—which would mean they were now safe.

Or—it could mean they were in more danger than ever.

If the killer had come down here to change out of his clown suit, Daphne realized, then he could still be in the basement somewhere. He might be hiding. In fact, he might be watching them at this very moment. . . .

"Come on, Christopher," Daphne urged again, and they walked quickly toward the corridor that led to the storage room.

Once there, Daphne first used the lamp to illuminate all the dark corners and assure herself no one had hidden there to surprise them. Then she bolted the door from the inside. But her next task was just as important as the first two. She lifted the lamp toward the place on the bottom shelf where she had removed the box marked M. At the time, she had been too focused on the box itself to look behind it. But now, sure enough, she saw a panel on the wall. This was where she and Christopher would have emerged had they taken the left-side passageway. And this was where the killer could still get in to kill them.

"Christopher," she said loudly. "Help me shove this chest against the panel!"

She quickly removed the box marked M that she had left sitting on top, and grabbed ahold of one end of the chest. Christopher joined her, and they began to push. It did no good. The chest was just too heavy to move.

"Maybe we can take some stuff out and make it lighter," Christopher suggested.

"We want it to be heavy!" Daphne cried. "So he can't move it if he tries to get in. Push again!"

This time they succeeded in moving it a few inches. Another shove produced another half a foot. The chest had been sitting there so long it had become stuck to the floor. With extraordinary effort, fueled by the adrenaline caused by knowing a killer was somewhere in the house, Daphne and Christopher managed to shove the chest across the room. Then they pushed it up onto the bottom shelf, pressing it against the wall and wedging it under the shelf immediately above. Doing so effectively sealed over the secret panel. Nothing was going to be strong enough to push that chest from the other side of the panel, not with it being wedged between the shelves in this way. And there wasn't enough room on the other side of the panel to swing the ax, either, so chopping through the chest wasn't a possibility. For the moment, therefore, Daphne felt relatively safe.

She sat back against the shelves and let out a deep breath. Christopher nestled in beside her.

"That clown can't get us in here?" he asked.

"Not here," she told him, slipping an arm around the little boy. "We're safe, here."

"Those voices were wrong," he said.

Daphne looked over at him. "What voices?"

"The voices I'd hear at night, telling me if I got rid of you, my mother would come back."

"You heard voices telling you that?"

He nodded, and the tears sprang from his eyes again. "That's why I locked you in the crypt. I thought . . ." His tears took over for a moment, and he couldn't speak. "I thought if you were dead, my mother would come alive again. I'm sorry, Daphne."

"It's okay, Christopher. It's all in the past now."

She pulled him in tighter.

What were the voices Christopher heard? Were they in his head, part of his deep emotional problems?

Or did someone—or something—deliberately try to plant that idea in his head to get rid of me?

Daphne closed her eyes. Her mind was having a hard time accepting everything that had happened this night. Everyone in the house was dead, except for the two of them. Her friends and her foes alike. Everyone she had met when she first came to Witherswood those few months ago—which now seemed like years ago—had been brutally murdered.

Every single one! Donovan, Suzanne, Louella, Abigail, Axel, Boris, Gabriel, Ben, Ashlee, and Pete. She could scarcely comprehend the fact that she and Christopher were the only ones left.

And how long would they have to stay in this room? Until the blizzard passed, she felt certain. And even longer than that, she realized, until the roads were passable again. Abigail had been right: no one could get up that twisting cliffside road until the snow and ice were removed. That might take days. And they had nothing in here to eat or drink. It was going to be difficult. But it beat being out there, in the house, where the killer waited with his long sharp blade.

"How long will the clown stay out there?" Christopher asked, as if reading Daphne's mind and anticipating her next question.

"I don't know," she answered, but she had her suspicions. Whoever he was, he couldn't get down the hill any more than someone could get up to rescue them. He was as stranded here as Daphne and Christopher, waiting out the blizzard. That meant their wait could be very long indeed.

Daphne glanced over at the box marked M, now sitting beside them on the floor. Reaching inside, she pulled out a letter at random, and opened it, reading it by the dim glow of the kerosene lamp.

This was the only solution, of course. My parents had turned me out. This was the only place that would accept me. She will have a good life here. I assure you.

Signed, *M.*

Daphne put the letter back into the box. What did Maria mean, "This was the only place that would accept me"? Had her parents disowned her because she had become pregnant by Pete—the son of the notorious serial killer?

Is that what Pete meant when he'd said to her upstairs that his father's heinous crimes had ruined all of their lives? He had looked at Daphne when he'd said it, implying his monstrous father had left an imprint on *her* life, as well.

Was she, then, Pete's daughter?

She looked over at the little boy resting his head on her shoulder.

Was Christopher her brother?

The lamp flickered and died at that moment, and they were left in darkness. Christopher began to whimper.

"It's okay," Daphne assured him. "It's okay."

The blackness was absolute in the room. There was no place where any light could seep in. They wouldn't be able to distinguish between night and day if they were forced to spend a long stretch of time in this place.

Daphne tried to keep her mind focused.

If Pete was her father, then what had happened to Maria? From the letters, it would seem that Maria had started off raising her daughter herself. But if Daphne was, in fact, that daughter, then at some point Maria had turned her over to the sisters at Our Lady. Why? Where did Maria go? Was she dead? Or was she—Daphne's mother—still alive somewhere?

Questions lingered, but so much was starting to make sense. Now Daphne understood why Pete would send for her out of the blue to come live with him. Now she understood why Mother Angela would say this place was her destiny.

But was it her destiny to die here?

Was it Daphne's destiny to die just as she had stumbled upon the first clues to her true identity, before ever finding out the whole truth?

No doubt the clown had slit Pete's throat upstairs just as he had done to everyone else. So there would be no answers forthcoming from Pete. If anyone in this house had known the truth, they had taken it with them to their graves.

She thought of Pete, slunk down in his chair with his face twisted from an apparent stroke.

Her father.

That was her father.

She started to cry.

All her life she'd longed to know who her parents were. And now that she had found out, it was too late.

But the truth seemed clear to her now. More answers might be found in the box beside her, and hopefully she'd have a chance to go through everything that was in there, at some safe, relaxed moment in the future.

But at the moment, she thought she knew the basic fact.

She was . . . a Witherspoon.

And with the thought came another one, immediately following.

So maybe that's why Gregory would want to torment me.

She reacted forcefully, arguing with herself.

Stop that! Gregory is not the killer!

But *if* he was, and *if* he knew the truth about her, maybe that explained why he'd put her through all this. He'd certainly carry his hatred of Pete toward his daughter. Daphne struggled against believing it, but if Gregory really was the one who'd put on the clown suit and slaughtered the entire family, then he wouldn't stop until the last Witherspoon blood had been spilled. Maybe he hadn't, in fact, spared Daphne. Maybe he was outside that door right now, waiting for her, waiting to slit her throat.

Daphne shuddered.

Christopher noticed. "Are you okay, Daphne?"

"Yes," she lied. "Just feeling a little cold, that's all."

"I'm cold, too."

She tightened her grip on him.

"Listen, Christopher" she said. "It's going to get colder. And we're going to get hungry. And we are going to have to get used to the dark. I don't know how long we are going to have stay in here—"

Her words were cut off by a rapping at the door. Both of them froze.

"Daphne? Daphne, are you in there?"

The voice was soft, difficult to hear, because the door was so thick.

"Daphne? Oh God, Daphne, are you there?"

"It's Ashlee," Daphne whispered to Christopher. Ashlee was alive!

"Ashlee?" Daphne asked through the door. "Is that you?"

"Oh, yes, Daphne, it's me! I got away! I got away!"

"Where is he?" Daphne asked, her ear pressed up against the door to hear better. "The clown?"

"I don't know," Ashlee replied. "But I've got the rifle, and I'm ready to use it!"

Daphne hesitated. "If I open the door to let you in, will you be quick enough to shoot him if he makes a lunge for us?"

"Oh, yes, Daphne! But I don't want to come in. I want you to come out! Jim has come back with his snowmobile. He can get us out of here. It will fit all of us!"

"We're rescued!" Christopher cheered, hearing the bit about the snowmobile.

"Thank God," Daphne breathed, and feeling with her hand along the door, she found the bolt and pulled it back.

As she promised, Ashlee was standing guard with the rifle, looking around the corridor to make sure no one lurked in the shadows. A giant, industrial-sized flashlight stood propped on the floor. Daphne, and then Christopher, stepped gingerly out of the storage room.

"Come on," Ashlee urged them. "He's waiting outside."

She picked up the flashlight in one hand, the rifle lodged under her other arm, and guided them through the dark. Yet as they headed down the corridor to the main part of the basement, something felt wrong to Daphne. Very, very wrong. She couldn't quite put her finger on it, but suddenly she wished that she and Christopher had never left the darkness of the storage room.

They passed the clown suit on the ground.

And then it hit Daphne.

"Ashlee," she said. "You told me the name of your friend with the snowmobile was John."

"Yeah," she said. "That's what I said. John. He's come back."

"You said Jim."

"I did not. I said John. You just misheard me." She looked over at Daphne impatiently. "Come on. Let's go!"

As they turned past a pile of old chests and boxes, Daphne gasped.

Ahead of them, Gabriel sat in his wheelchair.

"Gabriel!" Daphne exclaimed.

"Yes," Ashlee said behind her. "I forgot to mention. Gabriel survived too."

"Hello, Daphne, hello, Christopher," Gabriel said, in a voice that seemed different somehow.

Daphne's eyes dropped to the floor. Beside the wheelchair, she spotted something very odd. The feet and legs of a mannequin—a store dummy—dressed in men's pants and shoes. In her mind flashed again the scene in the hallway when the clown had appeared at the door of the study. Gabriel's wheelchair had been overturned, and from the darkness a pair of legs had protruded. Gabriel's legs, they had presumed.

But no.

It was the mannequin's legs.

"You look so surprised to see me, Daphne," Gabriel said, smiling broadly. "I would think you'd be glad to discover that I was still alive."

Daphne watched as he gripped the arms of his wheelchair.

Her mouth fell open.

Gabriel stood.

And then he began to walk—*walk!*

Daphne's eyes spun over to Ashlee, who, she saw to her horror, was now pointing the rifle directly at her.

Her gaze returned to Gabriel.

He was coming toward her, carrying in his hands the long, bloodstained razor.

TWENTY-TWO

"It was you!" Daphne breathed in terror. "It was you all along!"

"Yes, Daphne, I was the clown." Gabriel had paused in his approach toward her, running the long, sharp razor between his fingers. "Gosh, it's good to be out of that ridiculous suit and makeup and wig. You can imagine what a sweat I broke out in running around in that thing all the time!"

"How long have you been able to walk?" Daphne managed to ask. She realized Christopher was standing behind her, clinging on to her arm.

"Oh, years," Gabriel told her offhandedly. "The doctors always said they were hopeful I'd walk again, and seemed perplexed when I couldn't. I stopped going to see them, and practiced on my own. I got in good shape, too, planning for this day."

"Why would you do all this?" Daphne cried. "Kill your whole family!"

"Because they killed me!" Gabriel shouted, the veins in his forehead suddenly standing out in relief, highlighted by the glow of the large flashlight Ashlee had propped once again on the ground. "Don't you see? My whole life has been contaminated by these people. My cowardly uncle Pete, whose failure to turn in my grandfather meant that I'd forever be a pariah in this town, among my peers. His negligence meant my father was killed. And without my father, Uncle Pete was able to bully my mother into doing anything he wanted. And then to rub salt in the wound, he always preferred Donovan to me."

"But Ben! How could you let your own brother die? Your brother who was always good to you?"

"Good to me? Ben was part of the problem. Did he ever stand up for me to Donovan? To Uncle Pete? Never!"

"I don't think you're remembering correctly," Daphne told him.

His eyes blazed. "Why is that, Daphne? You think I'm crazy?" And he laughed. It was the laugh she had heard before, from the clown.

"Come on, Gabe," Ashlee said. "Let's get this over with."

Daphne spun on her. "I thought you were my friend," she said.

"Oh, sweetie, I *was* your friend," Ashlee said, sighing impatiently. "Look, I tried to get you to leave here many times. I encouraged you to go off with Gregory Winston. I gave you several opportunities to hightail it out of here. Neither Gabe nor I originally planned to include you in any of this. You just would never leave!"

"I tried scaring you," Gabriel said, "like that very first day you came to Point Woebegone. Ashlee deliberately didn't write your arrival in Axel's log until he was already gone, so that we could meet you at the train. On the deserted platform, I'd appear in my clown suit. A little ghostly vision for your first introduction to the place!"

"But Gregory Winston beat us to you," Ashlee grumbled, "and so we decided on a last-minute change of plans. Actually, it worked out to our advantage, didn't it, Gabe?"

"Yeah, it was perfect," he said. "I got to kill Maggie and give you a little glimpse of me in my clown suit at the same time!"

"Why would you want to kill Maggie?" Daphne asked. "She had nothing to do with your family."

"Yeah, but she had everything to do with me, see?" Ashlee said. "She was my friend. She knew too much. So . . . she had to go."

"Besides," Gabriel added, "we thought witnessing a murder on your first night here would definitely send you running back to Boston." He sighed. "But you just wouldn't leave! I tried again, scaring you that day in the village, when I jumped out of the Dumpster at you. Now, *that* was a filthy chore, believe me! But I figured if I got you to quit and go running back to Boston, it would have been worth it!"

"You see, sweetie, we really tried our best to not involve you in all this," Ashlee said, smiling over at her wistfully. "But you just never took the hint! Really, if you had left that time when you said you were going to, I'd have happily driven you to the train station myself and given you a big hug and wished you well on the rest of your life. You would

never have been dragged into any of this messi-
ness."

Ashlee's face turned hard.

"But then, a couple of days ago, Pete gave me a
bit of news that convinced me that it was better
that we kill you, too."

"Yeah," Gabriel agreed. "I already had too many
cousins anyway."

"What do you mean?" Daphne asked.

"Sweetie, come on! I know you figured it out!
You're Pete's daughter with that tramp Maria, the
great love of his life!" Ashlee frowned. "He told me
the truth the other night. He was going to tell you
himself. He figured it was time."

"So that's when we knew it was time to put our
final plan into action," Gabriel continued. "And
wow, this blizzard couldn't have been more timely!"

"So Gabriel was the one I saw you with earlier,"
Daphne said, looking over at Ashlee. "There was
no man on a snowmobile."

"Great deduction, Sherlock!" Ashlee said, laughing at her. "Yes, that was my sexy, adorable Gabe I
was kissing. Shit, that was a close one. We thought
you'd caught us."

"Ashlee, I salute you on your fast thinking,"
Gabe said, gesturing toward her with the razor in a
kind of perverted honor. "The lover with the gro-
ceries on the snowmobile . . . brilliant!"

"I learned pretty early in life how to think up
lies on the spot to get out of trouble, or to get what
I wanted," she said. "I didn't grow up with all the
luxuries the Witherspoons enjoyed in this house."

"How could you do this?" Daphne asked her, still

trying to make sense of this creature that stood before her, to reconcile her with the Ashlee she'd
thought she knew. "How could you allow all these
people to be killed in cold blood?"

"I hated them!" she shouted, her own rage now
obvious. "From the moment I walked into this
house, they all judged me, looked down their
noses at me! And Pete . . ." She laughed bitterly.
"Maybe, just maybe, for a minute, I could have
loved him. But it was clear his heart was with that
damn Maria. How could I compete with a memory? I understood what made sweet, sainted Peggy
jump out that window!"

"Now, now, babe," Gabriel said. "I made you feel
welcome, didn't I?"

"Yes, you did, sweet'ums," Ashlee cooed back,
making kissing sounds with her lips. "Really, Gabe
was my salvation here, Daphne. I don't know how
I'd have survived this crazy old house if not for
him. We'd meet in secret . . . oh, it was so romantic!"

"Maybe you hated the people in this house, but
why kill your friend Maggie?" Daphne asked.

"I told you," Ashlee said. "She found out too
much. One night, she came up to Witherswood,
and found Gabe and me together. And I knew how
that girl thought. We grew up together, remember! She came up here with me when I married
Pete. She hoped to snare one of the sons. Look, we
were both poor girls from the wrong side of the
tracks. But Donovan was with that bitch Suzanne,
and Ben was gay. So that left Gabe, and I remember Maggie said, 'Okay, so I'll take the cripple.'

But in fact, I'd already taken Gabe, and Maggie got pissed. I knew she couldn't be trusted, that she had knowledge that could blow our whole scheme open. So, she had to go."

"You're . . . both . . . reprehensible," Daphne managed to say.

Ashlee had moved over to stand beside Gabe, still pointing the rifle at Daphne and Christopher.

"What do you say, Gabe?" Ashlee asked. "How about if we just shoot them? It'll be quicker. And all this blood is getting me a bit queasy."

"No, dear, it has to be the blade," Gabriel replied. "Because the police have got to believe it was an intruder, a copycat killer, trying to re-create dear grandfather's crimes. Ben took a bullet, it's true, but we'll just tell the truth on that one. Uncle Pete was a lousy shot."

"So . . . you plan to tell the police that you survived the massacre?" Daphne asked.

"Of course, sweetie," Ashlee said. "We're going to hide in the storage room and wait out the blizzard. We'll tell the police we were hiding from the killer. It'll be just like you were going to do. But we've got some provisions to make it less of an ordeal." She nodded at a burlap sack beside Gabriel's wheelchair. "The sandwiches cook made for us, plus plenty of water bottles. Even a box of chocolate chip cookies. It will be kind of fun!"

"You're monsters," Daphne said, as Christopher's little hands dug deeper into her arm, his face buried in the back of her blouse.

"Of course, as Pete's widow, I get the whole estate," Ashlee said, "providing that little cretin behind you is dead. Oh, how that little brat annoyed me from the very first day I walked into this house, always whining about his sainted mother."

"You're cruel as well as monstrous," Daphne said.

"Not really," Ashlee said. "Gabe and I decided that after we get married, we'll name our first son Christopher. Didn't we Gabe?"

"I don't recall that," Gabriel replied quietly.

Ashlee laughed. "Oh, sure, we did. Christopher Peter Witherspoon. The town will find it so touching."

Gabriel looked over at Ashlee and smiled. "Actually, my dear, I don't recall ever deciding that we'd get married."

"Oh, but we did," she told him, an expression of confusion replacing her smile. "We talked about getting married many times."

"You talked about it," Gabe replied. "Not me."

"Well, we can discuss it later," Ashlee said, suddenly unnerved by the way Gabe was looking at her.

"No, we really can't," he told her, "because you see, there's not going to be a later. At least, not for you, Ashlee."

Her eyes widened in horror as Gabe took a step closer to her, the blade raised.

"Gabe, stop it!" Ashlee screamed. "You're scaring me!"

"I'm good at scaring people, it seems," he said, grinning wickedly. "You stupid bitch. Why would I share my inheritance, as Pete's only surviving heir, with such a common whore as you?"

Ashlee began to blubber, her words incoherent.

"Don't you understand?" Gabe asked. "I only loved one woman! And she's all I ever *will* love! Kathy Swenson! And this family took her from me!"

He lunged at Ashlee with the long blade. She lifted the rifle and pointed it at him, pulling the trigger and bracing for the blast.

But nothing happened.

Gabriel laughed. "You stupid, stupid bitch! Did you really think I'd hand over the rifle to you without first taking out the bullets?"

He whacked the weapon out of her hands. It went clattering across the concrete floor.

"I figure Daphne deserves to see you die before she does," Gabriel said, "since, after all, you were *such* a bad friend to her."

Ashlee screamed.

The blade swung.

Blood sprayed into the air like red paint thrown at a moving electric fan.

In the chaos of that fleeting instant, Daphne shoved Christopher away from her. "Run!" she shouted at the boy. "Run! Get out of here!"

The boy obeyed, his frantic footsteps echoing away in the dark basement.

But that was only part of Daphne's plan. She lunged for the large, heavy flashlight that was propped on the floor. Gripping it in her hands, she turned quickly and swung it at Gabriel's head—but found herself slipping in the pool of Ashlee's warm blood. Her swing went astray, and she toppled to the ground, falling over Ashlee's body. Her face came to rest only inches from her former friend, whose dead eyes stared at her.

Gabriel reached down and took hold of Daphne's arm. "I'll find the boy," he said calmly, seeming unperturbed by her attempt to overpower him. "Don't you worry about that." He flipped Daphne over so that she faced up at him. He was smiling. His smile chilled her to her soul.

"But first," Gabriel said, "it's finally time for you to die, Daphne. Pity, really, because you were the only one who was halfway decent to me in this house. But you're a Witherspoon, my dear. So that means you have to die."

He raised the blade over her throat.

TWENTY-THREE

Gabriel's furious eyes bore into her. Daphne felt the cold steel against her throat, much as she had the night in the crypt.

But then came a large thud, and Gabriel's face flew out of her field of vision.

She sat up.

Ben stood over her, the flashlight in his hands.

Gabriel was sprawled out beside him, moaning.

"Ben!" Daphne cried, astounded to see him alive.

Her friend stood looking down at her, his shirt drenched in blood. He swayed suddenly, as if he might fall down. Daphne jumped up and steadied him.

"You're alive!" she exclaimed, her arms tightly around his torso.

"Christopher found me," he mumbled. "He told me . . . you were in danger. . . ."

His legs buckled. He had lost a great deal of blood. Daphne was amazed he'd been able to get all the way down there without falling. She helped him sit in Gabriel's wheelchair.

"Where is Christopher?" Daphne asked.

Ben gestured with his head. "I don't know. . . . I wasn't sure if he followed me or ran somewhere else into the house."

Daphne looked back at Gabe, who was writhing on the floor, bleeding from his head, his fingers opening and closing as he seemed to claw the air.

"What should we do with him?" Daphne asked.

"Tie him up. . . ." Ben said, but the words barely made it past his lips.

Daphne knew if Ben's wound wasn't staunched properly, he'd die. That he was still alive at all was a miracle, a testament to his strong physique and stamina. But he was going to need a blood transfusion very soon. How they'd manage that, trapped in this blizzard, Daphne had no idea.

But the first order of business had to be securing Gabriel. If he came to, got his wits back, and managed to get back on his feet, he'd try to kill them again. And Ben was not in a condition to fight him off. Daphne would be on her own.

She began overturning boxes and pulling open cabinets in search of some rope. Anything strong enough to bind Gabriel's wrists and ankles to keep him immobilized. She shook the contents of one cardboard box onto the floor. Fragile glass Christmas ornaments shattered at her feet. Another box held only paper and canceled checks. She lifted a third box—and heard a small cry.

She looked. Behind the box, cowering in the fetal position, was Christopher.

"Christopher!" she called, and immediately bent down to scoop him into her arms.

"He didn't kill you!" the boy cried, wrapping his arms around Daphne as well. "You're alive!"

"Yes, I'm alive," she said. "I told you we'd get through this!"

He clung to her, crying.

Daphne stroked his hair. "You saved my life, Christopher. Do you know that?"

His little round button eyes looked up at her through his tears.

"You sent Ben down here just in the nick of time," Daphne told him. "You saved my life, Christopher! Now we're even, baby."

A gigantic smile suddenly burst forward on his face.

"Now come on," Daphne said. "We've got to tie Gabriel up and then help Ben." They stood up. "Do you know where there's any rope?" she asked.

The boy's eyes scanned the basement. Suddenly he made a beeline across the room toward a workbench.

"How about this?" he asked, holding up a tangled green electrical power cord. "Will this work?"

"It's going to have to," Daphne said.

The boy tossed it to her, and Daphne hurried with it back to the place where she'd left Gabriel and Ben.

But, though Ben was still slumped there in the wheelchair, barely conscious, Gabriel was gone.

A trail of blood along the concrete floor stretched on a few feet from where he had been lying, but then it disappeared.

He'd been able to stand up.

And get away.

Daphne felt the fear bubble up from her gut. She picked up the flashlight and swung its light around the basement to see if Gabriel was anywhere within sight. She couldn't discern him anywhere, but there were plenty of dark shadows where he might be hiding. She knew they had to act fast.

"Christopher, grab that burlap sack," she ordered the boy.

There was no way to get out of the house, or perhaps even up the basement stairs—not with Ben in such a weakened condition. They'd have to revert to the earlier plan. They'd hide out in the storage room. And this time, they'd have the provisions Ashlee had prepared in case their wait turned out to be a long one.

Daphne set the flashlight in Ben's lap, grabbed hold of the handles of the wheelchair, and began to push. Christopher followed along, his head moving left and right, on watch for Gabriel's return.

Daphne suspected their adversary was tending to his wound. Ben had smacked him pretty good with that flashlight. There had been a lot of blood. If Gabriel expected to finish killing them off, he'd have to make sure he had the strength. That meant wrapping his head and possibly resting for a bit. She hoped that interim gave them enough time to make it to the storage room.

Unless, of course, that's exactly where Gabriel had gone.

He'll be waiting there for us when we arrive, Daphne feared.

I might be able to fight him off, but he could get Ben and Christopher, she thought.

She vowed she would not let that happen.

But it appeared Gabriel had gone elsewhere to nurse his wound. Probably upstairs, where he could get water, Daphne presumed. Just to be sure, however, when they reached the open door of the storage room, she took the flashlight and used it to scope out every darkened corner. She looked behind every box, every shelf, and then made sure that the chest was still wedged against the passageway. When all seemed clear, she breathed a sigh of relief, and motioned to Christopher to wheel Ben inside.

Once the door was secured, Daphne set about rewrapping Ben's wound. Christopher gave her his shirt, leaving the boy in just his T-shirt. She tied it as tightly as she could around Ben's shoulder. His eyes flickered open to look at her, and he gave her a small smile.

"Now I want you to drink," she said, fishing out a plastic bottle of water from the burlap sack and twisting off the cap. Holding it to Ben's lips, she told him to drink as much as he could. "Then some crackers. We need to keep you from passing out."

Christopher tossed her a box of animal crackers.

"Here, Ben," Daphne said, feeding him a couple of lions and bears.

They sat there in silence for some time. The flashlight, propped up on its end, cast a much brighter glow than the kerosene lamp had. Every corner of the small room was illuminated. Daphne started to breathe more easily, convinced they were finally safe. At least for the moment. They had enough food and water to last a couple of days. But after that . . . she shuddered, knowing Gabriel could last much longer. He had the whole house, with its full pantry and kitchen.

But the blizzard wouldn't last forever. It might take a few days for the plows to clear the roads, but eventually people would start coming up the hill. Cook would arrive, expecting to start work. The mailman. And . . . Gregory would come. Daphne was certain Gregory would come.

Ben seemed more alert. The food and water had helped. He gripped Daphne's hand and squeezed it.

"Thank you," he whispered.

"Thank you," she replied, then reached over and took Christopher's hand as well. "We all took care of each other."

Ben grimaced. "My brother . . . I can't believe all this was my brother's doing."

"He's out of his mind," Daphne said.

"So much hatred he's been carrying around," Ben said. "I knew he was bitter, resentful . . . but never to this extent. I never knew how much he resented even me."

Daphne gave him a sympathetic look.

"I could try reasoning with him," Ben said.

"Reasoning with him?" Daphne asked. "Ben, he's just killed seven people in cold blood—nine, actually, if we count Donovan and Maggie. I think he's far beyond any form of reasoning."

Ben just nodded sadly. "I think of my mother,"

he said. "She was always fearful about Gabe. I remember she worried his depression might grow into something more malicious. She was right."

"How did you manage to get out the study?" Daphne asked.

Ben sighed. "When I came back to consciousness, I saw the room was empty, except for Uncle Pete. I managed to stand, and made my way over to him. He told me that the clown had killed almost everyone."

"Mr. Witherspoon was still *alive?*"

"Yes," Ben told her. "Though he could barely speak or move. He was slouched way down in his chair. I think he'd had a stroke."

"Yes, I'm sure he did," Daphne said.

"It was only when Christopher found me staggering through the house that I learned you were in any danger, and that the clown was actually . . ." He couldn't bring himself to say the name. "My brother." The pain on Ben's face was terrible to see.

An odd realization came over Daphne. "But then Gabe *didn't* kill Pete when he broke into the study," Daphne said. "Right before Christopher and I escaped through the secret passageway, I saw him smash through the door with the ax. I thought for sure he'd kill everybody who was in the room then."

Ben shrugged. "I guess maybe he thought that Uncle Pete was already dead. Clearly he thought I was, as he didn't bother with me, either. I guess he just grabbed ahold of Ashlee and took her with him, and then killed her down here."

"Ashlee was in on it," Daphne told him, as Ben's eyes widened in shock. "She was part of the whole thing."

She filled Ben in on as much as she had learned. He just kept shaking his head as he listened to the long, sordid tale.

"My brother," he moaned. "My brother . . ."

The fact that Pete had still been alive when Ben left the study made Daphne consider the possibility that she might actually see the master of the house again.

She might actually see her father.

Mr. Witherspoon really is my father.

The news still felt unreal to her. That man . . . that hard, stoic man who had nonetheless treated her fairly was actually her father. And now he sat suffering, possibly dying, a floor above her. How Daphne's heart ached to be able to go to him. All her life she'd wished she'd had a father, and now here she was, trapped in a basement while her father died slowly above her. She wished she had managed somehow to bring him down here to safety as well. Surely if Gabriel went back upstairs now and discovered Pete was still alive, he'd slit the old man's throat like he had the others.

Daphne started to cry.

Seeming to sense what she was thinking, Christopher put his arm around her.

"My father would want us to be strong," the little boy said. "That's what he was always saying. Be strong." He smiled sadly. "I never listened to him. But maybe I will start now."

Daphne hugged him back.

That's when they heard the scraping sound.

"What's that?" Daphne whispered.

They were all silent, listening for the sound to return.

Scraping. From inside the wall. From . . . Daphne moved closer to make sure . . . from inside the secret passageway.

"He's coming," she whispered. "He's trying to get in here using the passageway."

"God, no," Ben moaned. "I don't think I'm strong enough to run. You two, go—you two, get out of here while you can!"

"No," Daphne told him. "We planned for this. We wedged that chest over the entrance to the passageway. It's in there pretty solid. There's no way he can budge it."

"Don't underestimate the strength of a madman," Ben said.

They listened again. Footsteps now. Close. He was near the entrance to the storage room.

They all drew in a deep breath.

They heard the panel slide open behind the chest.

They were still as stone statues.

They heard the huffing and puffing made by their pursuer as he tried to dislodge the chest. He was pushing, shoving. The chest trembled ever so slightly, but it did not move.

"You've got to be ready," Ben whispered to Daphne. "If that chest moves, you and Christopher unlock this door and make a run for it."

"It's not going to move," Daphne said, praying she was right.

Would she even have time to get the door unlocked and open if Gabriel somehow burst in here? They were sitting ducks in way, just waiting for him, in this enclosed space. If somehow he managed to push that chest away from the opening and came flying in here, razor swinging, they'd likely all be dead in a matter of seconds.

The chest shook, more noticeably this time, as the man behind it threw his shoulder against it, desperate now to break in.

Christopher grabbed Daphne by the arm and buried his face in her shoulder.

But suddenly the chest stopped moving. The sounds of exertion ceased.

Had he given up?

But then—

A blast.

A gun.

And then another.

Shards of wood flew off the chest. Sawdust and the smell of gunfire filled the air of the storage room.

Christopher screamed.

Another shot, and the chest collapsed into itself, broken wood everywhere, linens and blankets tumbling onto the floor. The shotgun blast exposed the opening to the secret passage, and from that opening Daphne now saw a pair of protruding hands, shoving aside what was left of the chest.

Then, to her horror, she watched as the man himself stepped inside the storage room.

TWENTY-FOUR

Daphne was about to fling back the bolt on the door and make a mad dash out of the room with Christopher, her heart broken about having to leave Ben behind, when she took a good look at the man who was now standing in front of her and realized she didn't need to run. At least, she hoped she didn't need to run.

It wasn't Gabriel.

It was Gregory.

"Daphne!" he shouted, rushing over to her and throwing his arms around her, raining kisses down on her face.

Daphne hesitated for just a second—she had been through so much in the past twenty-four hours it was hard to know who she could trust—but then she wrapped her arms around Gregory as well. She felt his heart beating, and she knew he loved her. He would never hurt her. She had been wrong, so very wrong, to suspect him.

"Gregory," she gushed, "how did you find us?"

He sat back, taking her in and looking over at

Ben and Christopher. He wore a heavy winter parka, snow still clinging to the arms and hood, as well as his boots.

"I was worried about you," Gregory said, out of breath. "And from what I've seen upstairs, I had reason to be worried—and not just because of the storm."

"You've been upstairs?" Daphne asked.

"Yes," Gregory told her. "I came up here and when no one answered, I went inside—and I found the bodies of Suzanne and Louella."

"It's Gabriel," Ben said with difficulty.

"Gabriel?" Gregory asked, in utter astonishment.

They filled him in, explaining that it wasn't just Suzanne and Louella who'd been murdered, but everyone in the entire house, except for the three of them.

"And maybe, hopefully," Daphne added, "we'll find that Mr. Witherspoon is still alive."

"What was with the shooting in the passageway?" Ben asked.

Gregory sighed. "If I had known you three were in here, I might not have risked using the gun," he said. "But it was the only way I could think of to get that chest out of the way."

"How did you even know about the passageway?" Daphne asked. "Did you come down here from the study?"

"No, I came from outside," he told her. "There's a way to get here from the back of the house. You knew that, Ben, didn't you?"

"Yes," Ben replied, leaning back against a shelf, his eyes closed. "We used to sneak in here as kids, you and me and Donovan and . . ." His voice broke. "Gabe."

Gregory was nodding. "The secret passageways in this house go every which way, take all sorts of turns. Once I saw the bodies of Suzanne and Louella, I heard commotion down here in the basement, and I figured others—including you, Daphne—might be in danger. And I also figured I'd be more effective if I came in through the cellar, rather than just blunder down the stairs into the middle of a murder scene." He smiled. "I didn't expect to find you in here. You've saved me from having to go looking for you."

"How did you even get up here, in this blizzard?" Daphne asked, realizing they hadn't even inquired of Gregory that most basic fact.

"Snowmobile," he told her.

Daphne smiled. So their rescuer would come on a snowmobile after all.

Ben was starting to turn a deathly shade of gray, so Daphne held the water bottle up for him to drink again. "He needs a blood transfusion soon," she told Gregory. "He's lost so much."

Gregory looked concerned. "Problem is, I can't fit more than one other person on the snowmobile. Well, maybe I could fit Christopher, too. He's small enough."

The boy beamed up at Gregory, who tousled his hair.

Daphne nodded. "That's fine," she said. "You take Ben and Christopher back down to the village. Get Ben to a doctor immediately. Then you can come back here and get me."

"No," Ben groaned. "Can't . . . leave you . . . alone . . ."

"That's right, Daphne," Gregory said. "The passageway isn't even secure anymore. I blew the chest to smithereens. Gabe could get in here very easily." He looked behind him at the dark aperture in the wall. "In fact, he might be in there now."

He checked his gun. Daphne saw he still had plenty of ammunition.

"I'll push another crate up against it," she said. "I'll pile all these boxes, too. He would take him an awful long time to dig his way in, and by then, you'll have the entire police force coming up here on snowmobiles." She smiled weakly. "At least, I hope you will."

"No, I'm just not comfortable leaving you here alone," Gregory insisted.

"You must!" Daphne demanded. "Otherwise, Ben will die."

Ben tried to speak, no doubt to offer some form of protest that he'd be fine, but found he couldn't even form the words. Christopher scrambled over to him with another bottle of water.

"Daphne," Gregory said, "if anything ever happened to you—"

He stopped speaking. His nostrils were suddenly flaring.

"Do you smell that?" he asked in alarm.

"Smoke . . ." Daphne said.

Sure enough, from the passageway, plumes of gray smoke were now billowing into the storage room. Already the place was filled with a misty gray haze that burned Daphne's throat. All four of them began to cough.

"He's trying to smoke us out," Gregory said.

"I can see flames way in back of the passage," Christopher told them, scrambling over toward the opening, his hand covering his mouth and nose.

"Jesus Christ," Gregory said, "he'll burn the house down!"

"Maybe that was his intent all along," Daphne said.

Gregory was gripping her arm. "Whatever his intent, we can't stay in here. We'll asphyxiate. The smoke will overpower us before much longer."

He grabbed the burlap sack and dumped out the bottles of water.

"Rip off a piece of clothing, douse it with water, and hold it to your face," Gregory instructed.

They all complied. Daphne first tore a piece of her blouse, soaked it, and handed it to Ben. He managed to hold it to his face. Then she repeated the process for herself.

"We're going to have to risk going out into the house," Gregory told them from behind his wet cloth. "If we can stay real close together, I hope to be able to hold Gabriel off." He held his gun in front of him with his free hand.

"Ben, I'll help you back into the wheelchair," Daphne said.

He shook his head. "That would just . . . slow you down. . . . Leave me here."

"No!" Daphne insisted. "I won't leave you!"

"Ben, my old friend," Gregory said. "Can you walk at all?"

"I'll try," Ben replied. "But if I fall . . . if I can't continue . . . you've got to go on without me. Promise?"

"We're promising nothing yet, buddy," Gregory said. "First you get on your feet."

The room was now nearly filled with smoke. Daphne's eyes were stinging. She could hardly see. She realized the fire in the passageway could easily spread to the entire house, burning Witherswood to the ground. They might get out—she hoped and prayed they would—but what would surely burn along with the house were all the letters in the box marked M. All of her history, reduced to cinders. She couldn't very well carry the entire box, but she could save a random portion of it. In a flash, her free hand plunged into the box, grabbing as much as she could. Withdrawing the fistful of crumpled envelopes and papers, she stuffed them deep down inside her blouse.

Then, as the smoke obliterated the last of her vision, she reached up and placed her fingers on the bolt of the door, ready to slide it open.

With an assist from Gregory, Ben stood. He seemed steady enough.

"You carry the flashlight, Christopher," Gregory told the boy. "Make sure to keep it pointed in front of us, so we can see our way."

Christopher quickly snatched up the light.

"Okay, then, let's go," Gregory commanded.

Daphne slid the bolt and opened the door.

Her fear was that Gabriel would be waiting on the other side. If he had reloaded the rifle, he could have easily taken them all out on the spot, one by one, as they came out of the smoky room. If he just had the razor, however, he might only get one of them before the other three overpowered him. Either scenario was not one that Daphne hoped to encounter.

But to her great relief, Gabriel was not there when they opened the door.

They stumbled out of the storage room coughing and wheezing. Hot tears rolled down Daphne's cheeks. They gasped for breath, gulping down as much of the frigid basement air as possible, providing soothing relief to their smoke-filled lungs.

"Keep your wet cloths," Gregory ordered. "The fire might spread."

Daphne clamped the fabric back to her mouth. The smoke was billowing out of the storage room now and filling the corridor that led to the main part of the basement. She could hear the crackle and snap of flames behind her.

"Mr. Witherspoon might still be alive," she said from behind the wet cloth. "We need to stop in the study and see—"

She saw the look Gregory gave her, but it was Ben who spoke.

"Daphne, we can't take that chance," he said.

With a heavy heart, she nodded. She understood there was no time to waste.

They ran. First down the corridor, making sure to close to the door behind them, trapping the smoke for the time being, and then through the basement, passing the body of Ashlee, soaking in a large puddle of her own blood. Christopher did his part, making sure they had enough light to see their way as they ran.

When they reached the stairs, however, they saw

that the dawn was breaking. A soft, lavender light spilled down from above. As they made it up to the first floor of the house, Daphne started to believe they'd really made it, that they'd be able to get out of the house before Gabriel got to them. Just what they'd do *then*, of course, they hadn't had time to decide. Gregory's snowmobile couldn't fit them all, so they remained stuck with their earlier dilemma. Still, for the moment, all Daphne cared about was getting out of the house without encountering Gabriel. She'd take her chances in the snow.

But then, as they ran past the parlor and into the front foyer, which was filled with early-morning light, all of her hopes were dashed.

One instant, Gregory was running a couple of feet in front of her.

The next instant, he was down.

Gabriel was on top of him.

He had been waiting for them, anticipating their escape route. As they'd emerged into the foyer, Gabriel had jumped down from his perch on the landing of the great marble staircase. His aim had been impeccable. His feet landed squarely on Gregory's back, sending him down, face first— and his gun cannonballing across the room. Daphne could hear Gregory wheezing. The breath had been knocked out of him.

Quick as a flash, Gabriel leapt off of Gregory and onto Daphne, who screamed. He held her in front of him in the crook of his elbow. She heard, rather than saw, the razor come out of his shirt, and then, once more, she felt its cold metal on her neck.

"I had hoped to finish off Daphne last," Gabriel

said, rather petulantly, as if he was truly disappointed, "because she's the newest member of our little clan."

Ben was white-faced, holding on to the banister of the staircase to keep from falling. Christopher stood in front of him, big button eyes staring in horror. Gregory was gasping for air on the floor, his face covered in blood—a broken nose? He was trying to sit up but was not having any success.

"But I must admit," Gabriel continued, laughing now, "I'm delighted to have the chance to include Gregory Winston the third in our little family reunion. What an unexpected benefit. All of us, back together again!"

"Gabe," Ben said, his voice terribly weak, "you don't want to do this. . . ."

"Oh, but I do, dear brother, I do! I've waited so long for this!"

"Daphne's never done anything to you," Ben told him. "Let her go."

"Hey, believe me, I considered sparing Daphne. She had many chances to get her butt out of this house." He sighed. "But see, now that I know she's got as much of that sick, poisoned Witherspoon blood as the rest of us, well, she has to go, too."

"Don't hurt Daphne!" Christopher shouted.

Gabriel hissed. "You little brat. I never liked you. I'm going to enjoy cutting that throat, believe me!"

Daphne knew she had one chance.

She prayed that her aim was good.

She reached down with her right hand and grabbed Gabriel's crotch.

And she squeezed as hard as she could.

Gabriel screamed.

He could have cut her with the razor at the moment. It was right at her throat. Daphne knew she was taking an enormous chance.

But it was the only chance she had.

So she took it.

And it paid off.

As Gabriel screeched in pain, he let her go. She bolted away from him.

"You bitch!" he shouted. "You freaking bitch!"

Daphne was running across the room. She spotted what she was looking for, and dove for it. Her hands closed around Gregory's gun.

She spun around, pointing it at Gabriel, who was lumbering toward her.

He laughed. "As if you'd have the guts to use that, little convent girl."

"Come any closer," she told him, "and I will."

"You don't even know how to use it," Gabriel taunted her.

Daphne noticed that while he'd let her go, he hadn't let go of the razor. He still brandished it in front of him. Out of the corner of her eye, she saw Ben try to approach, no doubt hoping to overpower Gabriel. But he fell to his knees, and then onto his side. The tourniquet had come loose on his shoulder, and a waterfall of blood was again running down his arm.

Gregory, too, was still struggling. He'd smashed his face up pretty bad on that direct hit with the floor. There was a lot of blood. He seemed dazed, and was unable to stand.

Alone among them, it was eight-year-old Chris-

topher who stood ready to leap to Daphne's rescue, if only Gabriel weren't wielding that long
razor in front of him.

"Such gallant knights to the lady's rescue,"
Gabriel sneered. "Look at them. Pathetic."

"I will use this," Daphne insisted. "I will blow
your head off, Gabriel, if you take another step."

He stayed where he was.

"A stalemate then?" He laughed. "Because I
know you don't want to have to shoot. You don't
want the death of an obviously poor, deranged
soul like me on your conscience."

"I'll wait until Gregory and Ben can stand, and
then they'll tie you up," Daphne told him. "Unless,
of course, you make another move, and then I will
shoot you dead. I'll worry about my conscience
later."

He stared at her, obviously trying to intimidate
her.

But Daphne was no longer the little girl who
had come to this house, easily frightened and sug-
gestible. She stood her ground. Her fear was giving way to anger. More than anger. Outrage.

"I can't believe you did all this, planned all this
so meticulously for so long," she said, not flinch-
ing from Gabriel's gaze. "Your body had healed,
you had been given a miraculous recovery—and
yet instead of going out and living your life and
making something of yourself, making up for all
the time you'd lost, you squandered it all. You
squandered your second chance at life. Your bitterness and resentment turned out to be more important to you than even your own life."

"I don't need any lectures from a convent girl," Gabriel snarled.

"Dressing up as a clown, putting those disgusting false teeth into your mouth," Daphne said, shaking her head. "Jumping out of Dumpsters, hiding in the tower and Christopher's closet, following me down into the crypt . . ." She looked at him quizzically. "You know, I can figure out how you managed most of your ruses. You ran around the block to surprise me in the parking-lot Dumpster. You and Ashlee planned for me to see you in the tower the night you killed Donovan. But how did you get out of the crypt? Was there a secret passageway out of there that I didn't know about?"

Gabriel looked at her. "I was never in the crypt," he told her with a sneer of contempt.

"But you were," she insisted. "The clown came down into the chamber, and it cut me with the razor. . . ."

Gabriel laughed. "That one, missy," he said, "was your own overactive imagination."

But Daphne knew it hadn't been her imagination.

And as if to prove there really had been a clown in the crypt, the music began to play from above.

All around the mulberry bush . . .

The music came from the stairs.

They all looked up. All except Daphne, who kept her eyes and her gun trained on Gabriel.

The monkey chased the weasel. . . .

Christopher let out a gasp when the clown appeared at the top of the stairs.

The monkey thought it was all in fun. . . .

The clown took a step down.

Pop! goes the weasel!

Daphne saw Gabriel, his eyes fastened on the clown, stumble backward. He was muttering in fright.

The inane little tune started again, and ran over and over. Daphne was certain that, this time, there was no secret tape recorder hidden in the clown suit.

The clown, smiling its big blue grin, its terrible teeth exposed, made its way down the stairs. Gregory, Ben, and Christopher watched in open-mouthed amazement. But the specter paid no attention to them. Nor did it seem interested in Daphne. It stepped off the last of the stairs and walked directly across the foyer, its gaze firmly fixed on Gabriel.

"No!" Gabriel screamed. "Get away from me!"

All around the mulberry bush . . .

The clown reached out and snatched the razor from Gabriel's hands.

The monkey chased the weasel. . . .

The clown lifted the razor.

The monkey thought it was all in fun. . . .

The clown laughed.

Pop!

The clown swung the razor.

Goes the weasel!

The blade sliced clean through Gabriel's neck. His head went flying through the foyer, bouncing off the far wall and ricocheting back, rolling like a bowling ball across the marble floor and coming to a stop only a few feet from where Daphne stood.

Gabriel's eyes still held life, looking up at her, and his mouth was still screaming, "No!"—even if there was no sound coming out of him anymore.

Blood shot up like a geyser from Gabriel's severed neck. Seconds later, his body collapsed into a heap on the floor.

The clown turned its yellow eyes to Daphne.

TWENTY-FIVE

Daphne kept the gun trained on the clown, even though she knew a bullet wouldn't do any good against such a creature.

Staring straight at her, the clown laughed again, those revolting teeth gnashing.

And then it was gone.

She didn't quite see it disappear. It was just there one minute, and gone the next.

Slowly, without saying a word, she lowered the gun.

Christopher bolted across the room toward her, wrapping his arms around her waist. Daphne dropped the gun to the floor. It clattered against the marble. She placed both hands on Christopher's head, and began to cry.

Gregory had finally made it to his feet and he hurried toward her.

"We've got to get out of here," he said, in a voice garbled by his broken nose. "The fire . . ."

Daphne looked up. Smoke was now filling the corridor that led to the basement.

"Ben," she said.

Gregory nodded. "It will take about ten minutes to get down the hill on the snowmobile. I can take him and Christopher. There are paramedics at the fire station who can get Ben a blood transfusion. But after I drop him off, I'll be right back here for you."

"Yes, of course," Daphne said. "Just go. Hurry. Though you might want the paramedics to tend to your nose, first . . ."

"I think my nose can wait," he said. "If you wrap yourself in a blanket and sit at the front door, with the door open, I think you should be okay. The fire won't reach here that quickly. I think I could be back in less than a half hour."

"Yes," she said. "Go!"

Christopher wouldn't release his grip on her.

"Hey," Daphne said, stooping down to look into the boy's eyes, "you wanted a ride on Gregory's motorcycle. His snowmobile will be kind of like that."

"I don't want to leave you," he said. "The clown might come back."

"No, he's gone," Daphne said. "I'm sure of that."

"But the fire . . ." the boy added.

"I'll be safe from that, too," she assured him. "Come on, let's help get Ben on his feet."

Ben could no longer speak. Daphne wrapped his wound again with a scarf she found in the front closet, and then pulled onto him a parka that she'd found there as well. Christopher slipped into his own coat, gloves, and scarf, and then the three of them helped Ben outside, where the snowmobile was parked not far from the front door.

They got him on, strapped him in, and then Gregory got on behind him, nestling Christopher in between.

"Less than half an hour," Gregory called through the still fierce wind. The blood on his face was freezing.

Daphne nodded.

She watched them take off down the hill. The snow seemed to have stopped, though it was hard to tell, since so much drifting was still taking place. She crunched through the knee-deep snow, shuddering from the cold. Once back into the foyer, she pulled another coat down from the closet—whose had it been? Abigail's? Suzanne's? Ashlee's?—and put it on over the one she was already wearing.

Then she thought of Pete.

It wasn't likely he was still alive, but she had to be sure.

Taking a deep breath, she pushed her way into the smoky corridor. She stepped over the dead body of Axel and through the shattered remains of the study door. She found Pete where she had last seen him, slouched down in his chair in the study.

"Mr. Witherspoon?" she called.

He moaned.

He was alive!

Daphne knew she had to get him out of here before more smoke filled up the room—or worse, the fire made it up the stairs.

"Mr. Witherspoon," she shouted. "Can you walk at all?"

She saw that it was hopeless. So, she snaked an arm under his slight frame and lifted him to his feet. She gently eased him onto a small rug, and then, clearing the broken wood out of the doorway, she dragged him out of the study and down the hall. How she had the strength, Daphne couldn't imagine. But she was able to do it. She dragged the old man all the way across the foyer, past the bloody corpse of Gabriel, and to the open doorway. There, she wrapped him in all the coats she could find in the closet, and waited for Gregory to return.

She stared out into the frigid pink morning. Reaching inside her multiple coats, she found the papers she had stuffed into her blouse. Surely the rest of the box marked M was now burned to a crisp. But these she still had.

She discovered she had saved, quite randomly, one very important document.

From a yellowed envelope, she removed a folded piece of paper. Daphne looked down at it and saw it was a birth certificate.

She saw her birth date, and quickly read the rest of the details.

Born in Point Woebegone.

Daphne May . . . Witherspoon.

The daughter of Peter Witherspoon.

And . . . Maria A. Mastroianni.

But . . .

Daphne couldn't make sense of it.

Mastroianni was Mother Angela's last name.

She couldn't move. Couldn't think.

She stared down at the name.

Maria A. Mastroianni.

Maria . . . Angela . . . Mastroianni?

She looked over at Pete, propped in the doorway, his eyes closed.

What did it possibly mean?

The sound of the snowmobile drew her attention then. Daphne looked up, and not only was Gregory, still bloody-faced, bounding over the snowdrifts toward her, but so were three other snowmobiles, the front one driven by Sheriff Patterson. They stopped a few feet from her, snow flying. The sheriff asked her if she was okay, and Daphne just nodded. He and a deputy entered the house, guns drawn, while a paramedic loaded Pete onto an extra-large snowmobile. Gregory came over to Daphne and helped her stand.

"Let's get out of here, sweetheart," Gregory said, and helped her to her feet.

Daphne would barely remember the ride on the snowmobile down the hill. She seemed to come back to life when paramedics at the fire station examined her and pronounced her fine; then she faded out again, thinking only of the name she had seen on the birth certificate.

Maria A. Mastroianni.

Pete and Ben were helicoptered to the hospital in Portland. Gregory had his nose set by the paramedics, then brought Daphne and Christopher to his house. From his windows they watched the spectacular sight of Witherswood burning on top of the hill, bright orange and yellow flames cutting through the deep gray sky. No firetrucks could get up there in the snow, so the old mansion just burned to the ground.

They spoke very little. Gregory made up two

guest rooms, and both Daphne and Christopher slept.

In the morning, they dressed and, the roads having been cleared, set off for Portland. Outside Pete's hospital room, Daphne was startled to see a very familiar woman.

Mother Angela.

"I heard of the fire, and came right away," she told Daphne, taking her into her arms.

"I know everything now," Daphne said quietly.

"I figured you did." Mother looked down at her with sad eyes. "My poor baby."

"I know everything," Daphne repeated, "but I don't understand everything."

"My poor child," Mother said, cupping Daphne's face in her hands. "My parents disowned me when they discovered I was pregnant with Pete's child. They refused to have anything to do with me. Not only was I expecting a child without being married, but the father was a man they'd never *permit* me to marry—the son of a notorious murderer. So I became dead to them—unless I entered a nunnery."

Daphne looked up at all the pain that still shone from Mother's eyes.

"I was underage. I had no choice in the matter. They threatened to make Pete's life miserable. I expected to leave the convent when I was old enough, but then . . ."

"Then what?" Daphne asked.

"By then Pete had married someone else."

"Peggy," Daphne said.

Mother nodded. "I decided to stay where I was. I

loved the sisters. They had been so good, taking me in. Not only me. They took *you* in, too."

She kissed Daphne's cheek.

"But he never stopped loving you," Daphne said.

Her mother seemed near tears. "Nor I him." She took Daphne's hand and led her into the room. Standing beside Pete's bed, the three were a family, finally, for the first time. Mother stroked Pete's cheek, and Daphne held his hand, and he seemed to know they were both there.

He died late that afternoon.

Ben, recovering quickly once he'd had the transfusion, told them he'd been made privy to the contents of his uncle's will. "It was to have been divided among all his heirs," he said, "but there was one notable addition." He looked over at Gregory. "One quarter of his estate—which is considerable—is to be set aside as a foundation to help children whose parents have been murdered."

Daphne saw all the years of hatred and resentment suddenly evaporate from Gregory's face then. He walked into Pete's room and stood beside his body. Ben and Daphne joined him, standing on the other side of Pete's bed.

"Why didn't the ghost of his father kill him?" Daphne whispered, looking down at the peaceful expression on Pete's face. "Why didn't he kill all of us, in fact? Why kill only Gabe, and spare us?"

"Who can say?" Ben asked. "But remember, he only killed one family member the first time. My father. And only when Dad had discovered his crimes. He killed his son only as a form of self-protection, so that he could keep his killing spree going."

"So . . . why kill Gabe this time?" Daphne asked. "Was he . . . trying to make up for all the shame and horrors he'd left to all of us?"

"I hardly think that monster capable of good intentions," Ben said. "I think, in fact, it's the opposite. If he'd killed us, there'd be no one left to remember what he did. And killers like him, after all, are all about the notoriety. He wanted the credit."

"Will he ever come back?" Daphne asked, shuddering.

"I don't think so," Gregory said, looking up from Pete's face. "I think his spirit was exorcised when the house burned. He's gone. I'm convinced of it. Into the flames where he belongs."

Daphne wasn't sure why she was so certain he was right, but she was. The ghost of Pete Witherspoon Senior was gone.

But now, of course, there were other wandering spirits on the top of that hill. . . .

That evening, they all returned to Gregory's house. He had more than enough room to put them up for as long as necessary. Charlie arrived from Portland, worried about Ben's condition, and was overjoyed to see him doing okay.

That night, they all ate together, a new family arising from the ashes of the old. As the skies cleared above them and the moon slipped out from behind the clouds, Gregory took Daphne out onto the deck, and held her there in his arms as they looked out over the crashing sea.